CW00570731

The Secret Lives of Neighbours

James Russell

Although this book is based on a real person, it is a work of fiction.

Any references to historical events, real people or places are used fictitiously.

Other names, characters, places and events are products of the author's imagination.

Any resemblance to actual events or places or persons is entirely coincidental.

ISBN:9798397372312

Dedicated to Andy & Margaret

and to all the women whose stories are never told.

The Secret Lives of Neighbours

Chapter One

Ibiza 2016

Her life was grinding to an end. Living was just something that happened, but it hadn't always been this way. She had had a life and it had not been without incident. Sometimes she felt it was only her stubbornness that had kept her going for so long. As another summer began she wondered if this would be her last, if it was, then there was something she had to do.

"Baby, let's go." She didn't look to see if her command was being followed. She didn't need to. As she left her sanctuary she paused by the window to study the reflection, the glass muddied by years of dust and dirt. It was hers but she was tired of this image, this haggard old woman. With a slow, deliberate hand she shifted some of the grime, looking for the face of the beauty that had arrived in Ibiza some 60 years earlier. Try as she might she saw no signs of it, nor of the innocent mountain girl that had preceded her. Her gaze fell and concentrated on her spindly fingers, closing them around the door handle. "Come on Baby. They're waiting for us." The door scraped open and the two old ladies shuffled into the low morning sun. She wasn't perhaps the woman she used to be but she was still Maria Dolores.

The house was easy to locate. It sat in the shadow of a well preserved old windmill. The twisted Stone Pine tree that obscured most of the entrance was older than the building itself. The scarred trunk threw branches out over the road forming a canopy over the gate. Layers of pine needles piled up like rudimentary nests in the crevices where branches diverged from the trunk; Mother Nature neglecting the spring cleaning. A heavy chain that Maria Dolores struggled to wrap around the fence post secured the gate. It had no lock. The once white paintwork was cracked and fragmented. A rusted fence, buckled by the weight of a vast bougainvillea, was an eye height hazard to any passer-by. The impressive plant with its plethora of fuchsia flowers hung around the pine tree like a billowing skirt hiding the entrance to the dilapidated house. That was the way she liked it. Maria Dolores didn't want anyone seeing how she lived.

Even behind dark glasses the morning glare made her squint as she stepped into the street. She stood to steady herself, took a deep breath then closed the gate, laboriously fastening the chain behind her. The breeze that came up from the Mediterranean brought with it lavender and rosemary that grew untamed across the hillside. It was a welcome, if brief, respite from the morning's mugginess. The stillness was interrupted by the squeal of a moped as it sped past. Yanking Baby closer, Maria Dolores spat in the bike's general direction. That it had flown by in the middle of the road was of no consequence, it was still too close for comfort. Her eyes bore into the driver as he tore away unaware of his offence. "Come on Baby, it's safe now." She tottered on down the incline with her characteristic limp, pulling the more or less compliant mongrel behind her. Sometimes her gait tricked her, the forward motion moving her feet quicker than her brain could register. It compelled her to take a dance step; a hop or a shuffle before recovering again. The sweet sickly odour of the warming tarmac irritated her and she screwed up her nose to show her disapproval as she crept across the street.

That forgotten, decrepit building had been her home for over 30 years; its deterioration mirrored her own. The area had remained quiet but had flourished around her. Half a dozen residential streets wound their way round, and down the hillside. Neighbouring houses with sea views sold for hundreds of thousands. A series of criss-crossing paths connected the town to the beach and now the warmer weather had arrived more people would be traipsing by her house much to Maria Dolores' annoyance. There was little she didn't know about the area, although at 86 years old there was also a fair amount that she had forgotten.

She paused just before the junction of her narrow street and the busier thoroughfare below. Pulling Baby into the shade she took advantage of the moment to straighten her sunglasses. She had never got out of the habit of primping herself whenever she had the chance. If asked, she wouldn't be able to say how long she had worked as a prostitute, but she did know that one never knows when one might be propositioned. Take a trick when you can.

The cropped wall that overhung the main street was the perfect place to rest and take in the morning hubbub, as tourists emerged into a new day. Barely clad youngsters whipped by on rented mopeds. The first-timers tentative and cautious. The foolhardy speeding, weaving between imaginary obstacles, accidents waiting to happen. A dusty goods van stopped below her blocking off one lane, the driver ignoring a parking space only 15 metres away. He jumped out and without looking threw a dismissive arm in the air at an affronted taxi driver.

Immigrant Latino women in prim uniforms swept the entrances of the street's brassy hotels. They made light work in clearing away the previous night's debris, thankful for the opportunity to earn minimum wage. Close by Latino men carried sacks of sand and cement up a path to one of the numerous building sites. These exploited labourers trudged through the heat, grateful to receive fifty euros in black at the end of the day. A couple of tourists rotated a cheap pop-up map and squabbled over which was the easiest route to the centre of town. Maria Dolores had seen it all before, this was just Ibiza stretching and yawning, a daily ritual of which she was a part.

She sat there expressionless. Thick rimmed sunglasses generously covered her eyes, pearly hair pushed up into a rose-pink sunhat. The creases that tapered from the corners of her mouth, however, established her as a woman of a certain age. She didn't envy the young women as they paraded along the street in tight shorts, bikini tops and flip-flops. She had had her life. Decades had passed since she, or anyone else for that matter, had considered her beauty. In those days her blue-green eyes, unusual in an Andalusian woman, combined exotically with her flawless olive skin and jet black hair. Her looks had brought her many admirers over the years, but also unwelcome attention. Let the young enjoy themselves whilst they can she thought, life will catch up with them.

In the near distance the Church of San Salvador de la Marina reared its square shoulders above the old port, the bell tower surveilling the quotidian life around it. These days nothing much intimidated Maria Dolores but she stared at that morning's destination with some trepidation. The church's priest, Father Gabriel, gave out food at the various food banks around town. This open display of benevolence irritated Maria Dolores but unlike others she had known, Father Gabriel hadn't seemed sanctimonious. Something in him comforted her, she saw a man she could talk to. Since first observing him at the food bank she had tracked him down and regularly visited his church, deciding if he was the one she could open up to.

She was brought back to the present when Baby lumbered to her feet and took cover behind her mistress's legs. Maria Dolores looked up to see a neighbour whose French bulldog was sniffing around. They had been neighbours for five years or so but had never exchanged more than cursory greetings. She thought maybe he was German from the accent. Anyway not one for talking a lot.

"Buenos días Señora."

She nodded curtly. "That dog not get hot?" The words were aimed at the snuffling little canine. Maria Dolores didn't lift her head, not wanting to directly address the person standing a little too close to her.

"He does, but, you know, he stays in during the day." Jimmy was in fact English but that was irrelevant. Maria Dolores didn't care and had no interest in him nor his dog. Late-night antics, noise and too many comings and goings had left her disgruntled with this particular foreigner.

"You'd think he'd get hot with all that black hair," she repeated, regarding the dog with a little disdain. She had considered leaving Baby at home during the day, out of the heat, but how could she? The thought was ridiculous. They were companions.

5

"Well, I guess." Retorted the neighbour beginning to take the line of questioning personally. A retaliatory tug on the leash stopped the bulldog getting too close to Baby. The exchange was over, the conversation killed before it started. The neighbour said goodbye and headed back up the hill. She watched them go, man and dog, the neighbour she hardly knew. An uneasiness she hadn't been fully aware of in his presence began to ebb away. Maria Dolores took one more glance up the street then crossed over to continue her journey.

An hour or so later they reached the narrow pedestrian streets around the Church of San Salvador de La Marina. Life here was already underway. Waiters wiped down tables for the anticipated lunchtime rush. Others lowered canopies to protect customers, at least from the direct glare of the sun if not from the midday heat. Familiar greetings and jocularity echoed off the walls. The streets without restaurant terraces were crammed with stalls selling anything a tourist might need, and many things that they certainly didn't. Classic linen clothing from the 'White Isle' and cotton t-shirts with lizards, a Volkswagen camper van or a Vespa scooter. Throwbacks to the island's hippy past. The constrained side streets forced passers-by into single file and the inevitable impasse. A deliberate strategy to slow the procession, maximising time spent exposed to the merchandise. Maria Dolores and Baby skilfully negotiated these same streets, she occasionally raised her head to acknowledge a familiar face. Her apparent disinterest though was a pretence. She was a bedouin of these medieval alleyways. She saw everything she had to see and more, she absorbed it, habitually vigilant. The tourist season offered everyone opportunities. If she cleared a table or two at Miguel's bar after breakfast, it would earn her a coffee and croissant. This was a small price to pay for her silence. She found that old customers always found a way to be generous.

Today, however, wasn't one of those days. On reaching the Church of San Salvador de la Marina she tied Baby to a bike rack and scratched the little dog behind the ears. "Watch out for rabbits. I won't be long." Baby looked up at her aged mistress and cocked her head briefly before lying down. The exterior of the church had no remarkable architectural features. The small, gothic arched windows contained opaque glass but lacked colour or artistic detail. The interior was equally insipid. An enormous off-white concha shell which contained Holy water was mounted to the wall. In the dark recess of the chancel a three metre tall Christ was lit from below, its shadow stretched to the ceiling. It fascinated Maria Dolores because it lacked facial features, wore no clothing yet had no genitalia and no crown of thorns. There was nothing to indicate that it was actually a representation of Jesus except for the crucifixion and its lofty position above the devotees that convened below.

Deeper into the church she was greeted with cool but stale air, quite a contrast from the humidity outside. She made her way down the nave to the wooden chairs in front of the transept. Her arrhythmic footsteps, and the faint whir of electric fans the only break in the silence. She sat there a while thankful for the break and respite for her gout-ridden feet.

"Good morning Dolores, how are you today?" Maria Dolores didn't acknowledge that Father Gabriel Ferrer had spoken to her. This was another ritual that she had little interest in. He usually greeted her in this manner but had given up any notion that she might offer conversation or give him more than a sardonic look. People sought refuge in churches for different reasons, he accepted that. He smiled and moved on. Dressed in church issue black trousers and pale blue shirt he still managed to look elegant, too elegant to be a priest. He was immaculate, his tanned skin radiated youth and vigour, his hair always perfect. Had she not seen him in an ecclesiastical setting, Maria Dolores could have mistaken him for one of the moneyed tourists commonly seen in the marina. She had never seen him in a cassock, but then Sunday mass had never been high on her list of social engagements.

"What day is it today?" The croaky words forced themselves from her parched mouth, apparent strangers to her tongue. Father Gabriel, paused a second, surprised at the voice coming from behind him. He turned and made his way back towards the old lady, keen not to miss anything. He sat in front of Maria Dolores, who still hadn't looked up.

"What day is it?" This time her words had more strength.

"Well, it's the 9th of April. Tomorrow is Saint Michael of the Saints."

"Then it's his birthday. They said it wasn't but I'd know," she paused. "I'm his mother." Maria Dolores raised her head, but looked past Father Gabriel to the Christ without a face, searching for something in him, a recognition of her pain. "I'd know, I'm his mother," she repeated.

Chapter Two

Father Gabriel turned his chair around to face Maria Dolores. They were still seated in front of the altar in the church of San Salvador de La Marina. He wasn't sure how to proceed, which was out of character for him. He believed he had a good rapport with his parishioners and considered himself an accomplished facilitator. The old lady sitting in front of him however, was a different story. Visual clues were scant, no eye contact, no pleading look for help or approval. Maria Dolores was a closed book. So he decided just to wait. She had, after all, sought him out. When the time was right she would continue. So they sat in silence. Outside traffic passed by, people continued their daily routines, unaware of the drama about to unfold only metres away. A motor starting or the occasional raised voice broke into the church amplifying the silence. Then Maria Dolores took an audible breath and started her story.

"It was a Wednesday. I remember the day because later we had to go back to the church. In class all day with Father Alberto then Franco's speech to the nation at night. The church had one of the two radios in the village so that's where we went. It was 1946. In those days nobody had anything. Father Alberto wasn't much of a teacher; he talked about Jesus and the scriptures just like he did on Sundays. And the war, he talked a lot about the war, all the men did. But with the road through the mountains closed by the snows, the church hall was the only place we could have lessons, and that man the only teacher."

"When class finished all us kids ran outside. It was a beautiful sunny day, the first day I'd felt the warmth all winter. I closed my eyes and let it soak into me. We were all in a good mood, the young ones screamed and shouted, happy to be out. Conchi ran ahead of me, looking for the bits of snow that we hadn't already stood in and jumped on them. Every time she broke the hard snow, it cracked and she squealed. She loved it. That's the way I remember her, that happy girl playing in the snow."

"It was only a few minutes to our house and I could see Mami up the hill standing in our doorway all lit up in the sunshine like an angel, letting the sun warm her, just like I did. She waved at us to hurry up. Grey clouds were coming over the hilltops. It wouldn't be long until the sun sank into them and our valley would become cold and dark again." Maria Dolores took several pauses whilst talking but her emotions stayed buried. Her voice, still with it's subtle Andalusian accent, grew in strength but her tone was prosaic and unwavering. She avoided talking directly to Father Gabriel, occasionally she glanced up at him but seemed unconcerned if he was listening or not.

"Our house was like most of the others in the valley, it was small and cosy. It had very thick walls and small square windows and was warm in the winter and cool in the summer. They were whitewashed with lime paint and some had a bit of colour around the windows and doors. Ours was just white. The pen for the animals was bigger than the house but only had three stone walls. One wall was held up by some old tree trunks. The roof and gates were more solid. Papi built them with wooden beams he and some other men took from the old Jimenez house. Poor Señor Jimenez had been killed in the fighting the summer before. I didn't even know the men were still fighting. Ha! What did I know? A week after that Father Alberto told us in mass that Señora Jimenez and her daughter had gone to live in Seville. Rocio, that was her name. We were the same age and I was so sad when they went. My best friend just disappeared. She came back into my life though. Papi said it wasn't doing the Jimenez family any good so it might as well keep our animals protected. Like I said, no one had anything in those days."

"We lived in that one big room that had a stove and a fireplace. We moved the table and benches around depending on which was burning, they were never lit at the same time. Papi's big armchair was always closest to the fire. One bedroom for us with the bed we shared and the one next door for Mami and Papi. That's all there was. There was no toilet, no water inside, no electricity. By the end of the winter, the *dispensa* was pretty bare but there were usually dried beans, lentils, almonds, and olive oil, things we made ourselves. Sometimes Papi would kill a chicken or even a goat and we would have some meat and a stew that would last a week. We would make sausages that hung there to dry, they dripped fat on the floor and Mami had a plate to catch it and we spread it on bread." Father Gabriel noticed Maria Dolores' lips thinned into the faintest smile as she remembered her impoverished childhood.

* * *

"'How was Father Alberto today?' Every day Mami asked the same questions. She stood by the stove stirring some blood sausage and beans. Fresh bread sat on the table but heaven help you if you touched it before Papi got home. I sat with my elbows on the table staring at it. It was always so tempting. Conchi giggled.

'Father Alberto made Pepe Gonzalez kneel on some dried chickpeas because he didn't know the capital of Extremadura. It's Merida. I know it. And when Pepe got up his knee was bleeding, then Pepe peed himself and Father Alberto slapped him on the head for making a mess on the floor.'

'Conchi, don't laugh.'

'But it's true.' Conchi giggled again, excited to be telling Mami some gossip. 'All us kids were laughing at him.'

"I saw Mami wince, I wasn't sure how much she liked Father Alberto, everyone knew him and how cruel he was, but he was our priest. He was only our teacher because señora Álava left suddenly and they didn't send us another one. But Mami was very religious and she said we had to respect him. 'Poor Pepe.' Conchi stopped jumping around and came to sit with me at the table. We sat there in silence for a while, Mami by the stove, lost in her thoughts, the only sounds coming from the simmering pot and Conchi scratching at the table."

"Everything changed when Papi opened the door and our dog, Pirri, rushed into the house. The cold air from outside gave me goosebumps and Conchi shivered. Pirri ran around the table a few times sniffing, then jumped up on me, licking my hands.

'Hello, Pirri. Where have you been? You catch any rabbits?' I bent down and rubbed behind his ears, it was what I always did, our little ritual. He loved it. I could see it in his eyes, his tail wouldn't stop. Behind me, Papi said something to Mami then he came over to say hello to us. He kissed Conchi on the head and messed her hair. She wriggled and squealed; their little ritual. He walked around the table, telling Pirri to go to his basket. Pirri ignored him, he was digging his teeth into my forearm but he would never bite me. Suddenly Papi's huge hand reached across and grabbed Pirri by his neck and threw him across the room.

'Basket' Papi yelled. Poor Pirri landed on his side, rolled over, scrambled to his feet and into his basket. I could tell he was scared. Conchi jumped in her seat, catching her breath.

'PAPI!' I shouted and I stood to face him. He turned to me and raised his hand, raised his hand like he was going to slap me. 'Papi,' I said again but that look in his eyes was my warning not to say anything else. I still remember the smell of brandy coming off him. Papi got angry really quickly, but he never beat us. Then the house was still again, the only noise was the crackle from the stove. Papi stood there with his hand raised, I looked to Mami, but she was staring at the floor. Then I looked back to him. Without lowering his stare, without a word he put that massive hand around the back of my neck and pulled me towards him. He kissed me on the forehead, and still without saying anything, turned and went and sat in his armchair."

Maria Dolores shuffled in her chair and blinked; opening and closing her heavy-lidded eyes, a drunk trying to stay conscious at the end of the night. The wooden church pews and chairs weren't built for comfort, a subtle penitence before the eyes of God. Father Gabriel listened as Maria Dolores recounted the time in her childhood village. He had moved a row and now sat beside her. He placed a cautious hand on her knee.

"Dolores, would you like a glass of water?" She sat contemplating this for a minute. The feeble current of air from an electric fan rippled her hair. Then she shook her head. She did want water but didn't want Father Gabriel to leave her, not now that she had started to unburden herself.

"The dark clouds had gone and the sky was all clear and starry. The village always looked far away at night but it was only 20 minutes. All you could really see was the church, the bell tower and that big cross. There weren't many streetlights but that wooden cross was always more evil lit up. The shadow made it look bigger. I always felt that God was watching over us, waiting for us to sin so he could send Father Alberto after us."

"Our village, Los Caballeros de La Sierra, was just a few streets coming off the main road through the Sierra Morena Mountains. Hah, and the asphalt didn't even stretch to the side streets. The only one that wasn't a dirt track was the cobbled street that Papi helped build. It ran up past the bar and the plaza to the church. Señor Miguel Guerrero and his fat wife ran the bar with Ana. She was their daughter, I knew her well. She left school the year before although we were the same age. She always wanted to be a teacher but Miguel made her stay at home to make food and stuff for the bar. He would never let her out of his sight. Always asking where she was. Strange that, what could happen to her in that place? She was chained to the bar and was starting to put on a bit of weight as well, she wasn't happy working there, she told me often enough. Like I said, she was desperate to get out of there and be a teacher, not work in that stinking bar every day. She was lucky though cause it was the only other place that had a radio and one of the few that was connected to the electricity. All we knew about the outside world came through the bar or, of course, from Father Alberto and The Church."

* * *

"We crossed the main road where the streetlight was and as we neared the church I watched my shadow stretch up the street before me. I felt like it was pulling me in. Some things are still so clear to me. Inside we separated, of course we did. After mass we would sit in families but now the men sat together, their arms hanging over the backs of the chairs, their chests all puffed out, each one taking up as much space as they could. They shouted to Papi although most of them had probably seen him earlier. They shuffled chairs around to give him a place at the table. José Blanco was the loudest of all. How he loved his own voice. He saw me look at him and stopped talking, his eyes followed me as I passed their table. That creepy smile and yellow teeth sticking out that dirty beard. He licked his dirty finger and wiped away the greasy black fringe. All the time staring at me, grinning and staring at me." As attentive as Father Gabriel was he couldn't have detected the deep revulsion Maria Dolores felt at the thought of that man. Still after all these years bile rose in her throat. But her hard exterior remained unruffled. She continued.

"All the men smoked. Those that had tobacco shared and rolled for those that didn't. The blue cloud that hung around their tables swirled around when someone moved or blew smoke through it. All the time the men talked, and threw their arms around. Some pointed to the portrait of Franco and always loud in the typical way of the Andalusian men. The blackboard and the maps we used for classes had been hidden behind a large curtain. Only pictures of the Virgin Mary and Jesus the shepherd hung on the walls. El Caudillo Franco was mounted in the space where the portrait of King Alfonso used to hang. Franco's frame was smaller than our old king and left a white border where the smoke hadn't yet stained the paint yellow."

* * *

"The women sat behind the men and us children at the back, out the way of everything. This was gossip hour. Not that there was much to talk about, huh, especially in the winter, but chatter they did. All of the village was there, it would be suspicious if anyone was absent and missed Franco's address: they could be considered an enemy of the State, and no one needed that, not even as a joke. We knew we had to be quiet but until Father Alberto arrived we chatted amongst ourselves.

"When Marta Perez came in, my friend, Encarni, nudged me. Marta was only two years older than us but was married and already had her first child. She loved Raul but she hated being alone all day with that baby and Raul wanted more children. It was awful, so she told us. You could see it in her eyes and how she held the baby. She sat there with the women, all quiet, looking like she was lost. I told Encarni I'd never treat my baby like that, I'd be a more loving mother."

"Then when Señora Guerrero came in I nudged her back. 'Look.' I whispered. 'All those years making pastries, she's as fat as a pig ready for the slaughter. She eats more than they sell.' Encarni giggled. 'When she smiles her eyes disappear inside her head. Her arms and neck are like a bull's. Ole! Ole!' And I pretended to wave a bull-fighter's cloak. 'One day a matador will get her and cut off her ears and they'll end up in a pie.' We leant into each other trying to control our hysterics. When I looked up I saw Mami watching me. She urged me forward towards her. I gave Encarni's hand a squeeze and got up. 'You're not a child anymore Dolores. Come and sit here with the women.' And it was as quick as that, one minute I was giggling with the girls, the next I was at the women's table. I didn't realise it then but being accepted as a woman had its consequences."

"We sat hushed whilst General Franco addressed the nation. Sometimes the men exchanged glances and nods, flicking their cigarette ash on the floor. The General's voice was small and far away and got broken up by the crackles, cause of the reception up in the mountains. He celebrated victories over the guerrilla fighters in Albacete, Lérida and Valencia but said there were many hiding in the mountains and they would be hunted down. He told the men of the New Republic to always be vigilant. Half an hour later when the General had finished, Father Alberto spoke and shook hands with the men and thanked them for coming and again warned us all to be on the lookout for communists and monarchists alike. There were bandits everywhere. He asked the men to stay behind and dismissed everyone else. 'Go with the grace of God and the protection of El Generalísimo.' I bet he wore a soldier's uniform under that cassock of his."

"Later, I heard Papi come home, he had been drinking and made a right noise. He woke Mami as well. They said something but I couldn't hear what they were saying because of the noise Papi made. Once he was in bed though, I could hear they were talking about the Jimenez family. Father Alberto had told the men he had confirmation that Señor Manolo had been a fighter with the Popular Front in Seville in the Civil War. His death was unfortunate but was the price paid by traitors against the State. José Blanco cheered when Father Alberto announced it. Mami gasped when she realised what had happened.

'Manolo was shot? He was executed? On the word of whom? It couldn't be Father Alberto, I don't believe it, he's a man of the church.' I could hardly hear her croaky voice cause it was breaking up with emotion. Papi said nothing but that was answer enough. 'And Esther and Rocio?' Papi didn't answer. 'Pascual, tell me! Tell me what happened to Esther?' Papi paused again as if trying to remember, although this wasn't the kind of thing you forget.

'They got away. They did go to Seville. I watched them go.' Papi explained a few of the men but mostly José Blanco, thought they were fair game, the family of rebel scum. 'Esther begged on her knees to Father Alberto to save her girl but he turned his back on them.'

'No. No Pascual, I don't believe it. Why didn't you tell me before?' Mami gasped again, she was shocked.

'No. Dora. Nothing happened to them. I told José no way he or anyone else was to touch them and I stayed with them until Miguel Guerrero came and took them away in his truck. José knows better than to cross me.' I lay in bed with Conchi beside me, her breathing faint. I stared up at the ceiling into the blackness thinking about what could have happened to my friend and her mother. Miguel Guerrero had taken them away, but then what? There was no light in our room, all there was, was darkness and Mami's sobs."

"Mami hardly said a word for the next few days. Life just went on but every time I passed the old Jimenez house I thought of my friend Rocio and her mother, and every time Manolo's face filled my head, frightened and all bloody. Did Miguel really save Esther and Rocio and take them to Seville? I had never thought of our valley as a dangerous place before. I was born there, in the village, I knew everyone, we all knew each other. It really scared me. I noticed more the look on Father Alberto's face as he bullied the children in class. The contempt he had for us, the delight he took in punishing the boys, always the boys, sometimes he could hardly hide his excitement. He caught me once staring at him, watching him enjoy himself. When he noticed me a big grin spread across his face, standing there all dressed in black, the uniform of The Church. No matter what Mami said, he was not a man of God. He was not a man of God."

Chapter Three

It was mid morning and ominously hot for spring. Jimmy was sprawled on the sofa, trying not to think of the looming afternoon shift in the city's Accident and Emergency department. One positive was that the hospital had air conditioning. The heat and the humidity of the apartment would be murder later in the afternoon. He looked down at Wayne who was biting his left paw.

"Hey, stop that." Wayne took no notice and continued gnawing. "Take you back to the vet." Jimmy leant over and hoisted the chunky dog onto his chest so their faces were only centimetres apart. Wayne harrumphed his displeasure at being lifted. His breath smelled rancid, but that was Wayne and Jimmy accepted it. "I said quit it, you'll get another infection." Jimmy dug his fingers into the space behind the dog's disproportionately large ears, making his head rock with the rhythm of a vigorous massage. This was their ritual, their daily bonding. Wayne's eyes flickered closed with pleasure, his breathing purred. "Listen, I'm going to work. I'll not be long then we'll walk down the pub for a night cap. What d'you think? Eh? Yeah, I thought you'd say that. Right down you go you're making me too hot." Wayne harrumphed again then waddled off to look for a cool corner to settle into and peace to continue chewing his paw.

After another refreshing shower Jimmy felt ready to face the day. "Bye Wayne, I'll not be long." He waited for a response from the other room, knowing none would come. As he grabbed his keys from the tallboy he repeated "Bye," this time to a photo of him with a toddler sat on his knee. Both of them smiled into the camera. "Miss you mate." Again he waited, staring at the photo. Nothing. He took a deep breath and locked the door behind him.

As he left his apartment building he looked across the road to the hovel where the old woman lived. He couldn't not notice it and again he wondered how anyone could live there. The house to its left was only marginally better. Both were a stain on the neighbourhood. As usual the albino wolf dog was sitting to attention at the top of the stairs. She turned her head as Jimmy's gate swung closed but her stare didn't linger. There was something unsettling about that dog and Jimmy was thankful that the kid who owned it controlled it so well.

He had only advanced a few steps when he stopped. A dusty Toyota was reverse parking in front of him. A dozen or so stickers from the island's discotheques and parties adorned the periphery of the rear-view window; Matinee, Cocoon and CircoLoco. A testimony to the car's summer expeditions and an obvious impediment to any driver's vision. A less dirty semi-circle revealed that the back windscreen wiper had at one time worked. Jimmy stared, his eyes narrowed against the morning sun, as the car jostled into place. Wheels screeched as it mounted the kerb, scraping the car in front. The driver screamed something in Italian to no one and everyone. He finished his manoeuvring with another double bump. Heavy bass boomed from the car as Jimmy edged past. "Fucking Italians," he muttered. He hoped that a door might open so he would have an excuse to kick it shut again, perhaps catching a leg in the process. The possibility of it both scared and excited him. He noticed the passenger pass a yellow flame under what looked like Moroccan black and crumble it onto some tobacco precariously balanced on his thigh. A quick smoke would bring them down from their MDMA or cocaine high. Jimmy barrelled his fingers and pointed them towards the men inside. 'Pow!' he spat, in a poor impersonation of Dirty Harry. For Jimmy this was a seasonal plague and summertime hadn't even started.

The fifteen minute walk to the hospital was torturous, it felt about 30 degrees. Breezes this far from the sea were sparse and offered little relief. As usual the sky was cloudless and the sun had already chased away the shadows, stealing the streets of their shelter. The older men that gathered in the morning to smoke and repeat yesterday's stories had already retired home. A few women braved the midday, scuttling between their home and shops with provisions for lunch. Serious shopping could wait. No one walked in this heat unless they had to.

The temperature change once in the hospital was marked. Jimmy's skin prickled with goosebumps. "Thank God for air-conditioning," he muttered to himself. He had arrived late but still sauntered into the ward area. He flashed a few insincere smiles at colleagues whom he had no intention of being otherwise cordial to. He had never got comfortable with the manner in which the Spanish greeted each other. Kisses and a catch up with people they had seen only the day before. It felt false, Jimmy preferred his English reserve.

* * *

"Buenos días." Jimmy chirped as he pulled over a chair to the nurses' table.

"Piss off, 'buenos días' Jimmy?" Eva Batista mocked his English accent. "You're late. I told you yesterday I had to be at my kid's school at 12 and it's 10 past already." She stared at him, lips tight, daring him to refute what she had just said.

"I, erm, never mind." Jimmy cut short his reply.

"Well, this is what there is," and with a certain amount of animosity she continued, giving Jimmy a name, diagnosis and treatment summary for each of the 14 patients in her charge. The bare minimum. He listened disinterestedly looking down at the nursing admission sheets that she snapped before him. She dropped them onto the desk but thrust the last one at him. It was blank. "You can do that one, he arrived about half an hour ago. When *you* said you would be here. He's in bed 12. I'm off." Eva stood, slammed the chair under the table and left without another word.

"*Adios*." Jimmy sighed and watched as she strode towards the door. Unusually for a Spanish woman she was a natural redhead, with olive-brown skin, heavily punctuated by chestnut freckles. She was pear shaped with substantial breasts. Her tight scrubs accentuated her backside. The tunic top, not wide enough to be pulled all the way down, sat wrinkled around her waist. Jimmy smirked to himself. Eva could be a bit of a bitch, but that just added to her attraction. He had masturbated more than once thinking about little ginger Eva. She stopped to talk to another nurse at the door, no doubt exchanging pleasantries about him. He didn't care, he too could be a bitch if he wanted to.

Satisfied there was nothing immediate to take care of Jimmy took the blank admission sheet and sought out the new arrival. His shoes squeaked in protest at the cheap linoleum as he padded down the ward. Behind drawn curtains he could hear the muted voices of private whispered conversations. The harsh fluorescent light and the off-beige drapes made him feel he was in some science fiction movie. When he reached bed 12, he pulled back the curtains he was faced with the half dead. Light breathing sounds the only signs of life. Jimmy recognised this man as Klaus Frimbold. Klaus's head was heavily and amateurishly bandaged with an ineffective under-chin strap. Whoever had bandaged the wound had neglected to clean the blood from his face. Blood that had since dried out, blackened and cracked and was now flaking onto the pillow case. Klaus's story wasn't unusual for an alcoholic; get drunk, fall over, injure yourself and end up in A&E. "For Christ's sake," Jimmy muttered knowing Klaus' stay wouldn't be a short one. With so much paperwork to be started it was no surprise Eva had left it for him. Just as he was about to go Klaus's eyes flickered open. Jimmy shuddered and stared, waited a moment, then took a step to the left. The vacant orbs didn't follow. The gaunt, bloodied face looked straight ahead, eyes open but sunken and inert. No recognition. No light. Klaus was one of the forgotten souls of Ibiza. Many people arrived and were seduced by the island, the magic, the hedonism. Many people stayed when they should have gone home. A disconcerting thought highjacked Jimmy's consciousness. What if Klaus was the ghost of his future? Lost on the island, abandoned in a foreign land, with no one to look after him, with no one to care. Is this what was awaiting Jimmy? Pangs of regret started to surface but he didn't give them air turning his attention back to the matter at hand. "Glasgow Coma Scale, umm, let's say 11." A measured guess that allowed him to take no immediate action. He made a mental note to get the nursing auxiliary to provide Klaus with some personal hygiene and remove the blood from that tragic face and with that he let the curtain fall again.

* * *

The rest of the shift went without incident but he was glad to be home. Wayne was waiting behind the door. "Hi champ, ready to go out?" Wayne stood as Jimmy bent to scratch his head. "Just pick up something and we'll go." The dog watched as Jimmy rummaged through a drawer, then they were off. The walk to the pub would be slow, Wayne's pace as he marked almost everything he passed. When they arrived at the Italians' dusty Toyota, Jimmy bent over and pretended to pick up Wayne's excrement but instead punctured both pavement side tyres with a screwdriver hidden in the little collection bag. He hadn't expected the noise of the air escaping to be so loud, but grinned to himself anyway, delighted at the small victory. He gave Wayne a gentle tug, the beer waiting for him would now be all the sweeter.

Chapter Four

Ibiza 2016

It had been a long and hot spring day so Paco had taken Tyson down to the shore after school. The faithful dog watched as her master and his friends flaunted their acrobatic and clownery skills jumping into the cool water. In the afternoon sun her white coat contrasted sharply against the dark volcanic rock. She never took her eyes off him, occasionally rising to her feet when the play-fighting appeared a little too boisterous. Tyson maintained this same vigilant pose most of the day whilst Paco was at school, standing guard on the porch, a single headed Cerberus. This unwavering devotion to Paco didn't enthral his mother, who recognised the potential for violent reaction if provoked. It was in the DNA of such dangerous dogs, it was to be expected. His father, Sebastian, on the other hand, was counting on it.

After an hour or so by the water, the friends went their separate ways. Paco remained on the rocks, allowing the sun to dry and warm his robust yet athletic body. He flexed his biceps, then his pectoral muscles and grinned to himself. Not bad for his age. He lay there in the near silence, one arm across the dog the other behind his head and watched the seagulls and falcons in their respective strata patrol the shoreline. As the sun sank behind the hills he returned home where dinner and homework would be awaiting him.

As he approached his house he saw the elderly neighbour standing by her gateway with her scraggy mutt. The giant Tyson loped over to investigate. Baby cowered as was her custom but Maria Dolores stood firm, knowing there was no threat. Paco had known the old lady all his life but, although he was curious, he knew little about her. His mother, Bernarda, was the only one in the family that had anything to do with her. He nodded his acknowledgement and stopped a moment watching the dogs. The old woman seemed harmless to him. It never crossed his mind to judge her for being unkempt or living like she did. That was just her way. As he stood watching, without warning, she half kicked Baby towards the wall. The rapid action caused her to lose her balance just as a moped sped past them missing Tyson by less than a metre. Baby yelped in disapproval as Paco sprung forwards motivated as much by his dog's closeness to the moped than the old lady's fall.

"You alright?"

"*Hijo de puta,* That's the second time this week," Maria Dolores seethed having noticed the oncoming vehicle before Paco or the distracted dogs. He offered his arm and helped her up. Once on her feet she brushed herself down. The pair faced each other, a brief nonverbal exchange that neither needed to clarify. She nodded and grunted again then opened her own gate and followed Baby in. Paco slapped Tyson roughly on the neck and glared into the half-darkness but the moped was nowhere to be seen.

A few hours later the roars of 'Paco! Paaaco!' reverberated

along the narrow, empty street. Darkness and humidity fell in equal measures along the hillside, the warmth of the spring sun already a memory. "Pacoooo!" This last cry hung longer in the air, heads in neighbouring houses turned. Paco switched the outside light on and stepped out onto the porch, Tyson trotted out after him. The naked bulb swung in the night breeze. "Ay, Paco. Thank God you're here. Help me." The desperation in his voice battled with an alcohol induced languor. He let his heavy head drop back on the asphalt. "Help me," he repeated, staring up at the dark sky.

Paco plodded down the stairs, indifferent to his father's predicament. After apparently managing to navigate his way home safely, his drunkenness hadn't allowed for either a dignified nor coordinated dismount and had been trapped by the weight of the scooter.

"Papi, did you hurt yourself?" Paco asked more out of obligation than genuine concern, having witnessed this scenario before. He lifted the scooter up, first with his strong arms, then shifted his weight to push it with his shoulders, freeing his father. Sebastian crawled out and pulled himself up on Paco's leg. "You're lucky the exhaust didn't burn you." But Paco's words fell on deaf ears.

"Thank God, thank God. I thought I was gonna be stuck here all night." The slurred words trailed away as he swayed with the breeze. Paco watched his father stutter forward. Slow, calculated steps carried him inside the gate and then he was gone. A quick scan of the street didn't reveal any place to park so Paco hoisted the scooter up onto the pavement for the night. Tomorrow it would be his father's problem. With as much urgency as he had descended, Paco re-climbed the stairs to the house, wiping his hands on his bare chest. He was a sturdy 15-year-old, certainly broader than the other boys at school and walked with a swagger and confidence that belied his age. Heavyset men with broad shoulders, a family characteristic that Sebastian had passed onto his four sons. A fried and processed food diet, their mother's contribution, completed their corpulence.

If Bernarda, had chastised his father it was over before Paco re-entered the house. Sebastian was already asleep on the one armchair the family possessed, the same one Paco had vacated when called to the rescue. The room was noticeably cooler than the air outside and he felt a chill as he sought out somewhere to sit in front of the 71 inch plasma television. It was inordinately large and dominated the small living room but there was little negotiation when 'gifts' arrived in the night.

The fireplace that kept the small room warm and humidity free in the winter lay dormant. Evidence that Sebastian tried in his haphazard way to repair damages or incorporate renovations was abundant. An extension in which Paco's parents slept had been constructed at a leisurely pace by his father and friends. So far it was still standing. The house was, like Maria Dolores' next door, old and decrepit. The torrid Mediterranean sun, the all-permeating humidity and the harsh alkaline sea wind were a potent cocktail that caused the paint to flake, the walls to crumble and the wooden window frames to rot. These houses on the hill weren't built with modern materials nor were they designed like the centuries old Ibizan houses which still dotted the island. Sebastian was no skilled tradesman and with little monetary recourse was fighting a losing battle.

Paco took his can of store-brand cola and sat on the floor at his mother's feet. Tyson came and rested her head on his lap. An automatic hand reached across her and started to massage her neck, Paco's eyes not leaving the television.

"Bed soon." Bernarda attempted to ruffle his hair but he pulled away, throwing up his hand as if batting away an irritating mosquito. "School tomorrow," she added more sternly.

"Yeah, alright." But Paco knew better than to argue. Every morning she prepared breakfast for her three sons, the three that still lived at home. Every morning she impressed upon them the importance of paying attention in class. Every morning the same ritual, the same lecture. Bernarda hadn't attended school after the age of 12, not many of her contemporaries had. In the those days Spain still suffered the hangover from Franco's regime, there was no presumption that gitano children attend school. That it had been written into the Constitution was a concession to the liberal left, an empty conciliation, a pretence to a new united Spain. Social progress had been lethargic to say the least. Gitanos were second class citizens, nobody cared. But she was adamant that the children have an education, the opportunity to have what she had been denied. Much to her embarrassment, Bernarda could only read what she needed to but was far from able to help with homework. Their father even less capable.

"You listening?" Paco didn't answer but got up and went to the bathroom. The lights momentarily flickered and the TV switched itself off; someone must have turned on the communal lights of the building next door. The building from which the Moreno household's electricity had been 'diverted'. Paco left his mother sitting in the stillness with only the company of her husband's laboured breathing. With a subtle click of his fingers Tyson stood and trotted behind him. A few minutes later he heard another nightly reprimand. "And the dog doesn't sleep on the bed." Tyson was indeed on the bed. She lay to his left, her black eyes still open, fixed on the door, 40 kilograms of canine security. Unlike all his classmates he didn't have a smart-phone, Nintendo Switch, or even an old Gameboy but he didn't care. He had his dog and he wouldn't have it any other way. He closed his eyes and let sleep take him, one arm still draped over Tyson.

Bernarda looked around the room but she didn't see the home she had dreamt of. Drapes that could not be described as curtains hung by the windows. A crucifix and a weathered portrait of Saint Anthony the only adornments on the cracked stucco walls. That television was the only sign that the 21st century had graced their house. A wooden side dresser, reclaimed from the street, stood against a bare wall. She didn't know how many family photographs stood to attention across its surface. Faces stared out from their varied wooden and faux-metal frames: cold poses and serious looks, nothing natural, no one laughing. If she counted them she would find that there were 14 but there was only one of Sebastian Jr, and it was this photo that always cried out to her. She knew she had let him down. He was her first born, the first to drop out of school, the first to work his way into The Clan, the first one to be lost to her. She was determined that he would be the only one to go down this path. Paco was a good boy, he had looked tired and would be sleeping already. That dog was probably on the bed with him, but Bernarda didn't care, she wanted him to be happy. She stood and headed to her own bedroom, leaving her inert husband unconscious on his armchair.

Chapter Five

The Mountains 1946

A few days later Maria Dolores returned to San Salvador de La Marina to continue her story. As she sat with Father Gabriel under the relentless presence of the Christ without a face, the last of the snows in the valley around Los Caballeros de la Sierra melted and sank into the yielding ground. Patches of green broke through and expanded, spreading up the hillsides. As she recounted tales from her childhood, the first shoots of revitalised life emerged giving optimism to those in the valley. It restored sustenance to the livestock and their unborn young within, and after another severe and ruthless winter the cycle of life yet again triumphed.

The more temperate weather allowed the mountain pass to open again. Cars and trucks seldom stopped as they headed to the coastal towns. Buses were more regular but if they did pause, there were few that had reason to alight here. Occasionally men passed through the village looking for seasonal work. Sometimes in small groups, sometimes alone. Wasted figures, malnourished and diseased, they were treated suspiciously and encouraged on their way. Physically fragile men had no place on the mountain pastures or tilling the uneven plots around the farmhouses. They left the village as quickly as they had arrived, on to unknown destinations or occasionally dying alone along the roadside in the unforgiving cold of the night.

Juan Diego Martos Gutierrez was one young individual who happened to pass through Los Caballeros de La Sierra on a bright sunny day just as Pascual Benitez was gauging the size of the imminent and seemingly immense task ahead of him. The shearing of the 20 or so Segureña sheep followed by lambing season as well as general springtime maintenance. Then there was the huerto which had been amplified since last year. With some luck and hard work the huerto would deliver enough food to make preserves which would last them deep into next winter. He realised with some apprehension that this year it would be way too much for one man; especially now that Manolo Jimenez wasn't around to help out.

The two men's first encounter came at the entrance of Guerrero's bar. The shadow of the nearby church reached across the plaza, engulfing them. Cold oppression hung in the air in stark contrast to the blue skies and sunlit hillsides surrounding the village. The shadow would soon pass and the bar's few customers would have midday coffee or aperitif in the sun and forget for a moment the quotidian stresses of life in the mountains. The heavy set proprietress, who had just refused the outsider's offer of assistance, was explaining that it was unlikely that anyone 'around here' would be looking for workers. Pascual, however, took one look at Juan Diego and knew immediately that this young man was exactly what he needed.

"Buenos días Maria." Pascual approached the bar door but

feigned not to notice the other man standing there. "How is everything today?"

Maria stopped manhandling a small wooden table and brushed down her pinafore, a polite but unnecessary gesture. "Buenos días Pascual. Just putting a few tables in the sun. We should make the most of it don't you think?"

"Quite right Maria."

"You want a coffee?" Maria enquired. Juan Diego witnessing the exchange took a small step back, an innate timidness directing him not to intrude on this private conversation.

"I'll take a quick cognac thank you, and eh, just a word with Miguel if he's around."

"You've just missed him. Gone to buy a few things, well that's what he tells me."

"Hah, more brandy I hope and cigarettes. He still not smoking?"

"Nope and he's a pain for it. But he's determined he'll never smoke again after what that doctor told him." Maria shrugged her shoulders.

"He's some man. What do doctors know anyway. I've smoked for 40 years."

"Back about four he said. After lunch. Hah! Just like him, coming back when the work's done." Maria managed an unconvincing smile, there was no sarcasm in her voice, just a tired acquiescence of the situation. Her brown and black mongrel dog trotted over to Pascual and investigated his left leg, sniffing up to the knee but quickly lost interest, the scents of the country all too commonplace and unexciting.

"Hmmm. OK, gracias." Pascual considered the information and turned towards Juan Diego. For the first time he acknowledged the younger man, looking him up and down without directly facing him. He saw someone who looked like he could certainly cope with the oncoming season; wide shoulders, sturdy body and youthful. A dirty flat cap sat tipped back revealing the roots of his black hair, which at the back had been tucked into an equally dirty neck scarf. Clearly, the woollen jacket he was wearing wasn't originally his, although the shoulders and chest were a good fit, it was too long and the sleeves were rolled up at the wrists. The chestnut-brown trousers were a tone or two darker than the jacket but were a better fit. The worn-in black boots had also seen a few seasons' field work. All in all Juan Diego was a bit unkempt but was certainly a class above those that normally passed through the valley looking for work.

"Buenos días señor." Juan Diego removed his cap, holding it tightly in front of him with both hands. He gave a slight, nervous nod towards Pascual.

"What's your name son?"

"Juan Diego Martos Gutierrez, señor," he replied still not completely lifting his head.

"What you doing around here? Not much work here, you know." Pascual took a few steps towards Juan Diego's left making it obvious he was again giving him the once-over. Juan Diego didn't answer, keeping his head bowed, avoiding direct eye contact, not wanting to seem disrespectful. "You ever worked as a farm-hand?"

"Yes, señor, my uncle has a farm outside Oviedo. Mainly cattle. Heavy work in calving season," lied Juan Diego. The deceit an innocent but necessary one. He straightened his back, pulling himself up equal to his examiner, spirited by the interest.

"So why you not up there working with him?"

"I have cousins there, his four sons. There's not so much work in the winter for everyone," Juan Diego improvised.

"Hmmm, and you're not heading back north?"

"No señor. I'm here now and want to work." The two men

now stood facing each other. Juan Diego knew he was supposed to be intimidated by the intense stare of the older man but he felt safe. When you smile, when a smile is truly genuine it emerges first in the eyes, not the mouth. Layers of orbital, temporal and zygomatic muscles combined to send the message that both men subconsciously recognised.

"I work hard, señor. You can rest assured of that."

"Hmmm," Pascual repeated. "Well, come with me then." And this was how their first encounter ended, with Pascual leading Juan Diego away from the village and towards his home, towards his family and towards Maria Dolores.

Chapter Six

Ibiza 2016

The metal blind that normally very effectively kept out the morning sun hadn't been fully lowered the night before. Light streamed into the south-facing bedroom. Wayne's gravelly breathing rose from the floor to his left. With his face still in the pillow, Jimmy stretched out his arm and let it wander until it located the dog. He followed the contours of his back until he reached the head and then scratched around the ears. Wayne shook his head then groaned as he pushed into Jimmy's hand. Another daily ritual completed, their morning greeting realised. Outside the faint rumble of traffic and the buzz of a grass strimmer told Jimmy the world carried on even if he wasn't fully present. He allowed his senses to awaken him but cursed his own negligence at not closing the blind properly. His mouth tasted disgusting, a fur coated his teeth and his shrivelled tongue stung. It was painful to swallow. It crossed his mind that he had vomited the night before but that wasn't like him. The night had been more about drugs than alcohol, although one normally accompanied the other. He didn't use cocaine much but when he did he had a tendency to overdo it, especially in the wrong company. He became aware of his left calf jerking. It tensed then relaxed, a surge of cramp was imminent. It was time to get up and move before the real pain set in.

As he left the apartment he noticed the picture of his son wasn't in its usual place. A bolt of anxiety stabbed at his chest. A glance around the small kitchen revealed nothing. The anxiety doubled. "Fuck," he muttered and quickened his step to the living room. And there it was, face up on the coffee table. He picked it up and and blew away a few flakes of tobacco. He didn't remember how it got there, but it wouldn't be the first time he'd carried the photo around the house, talking to it. Alcohol brought out his melancholic side. He placed it in its rightful spot and opened the front door. "Come on Wayne. I need a coffee."

It was just after ten as Jimmy made his way down the winding path that ran past his building to the promenade. He had had only five hours sleep and the sunlight was cruel. Wayne bounced after him navigating the steps with more agility than his stocky frame might have suggested. Two minutes later the Mediterranean stretched out before them. The sister island of Formentera a dark ridge on the horizon. The water was a translucent green and aquamarine, colours which emanated from the Posedonia flora below. Jimmy paused and managed an appreciative smile, absorbing the calm beauty of the morning sea.

He passed the waterfront's tourist-laden terraces and was soon sitting in his favourite cafe on a quieter corner in Figueretas. An elderly Moroccan with brown teeth served him a strong sweet coffee with a semolina biscuit. He downed them both and ordered more, convinced that the caffeine and the sugar were exactly what his wrecked body needed. Wayne snuffled around at his feet hoovering up crumbs.

Jimmy enjoyed the lack of pretentiousness here. Men in faded djellaba pushed dominoes across cheap formica tables with nicotine stained fingers. They goaded each other and smiled toothless grins, all the time chatting incessantly. Jimmy didn't understand a word. How good it felt to be lost and disconnected. His neighbour, the old woman, with her scrawny mutt, passed by on the other side of the street, but their eyes didn't meet which was fine with him. Half an hour more then he'd head home. It was hot and he needed to be horizontal.

Much later Jimmy found himself in Jock's bar. At home he had tried to sleep again but his mind was still chemically active and his body fidgety, the apartment hot and stuffy. The sweltering heat was doing nothing for his hangover. Jock's was where he often ended up when at a loose end. His phone pinged in his hand. Santi: 'Where r u?' Jimmy wanted to say he was in bed but instead replied. 'Jock's'.

Twenty minutes later Santi sat two fresh pints of Guinness on the table. Jimmy gulped at the cold beer, gratefully accepting the buzz. The gnawing sensation he had behind his eyes all day was starting to ease. He stared at the painted black decking. It was smattered with burn marks and unsightly blisters, an indelible record of the hundreds of cigarettes that had been extinguished there. Santi continued talking.

"But you remember Castro's right?"

"I remember getting there." Jimmy sighed, the interrogation was getting tedious. Santi grunted a laugh.

"Well you were in the toilet every 10 minutes, and asked me for another gram." This explained Jimmy's physical state. "And they kept bringing us shots of Hierbas, and you drank Arantxa's cause she was driving."

"Arantxa? That works in outpatients?"

"Yeah, the pair of you disappeared. I thought you were just having another line but then you didn't come back."

"Kinda rings a bell." Jimmy's groan tickled Santi.

"Well you will get drunk and take drugs." The patronising tone was beginning to grate. "Anyway when you got home, you fell asleep."

"Santi!"

"She messaged me earlier. I asked her." Jimmy clenched his teeth, annoyed that Santi already knew more of the night's events than he did. "Come on. Don't be like that. Don't worry, you didn't shag her." Jimmy slapped his pint glass down on the table. A lick of white froth leapt up but splashed back into the glass again. "Didn't even try," Santi laughed louder.

"The hell you ask her that for?"

"Calm down Jimmy. She likes you that's all I'm saying." They sat in silence. Jimmy clenched his jaw but knew Santi was just being Santi, indelicate to say the least. Other people's feelings weren't a priority. It was his own fault for overindulging. It was an old habit that wasn't about to die. He swilled the black beer around in the glass.

"I'm gonna go."

"Listen, is this still about Jenni?" Jimmy visibly tensed then slumped forward over his glass. He didn't understand Santi's continuing animosity towards his ex.

"Here we go."

"I'm just saying."

"Yeah, you're always 'just saying'. You need to give it a rest Santi it's got nothing to do with you."

"And you need to get over that cow. She ran away with your kid."

"She didn't run away, we split up."

"Whatever Jimmy, she's not here, neither is little Pedro *and* you're still whining about it." An edginess had crept into

Santi's tone.

"*And* maybe I'm not like you that shags anything that moves, only thinking with my cock. *And* maybe that's why you screw up all your relationships. So maybe *you* should keep out of it." Santi sucked his teeth, smarting from the force of Jimmy's outburst. The two of them stared at each other, neither sure if retreat or attack was the wiser option. After a long minute, Santi stood and went inside. That they argued wasn't unusual but tempers seldom frayed. That things got heated so quickly surprised Jimmy. He took a controlled, deep breath to stop him hyperventilating and watched as Santi paid the bill. Was this anger warranted? After all there was some truth in what Santi said. Jimmy just didn't like to hear it.

Santi returned. "I'm away. Talk to you later." When Jimmy didn't respond Santi added, "But Jimmy, think about what I said. You need to move on and get over that bitch." Then Santi did walk away leaving Jimmy gazing down at the black decking.

A bench overlooking the sea seemed the perfect place for Jimmy to pause on his return home. He let himself be soothed by the rhythmic sound of the waves. But the calm was momentary, his tumultuous thoughts soon took him back to Jenni and his son Pedro. Santi's words had exposed and gnawed on a raw nerve and after a few more beers Jimmy had become even more morose and melancholic. It was true that they had split up but the real reason was Jimmy's philandering. His anger with Santi was a projection of the anger he felt towards himself. His own behaviour was exactly what he had accused Santi of. He had chosen sexual gratification over his relationship and his son and had quickly lost both. 'Lost' He thought. 'Lost, no. Thrown away.'

Chapter Seven

The Mountains, Spring 1946

Pascual persevered with the interrogation on their short journey up the hillside from the village. Juan Diego, who continued to impress, matched the purposeful stride of his new employer. He wondered if his body odour was noticeable and thought of the detachable shirt collar he had folded in his bag. Finding opportunity to attach it before reaching their destination would surely be an impossible task. He needn't have worried however, his humility and eagerness both to work and to learn had already struck a chord. His youthfulness suggested a physical capability that Pascual sometimes felt was waning in himself.

The door opened as the two men approached the house. Dora made a brief appearance throwing some scraps to a couple of chickens scratching at the hard ground at the front of the house. Their relentless search for food proving at last to be fruitful. She watched them for a second or two before returning inside. On their arrival, Pascual introduced Juan Diego to Dora as his new farmhand. Juan Diego allowed himself the merest of smiles at his newly announced position. It sounded almost permanent. A stability that he had been lacking for some time.

"First we eat, then up to the pastures. You can sleep on the floor by the fire for now. There's blankets somewhere. Maybe fix up the Manolo's place when the nights aren't so cold." Whenever Pascual mentioned his old friend his voice dropped, almost imperceptibly but Dora noticed the regret, that soft tone of remorse that refused to fade away. "Well, see how things go. Let's see if you can work first eh?" He smiled at the attentive Juan Diego, but it lacked the same intensity as before.

They sat at the kitchen table where Dora began her own interrogation and again the young man continued to impress with a politeness and respect which contradicted his dishevelled exterior. She laid a motherly hand on his forearm. "Call me Dora, señora makes me feel old." She rewarded him with some fresh unleavened bread. It had been sitting on the table tantalisingly close, but it hadn't crossed Pascual or Dora's mind that he might be hungry. He was in fact ravenous. In the end, it was a prize earned for being himself and the first real sustenance he had had in days. The rough crust hurt his inflamed gums as he bit into it. Its baked dryness rasped his already parched mouth but this elemental food was, for Juan Diego, manna heaven sent. He revelled in his surroundings: the warmth from the stove, the wooden chair treated him like a throne, feeling returned to his feet. In the moments of silence, again, he feared that he smelled; how long had it been since he washed or changed his shirt? He felt embarrassed by his condition but nevertheless welcomed by these two strangers. He thanked Dora for her kindness, she smiled and said something about Saint Luke and the good samaritan. Beside him Pascual rolled his eyes.

Shortly afterwards Conchi crashed through the door, as

always eager to recount the day's events in the classroom. She ran towards Dora who was standing by the stove, the words spilling from her just as fast as her feet were carrying her. The two men sat at the table went unnoticed.

"Mami, Mami, Father Alberto says we're to go to the big school next week. A bus'll take us every day."

"Oh that's exciting Conchi."

"I've never been to the real school before."

"Yes, I know." Conchi's tale was broken by her father's laughter from across the room.

"Ayy, Papi. I didn't see you." The gaiety in her voice dropped off as she suddenly registered the other presence.

"How could you not see me little one? I'm over 6 foot, come over here. Come meet Juan Diego. If you're going to the big school I'll need another helper with the animals. Won't I?" She held onto her mother's apron unsure of the stranger but then relented, and ran to her father's side.

"Hello." Juan Diego stood and held out his hand.

"This is Conchi."

"Hello, Conchi." Juan Diego repeated. She softened a little and echoed his greeting but didn't take his outstretched hand.

"Don't let this little one trick you. She's not so shy." Pascual laughed again, pulling her closer, his huge arm wrapping around her waist.

Moments later the door opened again, bringing with it a burst of sunlight. The relative darkness resumed as Maria Dolores closed the door behind her. Like her sister before her she was keen to update her mother on the day's business.

"You'll never guess. Well, I suppose Conchi's already." Unlike her sister, her tone was composed, and unlike her sister, she immediately noticed that there was a stranger in their midst. Her words halted in mid-sentence. She paused by the door, unsure whether to enter her own home or not. She wasn't accustomed to seeing outsiders in the house. Without taking her eyes off him, she unwrapped her headscarf and placed it on the door-side dresser.

"And this is Maria Dolores." Pascual left his introduction hanging in the air, the words for him insignificant and uncomplicated. Conchi giggled again and nuzzled into her father as he tickled her and Dora turned her attention back to the lentil stew. Juan Diego stood again, this time more slowly. The chair scraped loudly on the stone floor, a log cracked in the fire behind him. His eyes, now fully re-accustomed to the duskiness of the room, focussed on the frozen Maria Dolores. He felt a sudden activity in his chest, an uncontrollable hormonal reaction to what he saw before him. He wanted to remove his hat as one should do in the presence of a woman but it already lay on the dresser beside Maria Dolores' discarded scarf. He wanted to take a step forward but his feet were rooted to the floor and didn't obey his commands. He wanted to approach her, to herald her beauty but no words came. The space between them was somehow closing in, but still beyond him. Maria Dolores broke the silence, that charged atmosphere only she and Juan Diego seemed to be aware of.

"Buenas tardes señor."

"Buenas tardes. Ehh, Juan Diego, señora, err señorita. Juan Diego Martos Gutierrez." He stuttered his introduction, the words tripped over each other as they clunked noisily into the room. He dipped his head again but maintained eye contact, an intense stare. Eyes that penetrated Maria Dolores and she felt herself flush. Frightened that she would betray herself, she also bowed her head, but to hide her face.

"Juan Diego is going to help me this spring." Her father interrupted by way of explanation. "Ha, he doesn't know what he's letting himself in for. Isn't that right little one?" He said to Conchi as he dug his thick fingers into her ribs tickling her again. She squealed with delight.

"Hang your coat up, Lola. Take the plates to the table, don't just stand there." Dora's instructions snapped Maria Dolores back to the present. Without further hesitation, she began to assist her mother. This was her normal routine, her actions unmeditated, but those actions were incongruent with what was actually coursing through her. Her thoughts were on this new person in her house. She couldn't recollect ever seeing a man that she would call handsome before. The men from the village were, well, just men from the village. What was this physical attraction? What was happening to her? She had never blushed before, nor wanted to hide her face. What was this unsettling feeling deep in her stomach? Did she even know anyone with such blue eyes? Or was it just the way he looked at her? Like no one had ever done before.

For the next hour the family ate. Dora and Conchi exchanged ideas about going to a 'proper' school, Conchi's excitement relentless. Maria Dolores, suddenly without appetite, forced herself to eat. She sat in a self-imposed silence, stealing glances at Juan Diego when she felt no one else was looking. Pirri padded around the table, briefly taking an interest in Juan Diego then went to lie by the fire, a berth he was soon to be ousted from. Pascual revelled in his own voice and his new audience and outlined exactly what was expected from his new farmhand. The sheep were to be taken to pasture every day now that the snow had almost gone. He was to help with chores and maintenance around the house and stable. Once the earth was tillable, there would also be sowing to do. If he had any spare time he could repair what was left of the old Jimenez house. It was mostly in good condition even though some materials had already been appropriated for other purposes. After lunch, before the early spring sunset, Pascual kept his word and took Juan Diego to show him the valley, where he was to work. Maria Dolores watched as they left the house, suddenly able to breathe again.

Life as a farm-hand starts before the sun hits the pastures, before it can impart any heat to those that labour on them. And so it was for Pascual and Juan Diego; rising before dawn and most days not returning until after dark. Pascual savoured the youngster's company and regaled him with anecdotes about the village and the mountains. Juan Diego, in turn, worked hard, both on the hillsides and on making the Jimenez place habitable. He felt the mountain air breathe life into him, the physical work invigorated him and the regular food replenished his yearning body. His acceptance by the Benitez family humbled yet heartened him and after his time wandering he felt their humanity touch him and he began to relax and be himself again.

Although very aware of his presence, Maria Dolores seldom saw Juan Diego. He was gone before she got up, his blankets and pillow folded and left beside the fire. If he came home at lunchtime her father consumed his attention asking about his day on the pastures and the state of the animals. Mostly he didn't return until dark when the family ate then sat around the table with oil lamps, the girls finishing homework and their mother sewed or read the bible. It was Pascual's custom to take a large brandy, something Juan Diego always declined.

As Easter approached Maria Dolores joined her mother and the other women as they busied themselves with the spring clean of the church and the preparations for the Procession of the Virgin. They sewed black painted wooden buttons onto bolero jackets and embroidered lace frills on their *mantillas*. For the marching costaleros, they darned and pressed their suits and stitched the long cassocks for the lucky six ready to carry out their exalted duties. For now, the Virgin remained in the comfort of the church whilst the chosen costaleros carried a customised old cart on their shoulders, sometimes loaded with a child or two, down from the church to the old well. They passed through the shadows of the aged olive trees, those ancient creatures that twisted and violently contorted in on themselves, as much by their own volition than by the elements around them.

The tiresome work was overseen by the idle Father Alberto who, on occasions like this, reflected upon his circumstances in this isolated community. He thought of the procession of the Virgin of Hope of Macarena in Seville, lauded and applauded by thousands as she was carried through the streets in a procession that lasted all day. The dignitaries that saluted her, the archbishops and probably a cardinal. That was the company he deserved. He craved the grandeur and the opulence of the parade. He yearned for the reverence that he too would receive from the devotees of the Virgin. He felt castigated in the valley and knew that in middle-age it was less likely that he would be rewarded with what he coveted most; an affluent parish and the power that accompanied it, an escape from this obscure hinterland. But he remained hopeful, an opportunity would arise and he would be ready to seize it. He compensated for his lot by overtly moralising to these simple parishioners. He could, quite literally, beat them into submission from a young age. Not having a bishop closely monitoring his activities had its advantages. The insignificance and remoteness of Los Caballeros de La Sierra also precluded its regular policing by the Guardia Civil. This was another unofficial responsibility that Father Alberto secretly relished, leading the fight against Franco's, and therefore the Church's, enemies; spiritual, political or otherwise. All in the name of God and Country, of course.

For over a decade Pascual had been the chief costalero, serving always at the left hand of the Virgin. It was his responsibility to control the pace and rhythm of the procession and only he decided when to set Her down to rest. One afternoon before the sun had set, a bank of low cloud descended upon the valley bringing with it a chill. It reminded the villagers that despite the daily sunshine, the summer had not yet arrived. Normally Father Alberto didn't interfere with the practice, his role was to walk behind the Virgin, leading the parishioners in their penitence. That day, however, as the costaleros prepared the wooden platform that would carry the Virgin, he approached Pascual.

"Good afternoon. How is everything going?" The priest peered down his nose to the working men, his inspection of their labours obvious.

"Good afternoon, Very well thank you," Pascual stopped to wipe his brow but kept his eyes on the priest.

"Looks like hard work and it's not so hot today is it?"

"No, not at all Father. It's not too bad"

"Hmm, a man of your age though." Father Alberto smirked, his fat cheeks rose in his face half-obscuring his piglet eyes.

"Ha! A man of my age? A man that has worked these mountains all his years. Plenty life in the old dog yet."

"Nevertheless Pascual, have you ever thought about handing over the mantle to a younger man?" It was then that Pascual noticed José Blanco looking on from the church door. He laughed realising where this conversation was headed. The thought of that cretin having more civic standing than him was preposterous.

"Father Alberto, José might have the years of a younger man, but he still has a long way to go to fill my boots."

"Pascual, I just think."

"No need to think of me Father, thank you." Pascual interrupted, "Like I say, I still have a few years left in me yet. I'll let you know when the time is right."

"Pascual, it's just that." Father Alberto's grin fell and was replaced by a sternness he normally reserved for the classroom. Pascual reacted to the change in tone and took a half step closer to the priest who did not move. Garlic and red wine rose from the priest's breath. He placed a hand on the cassocked priest's shoulder and leant closer as he spoke.

"I said, Father, I am very happy to continue to lead out the Virgin, it is an honour and a privilege." He conspicuously nodded towards the church, "And if José Blanco believes otherwise you can tell him to come and talk to me about it." They stood in silence, staring, each waiting for a retreat. The other costaleros had stopped arranging the platform, their attention now on the two men, the general hubbub abated. The priest yielded first, his stoney face turning again to a caustic smile.

"Very well Pascual. I can see you are eager to get on. I'm sure everything will turn out just fine." And with that, he departed feeling the eyes of the other men follow him back to the church.

Easter Friday of 1946 began as a bright cold day. The cloudless sky was a never-ending piercing blue, a pathway to heaven itself. The Virgin sat on a small plinth in front of the chancel awaiting her call. Since first light a few of the more devout women had been attending her, dusting again her adornments, straightening her lace, pampering this earthly effigy. Dora was conspicuous by her absence.

Father Alberto's late arrival was generally ignored by the

women. They paid no attention to his dishevelled state nor his bloodshot eyes. He approached and feigned an interest in their work but was brushed aside by the clucking women as they added their finishing touches.

Miguel Guerrero and his wife Maria applied the same industry to the bar and the preparation of food, whilst their daughter Ana arranged tables and cleaned glasses. They were sporadically interrupted by villagers bringing their own edible contributions.

José Blanco kicked Miguel's dog, who had had the bad judgement to stray a little too close. He continued to hang bunting and other faded little pennants outside Guerrero's bar. He took great pride in placing the State flag complete with its Francoist motto; *Una, Grande, Libre,* in the centre dominating the display. A symbol of strength he savoured.

Maria Dolores and Conchi had finished their chores, the chickens fed and the water trough in the animal outhouse replenished. They sat pristine in matching navy frocks, white headscarves tied below the chin, concealed their tightly braided hair. The headscarf's knot irritated Conchi, she pulled on it to relieve the pressure. Pascual, who had bathed and shaved, was dressing. Behind the closed bedroom door, they heard their parents share a private joke. Their laughter warmed Maria Dolores. The front door opened allowing Pirri to dash through. As always he sought out Maria Dolores who greeted him with her usual enthusiasm.

"Pirri, Pirri, did you catch any rabbits?" Pirri jumped up and licked her hands. "Down, you'll get me dirty." She dug her fingers under the dog's ears. In a feigned haughty accent she asked the dog, "Pirri, don't you think I'm beautiful in my finest dress?"

"You certainly are," came the unexpected response from the doorway. Maria Dolores blushed and turned away from the door recognising the voice of Juan Diego.

Conchi sniggered. "Juan Diego," she sang. "We're ready for the procession. Are you coming?"

"Yes, little one, of course. I'll have to wash and shave first but I'll be there. I wouldn't miss seeing all the beautiful women of the village in their finest dresses." His intonation mocked Maria Dolores. He entered the house, rolling down the sleeves of his working shirt. "Are *you* going?"

"Of course. Why do you think we're dressed up like this?" Conchi furrowed her eyebrows misunderstanding Juan Diego's tease.

"Ah. And you Maria Dolores, will you be there?" Maria Dolores didn't answer, she felt him sit down opposite her. His presence so close flustered her and she felt her face redden again. She could smell the exertion of the morning's work, feel the heat from his body emanate across the table, she sensed his eyes on her. "Maybe someone has stolen her tongue Conchi, eh." Conchi giggled again, stirring Maria Dolores into action.

"Actually, no one has my tongue, I just prefer not to use it answering stupid questions." She looked directly at Juan Diego trying to subdue her own smile.

"Well, it was worth the wait, don't you think Conchi?" He beamed back at her, raising his eyebrows, flashing those crystal blue eyes.

"Ah, Juan Diego, you're back," interrupted Pascual, his voice booming from the bedroom door.

"Yes Pascual, good morning."

"Everything all right? Good," he continued without waiting for an answer. "Dora has ironed a good shirt for you. I'm sure it'll fit fine. Oh, my beautiful daughters, what a sight you are." Conchi got up and ran to hug her father, leaving

Juan Diego and Maria Dolores staring at each other across the table, neither one wanting to let go of the moment.

At precisely two o'clock, Father Alberto led the selected few out of the small church. He was, as was customary, completely dressed in black; his cassock perfectly ironed, his polished shoes clicked the ground as he walked, a soft felt cap clung too snuggly to his round head. What was not customary was the opulent purple silk stole that crossed his shoulders, a garment and colour reserved for higher ranked clergy. His eyes flickered with apprehension as the costaleros lowered the Virgin delicately so she could pass through the narrow church doorway, her halo missing the apex of the arched frame by millimetres. Although they were all very familiar with the Virgin, the congregation, some 30 people, gasped then clapped as she came into the light, the sunshine sparkled off the tin-plated peaks of her crown. They gaped as Pascual and two other men delicately mounted Her onto Her platform. A few women came forward, crossed themselves and laid meadow flowers at her feet. Once in position, Father Alberto recited a benediction, dramatically flicking Holy water from a small silver phial. He splashed the Virgin, then the bearers' obeisant heads. On Pascual's command the costaleros lifted her, resting the wooden platform on their shoulders.

Murmurings smattered the courtyard as nervous onlookers watched the Virgin take to the air and the costaleros confirmed they were in position. Once settled Pascual nodded to his neighbour, who began to beat the slow tempo on his *tambori* drum. The Virgin gently swayed to the left, then the right as the costaleros found their rhythm below Her. Then on Pascual's mark, the procession began.

They carried Her down the gentle slope away from the church in silence. The scuffing of shoes the only sound to accompany the drum beat. They passed Guerrero's bar which was already prepared for the fiesta and towards the old well, where Her presence would bless the water and coming crops. Closest to the Virgin, the priest led his parishioners, followed by the men with the women and children bringing up the rear. It was their way, their custom but it was no more than patriarchal propagation. The women were sombre in their long dark dresses. Black macramé tasseled shawls which hung down to the waist and matching black head scarves completed their costume. Some, like Dora, mouthed quiet prayers.

Father Alberto walked with a pompous stride, exhibiting a self-importance that belied his station. He conveniently forgot for a moment that hubris was a sin, dismissing the expected humility in the presence of the Virgin. Maria Dolores noted his arrogance but was distracted, she hadn't yet seen Juan Diego. She slowed her pace allowing the other women to advance without her. Once they had passed she was able to look around less discretely but still saw nothing. A sudden prod on her right side made her jump.

"Shhhh," came the sharp caution as Juan Diego appeared to her left. "Huh, Maria Dolores. Please forgive me. I thought you were Ana Guerrero. You all look so alike dressed like this."

"Ana is twice the size of me, Juan Diego Martos," hissed Maria Dolores and she turned away to hide her smile.

"But you have to admit, she is a beautiful woman."

"Well, I suppose she is if you like a girl with the hide of a cow," Maria Dolores retorted.

"I'll be sure to pass on your compliments when I see her later," he teased, enjoying the game.

"She'll be there, right beside the cakes." Juan Diego this time laughed louder, attracting the attention of a few of the congregation.

"Perhaps Dolores, I'll see you there as well." And with that he left her as quickly as he had arrived. Maria Dolores trotted a few steps to regain her place at the tail of the procession, intoxicated with their flirtation. From a side street next to the bar, a wry grin spread across José Blanco's weathered face, having observed all that had gone on behind the Virgin's back.

Chapter Eight

Ibiza 2016

The return of the prodigal son to the Moreno household had been a happy occasion for all involved, at least to begin with. Sebas' disappearance three years earlier had been sudden but not wholly unexpected. It had been followed by the entirely expected police visits but their questioning, as everyone knew it would, proved to be fruitless. The gitanos were a closed community. The upheaval caused by his sudden reappearance had gone mostly unnoticed, lost in the midst of the party atmosphere that had pervaded their home. Bernarda hadn't stopped fussing whenever he was around, indulging his every whim. Their father had been a little more subdued, but he too, despite his inherent indolence, couldn't do enough for their first born. The twins were discovering a brother whom they had never really known, he reacted kindly and generously to their demands. Paco on the other hand didn't concur with the family's misplaced idolatry. He remembered well the Sebas of old. He remembered how that Sebas had treated him and the rest of the family before his exile; the drunkenness, his violent temperament, the beatings. In short, the nightmare it was to live with him. But he was back now and seemed to have mellowed. Paco hoped it would last.

Sebas came and went, never keeping regular hours. It wasn't uncommon for Paco to see him arrive as he left for school. Their greeting usually included some derisible comment regarding Paco's appearance or supposed educational needs. Paco was, however, a model student; academically intelligent with exemplary behaviour and despite a little prejudicial stereotyping, managed to flourish at school. In actual fact he found it all a bit too easy. His careers guidance advisor was convinced the upcoming exams wouldn't present him with any problems and had already discussed university options. It was a discussion Paco was hesitant to broach at home.

One stifling afternoon, soon after Sebas' return, Paco walked into what had been his bedroom to find his brother sitting on the bed in only his underpants. He was counting a pile €50 notes. Paco's instinct was to about turn, knowing he had stumbled upon something that he shouldn't have seen, but as he turned Sebas called him back.

"Come in lil' brother. It *is* your room." Paco hated being referred to as 'little bother,' like that, it was demeaning, he wasn't a child anymore.

"Hi," he mumbled and stood in the doorway watching as Sebas continued to flick through the crisp, pistachio coloured notes.

"Shut the door." Paco stepped inside. Tyson remained in the livingroom staring at the door waiting her master's reemergence.

The room was warm and stale, the air dense and malodorous. Cigarette ends overflowed a small decorative saucer sitting on the floor next to the bed. It was a souvenir that Paco's grandmother had brought back from Granada. It had a gaudy image of the Alhambra on it. It was stupid, nothing so important nor expensive, but before Tyson's arrival it was the only thing that he could have called his own.

"Y'ever see so much money?" Sebas hadn't meant the question to be rhetorical but the answer didn't need to be stated.

"How much is it?"

"Better be 12 grand or there'll be trouble." He chuckled at his own words. Paco watched as he expertly banged them into a compact wad, like a down and out croupier practicing his trade. He slipped a rubber band round the small brick of notes and slid it under the bed. "It's not all mine," he offered as way of clarification. The lack of full ownership somehow making it acceptable to be handling so much cash. "But all going to plan I'll soon have it back in my hand again and it *will* be mine." Paco hoped he wouldn't say any more. He wasn't really interested in shady goings-on, but he also knew he was a bad liar were anyone to ask him questions. He already felt guilty by association. Sebas sensed the apprehension.

"What's up?"

"Nothin'."

"What is it?"

"Just tired. School shit."

"School?" mocked Sebas, "What's tiring you out at school?" Again he chuckled to himself shaking his head. He reached down and pulled a cigarette packet from a half empty carton, opened it, let the cellophane wrapper fall to the floor and lit one. He lay back on the bed and for the first time looked directly at Paco. Grey-blue smoke floated between them. "Ahh, I get it. A girl." He rolled his eyes as he exhaled.

"No," Paco scoffed.

"A boy then."

"Fuck off."

"Good, better not be." Sebas inhaled again then blew the smoke up to the ceiling, a slow exaggerated exhalation, resting his head deeper into the pillow. Nothing passed between them for a long minute, the only noise Sebas sucking on his cigarette.

"So?"

"So, what?"

"So, if it's not a girl what is it? You getting bullied?" To Paco this suggestion was even more preposterous than being gay. A sneer and a sharp suck of the teeth, the reply that the accusation merited. Sebas swung his legs round and sat up already bored with the tedious and futile interrogation. He reached under the bed again and pulled out a box which he placed to his left so it was partially hidden.

"Here." He threw Paco a pack of condoms. "If you don't know how to use them ask your boyfriend," he sniggered. Paco caught the small packet but maintained his broody silence. "Go for girls on holiday in a group. Give 'em a bit of gitano charm. Get them a bit drunk." Sebas stared at the floor as he talked. "They'll have a guy at home and just want a holiday fuck. Something to brag about. You'll not need condoms, but keep one handy incase they get arsey with you." Paco considered his brother's advice. Of course he masturbated but wasn't quite sure why. When he had an erection he just did it. He never thought specifically about girls, he didn't think of anything in particular. He had never considered sex as a high priority, even less so now that his brother had presented it like that. Slightly embarrassed he slipped the packet into his pocket.

"An' take this." Sebas half rose and slapped a handle into Paco's outstretched hand. He looked down at what he thought was a kitchen knife. As he turned it in his hand he noticed the shark's fin curves of the double edged tip. He pressed the tepid metal between his fingertips, hesitant to touch the edges of the blade although it compelled him to do so. He sensed the strength of it, its power, realising immediately the potential for damage. The weight of it somehow seemed right to him, it felt comfortable, natural. This was no cheap and nasty knock off this was a bona fide hunting knife like he'd seen in Hollywood movies. Sebas saw his brother's face light up and knew that he had done the right thing in arming the boy. His eyes glinted as much as the steel of the blade.

"Bro, be careful eh! You could really hurt someone with that. Paco, I'm serious." Paco glanced at him, neither confirming nor denying what had been said. "And you better have this as well." Sebas threw him the first box he had taken from under the bed, an iPhone. "All your friends have got one, don't they?"

"Seb. Thanks." Paco tried to control his emotions, remain aloof, but his delight was obvious. Despite his indifferent adolescent exterior some part of the child remained. He slipped the knife back into its sheath then hid it at the foot of the bed, took the mobile to the sofa and ripped the box open. Perhaps this new Sebas could grow on him.

"My pleasure," his brother called after him as he stood to slam the door closed again.

Chapter Nine

The Mountains, Spring 1946

With the Virgin safely reinstated in her rightful place behind the altar in the church of Los Caballeros de La Sierra, the townspeople celebrated an afternoon mass under Her benign gaze. Under Father Alberto's ebullient instruction, they shared the Eucharist; the body of Christ, the blood of Christ. The low sun now shone almost horizontally through the stained glass windows, illuminating the length of the small church. Father Alberto dismissed his congregation with a reminder that mass would continue twice daily for the remainder of the week. Outside the church they separated; the men hung around and smoked whilst the women crossed the courtyard to Guerrero's bar to finish the preparations for the village fiesta. They bustled around the tables cutting bread and setting out dishes of marinated olives and homemade ajiaceite, dropping approving comments or raising a scandalised eyebrow at what other women had brought. The dishes were divided amongst the dozen or so differently sized tables spread out on the street. Estofado with beans, migas with garlic and peppers, rabbit with lentils. Their smells mingled in the rising vapours then quickly dispersed in the last of the afternoon light.

* * *

When the tables were finally prepared the men, who had been joined by Father Alberto, were called. The priest sauntered over, still basking in self-importance. Until he blessed the food the festivities couldn't begin. He stood by his assigned chair with a supercilious smile, his hands behind his back exaggerated the size of his substantial paunch. After an ample pause he blessed the food as if it were The Sacrament itself, continuing the sombre ecclesiastical air from the previous mass. Then he sat. The rest of the village followed his lead in silence and together they began to eat. As usual the proceedings commenced with a subdued atmosphere. The religious formality that he insisted upon was almost tangible as it hung over them. It was how the twisted priest liked it, it asserted control over his village.

To begin with, the only one that defied the solemn mood, and by default Father Alberto, was Pascual whose natural disposition didn't indulge this cheerless atmosphere. His voice carried across the square as he joked and teased. His laughter was infectious but it provoked contention from the table of dignitaries. He had a way of making those around him relax and facilitated without knowing it, the release of emotions. People could feel drained after being in his company and not know why.

As afternoon slipped into night the mood changed. Fuelled by consumption of homemade wines and orujos, more of the villagers began to find their voice. The general chatter changed from the perennial topics of crops, livestock and the threat posed by wolves to politics. Falagistas and Republican sympathisers, the concentration camps and the notorious state approved vigilantes were all topics to be discussed. The candour by which their respective virtues could be truly deliberated depended upon the immediate company. Pascual knew this as much as the next man and even though he had spent his entire life in this village, he was wary. During these discussions, Franco's name was always affirmed proudly regardless whether the sentiment behind it was authentic or not. People had disappeared for less and the memory of Manolo Jimenez still hung like a shroud over the village.

Juan Diego tentatively entered into these conversations, skirting around the edges, knowing he was very much considered an outsider in a suspicious landscape. He treated with equal caution even the most innocent enquiry into his own background. A history that was still to be divulged. His thoughts were focussed more on Maria Dolores, who sat but one away with Dora, the unwitting chaperone, in between. Their relationship was cordial, their paths crossed mainly in the evening and always in the presence of her parents. He paid attention to her when she talked, offered his assistance, whether it was required or not, and when she became flustered by his closeness he retired with a smile. Her parents still treated her like a girl but she was not, she was clearly a woman. He could see it, he could feel it and he spoke to her formally always addressing her by her full name. Conversely, he called Conchi 'little one,' adopting almost immediately the family nickname. It was a slow fumbling courtship but they were both young and inexperienced, naivety a barrier neither knew how to overcome.

When the sun had fully set, the fresh mountain air turned to a cool breeze that crept through the narrow streets and sneaked up on the revellers and slipped inside their skin. They chattered excitedly as Miguel Guerrero announced, with Father Alberto's permission, the bar officially open. The men jumped, carrying with them the bar's chairs and took up their

usual positions and waited to be served. The beer was flat but
at least it was served cold. Ana served fried churros sprinkled
with sugar and hot chocolate for the children. A genuine
extravagance in such impoverished times.

Juan Diego's instinct was to remain outside and help Dora
and the other women in the general tidy of the plaza. Maria
Dolores, however, dismissed him with a playful smile taking
a bottle of olive oil from of his hand, so he wandered into the
bar and automatically to Pascual's side. Pascual welcomed
him with a slap on the shoulder, he was turning into the son
that he had never had. Juan Diego sipped the beer looking
around the brightly lit room. Posters with withered edges
advertised past bullfights starring Domingo Ortega and
Manolete. The men had only been in the bar half an hour but
smoke already settled in blue layers across the room. The
atmosphere was jovial, Estrellita Castro sang along to copla
music on the radio. Everyone smiled as they talked and
raised their voices over the hubbub desperate to be heard.
Everyone except José Blanco. He flicked his right pinky nail
against an empty beer glass. The tool, more akin to a dog's
claw which he used to scoop out the inside of his ear, emitted
a dull ping. A slow metronomic countdown. His beady-eye
glare didn't deviate from the oblivious Juan Diego. He sat
silently as the fervent discussion went on around him. There
had been incessant rumours since the end of the Second
World War that Monarchic sympathisers and other anti-
fascist groups were gathering in south Portugal. Their aim, an
attempted rising against the Nationalist Francoist regime.
Such stories were abound in volatile Spain, especially in the
mountains where news was slow.

José Blanco's stare was broken when Dora came into the bar
along with some other women. When Maria Dolores didn't

follow after a few minutes, he rose without saying anything and left. He pulled up the collar of his jacket as he stepped out into the cold and now deserted street. The tables had been cleared and sat huddled under the bar window, safe from the strengthening breeze. The coloured bunting, that looked as if it would be despatched at any moment, the only evidence that there had been any festivities in the plaza. The gusting wind, an invisible and unknowing accomplice, carried the slam of the church's side door. As he rounded the building he saw the lights on in the church hall. Someone moved inside.

Juan Diego had also noticed Maria Dolores' absence. When he asked Dora, she answered, unconcerned, that she hadn't seen her.

José Blanco stopped at the church hall's window. The lace curtains were closed but he could still see Maria Dolores folding tablecloths and laying them in a pile on a table. He stood a metre and a half from the building, far enough away to be out of the light and observed her every movement. She sang to herself, a song that was impossible for him to distinguish in the rush of the wind.

Through the noise that surrounded the bar, Juan Diego asked Ana if she had seen Maria Dolores, but she had been busy helping her parents. She didn't know where she was.

Maria Dolores placed the last of the tablecloths into a box on the floor and looked around the room. Satisfied that her work there was finished for the evening she turned to the door.

Juan Diego sought out Conchi who was gossiping with some other younger girls, but she had last seen her sister when they had finished the meal.

As Maria Dolores grasped the door handle she simultaneously flicked the light switch in the little church hall. Darkness immersed her. There was an almost imperceptible light off to her left, probably coming from the streetlight outside the bar. As she pulled on the door, it flew open pushing her back. She thought it was just the heavy wind, but then something pushed hard against her face. A slap smothered her mouth. She tried to breathe in but her lungs didn't fill. She gasped but the air didn't enter. The force of it made her take a few hurried steps back into the room again.

"Shut up. Not a word." But Maria Dolores didn't comprehend what was happening. Her instincts made her struggle against the aggressor, ineffectively pushing against him, her muffled cries futile against his rough hand. "Maria Dolores," the voice mocked. "You're not so special. Not you, not your father. Shut UP," the voice spat again at her. She felt the beer and cigarettes on his breath as she tried to turn away from him. Then a hand grasped at her inner thigh digging a thumb into her flesh, pulling at her dress.

His strength knocked her back and striking one of the tables she lost her balance. A chair screeched across the stone floor. As she fell her assailant's hand slipped from her face allowing her to gasp for air, but before she could call out, the blow from the hard floor took that breath away again. Then he was on top of her as if he had orchestrated her fall, and through her clothes she felt him grope at her groin. She jerked back in pain as a finger or two partially penetrated her, tried to force their way into her, his weight pinning her down. His other hand pushed her head against the hard floor, fixing it there. She kicked a table and felt it move as she struggled but he was too heavy, his weight too oppressive. She grappled at him; one hand floundered at his face, the other, grabbed at the floor, searching for some non-existing weapon or escape route. Then her dress was up around her waist, the cold floor shocked her bare thighs. She sensed him react as her knee hit his flank but the pressure on her remained. Then in a burst of light, he was off her. She heard a throaty groan and turned to see him writhing beside her and for the first time, as her eyes adjusted to the brightness, Maria Dolores saw that her attacker was José Blanco. She sat upright and scuttled backwards across the floor, eyes wide, spitting blood from her mouth, pulling her dress down. In the same instance, someone else threw himself on top of José and began to strike him hard on the head shouting something she didn't understand. Gallego? Catalan?

She heard a hard crack as José's head was smacked against the floor again and the shouting continued. And as she recovered she breathed 'Stop,' an instinctive reaction against being so close to such violence. She pleaded with them but her voice was broken. She swallowed and tasted blood, tasted tears although she hadn't realised she had been crying.

"STOP" Now she screamed. "Stop, stop." With one last blow to José's head, Juan Diego did as he had been commanded. He stood up and looked down at the excuse of a man that lay before him. The fury in him expelled in his rapid heavy breathing, his energy filled the room. Spittle flew from his mouth with every exhalation. Juan Diego had repelled her attacker with ease and precision, with an experienced hand. José Blanco didn't fight back, his limited physicality only adequate for attacking those less able to defend themselves.

"*Hijo de puta.*" Juan Diego shifted his weight and drew back his leg then released, kicking deep into the crumpled man's chest. "*Hijo de puta.*" Those last deliberate words hissed through clenched teeth accompanied the sounds of a rib cracking and the would-be rapist's sharp groan.

As Juan Diego lifted Maria Dolores from the floor, she felt weak, her legs spent but she didn't want him to carry her. She had to concentrate on walking but everything had happened so fast. Why had José Blanco done this? What had she done to offend him? Her mouth stung and her ribs hurt where she had fallen against the table. She was aware that Juan Diego was talking to her but not what he was saying. He had his arm around her waist as they left the small hall, the same room that she had schooled in, the same room where they listened to the dictator's speeches. The Virgin Mary's expressionless eyes looked down on the three of them dispassionately, as Juan Diego turned off the light.

Juan Diego felt her tremble as they stumbled into the narrow street and the howling wind. He pulled her closer to him and steered her towards the plaza.

"We have to go and tell your father." Maria Dolores didn't respond, she placed one foot in front of the other to keep moving. Her face completely hidden by untamed hair that had just been ripped out of its neat braids. The fresh air revived her, pulled her back to the reality of the situation, but she couldn't reconcile what had happened. He had come out of nowhere. It had all happened so quickly. And Juan Diego, where had he come from?

"Come on, let's get your father." Maria Dolores bestirred herself, starting again to comprehend Juan Diego's words.

"What? No. No, we can't see Papi."

"What are you saying? Of course, we have to see your father. We have to tell him what happened."

"No. Papi will kill him."

"Good, that's what he....."

"We can't tell him." She interrupted. "Juan Diego, NO. Papi

can't control himself."

"You're not thinking straight Maria Dolores, you're in shock." She halted and turned to confront him.

"He'll kill him, they'll send Papi away. NO."

"Maria Dolores," he pleaded as he lifted the hair away from her face. A blemish of blood smeared her bottom lip, but he was still taken by her beauty even in the dark blustery night. He saw fragility but he also felt her strength. With his thumb, he touched the cut on her lip, wiping away the blood. She let him touch her but her stare didn't waiver. Eyes that dared him to challenge her, tearful but bright with determination and defiance.

"Lola. Listen to me." It was the first time that he called her by the intimate name reserved only for the family. In that moment it came naturally to him.

"No Juan Diego." Now it was she that spoke softly. "I know my father. I'm OK. He didn't hurt me. I'll go home. Tell Mami I went home but nothing else. Please, Juan Diego." His instincts told him to return straight to the bar and let his host deal with it. It was Pascual's right to know and let him exact revenge for her honour, but Juan Diego wanted nothing more than to please Maria Dolores.

"OK." He capitulated. "I'll talk to your mother, tell her I saw you go." He hung his head, knowing this was against his better judgement. Maria Dolores reached up and lifted his face with both hands and pressed her lips against his.

"Thank you, Juan Diego." Then she turned and walked away from him.

Chapter Ten

Ibiza 2016

After lunch had finished but before the family could disperse and Sebastian take an afternoon siesta, Bernarda marched them down to the supermarket. Sebas had been generous enough to pay the groceries and she was keen to fill the fridge as quickly as she could. Once there, Paco waited outside and watched his father drink a cold beer at a neighbouring bar until the rest of the family returned laden with grocery bags. Once they were distributed the family began the trudge back up the hill in the full heat of the afternoon. The twins marched briskly ahead, amusing themselves with a walking race, each trying to outpace the other. Stuffed shopping bags swayed at their sides. Paco was sweating and becoming increasingly irritated that he had been cajoled into physical work at this hottest hour of the day. He planned to lay the bags in the kitchen and disappear with Tyson to the sea before he could be coerced into any other form of labour. His parents brought up the rear some 25 metres behind.

He watched as the twins, still giggling and intoxicated at ending their race, disappeared through the gate. The gate whose door swung first inwards as they passed through it then out again. Paco saw Tyson's white snout poke through the gap. Then push the metal barrier wider. He saw Tyson recognise him. Saw her lift her head and run towards him, run across the road. Then the explosion of noise in the quiet street as the red Seat screeched to a halt and Tyson yelped in pain. A high pitched squeal that shouldn't come from such a big animal. But he didn't hear the glass break as he dropped the shopping bag. Didn't hear a jar crack open allowing the contents to spill. Didn't see those contents slide down the asphalt road towards his dumbfounded parents. He ran faster than he could have imagined. In the seconds it took to reach the scene Tyson had turned and fled back up the stairs. He barged past the startled driver, a man he knew but refused to recognise and ran up the stairs to find the dog, his dog, lying in her basket frantically licking her groin. A constant trickle of urine escaped her.

From her terrace next door, Maria Dolores witnessed everything. The car that came around the corner too quickly, as it always did. The idiot neighbour bumbling excuses in his pidgin Spanish. It would be different if it was his dog. Had he smiled as Paco brushed past him? He certainly wasn't smiling when their father caught up with him. Sebastian took his hand and stared at him without saying anything or at least nothing she could hear. Fear then replaced that smirk. She smiled to herself glad to see he was feeling uncomfortable. Then she stood and craned to see the ruckus on her neighbour's porch. Baby nuzzled into her calf perhaps in response to hearing the other dog's anguish. Paco's distress touched her and brought back memories of her own losses. His cries turned to rage and she winced as he held that wolf of a dog, his dark hands sinking into the white pelt.

For Jimmy the initial incident was over before he had realised what had happened. A thud and vibrations that juddered his whole body as much as his car. His panicked passenger, Charlie, screaming that he had hit a child added to his confusion. What child? Jumping out of the car he dropped to his knees to investigate the undercarriage of the car, relieved to see there were no body parts. Adrenaline fuelling an instinctive but futile reaction. One of the kids ran past him.

"I'm sorry. I don't know what happened," he spluttered to no one. Then the father was beside him, looming over him, saying something that didn't register. Sebastian took his hand, his grip vice-like and held it there. Jimmy didn't know how to respond so he stood facing Sebastian but was distracted by the commotion coming from above. He became aware of the sweltering heat of the afternoon, sweat trickled down his back. A wave of dizziness enveloped him. The air heavy and suffocating. Then suddenly Sebastian released him so he turned and climbed the stairs not waiting to be invited. As he reached the little terrace in front of the Moreno house, he saw the crumpled animal lying uncomfortably in her basket. "I'm so sorry," he repeated, time and time again. Words sometimes whispered directed at the injured dog. He had hardly noticed Paco until he stood and pushed him in the chest. One explosive, aggressive movement that caught Jimmy unawares. '*Hijo de puta,*' was screamed in his face but the words, again, hardly registered. Jimmy stood fixated on the still whining Tyson, frantically licking her groin. Her hind legs looked intact but awkward against her muscular body. A broken pelvis? The dizziness returned but he remained upright. He wanted to approach the dog and comfort her in a human way that dogs don't understand. Even through her distress, or perhaps because of it, Tyson growled and bared her teeth, fuelled with the innate knowledge she was facing her aggressor.

"I'll take it to the vet. I'll go now. In the car, my car."

Jimmy's invigorated words burst from his mouth but as he took a step closer Sebastian moved between him and Paco.

"Yes," shouted Paco enthused by the suggestion.

"No. We'll take her later. You should go."

"No, Papi. No, let's go now." Paco's eyes widened in disbelief.

"Just go now," Sebastian repeated to Jimmy and inched closer, his composure countered the tension around him. Jimmy stuttered backwards beginning to feel intimidated by this intrusion into his personal space.

"But Papi." Sebastian turned and met Paco's protestations with a glare. Nothing else needed to be said. Paco pushed by Jimmy again and returned to his whimpering dog. Jimmy found his balance and repeated his apology. An honest sentiment that fell on deaf ears. He shared Paco's bemusement about not going to the vet but he didn't understand the gitano ways. They would sort this out themselves. Jimmy owed a debt and would pay but that was for another day. As he turned to leave, Bernarda lumbered past him arriving late after collecting the remains of the shopping. She had nothing to say. This was an issue for the men.

Jimmy retreated home and told Charlie she had to go. He was in no mood for partying. She insisted on staying much to Jimmy's irritation. Ignoring her, he poured himself a large whisky and waited for news from across the road. As the adrenaline subsided he felt his body weaken and crumple. Thoughts of gitano retribution flooded his mind but they were always superseded by images of the broken dog. When there was still no news as the sun set, he poured himself another whisky and took 10mgs of valium. He lifted Wayne and carried him like a baby to bed. An exasperated Charlie watched in silence as her host left. In the bedroom the electric fan did little against the stifling heat of the night. A restless Jimmy tossed and turned and waited for the medication to kick in but sleep was slow to come.

For the rest of the evening and into the night Paco seethed. Sebas arrived home and took Tyson away. Paco had naturally assumed he would accompany his dog but the two adult men had overruled him without much of an explanation. When he tried to get into the car Sebas grabbed him by the shirt and threw him back. For a moment Paco was transported back to his childhood and the physicality he had experienced at his brother's hand. Sebas reminded him that since he had bought the dog, technically Tyson was his. This didn't wash but when Sebas grabbed him again and pulled him close so they were nose to nose, Paco knew he was on a hiding to nothing. But something changed that afternoon and Paco felt it. He realised he wasn't the child he had been before Sebas disappeared. He was now a young man and his day was coming.

Chapter Eleven

The Mountains, Spring 1946

Pascual and Dora had no reason to believe that Maria Dolores wasn't telling the truth about the cut on her lip, about the scratches on her face. It wasn't inconceivable that she had tripped on her dress in the darkness. Juan Diego chipped in that it had been a very windy night. Pascual nodded in agreement. Dora promised to help mend the dress. Maria Dolores feigned abdominal cramps when Dora mustered them to attend Easter mass. Her devout mother, however, insisted that all the family, and Juan Diego, accompany her. Maria Dolores needn't have worried, José Blanco's absence went unnoticed by everyone else.

Over the following days, Maria Dolores tried to avoid Juan Diego which proved to be difficult. The normally assiduous Pascual had for once decided to observe a religious festival. According to Dora, it was a timely and opportune excuse not to work, she asked if it was related to his hangover. Maria Dolores laughed at her mother's teasing but she was unconvincing, at least to Juan Diego, who observed her more keenly than ever. Every day after lunch, when Pascual had sufficiently roused himself, the two men set off for the old

Jimenez house, which was becoming habitable again. They spent the afternoons bonding, Juan Diego more eager than ever to impress. He was desperate to tell Pascual about the events of the previous Friday but didn't dare lose favour with Maria Dolores. He also knew that the longer a secret is kept the more difficult telling it becomes. He swallowed his own pride and better judgement and accepted his role as a deceiver. He spoke of the future, of staying in the valley after the autumn when there was less need for him. Now that he had somewhere to live he would be less of a burden and could maybe keep some animals of his own. Laying some groundwork for permanence in the valley. Pascual nodded but remained sceptical; a young man should go out into the world and enjoy life before settling down. But Juan Diego's intentions were fully honourable: a life there with Maria Dolores, he just wasn't convinced Pascual would share his enthusiasm.

Like Juan Diego, Maria Dolores was consumed by the events of that night. Thinking about the incident infuriated her; how could José do that? How could anyone? But when this anger subsided she felt anxious, an anxiety coupled with fear. Her own perceived weakness, in turn, enraged her. Then there were her feelings for Juan Diego. She didn't know how to explain that kiss, even to herself but she knew it was right. A kiss that she had initiated, one he tried to reciprocate before she pulled away. She wanted to talk to Juan Diego about it, but what was there to say? Thoughts once formed refused to convert themselves into words and so remained unspoken. The change in her temperament didn't go unnoticed. When pressed, Maria Dolores lied and said her period pains were bothering her. Dora made her infusions of chamomile and told her to lie down. In the silence of her own room, Maria Dolores' mind raced even more.

* * *

The day came when Pascual announced that Juan Diego would go and live in the old Jimenez house. He stood in silence, knowing his host's words would distress Maria Dolores, whilst Pascual, like a proud father, slapped him on the shoulder. A sharp pang of dread shot through her but she remained composed and carried on chopping vegetables with no more than a darting look at Juan Diego. A glance that conveyed her angst. She had felt safe with Juan Diego under the same roof and now so soon after the attack he was leaving her. Perhaps it was for the best. Hardly a word passed between them as the family ate lunch, then he took the few belongings he had, and with Pirri trotting behind him, Juan Diego headed off to his new abode.

A series of small knolls where the mountain turned into valley ensured that the two houses were out of sight of each other. As the crow flies, they were separated by under a kilometre. The rough terrain between them, however, meant the quickest and easiest journey involved walking first down towards the village then skirting around the rocky outcrops. For Maria Dolores, the space that divided them felt infinite. Juan Diego might as have well moved to the other side of Andalusia. The reality wasn't so dramatic. Juan Diego passed by the house a few times every day, mainly on the pretence to discuss work with Pascual and of course to eat. Maria Dolores allowed Conchi to make a fuss when he arrived, preferring to remain in the background, but she was relieved to have him close, to be in his presence again.

The weeks passed and the lengthening summer days brought warmth and more growth to the mountains. The new shoots of the spring were now giving volume and colour to the landscape. Deciduous branches were again reclaimed and repopulated by greenery. Chattering flycatchers skimmed the wild flowers that poked through the long grass picking off insects for their incessantly hungry young. For the girls, school finished and Pascual was quick to put them to work, as he had done ever since they were little. Conchi mischievously complained about the work to be done around the house and Dora threatened to send her back to school. It was a variant of the game they had always played. The previous summer Maria Dolores had mostly helped Pascual on the pastures but now she had been supplanted by Juan Diego. She seemed to be more occupied running errands to the village or cooking, a skill she had little interest in and even less aptitude. Dora warned her that as a wife and mother she would be responsible for the household, which included feeding her family. She suggested she practice and make bread and take it to Juan Diego. Maria Dolores jumped at this idea but became suspicious that her mother's words had ulterior motives. Had her mother guessed what had been obsessing Maria Dolores the past few weeks? Had she concealed nothing? Was her infatuation so glaringly obvious? Her heart bounded in her chest as she sought the ingredients needed.

Ninety minutes later Maria Dolores was on her way to the old Jimenez place with warm bread wrapped in cloth. She didn't expect to see Juan Diego, considering there were still quite a few hours of light left. The cottage was eerie and soulless as it came into view: perhaps because of the heavy cloud cover or perhaps because of the obvious absence of her friend Rocio. There were no clothes hanging on the line, no dog, no smoke coming from the chimney. No life. A feeling of despair and foreboding came over her. She hadn't been this close to the house since their disappearance. Manolo in the cold ground sprang to mind, it added presence to the bleak atmosphere. Her pace slowed as she approached the door. She remembered the night she had heard her father explain, in whispered illicit tones, the news of the family and their escape. The house now stood before her, a void where life should be and she wondered where Rocio and Esther could be. Then she felt something brush her right shoulder, she gasped and instinctively swivelled round. There was nothing there.

"Hah, Maria Dolores. Got you again." She swung to her left and there he was, Juan Diego standing right beside her. His breath touched her cheek.

"JUAN DIEGO!" The adrenaline surged dilating her pupils, her reaction was to lift her hand to him but he was ready and caught it in mid swing. She yelped in frustration and felt like stamping her feet to prove it. "Juan Diego, that's not funny. Stop laughing."

"I'm sorry Maria Dolores. I just couldn't resist it when you didn't hear me." He tried unconvincingly to hide his mirth. Maria Dolores tried again to strike him, frustrated by his reaction. This time he partially recoiled but allowed her contact with his shoulder. "Maybe I should take that bread from you before you hit me with it."

He reached out to her but Maria Dolores took a step back and held firm, holding her package like it was her own dignity. Juan Diego followed her move and stepped closer. This time she didn't yield. Holding her stare, he reached out again, lightly laying a hand on top of hers, his dirty fingertips resting on the white cuff of her shirt sleeve. Again she didn't resist and allowed him to prise open her fingers. Her boldness challenged him and spurred him on. He knew her first instinct would be a show of defiance, he had seen it often enough. She looked up at him but the blushes on her cheeks betrayed her. Her face remained stern but her eyes smiled. As Juan Diego took a step closer he pulled her into him. The bundle fell and the bread broke free of its cloth. Their bodies pressed against each other, each knowing the other wanted the same, their fate already sealed. Juan Diego's grip tightened around her waist as she grabbed his head with both hands and as they had done that night in the village, they kissed. This time neither broke free, neither wanted to, their passion compelling them on. They kissed like two clumsy strangers yet to find their rhythm, tasting each other for the first time. After what seemed an eternity, Maria Dolores pushed him away. She held her hands to her mouth, and bent forward with laughter. Juan Diego looked at her bemused.

"Lola, What is it?" That family nickname slipped easily from his tongue.

"Nothing Juan Diego, nothing at all." Then she grabbed his hand and led him inside.

They were virgins the both of them. When Juan Diego whispered it into her ear, Maria Dolores had been surprised. Surprised also that he had been quite so candid; as if preparing her for disappointment. But she thought everything had been wonderful. Years later after she had lost count, when contact with men numbed her, she took herself back to these days and remembered them as the best of her life. Not only for the sex but their physical connection, the simplicity of it all. She had never felt so comfortable in her life. Lying naked with him on an old straw mattress. Kissing him. Running her fingers through the hairs on his broad chest. Exploring each other's bodies firstly with the innocence of children, then becoming accustomed to each other's movements, discovering how to give and receive pleasure. The gentleness with which he always treated her. She never knew the compliments Juan Diego gave her as she lay sleeping in his arms. The kisses stolen, the whispered promises, the hearts and words traced on her back. He stared whilst she slept, watched the muscles in her face relax as it took on a serene air. He was entranced by her beauty, by her sleek black hair, like an Arabian stallion's mane. They both knew from that first tryst that it would not be the last, and so they continued throughout the blistering summer. They couldn't school each other in love nor sex but pioneered their own desires, not knowing nor caring where it would take them.

The family and Juan Diego carried on with their respective duties, but the heat of the Andalusian summer, even in the mountains, wasn't conducive to working. Neither man nor beast could tolerate it. It was perfect weather for afternoon siestas and the two young lovers took advantage of the time, being careful not to arouse suspicions. Maria Dolores started to think of the old Jimenez place as Juan Diego's. It took on another character, the unease she felt before was replaced with joy and excitement, anticipation and exhilaration.

These were the days when she dreamt about her future; the children and grandchildren. Working a farmstead as her mother did. That teenage girl didn't have the capacity to contemplate what the future really was, her dreams were in the present, her ambitions modest. When she was with him, when she thought about him, something awoke in her, emotions she had never before experienced, an awareness of herself and her femininity that she couldn't explain. She did not know what love was but perhaps the thrill and trepidation and these tumultuous feelings that coursed through her were how it begins.

Chapter Twelve

Ibiza 2016

"Father, I'm 86 years old and I've only ever loved once. I still miss him, sometimes I even talk to him. He was the only man that ever wanted me for more than ten minutes. He's dead over 60 years and I'm still here. Even now if I think about him for too long I want to cry. After all this time I still have him in my heart, all this love and only a dead man to give it to. I can't get rid of him." Maria Dolores talked as Father Gabriel had come to expect, despite the subject matter, with only the merest trace of sentimentality. Her voice grainy yet unwavering. He had learned to read her face, those crystalline eyes, a chink in her armour, a minute gateway to her emotions. She had first opened up to him a month or so earlier and almost every day since then she had returned to the church of San Salvador de La Marina. Sometimes she talked, sometimes she left again without explanation. But the priest had become completely captivated by her story, by her and the unravelling of her life. Day after day the woman that sat before him revealed more of herself as she peeled back her harsh exterior. He had wondered if this was a confession of a dying lady, making peace before meeting her maker but she hadn't repented anything. Well, not yet. She had only asked that someone listen to her story. She showed no hesitancy, no reluctance in exposing herself for who she was and what she had done. He saw no reason to disbelieve her. Her edges were rough, but he was beginning to see that they had been roughened for her. Being a man of the cloth he believed that there was humanity and compassion in everyone. He was used to his own parishioners self-eulogising, seeking his approbation, beguiling their way to absolution, but this wasn't what motivated this old woman. The truth was that despite everything, Maria Dolores felt safe there in that church. With him she had company, someone to listen and she talked openly with no concern that she might offend God in his own house.

"I was so naive Father, we both were. I never even thought I might get pregnant." At this Maria Dolores allowed herself a smile, recognition that her younger self had been so unprepared for life. "My bleeding was always regular but when one didn't come I didn't even notice. Then when the second one didn't come I couldn't remember when the last one had been. I think now maybe I was in shock. I was 16. How could I have been so dumb? I thought about getting rid of the baby. Can you imagine that Father, I wanted to get rid of my baby? I didn't want it." Father Gabriel took a breath ready to assuage her. This he had heard in confession; teenage pregnancy, seeking dispensation for abortion or forgiveness for the sin of just thinking about it. They were moving onto ground where his experience might be of some use and he could at last offer some consolation. But as he started to speak, he realised that the woman sat beside him was the elderly Maria Dolores, not the newly pregnant adolescent girl that seemed so present. There was nothing he could say now to alleviate those worries. Any trace of a smile had left her stoney face and she stared once more at the cold concrete floor.

"I was petrified, I didn't want to tell anyone. Finally, I told Juan Diego. He was so happy, he said we could get married. I laughed so much I cried, then I cried so much I couldn't breathe. He felt the possibilities, a future together, he was young, he had all that in him and I couldn't see it. Of course I was much younger than him but I was carrying those possibilities inside me and I still had to face Mami and Papi. He wanted to go and tell them straight away. That was the only time we ever argued. We saw things so differently. I wanted to run away, he wanted to tell everyone. I didn't know what to do and he had all the answers. I knew I had to tell them but I wasn't ready for that."

"Time went so slowly, every day with my secret growing. Conchi returned to school. The snow came back to the mountains. Papi sold some pigs and picked out the ones we would keep to butcher that winter. Family life continued as if nothing was happening. Juan Diego came to the house more and more and I had to tell him to stay away. I thought I was going to explode. Every time Mami looked at me I was sure she could tell. I felt the baby inside me, how could she not see it and unburden me? Tell me everything would work out? Then one day I did tell her. It just all came rushing out." Maria Dolores paused again. The damp air in the church clung to her skin. She looked up and focussed on the Christ with no face. "After that everything happened so quickly."

"Mami was shocked but didn't get angry. She said a Hail Mary as she tried to calm me down, I was hysterical. 'Juan Diego?' she asked. I nodded but couldn't say anything else. She shook her head from side to side all the time squeezing a kitchen towel, her strong hands rolling it into a ball then stretching it out again. I wondered if she was imagining it was Juan Diego. She stared at the smouldering fireplace for a while looking for answers. She muttered prayers to herself then spoke directly to the Virgin, asking for guidance. She pulled me down on my knees and we prayed together. 'God will protect us,' she said, 'God will protect the children.' Then she hugged me, caressed my belly and talked to the baby. Then we cried together. Telling her was such a relief, weeks and weeks of holding it in." Maria Dolores paused in mid-sentence as if replaying the whole scene in her head. "We decided not to tell Papi until I had seen the doctor. 'Go and see Juan Diego' she told me. 'It's a baby, it's not the end of the world', but there was something in her eyes, something that scared me."

"Can you imagine what a relief that was? I ran to see Juan Diego and jumped on him when I got to his house. I was so out of breath but I didn't care. And for the first time, I thought that maybe we could have a life together, a future. He had already started to make plans and showed me where the baby would sleep. How he could build a chimney to keep us warm, maybe with an oven attached. He wouldn't stop talking. We kissed. We forgot our worries, we forgot about Papi. For a moment it was like the first time all over again. I was so happy. I kissed him goodbye. That's how I remember him. His white shirt was so dirty with the sleeves rolled up his muscular arms. His hair was a bit long and untidy, it needed cutting. I thought to myself I would do it later. He was smiling his big grin, as he waved to me from the door of the little cottage, what I began to think of as our little cottage. Father, that was the last time I ever saw him."

Maria Dolores stood up, steadying herself against the chair in front of her. Father Gabriel, a little surprised, rose with her, taking her arm. Through her clothes, he felt the bony protuberance of her ulnar bone sticking out at the elbow and her physical frailty struck him. She exhaled loudly but as she inhaled again the breath tangled with her emotion and seemed to catch in her throat making her cough and tremble. Father Gabriel, as he was now accustomed, felt quite inadequate and helpless.

"Have you eaten anything today?" She turned and looked him in the eye, then shook her head. He took her by the hand and led her through the chancery into his office. It was sparse but felt warmer than the damp church. He guided Maria Dolores towards the only armchair in the room, the tan leather creaked as she sat down. Then he turned a smaller chair from the desk for himself and placed it opposite her.

A photo of Pope Francis hung beside that of his predecessor, Pope Benedict. The current pontiff's smile filled his face as though someone had just told him a joke. He looked like someone you could talk to, someone to trust. Conversely Pope Benedict's slightly smug and wry grin gave him a suspicious air, eyes hinting of dubious intention. Maria Dolores distrusted that face, there was something dark in it. Father Gabriel poured her some water and made a phone call. A few minutes later a young nun, dressed in a long grey habit with a stained working pinafore, brought in some sandwiches and coffee. She smiled at Maria Dolores without saying anything. Maria Dolores stared back, her look piercing, malevolent. The nun, a little perturbed, laid the refreshments beside Father Gabriel and left. The priest watched the exchange in silence.

Maria Dolores ate noiselessly, taking small bites and chewing deliberately, protecting her delicate, chronically inflamed gums. Almost immediately she felt revived. She couldn't be sure when she last ate but was sure this was certainly the first nourishment of the day. The priest sat and watched, taking an occasional sip at his own coffee. She looked dehydrated, her aged skin sagged around her jowls. Although her eyes were slightly sunken they sparkled, but her face was tired. He tried to imagine how the teenage Maria Dolores had looked without the grey hair, without the curved spine and leathery skin. Whilst he studied her, she broke the silence.

"In those days we had no doctor. The only time I ever saw one was when old Señor Santos was crushed when his horse fell on him. They carried him to his house and he never came out again. Esther Jimenez helped Mami when Conchi was born. I remember that though I was very young." Her voice trailed off as if trying to work out how old she would have been. They sat for a moment, Maria Dolores lost in the past, summoning another memory. Then she continued. "That was the way it was in the village. Next morning Mami and me took the bus to Cardeña, it took forever. The doctor there, Dr Gonzalez, was a gross man, his black hair combed over his head to hide his baldness. He lit a cigarette when we went into his office. He didn't smoke much of it, it just sat there, the orange ash growing and falling, filling the room with smoke, the ashtray overflowed with disgusting cigarette butts."

"I had to put on a hospital robe and lie on a table, it was hard and freezing. His fat little fingers pressed around on my stomach and he listened to my baby with that thing doctors use to listen to your insides. He asked Mami to wait outside, then he examined me below. That hurt, those fat fingers pushing inside me, he was so rough. He looked at them when he took them out, they had blood on them. He spread the blood around on his fingers with his thumb, just staring at it. He wiped his hands on a towel and then looked at me again, his fat face swallowing his eyes. I don't think he liked his glasses; he couldn't decide if he wanted them on or off. When he had them on they sat funny on his face, one side higher than the other. He kept moving his head so sometimes he looked through the glasses and sometimes over the top, like he was nervous about something."

"When Mami came back in he asked if we had seen the village priest. Mami didn't answer. The priest had to organise the hospital, he explained in a voice like he was talking to a child. I didn't understand what he meant. Hospital? I wasn't sick. He sat and played with those glasses. I remember his white coat had blood stains on it, the sleeves were dirtier than Juan Diego's working shirt. He explained that I could be about 5 or 6 months pregnant and should spend the rest of the pregnancy in a hospital. For a young girl, my blood pressure was very high and I had bled when he examined me, this might be a problem. There was a hospital for unwed mothers in Seville; The Sisters of Clemency and Grace. The priest had to write a letter so they would accept me. It was for my own health and that of the baby, he said. It took me a minute to understand what he meant, that I had to be taken away, to stay in a hospital. I stood up and told him no, I remember screaming, 'NO.' Even to Mami. I grabbed her arm and told her again 'No, Mami no.' I was so frightened, my heart was jumping out my chest. That doctor got angry, his face went beetroot and he called an orderly. I thought the old bastard was going to explode." Maria Dolores almost allowed herself a human reaction; the corners of her mouth turning up into the faintest of smiles. If she realised her profanity in the house of God she didn't acknowledge it.

"I don't think he liked being spoken to by a woman. A woman? Hah! I was just a girl. I remember the way he stared at me like he hated me, like, like I was an animal. 'You are a minor señorita, a child,' he shouted at me, 'I could have you sent there right now if I wanted.' I wouldn't let go of Mami's arm, I dragged her out to escape him as quickly as we could. The doctor came after us in the corridor and handed Mami an envelope. 'Sign the letter Señora, and think of the baby,' he said to Mami, but he spat at her, like Mami had done something wrong, like everything was her fault. Never, I thought. Never. Mami took the letter and thanked him, then we left."

"On the bus back home Mami just stared out of the window. I could see that doctor's letter in her bag, it was stuck in the pages of her little bible. I asked her what it said. 'It's nothing Lola, It's just something for Father Alberto. Don't you worry about it.' I wondered if I should take it and read it, or maybe even just throw it away. If only I knew. I held Mami's hand all the way to our village. There was so much to think about, my head was spinning. Five or even six months pregnant? That couldn't be right. I had hardly known Juan Diego that long. That pig doctor must have been mistaken. My belly didn't even show that much. When we arrived home it was late. Papi was sitting in his chair waiting for us."

"Papi didn't look angry at all. He was drinking something hot, I remember the steam swirled and floated out of the mug in front of him, his brandy bottle as always by his feet. Although it was late it wasn't yet night outside but the house was dark and really quiet. Where was Conchi? Why hadn't Pirri come to greet me? I stood by the door and took my coat off, I didn't want to go inside. Afraid that if I got too close to him he would see me trembling or see the new life inside of me. Mami told him we had been to the doctor in Cardeña, women's matters, and started to prepare something for dinner. Just like that. 'You too old to kiss to your Papi?' he asked me. I couldn't believe that was all he said. I walked behind his chair and kissed his cheek. I could see the corner of his mouth in the firelight, he was smiling. A little later Conchi and Pirri returned from saying goodbye to Juan Diego. Papi had asked him to go and buy supplies, he wouldn't be back for a few days. Then it hit me, that I wouldn't be able to tell him what had happened in Cardeña. I just wanted him to tell me everything would be OK. After that we had a night like every other night. My whole world was upside down and we ate eggs and potatoes and went to bed as if everything was normal."

"I hardly slept. I kept thinking of Papi's reaction. What he would say to me. And worse, what he would do to Juan Diego. I could hear his heavy breathing in the next room, he was so close to me. He was so close. I didn't feel like his little girl anymore. I dreamed an angel pulled my baby from my stomach. It didn't cry as it was taken away and the angel's hands were dripping in blood. I woke up sweating. I thought my baby had died inside me. Maybe I even wished that it had." She stopped and took a few laboured breaths. Father Gabriel saw in that painful pause that the events of those days still weighed heavily upon her, that despite the years some memories remained raw.

"When I woke again the house was like the night before, quiet. Only Mami was there. Conchi was at school and Papi had gone already. With Juan Diego away there was more for him to do. She told me she would tell him everything when he came back for lunch, we couldn't wait any longer. I wanted to cry, part of me wanted to stay and face him but mostly I wanted to run away, find Juan Diego and never come back. She said it would be best if I wasn't there. I was to go and see Ana when the bar opened and wait for her there."

* * *

"That morning took an age to pass, but when the time came I didn't go to see Ana, I went to the cottage. The door was open, it never had a lock on it, but I always felt safe there. The front door scraped across the stone floor every time it opened. Juan Diego explained it was a part of the house's foundations. I stepped down onto the wooden floor into the living area. Even though it was daytime, the house was in darkness. I didn't want to open the curtains, darkness seemed right. Juan Diego didn't have many things but I could feel him in there. There was no bed, just a mattress with blankets on the floor near the fire. And a chair, a chair like Papi's but smaller. I swept up the ashes and propped up the heavy poker just beside the hearth, it always surprised me how heavy it was, it looked so thin. I wandered around and in the bedroom I saw some planks of wood and he had started to build a crib. Just a simple wooden box. Building it there so I wouldn't see it. I remember smiling at that, my heart was burning, I loved him so much. He was doing that for our baby but then I cried again. How could I be happy with what was happening to me? I waited and prayed he would come through the door. He didn't."

"Just before it got dark Mami came to the cottage. She knew I would be there when I hadn't gone to the bar. She had told Papi everything but he had taken the news badly. We sat on the cold stone step, her arm around me, holding me. She told me I had to go to that hospital until I had the baby. It was the only way. My heart sank and I protested but I knew it was no use. Papi was angry but I should go home with her now, but be prepared. We walked slowly back to our house, Mami's arm around my shoulder the whole time. My legs were heavy, every step was an effort. My heart was pounding, the butterflies in my stomach turned into wild bats and I wanted to be sick. It was awful Father. I had never been so scared in my life."

"Papi was waiting for me inside. Pirri ran across the room to greet me but Papi kicked him. Kicked him hard and he stumbled away, crying like dogs do, yelping in pain. I opened my mouth to say something but nothing came out and I started to cry. I couldn't look at him. He grabbed me by the shoulders and shook me, shook me hard like he had kicked Pirri. He screamed at me, his face right next to mine, but I can't remember a word he said. Then he hugged me and cried into my hair. He held me so tight I worried about the baby, I couldn't breathe. I think he held me like that because he knew if he let go, if he freed his hands he would have hit me. I was terrified. I wanted to tell him I was sorry but I didn't. The words were screaming in my head but couldn't find a way out. I couldn't stop crying. I couldn't open my eyes. Conchi came to see what was happening and called my name but he ordered her back to our room. I heard her and Mami crying, but I couldn't open my eyes. I held my arm out to her and she came to me and the four of us stood crying. After a long time standing there, the words did escape, I did tell him I was sorry. He kissed my hair, damp from the tears then he let me go, pushed me away, picked up his brandy bottle from the table and went to sit on his chair. Mami took me and Conchi to the bedroom where we sat and hugged whilst Mami said some prayers."

"I slept so much that night, all the time holding onto Conchi. I was so tired but it was such a relief. When I dressed in the morning Conchi came to me and without saying anything touched my arms at the top and pointed to the blue bruises from where Papi had held me and shook me. I still remember those wide eyes staring at me. I told her everything was going to be all right. I had to convince her to convince myself. Mami wasn't there, she had gone to see the Father Alberto. I knew what for and I started to protest. 'No Papi.' But Papi's look told me everything, I had no choice. Conchi came and stood behind me and squeezed my hand. I sat at the kitchen table not able to eat or drink, I just felt so sick. I wondered what Juan Diego was doing. I thought about running away to meet him, but how would I find him. And I had no money, I had nothing. I was so helpless."

"After what seemed like a long time, Mami came back, she had been crying. She had explained everything to Father Alberto but he still needed to speak to me. He wanted me to go to confession. My heart sank again but then I decided not to let him bully me. I would go and then to the hospital and come back with my baby, our baby. I was so foolish, I thought I could handle it. I thought I was strong enough. In those days I thought I was strong enough for anything. As I left the house Papi gave me a kiss as he always did on top of my head. "I love him, Papi. Please don't hurt him." He didn't answer, he didn't even look at me. I watched his back as he walked off towards the animal pen."

"In confession, Father Alberto called me a slut and a whore. I didn't even know what those words meant but the way he spat at me I knew it wasn't good. He told me to confess and I confessed. I would have said anything to get away from him. He told me to admit things I didn't understand but I did it anyway. I kneeled on the hard floor and asked God for forgiveness, forgiveness I didn't want. I felt his hot, rancid breath through the partition. He asked me who the father of the bastard was. I didn't answer but he knew. He told me Juan Diego was a traitor against General Franco and traitors always get what they deserve. 'Never' I told him and then I ran outside to Mami. He shouted that God would punish me. I still remember that."

"Maria Guerrero was closing the bar as we arrived, she came over to talk to us. I stood apart from her and Mami as they talked. Maria looked at me a few times and at the bag at my feet. I felt humiliated, I felt ashamed, I had done nothing wrong. How did that priest know about Juan Diego? Maybe it was obvious. I wished more than ever that he was there. She took us into the bar and disappeared upstairs. A minute later Ana burst through the door, her eyes like plates, as if someone had just given her a huge fright. 'Maria Dolores,' she breathed but nothing else. She came and stood next to me. 'I have to go to the hospital', I whispered squeezing her hand. We sat in silence for a while, four women, waiting, all sharing the same secret, not saying anything. Then Señor Guerrero, came in with his jacket on. 'Come on,' he said to us. 'I'll take you to Cardeña.'"

Chapter Thirteen

Ibiza 2016

The summer season had truly arrived in Ibiza and the neighbourhood of Los Molinos. Paco side-stepped an open pizza box which looked full of vomit. He understood the economics of tourism, it was something they had studied, but he didn't understand why people acted like pigs and treated the island like a toilet. Did these people treat their own towns and villages like this? He doubted it. He continued on the winding path, feeling the sea-breeze at his back. School would soon end and he would be able to spend the days with his friends by the sea, enjoying as he should, time away from his family and the space left by Tyson. He didn't believe his brother's story, that she'd had to be destroyed. Didn't believe it for a second but his own enquiries had proved to be futile. A further confrontation with Sebas resulted in a slapped face. Everyone he asked had said the same. Lying wasn't the gitano way but protecting their own was and Sebas had influence in the community. Paco, despite his size and attitude, was still not really considered an adult.

As he reached the house his heart grew heavy, the expectation that his dog would run to greet him almost overwhelmed him. Tears, however, weren't an option. That sadness was quickly replaced by anger and frustration. It wasn't fair and he felt powerless. He was powerless. Entering the open gate he heard his mother deep in conversation with another female he identified after a moment as the old neighbour. They were discussing a cousin of his, Carme. He paused to listen.

"So, of course she comes to me, I'm her godmother. She knows I couldn't hide her and she knows I wouldn't let her boyfriend in my house either. It was a way to get back with the family I think."

"So where are they now?"

"Each one back at their own. I persuaded her to go to her mother. She'd brought enough shame on the family running away like that. They was fighting in the street, y'know, family honour. Anyway, where was she going to go? In Ibiza? Everyone knows everyone." Bernarda sighed.

"Yes, you gitanos are everywhere." Maria Dolores' words carried no malice.

"It was me that made her to go back. But then I had to go with her and make sure she wasn't spoiled. She's fifteen but not married yet."

"What do you mean?"

"I had to see her blood." Bernarda explained, "You know stick the finger inside her, see if she bleeds. Her grandmother was there with us, to make sure there was really blood. How can she marry if she isn't a virgin?" The thought of his mother having to perform this ritual on his cousin forced Paco to make his presence known if only to stop the women talking. He climbed the stairs and greeted them with a grunt. The conversation stopped immediately. Maria Dolores, squinted as if trying to focus in the afternoon light although she could see who had arrived.

"Ah Paco," said his mother. "You want a sandwich?" She

was sitting on an old plastic armchair, faded and cracked by the sun, arms folded below her breasts. When no response came, she rose. "I'll see what there is." Paco started to follow her inside.

"Wait." Maria Dolores' voice rasped in her throat.

Paco stopped and looked at her. It was his turn to narrow his eyes. He stood and waited for her to say something. "What?"

"I saw what happened to your dog," her voice croaked again but with more strength. Paco visibly tensed, his back and shoulders stiffened.

"Well she's not here now is she?"

"It hurts losing a loved one. I know." Maria Dolores' use of loved one gave Tyson presence. Paco was surprised at the effect it had on him but he maintained his stern exterior.

"What do you know about it?"

"I've lost plenty companions over the years. And Baby is an old lady as well. She won't be long in going. She'll be my last one, I can't take on another one now." Something in her tone touched Paco, the sincerity of her words. Something that told him this old woman understood his pain. The weathered armchair screeched in protest as he sat down. "I still remember our first dog back in the village where I was a girl. How he always came to say hello when my Papi returned from working the land. Every day happy to see me, ohh, and that made me happy too."

"Have you had many dogs?"

"Oh yes, I don't know how many but I remember them all. They are so much better than people. You can rely on them." Maria Dolores nodded in agreement with herself. "People just let you down." Paco copied her nodding without realising it.

"Sebas gave me Tyson when she was a little puppy. He said she was mine but then took her away."

"Yes, I know. We've been neighbours all your life Paco and

I see a lot of things from over there." She gestured to her own terrace only a few metres away. Paco had never really considered this before.

"Said they had to put her down but she wasn't really that injured. I just don't believe it." Maria Dolores read his face and looked down. She knew Tyson's outcome, perhaps not the details but certainly her destiny. But it wasn't her place to say, so she stayed head bowed so that her face wouldn't betray her. The despondency in the boy's voice fuelled her loathing towards Sebas.

"Paco, like I said, I remember all my dogs. They never leave me, never will. Tyson won't leave you either. She knew how much you loved her, you could see it, the way she followed you everywhere. You gave her a good life, she loved you too." The memories of a lifetime of dogs now made Maria Dolores nostalgic. She shuffled a little, feeling the urge to reach out to the boy but she resisted, something stronger, deeper prevented her. She truly empathised with him and she could see Paco was a more sensitive boy than he liked to admit and certainly already more mature than his elder brother. But she also knew he would soon be a grown man and there had been few men in her long life that had surprised her. She prayed he would be different but only time would tell. So whilst Bernarda bustled in the kitchen they sat in silence. Paco with his head in his hands. Maria Dolores watching over him.

Chapter Fourteen

Ibiza 2016

"I need to see a man about a dog." Santi's cryptic expressions were nothing new to Jimmy. It meant he was up to no good, most likely involving the purchase of drugs. "Well, about a bitch really." Santi chuckled to himself. Jimmy was none the wiser.

"So go. Why do I need to come?" Jimmy swirled the last of his beer around the glass then swallowed it.

"You might like it. There's a guy there that owes me for a favour and he says I should collect soon." Again, information that didn't inform.

"Santi, I can't be arsed. It's late."

"Late? It's only midnight, what's wrong with you? If that's finished let's go," he said pointing to the empty glass. There didn't seem to be any more negotiating. A little later Jimmy and Santi were on their way to La Fragata, this time by taxi, abandoning their usual practice of mixing alcohol, drugs and driving.

La Fragata was the most notorious brothel on the island, frequented by tourists and locals alike. The building was a chaos of conflicting styles, unsure of its own identity, but that had little bearing on what happened inside. Ionic columns framed the main entrance like stern sentries. Their curved capitals reminded Jimmy of huge glaring eyes vetting approaching customers. The blood red door had the added security of a heavy metal grate, reminiscent of a medieval portcullis, hanging to its side. The door was open but not inviting. Once over the threshold, stiff purple curtains stood to attention. A glitter-ball spun slowly throwing chinks of light into every corner of the entrance and out onto the carpark. Another less impressive door with a porthole window held any interested parties there, penned in until they could be scrutinised by security staff.

A thin, smiling woman greeted them. She leant against the doorframe and spoke with an South American accent. Foundation lay thick on her face, already cracking and flaking around her eyes and down the marionette lines of her mouth. It made her look older than she was. She wore her platinum blonde hair up in a high pony-tail, which exposed her darker roots. Her vest hung on her, small breasts not full enough to hold it in place. Its faded colouring was as washed out as she was. Although she smiled and flirted, her eyes were at a different party. They flitted between Jimmy and Santi, not resting on either long enough to register any detail. What did it matter? They were just two more men, passing through, looking for thrills. This establishment wasn't a pay at the door type, at least not when entering. She opened the door and dramatically waved them through.

The relative stillness of the entrance was replaced with an assault on the senses. Strobe lights flashed from a bar at the end of the dark corridor. On top of a heavy bass, piercing beats jousted to be the principal act. Voices came from the bar but also from the doorways on either side of the corridor, forced giggles and heavy laughing. Perfumes, male and female, hung in the air; musk and floral mixed with citrus and chemical. Once in the main room the music didn't seem so oppressive. Men sat huddled around tables, some trying to keep their identities a secret from people who didn't care and who wouldn't be posting pictures on social media. Jimmy and Santi made their way towards the end of the bar. Santi ordered two beers and two whiskies then leant into the barman and said something that Jimmy couldn't hear.

Santi sipped the beer then gulped the whisky. "I'm going for a line, you coming?"

"Don't think so Santi, I'm,"

"Jimmy, fucking loosen up. Come on." Santi stood and strode across the empty dance floor with purpose. Jimmy followed but edged around the outside. Once inside the toilets, Santi pulled out a wrap of cocaine from his front pocket. A euro coin also fell to the floor.

"Just leave it," he barked, then less aggressively, "Roll a note an' I'll chop." Jimmy watched the escaping coin trail through a small puddle of urine. When it toppled over, the stern face of King Juan Carlos stared up at him. He did as had been ordered and began to roll a €20 note with both hands, simulating rolling a cigarette, tighter and tighter.

"Good boy." Santi congratulated him without sarcasm and without diverting his attention from the matter at hand. He had tipped some cocaine the size of a fingernail onto a small shelf below the mirror and was masterfully pressing any lumps out of it with his plastic health card. He then began to separate the white powder into 4 short fat lines: insert card, slide, divide, check for lumps, (the finer the powder the quicker the rush), slide again, make the lines neat, no straying grains. Done.

Ready.

He licked the remnants from the card then held out his

hand for the rolled paper tube without takings eyes off his bounty.

Steady.

"Two for me, two for you," he chanted still not lifting his head.

Go.

He deflated his lungs, then with a finger closing his left nostril, he inserted the note into the right and sniffed powerfully running the note along the first line, taking inside him every last grain.

"Whoah." He threw his head back, eyes closed thinking gravity would also play its part. Changing hands he repeated the actions taking the cocaine in the left nostril. Ready, exhale. Steady, insert note. GO, fully inhale. He turned to Jimmy handing him the note. His eyes shone brightly, his pupils dilated as he nudged his partner in crime.

"That....is....fuh-king....quality." Santi spluttered, a wide grin spreading across his face. A small white rock dropped from his nostril. After almost 2 grams of cocaine, he still felt the need to amplify and theatricalise the experience. Jimmy, encouraged by Santi's swelling euphoria copied him. One in the left. One in the right. He felt the cocaine burn and rasp the inside of his nose, then sting as it blasted his nasopharynx. The powder melted into the mucous of the trachea, it corroded the bronchioles and finally crossed the alveolar barrier and into the blood stream. This of course passed unnoticed by Jimmy, but as the dopamine built up in his brain, he began to notice the feel-good factor, the embryo of his own euphoria. The hairs on his arms stood to attention, a wave of warmth flowed through his body. He looked at Santi and grinned in return. The same white powder they had been using all night just taken in larger quantities to chase the high.

"Fucking hell," he concurred, then licked his finger and ran it along the shelf mopping up the remnants of the cocaine, rubbing it into his gums. A momentary tingle was replaced by a numbness any dentist would be proud of. Jimmy felt his heart pound faster in his chest, felt pulsations throb in his head. He gagged as a little dissolved cocaine slid down into his mouth, and collided with some unlucky taste buds. He turned and looked in the mirror, smiled to himself, licked his fingertips and ran them up through his hair.

"Cocaine makes me really horny. Where is that big fucker? He owes me something." Santi sang, focussing again on himself. Jimmy didn't answer but followed Santi back towards the main room.

When they reached the bar a few bouncers were hovering around their stools. Santi reached them first and started chatting as if he had always been there, part of their conversation. Jimmy had no idea what Santi could be saying but they accepted him immediately, an acknowledgement that they were united by their presence in that place. Brothers of the same fraternity. A wave of paranoia washed over Jimmy as one of the men turned to look at him. The tachycardia in his chest momentarily took his breath away. As the cadence of the music dipped, the synchronised light show followed suit, first dimming, then abandoning entirely their choreography. It illuminated the whole room. In the brighter light, Jimmy realised that one of the men was his neighbours' son. As he joined the group Sebas grabbed him roughly by the back of the neck and pulled him closer.

"You tried to kill my brother's dog, you bastard," he spat through gritted teeth. "He's in pieces." His tattooed hand held Jimmy's forehead against his. Nose to nose. Whisky soured breath filled the remaining space between them. Jimmy's response was to have no response. He stood rooted, bound to Sebas. "You got nothin' to say?" Then after what seemed like an eternity, Sebas released him. Then laughter, all of them laughing at Jimmy. Santi, exaggerating as usual, doubled over. Jimmy didn't join in. He was in shock, his body rigid, his mind blank, he felt a warmth circulate in his lower abdomen, he thought he might vomit and urinate simultaneously. He couldn't comprehend what was happening. Santi pulled him into the group.

"Your face. You nearly shit yourself. Sebas knows everything, he's cool with it." Then he pulled Jimmy closer and laughed onto his shoulder.

For Jimmy, the night continued in patches. Moments of clarity and lucidity intertwined with inebriation and bewilderment as his surroundings came in and out of focus. Surges of euphoria hit them at different times, as dopamine accumulated in neural synapses. Santi indulged his relentless appetite with more cocaine. He snorted with abandon, shovelling it in using a house key as little trowel, sometimes demanding Jimmy's participation. They talked amongst themselves incessantly, mostly at cross-purposes and with little cohesion, but they entertained each other. No one seemed to care that they were openly taking a class A drug. At one point Jimmy noticed Sebas was supervising the sale of said drug. Customers grinned and headed immediately for the toilets.

Sebas came and went, sometimes Santi accompanied him, sometimes he greeted other men. He looked to be well acquainted with a lot of people.

"I met him first in A&E." Santi explained when they were alone.

"Who?"

"Jimmy, who the fuck do you think? Sebas."

"Oh."

"He came in with his old man, both of them all suited up. Well suited up, you know the way *they* suit up. Thought he was having a heart attack." Santi laughed to himself. "Chest pains. Palpitations. He was in a right panic. Shouting the place down. Screaming his head off" Jimmy nodded earnestly ignoring Santi's casual racism.

"So?"

"So, I did his bloods, ECG, everything, n' all normal. Turns out he was just on a bender. A three day wedding and had severe heart burn, from all the booze and fried food. And the coke fucked him up, made him anxious and tipped him over the edge." Santi laughed again, shaking his head. Jimmy smiled in response not particularly amused.

"So no heart problems then?"

"Fuck no, just powder and booze problems. So the rest of the family arrived and wouldn't leave his side. You know what they're like. The mother went ape shit. Saying it was lies. Her boy didn't do drugs. I was pissing myself. After that they all left and went back to the wedding." Santi slapped his hand hard on the bar. "Anyway, I saw him about a month later. He was working a door in San An. He wasn't a bit embarrassed, thought it was hilarious. Gave me some shots for treating him so well."

"So what's this favour he owes you?"

"Ah Jimmy, can't tell you. Let's just say a few boxes of valium procured from the hospital is a good little earner for a drug dealer. Everyone needs a few downers now and then, know what I mean?"

According to Santi, it wasn't long before he and Sebas were joking and boasting about seducing drunken tourists that visited the West End bars, recognising in each other kindred spirits. Jimmy could see it: the two of them embellishing stories of their triumphs. But this kind of behaviour was nothing new, it was the same story every summer. Sometimes women threw themselves at the men, on their own private mission, desperate for a holiday romance. Just to feel wanted for a while or have a tale to take home. Younger ones arrived without their inhibitions, fuelled by cheap booze, flirting and giggling. Both men knew how to play these girls, a few well-chosen words, a compliment, a free cocktail and they had them on a plate. It was a cliche but that was the way of things. And if sex wasn't forthcoming, if persuasion didn't work, it was taken; girls that drunk were not difficult conquests. Consent wasn't an issue. Santi and Sebas watched each other in action and bonded over this exploitation, whisky and of course cocaine.

"He's not a bad guy," Santi said in conclusion, draining the last of his drink. Jimmy couldn't really argue, it was the first time they'd actually met, but he had his doubts. "He's gone up in the world, though. Told me he's been lying low cause some of his Clan got caught bringing stuff into Ibiza. Now he's back and moving in different circles."

A little after 3 am, another bouncer led Santi and Jimmy to a room at the top of the stairs. "Compliments of Sebas," he told the two men. There was no talk of payment, no negotiation. He opened the door and with the single word 'Valeria' presented to them their prize. The room was essentially bare, void of personal effects. A poster of a naked woman under a waterfall was pinned to the wall above the double bed. It had been made with a loosely fitted, worn looking sheet and two pink velour cushions. On top of a side table sat a lamp, a box of condoms and an open can of orange Fanta. Another poster of a bikini'd woman hung askew beside a tall frameless mirror. Valeria sat on the edge of the bed looking at them, expressionless, no hint of a welcoming smile for the next customers. Any vestiges of Jimmy's hesitancy had long evaporated, dispelled by alcohol and drugs. Santi rummaged in his pockets and as an introduction offered Valeria some cocaine, dangling the little plastic wrap in the air. She agreed immediately, without feeling the need to clarify what it was. There was no need either to formally acknowledge Jimmy. A cursory glance in his direction was all he was conceded. Her eye stayed on Santi who was setting out his powder. She wasn't used to small talk, it wasn't necessary.

She wore black lingerie with matching bra, cheap polyester frills masqueraded as lace. Although she was slender the underwear was too small for her, her flesh hung over the tight wings of her bra as it passed under her arms. Her flaccid breasts were pushed up into the small cups to give her an unconvincing cleavage, her sternum bony and visible. Lank brown hair hung thinly on her shoulders, a few inflamed spots on her cheeks had been lazily covered with foundation. In the dim light her pallor was difficult to see, it wasn't so noticeable, she just looked unwell. The makeup hid nothing, not even to the untrained eye. But the men that came through these doors came to enjoy themselves not worry about the employees welfare.

Sebas' generosity hadn't extended to the top of the range, or perhaps it had. She padded slowly around the bed in her bare feet to stand behind the kneeling Santi. Jimmy noticed a stripe of dirt along her foot which marked a low shoe-line. Freshly painted toenails, an efficient distraction from deficits in personal hygiene. She stood in line, a polite girl waiting to receive communion. She looked like someone displaced from her home and was still in transit, destination unknown, vulnerable, slump shouldered and barefoot, knowing her place, accepting it. Santi, not feeling the need to be a gentleman, ignored her and snorted first. Then as Valeria knelt down and hungrily busied herself with a line, Santi turned to Jimmy and forced something into his mouth. He immediately swallowed before he could taste it, thinking it was crystals of MDMA.

Santi held up half a blue pill. "Bit a Viagra," he confessed as he took his half. "A bit late but we're gonna be here a while." He grinned and nodded towards the kneeling woman. Jimmy was past caring what drugs he was taking. He returned the smile and started to undo his belt.

Chapter Fifteen

Seville 1946

Maria Dolores sat squeezed between her mother and Miguel Guerrero in the cramped cabin as they drove to Cardeña. The chill of the afternoon air permeated the truck but failed to chase away the smoke from Miguel's cigarettes. He smoked incessantly, like a condemned man. The only brief respite came when he pushed open the small triangular side window to dispose of the butt. They hurried on to Cardeña to catch the early evening bus to Seville which would mean they would reach the hospital that same night.

Every now and then, over the low rumble of the engine, Dora thanked him. Her gratitude sounded like an apology. Her fingers in an endless tic with her Rosary beads. A repentant mother's silent communication with the Virgin, a guilty admission of her child's condition. His unease was obvious, he smiled back, but it was an implausible smile that shied away as quickly as it had appeared. Maria Dolores sitting closest to him found it difficult not to stare but his discomfort filled the cabin as much as the cigarette smoke did. He scraped the nail of his index finger down the steering wheel, a nervous expression of an agitated man. It made no sound but he occasionally paused to flick away the accumulated debris.

Maria Dolores tried to concentrate on the long, winding road before her but was distracted by glimpses of the mountains in the truck's mirrors. Her mountains. They diminished into the background and faded into the dusk. The cabin felt restrictive, it stifled her so much so that she often took deep breaths to fight the oppression. It was, she reminded herself, much better than the back hold he had shown them before setting out. He had offered to store her bag there but she had been revulsed by the stale smell, it had reeked of damp and inhuman activity, she decided to keep the bag with her.

As the mountains gave way to pastures, trees to open spaces, Maria Dolores had time to reflect upon what had happened in the village. Father Alberto's unexpected rebuke had stunned her. He reminded her of that doctor only a few days earlier. His words consumed her, they jumped over and over in her mind, eluding resolution. Why was he like that with her? Had she deserved the hatred in his eyes, the vitriol in his voice? Her family was being split up and it was her fault. She had got pregnant. The self-reproach and guilt that she had tried to ignore started to overwhelm her again. She longed for Juan Diego and wondered what he was doing. At this time of day if he was at home he would be in the house, maybe working on the crib. She smiled to herself, thinking of him lifted her. He would surely come to Seville. She prayed her father's inevitable retribution wouldn't be too severe.

A little under an hour after leaving the village, Miguel stopped outside the bus station in Cardeña. He said goodbye to Dora without getting down from the truck and nodded towards Maria Dolores, who rebelliously stared back without repeating her mother's thanks. Miguel, not particularly surprised by Maria Dolores' reaction, leant over and closed the passenger door and drove off, leaving the two women alone on the pavement. Dora took her daughter by the hand and led her towards the ticket office. They didn't have to wait long for the next leg of the journey, another hour onto Seville. As soon as they sat down Maria Dolores relaxed and fell into a deep sleep.

She awoke just after 8 pm and the afternoon had slipped into night. A little disorientated she thought she had awoken at home but the buzz around her soon told her she was in a foreign place. She roused and stepped down from the bus and stared around her, she had never seen so many people. The Guardia Civil strutted around with their black tricornio hats, men with rifles in military uniforms stood in groups smoking, other sombre looking men in suits with briefcases sped to their respective destinations. A mother pulled a child by the arm towards their coach, shouting something that was lost in the general commotion. Uniformed porters danced past each other, pushing trolleys of boxes or luggage. They yelled expletives but at the same time laughing, only just avoiding what appeared to be an inevitable collision. A careful choreography practised daily. Others, dishevelled, displaced men in sagging caps huddled against the walls hoping to blend in, seeking the safety and anonymity provided by the crowd. Above them great pillars of steel rose and arched, reaching out, fusing into one another to form the frame for the massive glass ceiling.

"Lola. Lola, come on. Come over here," Dora, despite circumstances, smiled at her daughter's wide-eyed marvelling of the Grand Station and tugged on her sleeve bringing her back to the present. "Cariño, we need to get going. Lola." Maria Dolores forced a smile and followed her mother out of the building. Dora had been to Seville many times and she knew the area well enough but was still keen to get to the hospital as soon as possible.

Maria Dolores continued to marvel at this alien world as they snaked through the orange-tree lined streets. Interspersed between the fruit trees electric lights not only illuminated both the road and the pavement but the Renaissance buildings that towered above her. The interiors of almost every arched window were also lit. She wondered who lived in such luxury. The wide Avenida de la Constitución buzzed with noise and life. Trams full of people hurtled past, bells pinging above the din. Hanging from the tail of each was a conductor who occasionally shouted out what sounded to Maria Dolores like foreign destinations. Automobiles chugged up the middle of the street between the two tram lines. Bright shop fronts displayed suits and dresses, winter coats and top hats, Cuban tobacco and Asian silks.

A little further a street-vendor called out as he roasted chestnuts like her father did. As he tossed them in the pan they gave off sharp crackles to accompany his cries. A familiar nutty smell in all this unfamiliarity. Music floated out of a restaurant door as people chatted inside, immersing themselves in the day's gossip. A couple approached them, arms linked. The woman in a wide-brimmed hat tied delicately under her chin with a pale pink headscarf. Her hands in matching pink gloves were clasped around her partner's elbow. Around her own elbow hung a red parasol even though it was night. The woman's boots had elegant heels that clicked on the golden lustred pavement, announcing the couple's approach. They glided past without even a glance at the two visitors. The dumfounded Maria Dolores had never seen such finery, and for the second time

Dora took her daughter's hand to hasten her step.

Some moments later they crossed the Plaza de La Virgen de Los Reyes and arrived in front of the immense city Cathedral and La Giralda which rose up beside the church like some great Egyptian obelisk. The incredulous Maria Dolores stopped in her tracks, open-mouthed. When she had studied the pyramids in school they seemed other-worldly, but this was brick and mortar and it was right there before her. She could reach out and touch it. The furthest she had travelled before today was the town of Cardeña, and here she was in front of what could only be described as one of the wonders of the world. The square bell tower was lit from below exaggerating its monolithic dimensions. It was the tallest structure she had ever seen, it left her breathless. They approached the cathedral, taking care to avoid the plumaged horses and open carriages that lined up alongside the fountain. Dora watched her daughter's awe and wanted to be pleased for her, but she knew what lay ahead for her little girl. She allowed her a few more moments, gawping at her surroundings, a child's amazement, but this was the imminent end of innocence.

A few streets later Dora found the hospital, The Sisters of Clemency and Grace. The square masculinity of its form set it apart from its more ornate surroundings. There were no redeeming architectural features, nothing to allure would-be visitors. The grey of the building's facade didn't reflect the streetlight like its baroque and gothic neighbours did. Light shied away from it. Illumination was also conspicuous by its absence from the windows on the upper floors. Nothing indicated life beyond the first floor. Both mother and mother-to-be felt the air get heavier as they approached. They climbed the seven steps to the entrance in silence, still hand in hand. A bust of the Virgin, weeping, hung over the apex of the arched doorway. As they entered the building, Dora crossed herself, hiding her face from both her daughter and the Virgin, feeling the shame at being there. Conversely Maria Dolores looked up, not yet knowing what to ask for but the Virgin's eyes remained closed.

The Sisters of Clemency and Grace Hospital turned out to be a hospital in name only. As with the vast majority of health institutions it was run by The Church. Religious subjection hung on the walls. Portraits of stern looking Popes and Archbishops, painted in dark, colourless tones refused to welcome the two outsiders, preferring instead to gaze off into the distance. The smell of carbolic acid was overpowering. Everything was spotless. The floors sparkled and the skirtings glistened. Maria Dolores didn't know it yet but this would be one of her tasks, her keep whilst her baby grew inside her. A dopey looking nun in a starched brown pinafore greeted them politely but without much enthusiasm. Dora took two letters, from Doctor Gonzalez and Father Alberto, and handed them to the nun, who looked a bit startled. Without really studying the letters or giving much in way of explanation, the nun took them upstairs to a small room at the back of the building. This cell on the second floor would be Maria Dolores' room for the next few months. The narrow arched window was hidden behind a closed wooden shutter. Maria Dolores stared at it wondering how much of this wonderful city she would be able see. A sturdy wooden cross was nailed to the centre of the adjacent wall. Two single cots were pushed against either wall but only one had a thin mattress which was covered with a sheet. The partially mangled, uneven metal frame of the other an open reminder that they hadn't been procured for comfort. A worn blanket sat neatly folded at the foot of the bed where Maria Dolores had perched. She watched whilst her mother unpacked the small bag into the single drawer in the bedside table. The nun bit her nails and looked on from the open doorway, occasionally craning her head to see what was being taken from the bag. She was unaware or at least unconcerned that her presence might be considered inappropriate. Maria Dolores couldn't look at her. Her habit and scapular were pristine but she looked slovenly, her coif sat slightly askew, revealing roughly cut short hair. Her vacuous look, although not in any way menacing, was unsettling. When Dora had finished the unpacking she laid her own bible on top of the bedside table. She pulled from the Holy Book a small tattered photo of her daughter on her communion day. Maria Dolores had never seen the fragile image of her younger self before. A sepia toned photo, a white dress and small solemn face against the darkness.

"I remember that day so well," Dora told her. "Seems such along time ago now. Here you are, a woman." She turned to face Maria Dolores. "Remember Lola, God will always be with you. No matter what happens next. God will always love you."

"Mami," Maria Dolores started but stopped seeing tears forming in her mothers' eyes. Dora smiled and turned away and started to take off her own coat causing the nun to step forward.

"Señora, *you* can't stay here." The nun was genuinely alarmed that Dora had thought of doing such an outlandish thing.

"I'll be fine here on the floor beside my daughter, thank you." Dora had been expecting this moment of separation since they stepped off the bus and had rehearsed several answers.

"But Señora, you'll have to leave. You can't stay here," repeated the nun but with a bit more urgency, panic creeping into her voice. "These rooms are for the pregnant girls only." Those last few words over emphasised with a certain disdain.

"Thank you sister. We'll be fine," Dora took a step closer to the nun who shrank away as if expecting to be struck. "What time will the doctor come round?"

"The doctor?" Again the nun seemed to be genuinely perplexed by the question. "The doctor comes on a Wednesday."

"Well thank you, Sister, you've been very kind," and with that Dora closed the door, forcing the nun to take a quick step back. Dora turned to Maria Dolores and smiled, a little victory for them. "She's right Lola, I can't stay. I expect there'll be another around soon to throw me out." She sat down beside her. "But in the meantime, I'll be here right next to you." They held hands perched on the edge of the bed and waited.

In the end, no other nun came, and the two of them slept huddled together on that thin bed, fully clothed despite the warmth of the stuffy cell. Very early the next morning, hand bells began to ring throughout the corridors. Shafts of morning light tried to squeeze through the slivers between the window frame and the shutter. And although Maria Dolores was accustomed to an early rise, she sat bolt upright. It took her a minute to register where she was, then another few seconds to realise her mother's absence. Panic rose in her chest fighting her breath. She stood up and grabbed her coat, hugging it tightly in front of her, but there was nowhere to go. Then she felt it, she felt the first movement of the life inside her. A life that she thought hadn't wanted to show itself. And now this, the first stretch of an arm or a leg, the first communication with her unborn. A cautious smile started to break across her face but then a tear, and then another. She felt herself tremble, ecstatic but at the same time terrified. Sitting first on the edge of the bed she lowered herself down so she lay flat with her hands on her belly, awaiting further movement. The shifting inside her evoked the words of Dr Gonzalez. Maybe her panic had stressed the baby, had caused her blood pressure to rise and it would harm both of them. What if she started to bleed? She concentrated on her breathing, stared at the ceiling, wishing that Juan Diego was close by.

A few minutes later Dora returned. "I've spoken to one of the senior nuns. Lola, are you OK?"

"Yes Mami, em, I'm just tired." Maria Dolores looked away, knowing her mother would see through her pretence.

"Well, that bell is for morning prayer. You need to go. The Mother Superior will talk to you after breakfast. You can have visitors on Saturdays, apparently." Maria Dolores started to cry, then mother and daughter embraced until Dora broke away. "Shhhhh," she whispered "We mustn't scare this little one." She cupped her hands around Maria Dolores' belly. "I'll be back in a few days," she paused and lifted her daughter's face so they looked into each others' eyes. "Lola, be patient. Do as the nuns ask. Say your prayers. Think of the baby." Maria Dolores lowered her head, neither wanting to agree with nor defy her mother.

"I will Mami."

Dora hugged her daughter again and kissed her on both cheeks. Their embrace this time was disturbed by more ringing of handbells. "Go to prayer Lola. I'll see you Saturday. I'll bring Conchi." Maria Dolores kissed her mother's hands. An overwhelming urge to run consumed her, escape to the bus and a return to the mountains, back to Juan Diego and her life. But that girl's life had already been transformed beyond recognition, it was a life that she would never get back. A timely kick from inside her reminded her of that.

"Bye Mami. Don't worry, I'll be OK." Maria Dolores dropped her mother's hands and forced herself to retreat into the corridor without looking back. She then followed another pregnant girl, who had passed by her at speed without even acknowledging Maria Dolores, the newest internee in The Sisters of Clemency and Grace.

The dopey looking nun from the night before was called Isobel. She wasn't to be referred to as Sister Isobel yet because she wasn't actually a nun. And when she becomes a nun she would be given another name anyway. The other nuns of the order still hadn't even given her a new name, although she had been approved by them and was allowed to live there with them. She had been a postulant for four years and was still waiting to take her first vows. But she was confident that she would soon be fully accepted by the other nuns. She grinned as she explained her life story within the walls of The Sisters of Clemency and Grace. Maria Dolores was fascinated by this curious woman but found it difficult to follow Isobel's repetitious and erratic monologue. She struggled to articulate some words, and sometimes stammered to a complete halt. She stared at the table as if resetting her brain, smiled at Maria Dolores then blithely started again, divulging another part of her life with the Order. She seemed to have been there for a long time. Dark heavy bags under her eyes filled her face and pulled down on her lower eyelids, making her whole face sag. They didn't move when she smiled. Her skin was grey, superficial thready blue veins meandered across her cheeks. The two girls sat opposite each other at a small wooden dining table where they had had breakfast that morning. They spoke guardedly as they awaited the arrival of other girls before they could have an evening meal.

"How old are you Isobel?" Maria Dolores asked without really wanting to know the answer.

"I'm 18 now," Isobel proclaimed, as if this was some great achievement.

"And how old are you, Maria Dolores?"

"Just 16." Both young women stared at each other, expressionless, something unspoken passed between them. For the first time since she had left her mother that morning, Maria Dolores relaxed a little. She didn't see Isobel as a friend, but in those few words at least she felt she had connected with someone.

"My baby died." Isobel smiled again, but this was a different, tragic smile which stretched and thinned her lips. Those sad drooping eyes found a home and at last seemed to fit her face. Maria Dolores began to stretch out her hand towards her companion but was violently interrupted by a loud slap on the table. Both girls jumped and gasped with alarm.

"GOD took your baby, Isobel," boomed the voice from above them. "And we know why don't we?" Both girls ducked their heads in childlike dread. Two strangers flinching from a shared but separate experience.

"I wasn't truthful in my prayers, Sister," Isobel began to recite some well trodden answer to the hand of Sister Inocencia which had remained nailed on the table between them. But before she could continue Sister Inocencia, already bored with her harassing, commanded her to be quiet with a 'Shhh' and flicked her other hand up towards Isobel, as if commanding a dog.

"And who are you?" Sister Inocencia's question demanded more than just a name.

"Maria Dolores Benitez, sister." Maria Dolores answered still not daring to lift her head.

"Ah. I was told you were coming. The girl from the

mountains."

Maria Dolores still startled by the sudden manner of the interruption, didn't know how to respond, so nodded and mumbled. "Yes, Sister."

"Yes, Sister," repeated the older woman slowly. "Well, we'll see how you get on, won't we? Now both of you, go and announce evening prayers."

Without hesitation Isobel fled. Maria Dolores followed and grabbing a hand-bell joined her calling the others as had been ordered.

As Maria Dolores lay fully clothed on bed that night, the events of that first day within The Sisters of Clemency and Grace danced around in her head. Having never previously been in a hospital she couldn't really have conceived what it would be like. She hadn't expected to be put to work scrubbing the floors, nor had she anticipated being forbidden to talk to the other girls and she would never have believed that she could feel so lonely and abandoned. But she was strong-willed. She knew that although terrified by the whole experience, she could put on a brave face. In no time she would return home again with her baby. Through the closed window shutter, weak street light filtered into the darkened room. Above her the crucifix cast a long blurry shadow across the wall. She had no idea what time it was, but she was tired, exhausted. Had her mother spoken to Juan Diego and explained it was for the good of their baby? "It won't be for long," she whispered to herself, to her unborn. "Think of the baby." Repeating her mother's mantra as she gently stroked her abdomen.

There were seven pregnant girls in The Sisters of Clemency and Grace, all except Maria Dolores were from the city of Seville. Their accents were harsher and the rhythm of the speech faster than she was used to, but she attuned herself to the dropped consonants and the words that spilled from their mouths so quickly they ran over each other. They stole moments to exchange words and gestures or whispered behind the nuns' backs with a well-practiced ease that cheered Maria Dolores. It reminded her of school. But they also smiled, laughed silently and pulled faces when they could, amusing each other despite the oppression. After an initial buzz of attention over the newcomer, they didn't seem that interested in Maria Dolores. They got on with their work and did whatever the nuns ordered taking their swollen bellies with them. They derided poor Isobel who would occasionally tell them to do something then back down as soon as the girls refused, which they nearly always did. Isobel retaliated by taking Maria Dolores into her confidence, telling her each of their histories. According to Isobel, one girl was a prostitute and had been in The Sisters of Clemency and Grace twice already and another had become pregnant by her bother. They weren't all girls, she divulged, half of them were women well over 21, but they were to be called girls whilst in there, 'it avoided complications'. This indoctrinated phrase didn't fit her simple character. When she recounted each girl's story, her mouth contorted and eyes bulged in disgust, and although she ended each piece of gossip with 'poor girl,' her contempt was palpable. Maria Dolores wondered if Isobel thought the same of her.

One day when they were alone in the small laundry Isobel asked her about the father of her baby. As soon as Maria Dolores opened her mouth to reply she regretted it but the words couldn't be reclaimed. She regretted it not because she didn't want to talk about Juan Diego, nor because she didn't trust Isobel, which she didn't. No, the act of doing so dragged her back home and reminded her how far away she was.

Isobel comforted her and told her that the girls returned home with their babies and so would she. As Isobel mentioned the newly born, Maria Dolores suddenly realised that she hadn't seen nor heard any babies since she had arrived.

"That's right," Isobel chirped. "The *girls* are taken to another building. It's only a few streets away. It's part of the medical hospital, there's lots of doctors and nurses. I've been there. I've seen it." Isobel's voice trailed off. She stared past Maria Dolores with her wide drooping eyes. They were more vacant than usual.

"Isobel, what is it?" After a few seconds she prompted her again. "Isobel."

"I went there when my baby was born."

"But, I er, thought you had a miscarriage." Maria Dolores reached her hand out towards Isobel but she flinched and withdrew her arm. After another hesitation she continued, her voice flat and monotonous.

"My baby died inside me, but they had to bring it out." She lowered her gaze and looked directly at Maria Dolores. "They pulled my baby out and they sent me back here. They didn't even tell me if it was a boy or a girl. I wasn't allowed to give it a name. I only saw it a second when they wrapped it up and took it away. They wouldn't baptise it because I wasn't married, but I hope God has it anyway." Isobel slowly tilted her head forwards towards Maria Dolores, her face and those empty eyes swelled and bulged making Maria Dolores want to recoil. Then suddenly she returned from her ordeal to the present. "So, I've seen it. Adelaida is there now. She'll have her baby and then she'll go home." Her voice once again bubbly, normality resumed. Isobel returned her attention to a sheet she had been folding and continued as if the conversation hadn't taken place. Maria Dolores also turned to the work at hand peering at Isobel. Every time they spoke, it seemed, she became more troubled by her predicament.

That first Saturday Dora returned as promised but without Conchi. They concealed themselves in the sparse cell as Maria Dolores pressed her for news of Juan Diego. Dora looked into her daughter's eyes and lied. Juan Diego was well she said but had gone away on business again and would be gone a few weeks. She told Maria Dolores that they had fought about the pregnancy but that after a few days everything had returned to normal. Maria Dolores felt herself sink, the visible release that comes with welcome news. She cried again and her mother hugged her. The fear that she had been holding onto for the last few days slowly dissipated as she accepted her mother's news.

"Just think about the baby," Dora whispered. "You'll soon be back home with us."

"And Juan Diego?" Maria Dolores left that question open.

"We'll have to wait and see what happens Lola." Came the vague response.

As before, the two sat on the edge of the bed rocking gently. Maria Dolores overwhelmed by her mother's presence. Dora having second thoughts about the course of action she, and Father Alberto, had decided upon. The visit was brief and much of it passed in silence, once the little gossip from the village had dried up. When Dora left she said she would hopefully return the following Saturday.

At the pre-supper mass that evening, Maria Dolores noticed there was an unusual buzz in the small *capilla* next to the dining room. The priest who was taking the mass ushered them in and ordered them to kneel and to recite The Nicene Creed. 'We believe in God the Father,' they chanted as one. Once finished the priest continued on his own leaving the heavily pregnant girls on their knees, the weight of their bellies tilting them towards him in fake devotion.

"God our Father, we pray that you protect our children," his tone even more solemn than usual. Maria Dolores suddenly realised that Adelaida wasn't amongst them. As she looked round, her movement was greeted by a hiss from one of the nuns. She knew of course, as did everyone present, that Adelaida had gone into labour. She had been taken to that other building, a departure without farewells. Another girl poked Maria Dolores in the thigh.

"I wonder if she'll keep this one," she whispered to the floor.

"What do you mean?" questioned Maria Dolores but another 'Shhh' from the big Sister behind them prevented any further discussion. Again Maria Dolores found herself wondering what happened in that other place, a place so mystifying and suppressed that it didn't even have a name.

The days turned into weeks and the girls continued with their work. At first the nuns seemed more attentive and supervised the girls more closely. Isobel explained it was always the case when one of the girls gave birth. Gossip was sinful. The so called public areas were immaculate although Maria Dolores had scarcely seen any visitors in the building. The door knobs were polished, windows cleaned, stairs and bannisters, inside and outside were scrubbed and burnished. To begin with Maria Dolores liked to work outside; she liked the feel of the winter air on her face. It didn't compare to the freshness of the mountain but it was a relief from the stuffiness indoors. But with increasing frequency she noticed that people passing by looked at her with a disapproving eye. Contemptuous looks accompanied not-so-veiled whispers and the occasional haughty tut. Dora came most Saturdays as promised but always alone. The visits became shorter and the silences longer. A new girl arrived from Jerez, she looked more lost than Maria Dolores had been and was about the same age. Isobel's attachment to Maria Dolores soon wavered now that there was someone new to impress and she found herself more alone. She longed for her home, Juan Diego and her little sister.

Then one Wednesday morning, just as Maria Dolores was getting up from the breakfast table, she felt a sudden sharp pain in her lower back. It seemed to ease as she straightened up so she gave it little importance. Unbeknown to her, the oxytocin had reached critical levels, childbirth was imminent. The first contraction happened about 15 minutes later as Maria Dolores was filling a bucket of water to mop the latrines. She was alone but her cries and the clamour of the metal bucket falling to the stone floor soon had one of the nuns in attendance. Minutes later she was on her back in her cell. Sister Inocencia instructed her to spread her legs and hastily removed Maria Dolores' underwear. She groaned loudly as another contraction gripped her lower abdomen. The nun finished her inspection and announced labour had begun although the cervix was only minimally dilated. She held in her hand a dark brown mucousy lump, which she presented as evidence. She ordered Isobel who had been hovering just inside the open doorway to call for the male orderly.

"No chair Isobel, she can walk," she yelled as Isobel disappeared down the corridor. Maria Dolores thought she was going to faint. Even though she was surrounded by pregnant women, no one had prepared her for childbirth. It was something they had never talked about. Talking about it made it all the more real and almost all of them knew what was coming, it was a reality best confronted later.

The orderly came and aided Maria Dolores to the building's

side entrance. They waited until Sister Inocencia returned with an envelope which she handed to the orderly. He tucked it into his inside pocket and at last Maria Dolores left The Sisters of Clemency and Grace.

Chapter Sixteen

Ibiza 2016

The Moreno household was for once quiet. Sebastian had taken the twins fishing. A trip that included an igloo box which contained more beer than any other provision and a carton of white-bait that Sebastian had procured from the fish market. They were well passed their best but he was convinced this would help him land a substantial catch. The twins were, as always, enthused and shared their father's optimism. Paco declined the invitation to join them, preferring to stay at home to study, a decision that produced sniggers from the others but he didn't care. Bernarda was out cleaning at a local dance studio.

Paco's studying was interrupted by the unmistakable sound of his brother's car, or more accurately the car his brother had acquired on his return. Sebas entered the house with another man of a similar age.

"He'll be fine, I'm telling you. A couple of grammes and he'll be sweet," the other man stuttered to Sebas, mumbling his words. The slurred, drunkenness an all too familiar elocution for Paco. The party had started early. He also had apparently not realised they were not alone and Paco was sitting at the kitchen table.

"Yeah I know. He's a *guiri*, but he's not gonna say anything to me, is he?" Sebas' bullish tone dropped a notch when he saw Paco. "Santi, my lil' brother, Paco." The introduction served more to warn Santi of Paco's presence than an attempt at social etiquette. Santi grinned, understanding their conversation was on pause.

"What, ya doin?" Sebas asked, disappearing in to their bedroom without waiting for an answer.

"School stuff." This felt like ground-hog day to Paco, the continual pillory of his academic aspirations. Sebas wasn't the least bit interested and Paco answered out of convention and nearly always said the same thing.

"Don't know how you can study in this heat." Santi proffered. Paco looked at him a little bemused. "I couldn't concentrate when its like this," he added.

"He's a smart arse as well. Works in the hospital." Sebas had reappeared clutching a black leathery pouch. "What is it you are, a physio?"

"A nurse."

"Anyway I don't know why you fucking bother." Sebas continued, a disdainful look accompanied his vexed tone. Paco didn't answer. Sebas turned to Santi. "You call him yet? Is he coming or what?" Paco watched as Sebas fingered something inside the pouch, noticing the satisfied smirk it brought to his face.

"Just sent him a whatsapp. He'll be out in a minute. Just feeding his dog." Paco's ears pricked up. He looked to Santi. Which dog were they talking about?

"Don't know why he doesn't just get a babysitter for that mutt." They both sniggered. Paco stared at them, unable to see what was funny. Sebas grabbed 2 cans of beer from the fridge and chucked one to Santi. "Well, let's get going then." Santi nodded at Paco then followed Sebas out.

* * *

When the car hadn't roared into life Paco stood and walked to the door intrigued why they hadn't yet departed. His brother and Santi were leaning on the car bonnet talking in low voices. Curiosity was soon replaced with indignation when Paco saw the neighbour, Jimmy, come into the street and wave at the others. What was *he* doing with them? Did Sebas not remember what he had done to Tyson? As he approached the car they greeted each other with exuberant fist pumps. Jimmy said something that Paco couldn't hear but a wave of the black pouch was answer enough; Sebas was dealing drugs again. The three of them snickered as they climbed into the car. Once settled, Santi leant forward and slapped Sebas on the shoulder. "Well come on then, get the gear out." Alcohol had affected his capacity for indiscretion and subtlety. If Paco had heard him from inside the house, the whole neighbourhood probably had as well. Sebas tossed the pouch over his shoulder.

"Let's get this party started." Jimmy shouted as the car roared into life and sped off.

For a moment he stared at the space where the car had been, still not believing the men's association. Sebas really was hitting new lows. As he turned to go back inside he noticed Maria Dolores standing in her small garden, partially hidden by the huge bougainvillea. She had also seen the men together.

———

Life on the island starts early. In summer the refuse vehicles start their rounds before the sun rises and return to their garages before most tourists are even awake. Maria Dolores was, as usual, wide awake at this hour. In those summer months she rose with the sun, although it took her another hour or so to make herself presentable. The outside air was warmer and more appealing than in the damp dilapidated abode she called home. The humidity was not as dense in the summer, but it still gripped Maria Dolores. Like the roots of a thirsty tree it permeated her skin, infiltrated her body and seized her bones. They protested until she escaped that insalubrious cottage to seek refuge in the warmth of the sun and the slow abating alleviation of her pains. That morning, like every other, she stood and tried to stretch a little the kyphotic curve of her spine. Her body had once again vindictively contorted itself whilst she slept. In the breaking sunlight, she called to Baby who mimicked her mistress, with a stretch and a slow re-animation of her elderly frame.

"Hola cariño, did you sleep well?" Baby looked up and cocked her head, wide-eyed but not entirely happy about yet another early morning call. Maria Dolores looked down at the dog and wondered if they shared the same ailments. It distressed her to think that Baby could be in as much daily pain as she was. She opened the door, and still hidden by the parasols that covered her porch, she re-arranged her skirt and blouse and put on her sunglasses, already feeling some relief in the warmer air.

When Baby joined her, they took careful steps towards the gate and the morning that awaited them beyond it. As she was about to open it a car trundled to a halt on the street only a few metres away. The driver decided to abandon the car half on the pavement rather than look for a parking place. For a minute there was no movement although Maria Dolores heard a muffled voice, then the driver's door opened.

"Wake up faggot. We're here." Sebas stumbled out onto the street and stood for a minute, both hands on the car's bonnet. A moment later Jimmy got out the car. "OK, OK I'm coming." His words less coherent. Sebas walked round the car to stand next to his new partner in crime.

"Third time this week Jimmy, you'll get a reputation." Jimmy smiled back at Sebas. "Told you, the best girls in town. And I'm still owed a favour or two there." Sebas repeated his triumphant boast to make sure Jimmy knew he was indebted.

"Yip, I'm not complaining." A pause. "Can't believe we left Santi there."

"Now he *does* have a reputation. It's all that coke in't it. One of their best customers and one of mine as well." Sebas chuckled to himself, "Well, when he's not slapping them around, that is."

"What actually happened?"

"Ahh nothing really. She didn't like what Santi was doing so he hit her one. It's nothing, she's just a bitch." Sebas added condoning Santi's' violence.

"Maybe. Right, I'm off, t' take dog for a piss before I can sleep." Jimmy straightened himself, hit Sebas on the back and staggered towards his apartment with the poise of a hesitant toddler. Sebas turned and climbed the few stairs to his own house.

Maria Dolores stood there frozen, fearing any movement would have given her away, even though the men were so drunk they wouldn't have noticed. She took a huge breath in, filling her lungs. Without realising it her breathing had become slow and shallow during this brief encounter. Her skin still stinging from the overheard conversation. She suddenly became aware of the pain in her left hand. Her arthritic knuckles and deformed fingers had closed around the railing, the fusiform swellings in her joints burned. She stared at her hand willing it to open but it didn't obey her. With her free hand, she pulled on first her index finger then released her middle finger, the others followed liberating her.

* * *

Maria Dolores imagined the girl, their prey, helpless against their physicality, their carnality. She was thrown back to her own rape and she lived that pain again. When she inhaled, her ribs were reminded of the knocks she took. She remembered again the metallic taste of blood in her mouth. He hadn't struck her, he had simply forced one hand over her mouth and smothered her into silence. The strength of his grip had ripped her lip against her own teeth. A tear tried to burst onto her stoney face but she refused to let it free. She opened the gate and led Baby around the abandoned car, the exact place where the two men had spoken of that other poor woman. She stood there, furious yet cowed by their words, waiting for the emptiness to offer something more, to give up some other detail that might wound her, summon some other demon from her past.

Jimmy stumbled back out onto the street again talking to the black dog, who seemed to be ignoring him. Baby growled then looked up to Maria Dolores for affirmation but she was already staring directly at her neighbour consumed with silent rage. She had allowed herself to be taken back to a place she thought she had outrun but decades later it was still there, ready to pounce on her again. She was disgusted with him but also with herself. She had survived but it persisted as part of her, it lived inside her. Jimmy saw her watching and raised a hand in acknowledgement. She glared back, her mouth dry, teeth clenched but he was too far away to read her animosity. She turned and with a leaden gait led Baby to the steps and down to the sea.

They ambled their way ungainly along the Passeig de ses Pitiuses, two old ladies already looking for a place to rest. Sun sparkles danced on the waves which broke on the rocks below. The promenade was empty. A few seagulls rode the air currents switching their gaze from left to right, right to left scanning the sea for scraps. Maria Dolores sought respite on a stone bench which had been curved into an elongated S to mirror the waves that she looked down upon. She lifted Baby and sat her on her lap, primarily for her own comfort. Over fifty years ago Maria Dolores had come to Ibiza to be free. It was an island waking from its Mediterranean slumber, there was excitement, there was hope for a new start, new opportunities. But it had quickly become her confinement. Her destitution. Her shackles. The sea looked deep and dark in the light of the low morning sun. It was impenetrable. She sat there unable to escape her own past. It haunted her still. But neither could she escape her present. The weight of it overwhelmed her. Maria Dolores pulled Baby even closer, the little mongrel wriggled to avoid strangulation. She thought she suffered discretely but the scars she wore told a million stories or was it just the same story of a million different women? In an uncharacteristic moment of self-contemplation, she wondered how her life had brought her to this point. She was reticent to reflect upon her past, it reminded her she would never be free from the brutality of men. Every time the past reclaimed her, it robbed from her some of the vitality to live. The courage she always had to confront life, slowly ebbing away. She turned her head to the rising sun and closed her eyes letting her face feel the warmth. The anger slowly subsided, giving way to a melancholy and a heavy heart. She longed again for the mountains, her village. Time took her further away from those days but her age took her back there more often, to torment her. Despite having had to flee the valley she loved, she wanted to return there, to the last place she had seen Juan Diego, to the only place she remembered true happiness.

Chapter Seventeen

The Mountains, 1946

Juan Diego's return to Los Caballeros de La Sierra was uneventful. He sat on the back of a pick-up truck surrounded by the acquisitions Pascual had sent him to retrieve, unfortunately the battered Renault's suspension hadn't colluded with his plan to rest. The mountain air thinned and cooled as they wound their way up towards the village forcing him to nestle deeper into the rough sacks. For the tenth time he yanked up the collar of his coat, but it didn't yield and a sliver of neck remained exposed. The peaks grew around him and even though he had only been in these mountains less than a year, he allowed himself to think that this place could be his home. This was in no small part attributable to Maria Dolores. His enthusiasm for their future together seemed boundless. He made plans which he then changed, altered and improved. It made him restless, eager to start their lives together. But it also made him happy. An overabundant contentedness had permeated through him, it was something that he had never before experienced. He delighted in it. The novelty of it excited him, it added to his lust for life, an impatience to belong.

* * *

He was only a boy during the Civil War but he remembered it well. He carried the scars from the aftermath when Franco's grip on the discordant country tightened. His village, some 40 kilometres inland of Barcelona had, like so many others, been fractured. Republicans fought against Nationalists, neighbours argued with neighbours, friends denounced friends until, in the end, brothers killed brothers. He had witnessed death first hand, the sanctioned murder of men and women for their political beliefs. The rumours of disappearances became reality when one, then another of his uncles hadn't returned home from work. Their absence left a void, reflected by the local authority's unwillingness to investigate or condemn. House raids and night abductions were also commonplace. The Guardia Civil bolstered by the army's Carabineros were conspiratorial in it all; turning a blind eye, giving the orders and even providing firearms. There were no half measures, no mercy.

Juan Diego's father did what any parent would and tried to protect him, urging him not to get involved but the boy was turning into a man. Not long after his 17th birthday fearing for his son's life, he told him to go, flee the village and never come back. He stubbornly refused, outraged by his father's suggestion. A few days later, however, he conceded when his father lied and told him there had been rumours that they were also coming for him. Juan Diego didn't even ask who 'they' were or what they could have against a teenage boy, but he had known this day would come. He bade his father farewell and left before dawn promising to come back, but like his uncles before him he never returned to the village.

Since then he had been wandering aimlessly joining the vagrants and others displaced by war, looking for seasonal work; on farms, in factories and even in the cities. They were to a man compelled on in the search for food and shelter, many of them the walking half-dead. Malnutrition claimed their teeth and sallowed their faces. Undernourishment sapped their strength and ripped out their souls. Parasitic lice and scabies, their constant companions, attacked from the outside and burrowed into their skin and tormented them. Juan Diego ate when he could earn it and stole when he had to. He once searched the body of a little known companion who he believed had died in the night, only to be caught literally with his hands in the other man's pockets. There was no anger in his victim's sunken eyes, broken orbs encircled by dark rings of dirt driven into the skin by life on the open road. He blinked rapidly and watched too weak to resist, resigned not only to the robbery but also his imminent demise. Juan Diego continued his looting but found only self-contempt, the shame of it never left him.

Generally, his youth and relative strength gave him the advantage over the other transients, who were shadows of their former selves after years of displacement. His accent exposed him as an outsider in every part of Spain he had passed through. This was no less obvious in the Andalusian mountains but now it was nondescript and he had long ago become used to speaking in Spanish, forgetting his native Catalan. Franco's regime wasn't kind to Catalans, nor Basques nor Galicians to name a few but the Catalans had been the most difficult to subjugate. They were truly unwanted by the central government in Madrid but the industrial powerhouse of the north was too important to relinquish. Their political collective, however, remained a threat to a united Spain, and so they were denied their culture, their language, their leaders and if they didn't conform, their lives.

* * *

Juan Diego had been years without friends and even longer without the spiritual companionship of family. And as they approached the village again he began to allow himself hope. He wasn't naive enough to believe that Pascual would approve of Maria Dolores' pregnancy but he also knew that he loved his daughters. With her help they could persuade Pascual and the devout Dora to let them live together in the house that he was restoring. When they saw his dedication to Maria Dolores they would accept their relationship. As winter took hold the farm workload would be lighter. He would have time to focus on his house, on his new family. He was determined to prove himself worthy.

The old Renault ground to a halt at the corner next to Guerrero's bar. The late afternoon light was retreating across the rooftops and the church bell tower, leaving the village in shadows. Juan Diego scowled as he thought of José Blanco, who, as church caretaker also had the responsibility to turn on the few streetlights. The sky looked clear but the air seemed to be getting heavier. He had the feeling that it might rain soon, perhaps a storm was coming. Juan Diego arranged the 5 sacks and 1 small box against the wall, thanked the driver and watched as he pulled away. The sacks weren't too heavy but were cumbersome, he would need help to take them up to Pascual's or make three trips by himself. As he approached the bar he thought he saw a man speaking with Miguel. However when he entered, Miguel was alone. He didn't notice that the wooden bead curtain that separated the bar from the kitchen was swaying. The beads clicked quietly as they glanced off one another, whispering malignant gossip.

Miguel greeted Juan Diego enthusiastically, coming round the bar to shake his hand. He asked how the trip had been. Juan Diego was a little taken aback by the other man's uncharacteristic energy but the journey had wearied him. He perched on a stool by the bar and took his cap off. The smell of fresh cigarette smoke lingered in the air. Juan Diego ordered a coffee, into which Miguel added a splash of brandy.

"You look tired," he commented by way of explanation.

"Well, it's quite a trip on the back of a truck." Juan Diego added forcing a smile but was grateful for the drink. Like some bygone home remedy it warmed Juan Diego from within. He felt it course through his body chasing away the chill of the journey.

"Pascual been in?"

"Not yet, but you know him, it's early. He said you were picking some stuff up for him."

"Yes, just got back. I'm late because I had to wait for them to finish the order. It's out on the corner there." He indicated outside with a nod of his head.

"You want another one?"

"No thanks Miguel."

"Here, have a drink." Miguel held out the brandy bottle.

"No, if Pascual's not around I'll have to do a few trips to get this stuff up to his place." Just as Juan Diego finished the last of his drink Ana burst through the bar door. She didn't at first recognise him but as he swung around their faces met. She stopped dead in her tracks, almost jumping backwards and stared at Juan Diego as if she had seen a ghost. He realised immediately that she knew about the pregnancy. His presence there had left her dumfounded. She stood eyes bursting, mouth agape, poised to say whatever it was that had stalled in her dry throat.

"Ahh, Ana cariño, you're back. Your mother needs you in the kitchen," her father interjected before any exchange could be started. "There's stuff to be prepared for later, go on."

"Buenas tardes Ana," Juan Diego stood to greet her in his normal gentlemanly manner without taking his eyes off the stunned girl.

"Juan Diego!" His name escaped her before she could think of the words that were to follow. Did he sense an apologetic tone? If she knew who else knew? Did Pascual?

"Go upstairs Ana, please. See what you mother needs." His sharp tone softened mid-sentence, a little too congenial for Miguel. It seemed disingenuous. He danced around the bar and placed himself between the two. Taking Ana's arm, he guided her passed Juan Diego. Their stare, however, did not waver as Juan Diego looked to see what more he could read in her face. In that moment he resolved to see Maria Dolores as soon as he could. Dread shot through him, adrenalising every nerve and muscle fibre. What if something had happened to her. Or even to their unborn baby. Her father's intervention ignited Ana's body once more as she took control of her own movements, but he had guided her through the bead curtain before she had the chance to say anything else.

"Sometimes I wonder if she's all there, my Ana." Miguel beamed at the space where Ana had stood. "You know we took her out of school early to help us in the bar. It was for her own good really." But this futile justification fell on deaf ears. Juan Diego was already making his way towards the door and the street outside.

"Thank you, Miguel. I've left the supplies at the corner, there. I'll come back in an hour or so to pick up the rest. Just in case anyone asks you about them." But the last words were lost to Miguel in the noise of the closing door.

Twenty minutes later Juan Diego dropped two sacks outside the door to his cottage. They landed with a dull thud. The last remnants of light were some distance away, already behind the horizon. It left him in darkness. The cold sweat made his shirt stick uncomfortably to his back. A loud scraping noise echoed through the cottage as the opening door resisted against the stone floor. It had no lock. Inside he swung the sturdy cloth duffle bag with his few personal belongings off his shoulder and lowered it silently to the floor. He stood in the pitch black and listened, trying to sense if someone had been there in his absence. Some deep primal instinct or training learned wandering the roads told him not to go inside. But he took a step forward. His shoe scuffed the stone as it planted in the silence. Tentatively he progressed down onto the wooden floorboards which creaked back in disapproval.

Although it was too dark to see, he lifted his head turning his futile gaze from left to right, right to left, animalistic, hunting, hunted, waiting for the still air to bring him some information. He took another half step forward. The breeze sneaked in behind him. Then the gravelly strike of a match. The bright yellow burn of the phosphorus illuminated Pascual sat on the armchair, then faded again as he inserted the match into the paraffin lamp. The warm glow of the flame partially lit the room as he placed the lamp on the floor. The temperature however, seemed to fall further.

"Where have you been Juan Diego?" Pascual's voice was calm, his words deliberate although it was obvious he had been drinking. "We were expecting you yesterday."

"Pascual! Jesus! What a fright to give someone." Relief flushed through the youngster's body and as he let go of his breath he felt his shoulders relax and drop. He didn't yet see Pascual as an adversary and continued, the tension finding release in a flurry of unsolicited explanation. "They couldn't fill the order in one day so I had to wait and go back, then I missed the bus back to Cardeña but I managed to get a lift in a truck heading north." He spoke with the urgency of someone eager to be reassured. He took a sharp breath in.

"What are you doing sitting there in …..?" but his words were cut off.

"Don't give a shit about that," Pascual snapped as he clambered to his feet. The chunky Gran Duke d'Alba brandy bottle clunked loudly as it fell and bounced across the floor. The hollow chime echoed around the room. Juan Diego stepped towards him, holding out his arm to greet him as was their custom. Pascual batted it away and before Juan Diego could even register what had happened he had been grabbed by the lapels of his jacket and thrown backwards.

"She's a fucking girl Juan Diego. She's just a girl. My little girl." Juan Diego was surprised by the swiftness of Pascal's movement as he felt himself airborne. In that confused moment he felt his mind separate from his body as he saw himself disconnect with the ground and await some unavoidable collision, unable to brace for it. After what seemed an age, he collided with the heavy door side on. It jarred against its own hinges and stood up to him. Then it stuttered into action and swung away from Juan Diego's prostrate, groaning body with a creak. He lay there in shock, the air knocked out of him, gasping for breath.

Then Pascual was on top of him, his right knee dug into Juan Diego's diaphragm, pinning him there, disabling his breathing even further. Again he grabbed Juan Diego's jacket pulling it tight around his neck, his fury flowing through his clenched fists driving up into the young man's throat.

"I trusted you," he cried as he pulled Juan Diego up, closer to him, then slammed his head against the step. "I let you into my house," he screamed as he lifted him up and thrust him downwards, smashing his head again onto the cold stone. Juan Diego felt everything; the force of the scream and alcoholic spittle on his face, heard the crack of his own skull and the pain shoot through his head and into his neck. He tried to form words but the air was being forced from him as Pascual shook his body. He attempted to lift his arms to defend himself, to strike back but couldn't, wouldn't. Pascual was a man of few words but each word spoken was the truth. She *was* just a girl and he a man, and now she was pregnant. Juan Diego should accept this punishment and he thought of her now, his hands grabbed at Pascual's arms but he was reaching out to Maria Dolores.

"I love her Pascual." The words left him but were lost between cries of pain. Images of the life that he had planned for the both of them spun and departed through the air. The very life that was now on the brink of being taken away and deservedly. How could he have imagined that Pascual would have allowed it? How could they have been so naive? He felt something wet trickle down his neck. The room swam, became light and dark again as Pascual repeatedly raised his head up then thrust it down. Crack. That intense pain again.

"She's-only-six-teen," each word emphasised and accompanied by another pounding smack against the floor. Then Pascual stopped. He let go of Juan Diego whose body slumped to the floor. Two days ago when Dora had told him of the pregnancy he had felt cheated, that Juan Diego could have done this, a man he trusted and respected. A man he liked and who was growing to be the son he never had. His first thoughts had been to kill Juan Diego, exact revenge for what was a violation against his daughter. But it was also a personal affront, he wanted payback for this deeper betrayal, what had been inflicted upon him. A deception that ate away at him like acid. But now there was no fight left in him, the anger had surged, exploded but then dissipated. It was all over in less than two minutes. There had been no retaliation from Juan Diego as he had expected, he had acquiesced and let Pascual dole out his punishment. His listless body lay bleeding below him now. Even in the poor light Pascual saw a dark puddle seep from under Juan Diego's head, growing into the gap between stone and the wooden floorboards.

Pascual struggled to his feet, completely drained of energy. He wiped tears from his face, surprised to find them there. He corrected his posture, straightening out his shirt and jacket then ran his fingers through his sweat dampened hair. Deep inside the first seeds of remorse had already began to grow, and he felt it. He told himself his actions were not the violence of a rabid man but a father seeking some justice for his dishonoured daughter. It was within his rights. But looking down at the groaning Juan Diego, moaning in his own blood, he felt guilty that he had caused such pain. He stepped over his daughter's lover, his grandchild's father and without saying anything else, left the little cottage.

Minutes or an hour later Juan Diego opened his eyes. A dull light flickered across the ceiling but he was unable to focus on anything. He rolled onto his side and winced and coughed as he shifted his weight onto his bruised rib. The pain that seared through his head concentrated between the eyes looking for an exit. He grimaced and squeezed them shut. He had a perfect memory of everything that had happened. He remembered that Pascual hadn't punched him, nor kicked him. Had he wanted to kill him he could have. He thought of Maria Dolores and wondered if there could be any way for them to be together. Would she come to him now? In the morning? Had she also experienced Pascual's rage? The possibility that her father had in some way also harmed her spurred him on. He raised himself to his knees. The constant high pitched buzz in his ears the only discernible noise. A few drops of blood ran across his stubbled cheek and dripped from his chin to the floor, he watched as they melted into the background. He clasped his hand to the crack in his skull only to find sticky coagulated clots of blood matted into his hair. He tried to study them, his bloodied hand held a few centimetres from his face but still his eyes didn't respond to their commands. The floor seemed to open up under him. And although he was sure his supporting hand was well anchored, the floor distanced itself from him, his blurred hand melting into the wood. He drew in air, expanding his lungs as much as he dared, until another sharp pain barked at him to stop. He coughed and spluttered as the air escaped him again. A breeze entered the room and lightly kissed his left cheek, prompting him to lift his head. He wasn't sure if he saw a blurred figure standing inside the door, the low light that flickered from the paraffin lamp had decided not to illuminate that corner of the house.

"Lola?" The possibility that she might have come to him kindled something inside him, but the effort of voicing her name made him grimace again. He heard a soft step, a lazy-footed shuffle. The shadow moved across to him, getting closer. "Lola?" He repeated. Then searing pain again as a boot connected with his bowed head. A kick so forceful that it lifted his upper body off the floor and fractured the fifth vertebra in his neck.

"No, Juan Diego your little whore isn't here. Pregnant little whore." Juan Diego didn't register the voice, he couldn't, all his mind could inform him of was the intense pain. He became immersed in it, his whole being consumed by it. He felt ethereal, not just leaving his own body, but fleeing this savagery. A part of his spirit detaching itself. He didn't hear the delighted snigger of his assailant nor feel the tobacco stained spit hit his face after he collapsed onto his back again.

The shadow moved across the room towards the fire and picked something up.

* * *

The tap, tap against the stone fireplace sounded like a hollow knell. A moment's lull, an interlude void of external input, just Juan Diego and his shrieking body. Then more excruciating pain as his own heavy fire poker, thwacked into his face. A noise as violent as the intention behind it. Again all other sensation deserted him and he was left with only blinding agony. He absorbed the immense pain then nothing. His body reached a state beyond the sensory. For self preservation his cerebral cortex switched off. He howled a low guttural noise, not human but animal, a defeated animal that wished the torture was over. With each exhalation blood flew out of him like a volcanic explosion, scarlet lava, spattering his face with glistening crimson specks. Air rasped through blood, saliva and splintered teeth. His mandible shattered at the point of impact. It hung askew trying to make its own escape from the abuse. It remained connected to his face by masticating muscles, facia and bloodied skin, leaving his mouth shapeless and torn. His attacker knelt down beside him and spoke slowly, close to his face, pushing the dirty tip of the poker firmly into his chest.

"Don't worry, I'll make sure I see that slut of yours." There was no emotion in the words, delivered cold and measured by a man that knew he was in control. "This is going to be easier than I thought," he mumbled, standing up again, taking off his jacket. Through his stupor Juan Diego then recognised the voice of José Blanco. At the realisation of who his aggressor was sudden rage exploded within him.

"I'll kill you," but the sounds that escaped were garbled, unarticulated cries spat through a mouth full of blood. Adrenaline raced through him, propelling him on, and in that moment the pain was overcome. He managed to grab and pull on José's calf and swing at him with his other fist, but the punch didn't connect, glancing off the thigh. Juan Diego's grip and movement, however were strong enough to startle his attacker who was thrown off balance stumbling backwards.

"Go on then, fight me. Get up. FIGHT," José screamed, but he knew it was an empty challenge. He swung the poker over his head and with a roar, brought it down into Juan Diego's cranium. The impact smashed his skull, then a second blow, and a third, then he dropped the poker into the pool of the already congealing blood. Juan Diego lay crumpled on the floor beneath him. The contest was over before José had arrived, but the victory was his. The calmness he had when entering the cottage had given way to uncontrolled malice. Months of spying on Maria Dolores and this reptile that lay before him, days and nights spent scheming retribution. And now he had it. Given to him on a plate by Maria Dolores' own father.

With all the force his hatred could muster he kicked the broken Juan Diego again, this time in the chest, aiming through him. He delighted in the sound the ribs made as they snapped, the way his boot was absorbed by Juan Diego's chest before he was shifted across the floor and the noise the air made as it was expelled from his victim's crushed body. Juan Diego didn't move. The only sound in the room now came from both men's breathing; Juan Diego's breaths irregular, gurgling, increasingly shallow, his body fighting for any air it could manage. José's fast nasal snorts, teeth clenched, face grimaced, bulging eyes wide open in uncontrolled fury. The victor stepped forward until he stood directly over his prey.

"Adiós, Juan Diego." José placed his foot on Juan Diego's exposed and bloodied throat and pressed down. His own breathing becoming more settled, controlled, the grimace of battle replaced by a spreading grin. He watched Juan Diego's leg shudder, a final corporeal throw. He increased the pressure enjoying the slow kill. And when the spluttering stopped, when the life had left Juan Diego, José Blanco pushed again, and kept pressing, until he heard the trachea crack and give way beneath his foot.

Chapter Eighteen

Seville Spring 1947

The orderly walked his young charge through the hushed morning streets. The early spring air was clear and cool, even in the heart of the city. The low dawn sunlight crashed into upper floor windows. Reflected squares of white light inched across neighbouring buildings. The serenity broken only by the heavy steps of the pregnant girl. Their progress was slowed by the intensifying abdominal pains. A bullet of torture that didn't shoot through her but started in her lower back and clawed its way through to her belly. Each contraction brought with it a wave of anxiety which stalled them further and she had to be coaxed onwards. A few passers-by, factory or office workers headed towards their morning shift. They passed by her like ghosts, she was barely conscious of them. In the background they heard the pealing of church bells, the same bells she had heard on previous mornings.

"The Chapel of Saint Nicolas," the orderly explained as if reading her mind. "The Patron Saint of Children." Maria Dolores had never met this man before but as she looked up at him, something in his restrained delivery and fatherly air resonated with her. Perhaps the bells were announcing to

Saint Nicolas, the arrival of another child in need of protection. They edged across the road and onwards. Twenty minutes later they stood in front of their destination. The building was smaller than the Sisters of Clemency and Grace but more appealing, more optimistic. It sat at the end of the terrace but the main door was set back some 10 metres from the street, cutting the corner off the city block. A solitary car was parked by the entrance under a wild looking bougainvillea. A few boxy fuchsia-pink flowers lay scattered on its tan leather roof. Through the glass door Maria Dolores saw a man in a white doctor's coat say something to a young woman who then laughed. Their laughter made her smile and she was momentarily distracted from her own pain, her own predicament. Just as she was about to turn into the driveway, the orderly tugged her arm.

"The side entrance for us señorita," he mumbled and with a quick flick of his head indicated their path, the rolled cigarette hanging from his mouth didn't moved. She followed without questioning, head bowed once more. A small double door led them into a cramped corridor where they were met by a stout woman in a grey midwife's uniform and matching hat. Puffed pristine white cuffs rested on her wrists.

"You look like you're almost ready," she smiled at the new arrivals. "Don't worry it'll soon be over," she added noticing the anxiety on Maria Dolores' face. No introduction, no greeting, just another girl coming to give birth. The panic started to creep deeper and Maria Dolores noticed her heart start to beat faster. It felt like it was slowly climbing up out of her chest. Her clammy skin protested at the cool air.

"You feeling OK? You're looking a bit pale." The midwife took a step closer reaching out to her. "What's her name?" she asked the orderly without turning her gaze away from Maria Dolores.

"Don't know," he shrugged. "Here." He pulled out the

envelope he had been given by Sister Inocencia. The midwife opened it and digested the few written lines. Then took a minute to re-read and scrutinise the signatures and looked towards Maria Dolores. In that moment her face changed, she smiled again but it lacked the same warmth as before. Her eyes betrayed her, a subtle adjustment of the iris, barely imperceptible changes only the subconscious can discern.

"Maria Dolores? Well, come with me child." Again she took hold of the girl's arm and began to lead her along the corridor, the orderly following behind. They had only taken a few steps when Maria Dolores was gripped by another cramp. Her legs refused to carry her further and she stumbled across the midwife grabbing at the hand rail. This time the contraction was enough to burst the amniotic sac, it's warm contents slid down Maria Dolores' legs, pooling on the floor. The orderly took a half-skip back still holding onto Maria Dolores but with an extended arm. He stood there unanimated and failed to stifle a yawn.

"Oh, this is going be quicker than I thought," remarked the midwife. "I'll stay with her, you go bring a chair." The orderly sauntered off without reply, and without much urgency. The midwife replied to Maria Dolores' unspoken questions. "Dolores, that was your water breaking, it just means the baby is almost here. It's just making a bit more space for itself. Don't worry, it's all very normal. Did no one tell you about this?" The question went unanswered. Maria Dolores had been shocked into silence. The lights of the corridor seemed to brighten then dim again. Her legs started to tremble and she reach for the security of the wall but slipped on the amniotic fluid and slumped to the floor. The next few minutes passed in a haze, she felt hands on her, picking her up, pulling and grabbing at her, then lifting her onto a bed, undressing her. Voices gave her instructions which she didn't comprehend. She gave her body to those around her, trusting without question or resistance. When the cloud lifted after what seemed an eternity, Maria Dolores found herself lying on a hospital bed surrounded by activity. As she returned to full consciousness she withdrew her body, closing her already splayed legs.

"Dolores. Dolores, calm down. You're already fully dilated. Your baby is coming." It was the same midwife who had greeted her earlier, her voice remained composed, her tone steady. "Relax Dolores and just do what I'm telling you." Maria Dolores grabbed at the side of the bed, clutching the mattress as another contraction started.

"Mami, mami," she cried between clenched teeth.

"Breathe, Dolores. A deep breath then push." Maria Dolores' cries for her mother were suddenly overridden by shrieks of pain. Pulling up on the mattress for leverage she pushed down again. She had never experienced such agony, it consumed the whole of her, it stole her breath and blurred her vision.

"Good, good Dolores. I can see the head coming. Relax for a moment. Relax Dolores. Now another push, a big push." These last words now carried with them more urgency, more command that she do as ordered. Maria Dolores whined for her mother. Where was she? Hadn't she promised to be here? Hadn't she promised to hold her hand through all of this? To take care of her. Then with one last effort, she pushed again. She screamed as her perineum ripped, but it gave way to allow the head to pass, then the rest of the body followed in one gliding movement. Then it was over. The baby cried as newborns do. Wails of surprise and concern at being brought into the bright cold world. Maria Dolores expected to be handed her baby. She craned her head to see but was told to wait as the umbilical cord was cut. She saw the head of the baby poking out of the blanket that enshrouded it. Even through the blood she could see thick black hair. Her breathing became more relaxed, now the baby was here. A uniformed nun announced to the room in general but in an unexcited tone, that it was a boy.

"Dolores you need to stay still, the placenta is just coming. Can you push again?" But Maria Dolores wasn't listening. She raised herself up on her hands to have a better view. The nun was cradling her baby, softly cooing at her baby boy.

"Let me see my baby." Words gasped by an exhausted mother. "Is he all right?" The nun swaddling the newborn looked up as if she had been intruded upon, then turned her back to Maria Dolores. "Please, give me my baby," she pleaded. Then she addressed the midwife who was still between her legs. "Why won't she give me my son?"

"Lie back Dolores, I'm almost finished. Just one more stitch," she replied glancing up at the orderly. Maria Dolores obeyed the orders, she lay back taking a few deep breaths then winced and shrieked again as the midwife stitched the split tissue. A moment later when she lifted her head again the nun who had been holding her newborn son had disappeared.

"Where's my baby? Where is he?" She called out, to no one in particular and to everyone. She pushed herself up in the bed kicking the midwife's shoulder in the process. "My baby," she stuttered, the panic rising in her voice. The midwife stood up holding her bloodied hands out in front of her.

"Dolores, your baby is OK. He's well, he's healthy." The midwife's words trailed off, the two women looked at each other through the silence of the room. "You need to rest. The birth was very quick and you lost some blood," Maria Dolores searched the room as if she had previously overlooked the nun who held her baby. Dread started to take a hold of her, she felt it grip her chest, to restrict her breathing, the room closed in on her.

"My baby. My baby. My BABY." With each anguished cry her voice became more shrill. She tried to get out of the bed but felt a firm thrust, pushing her back down. She hadn't realised there had been an orderly at her side and looked up at him puzzled. He returned the gaze but his face remained expressionless.

"Dolores, your baby will have a good life," the midwife continued.

"No, NO," she screamed and again with more endeavour, kicking her legs, she tried to lift herself from the bed. The orderly this time forced her back onto the bed, still without talking. She turned again to the midwife and pleaded with her, "Let me have my baby. Please give me my boy."

"Surely you knew Dolores," the midwife interrupted. "The letter was in order. It was signed by your doctor and the priest." Maria Dolores stared at the midwife, puzzled by the news. She didn't have a doctor. "The adoption letter. Dolores, you're a minor. It was signed by your mother." The midwife's calm tone was in sharp contrast to Maria Dolores' distraught appeals but this was a scene she was used to. Young women tricked or coerced into hospitalisation, lied to in order to control the birth and take away their newborn. The Church and Government colluding to award children to Franco's allies and Spain's nouveau riche.

Tears streamed down Maria Dolores' face, she screamed for her baby, yelled frantically and tried to bat away the orderly's arm but she was no match for his strength. She protested that her mother would never do anything like that but her words were lost in her sobs. Her confusion overwhelmed her. Another orderly, the one who had brought her from the Sisters of Clemency and Grace, approached from the other side and touched her other shoulder. The midwife stood at the foot of the bed with her hands perched in front of her still stained and dripping with blood. She assessed the scene for a moment then, sensing a change of mood in the room, nodded to the orderlies. Maria Dolores felt a face-mask being forced onto her face, as she struggled and twisted her head she heard the flow of a gas enter the mask and smelled the sweet smell of chloroform. She fell asleep fighting and mumbling, not for her baby but for the first time that morning for Juan Diego.

Later Maria Dolores woke up in a different room. Even though the evening light was dim it stung her eyes and she winced as she grew accustomed to her new surroundings. And although her body felt light and disconnected she was conscious of throbbing pains in her abdomen and vagina. She also became aware of someone stroking her hand. Her first reaction was to flinch, breaking off contact with the other person. The sudden movement of her body refocussed her attention and intensified the stinging pains below.

"Lola it's OK, It's me Rocio." The use of her family nickname disorientated her even further. "Rocio, Rocio Jimenez."

"Whaaa, Rocio?" Maria Dolores gasped, her voice croaky in her parched mouth. "Rocio. Oh Rocio." She grabbed her hand squeezing it to her chest and started to cry again, the rawness of the memory savaged her. "Rocio, they've taken my baby." Rocio's face crept into focus.

"I know."

"Whaaat?"

"Lola, I've been working here since I left, over a year now." She paused. "I heard one of the nun's mention our village so I sneaked into their office to see if it was true. I saw your name. I couldn't believe it. I've been here with you all afternoon. Oh, Lola, he's gone already. I'm so sorry," her cracked voice unsteady, unsure if she should be saying these dreadful words.

"Nooooo. No, no, no." Maria Dolores screamed into Rocio's hand, tears mixing with saliva. She continued to cry for a few minutes then they sat in silence, interrupted only by the occasional whimper from the bereft mother. The window was closed against the night, a small lamp sat to the right of the bed, the only light in the cold, desolate room. It illuminated Jesus on the crucifix above Maria Dolores' head, throwing a distorted shadow up towards the ceiling. Her bag with her few belongings sat on a simple wooden chair below the shuttered window. A thin wardrobe with a missing door completed the furniture. Maria Dolores was first to break the silence.

"He's really gone?" she asked with a deep sob, steeling herself for confirmation of what she already knew to be true.

"They give the children to the new parents straight away Lola. I didn't see anyone but normally someone's here waiting to take the baby away," Rocio explained, as if she was revealing the death of a loved one. She felt her old friend's pain. "I wish I had seen you before but they don't let us mix with the pregnant girls, I've only been to that place once."

"Can I get him back Rocio?" Maria Dolores squeezed her eyes closed as she asked the question she knew to be futile, not wishing to see the words as they left her mouth. The question went unanswered.

The night took an eternity to end. Intermittently someone, perhaps a nurse entered the room but said nothing, indifferent to Maria Dolores' wellbeing. Or perhaps she was just too experienced with these young, distraught mothers to start conversations that would not end well. When Maria Dolores woke in the morning she was unsure if she had slept or not. She dreamt of children running around the garden in front of her house in the mountains as she watched on. Faceless children that shrieked with laughter as they chased one another around flipping her skirt as they ran passed her. Her waking thought had been the last image of her unnamed baby. She had only seen the top of his head, his black hair, still matted in her own blood. She felt panic rise again in her stomach and had to breathe deeply to control it. She lay there staring at the ceiling not knowing what to do. A little later Rocio returned with some breakfast. Maria Dolores had forgotten that she had been there the night before.

"You should eat Lola," her faltering voice tailing off as she said her friend's name. Maria Dolores winced as she sat on the edge of the bed. She looked at the small tray with biscuits and milk and pushed it away.

"I can't believe you're here Rocio. Where's your mami? Papi said you went to Seville to be with your family," and although it did intrigue her, Maria Dolores' manner lacked compassion or real interest.

"I don't know Lola. We don't have family in Seville. We came here, the two of us. The nuns said we could work here and have a room then Mami just disappeared. One of the nuns told me that she had gone to the Sisters of Clemency and Grace, but that can't be true. That place is only for pregnant women. I went there to look for her but they didn't know her, or said they didn't." Both girls sat side by side looking at the floor, neither knowing what to make of the situation. "Lola something terrible happened when we left the village. Just before we left someone took Mami and beat her." Maria Dolores turned to her friend but Rocio couldn't face her.

"What do you mean? Who would do that?"

"I don't know what happened. I was in Guerrero's bar waiting with Ana and she came back in all dirty and had been crying. Her coat was ripped at the sleeve and her lip was bleeding. Then when we sat in his van leaving the village she wouldn't talk to me. She just held me real tight. Wouldn't let me go. Lola, she really scared me." Maria Dolores pulled Rocio's hand to her again wanting to give comfort but no words came. They sat again two girls lost in the silence; one trying to think, the other trying to forget.

"I don't know what to …" but Maria Dolores' words were interrupted.

"Oh, Lola, I brought you this." Rocio pulled a folded envelope from her pinafore pocket. "I stole it from the nuns' office. I went back to see if I could find out anything about your baby."

"What is it?" Maria Dolores became more animated. She sat upright and grabbed the envelope from Rocio's quivering hand. The letter almost ripped as she yanked it from the envelope which fell to the ground. She read through it mumbling not enunciating the words. "I don't understand, it says I'm in perfect health," she looked pleadingly to Rocio. "That doctor said I had dangerous blood pressure."

"It's the adoption letter Lola. Look, it's been signed by your mother and Father Alberto," Rocio pointed to two signatures at the bottom of the page, they sat beside that of Doctor Gonzalez from Cardeña. Three names signing away her baby, a trinity of condemnation, determining the destiny of her son's life. Maria Dolores started to cry again but this time it was tears of rage that broke down her reddening face. Betrayed by her own mother. Her own flesh and blood had brought her to the Sisters of Clemency and Grace to have the baby adopted. Her own grandchild. The room spun around her, the walls seemed to get closer, the air tighter. Then she screamed with such force that Rocio jolted with surprise.

"Lola, Shhhh. The nuns will come," she flapped at her now almost hysterical friend not knowing how to stop the noise. "LOLA," she pleaded. Then Maria Dolores stood.

"Good let them come in," she raged. "Oh, they'll tell me where my baby is."

"Don't Lola," she begged. "Don't. They won't tell you. They'll beat you, they'll beat both of us."

"I want my baby," each word forced through gritted teeth.

"There's something else. Look." Rocio bent down to pick up the envelope. Hand written on the back were two words. 'Boy', then underneath in capitals, 'MARBELLA.' Maria Dolores grabbed the envelope, turned it over twice, then again in the hope that it would reveal more information.

"I need to go home," she said, "Juan Diego will help me get our baby back. He'll know what to do."

Chapter Nineteen

Sebas hadn't taken Paco into his confidence about what happened to the cash he had seen him counting that day and Paco hadn't given it a further thought. It was obvious that these were funds to further Sebas' drug deals. Paco didn't have firm views one way or the other about taking drugs but he knew that problems always followed. That, after all was part of the reason he had to leave so suddenly the last time. Perhaps, Paco thought, it wasn't such a bad thing after all.

The days strolled on, the nights became warmer until there was only a few degrees difference between day and night. This made for a very uncomfortable sleep for those on the island without air conditioning. The family's sofa's heavy jute upholstery made it durable but not particularly pleasant to rest on. The thick fibres trapped the heat emanating from the young man's growing body. More than once Paco woke sweating and had to escape to the small porch where at least there was a breeze if not necessarily a cool one. These were the times he missed Tyson the most, the solitary times before the rest of the house awoke, when her company was everything to him. It was one such morning that Sebas found his melancholic little brother sat on the steps. He called to him from the gate, the only human noise in the breaking dawn.

"Lil' brother." Paco didn't respond, he watched as Sebas staggered up the stairs towards him. His dishevelled t-shirt made him look as though he had been wrestling with someone. He reached Paco and threw himself down on the step. "What ya doin'?" He reeked of alcohol and cigarettes.

"Nothin. Can't sleep." Paco inched away from his brother and the smells of the night.

"Heyyyy. You can't fool me, I'm your brother," Sebas added throwing his arm around his sibling, drawing him closer. Paco turned his head away from the stench, which with the closer proximity now included body odour. "Come on," he drawled. "Tell me."

"It's nothing. I told you already." Sebas' drunkenness and sloppy coordination reminded Paco of times of old before his disappearance. He felt an irritation swell inside him.

"Listen lil' bro. You don't want me involved, fine, but remember I'm your older brother, eh!" Sebas' proclamation, not only an insincere sign of brotherly love but also a subtle reminder of the hierarchy. How things were within the family and the Clan. His head swayed, his eyes almost closing behind his sunglasses. Paco stared at the ground considering what he had said. Sebas hadn't been there to be a big brother for the last few years, but maybe it was time to forgive, now that he had returned home. Paco took a breath and hesitated, the words had formed but he was reluctant to release them knowing how feeble it made him sound.

"I just miss Tyson," he said not lifting his head, reaching down to rub between his toes.

"What? Tyson?" Sebas exclaimed struggling to recognise the name.

"I loved my dog. I miss her."

"That fucking dog. Is that it?" Sebas sat bolt upright overstating his surprise.

"Sebas!" Paco protested.

"You're moping around like a little girl about a fucking dog." Paco blushed and regretted having opened his mouth. He tried to stand. Sebas grabbed his arm pulling him down and started to laugh. "Really? You fuckin' serious?"

"I knew I shouldn't have told you nothin." Sebas continued to laugh, holding his brother even closer. Paco's ire began to rise, the resentment that had been building since Sebas' arrival finding a vent. The bonds of brotherly love dissipating.

"Stop being a pussy an' man up. It's just a fucking dog, I'll get you another one." Paco tried to free himself but his struggles were more than matched by Sebas' muscular arm.

"Get off." But Sebas had stopped laughing, and tightened his grip. Alcohol limited his ability to reason, on another occasion he might have been able to sympathise more with his brother. But some innate need to be assertive kicked in. He was the alpha male and with a physical struggle imminent this was an opportunity to impose his seniority. Paco tried to wedge an arm between them, leverage to push away, his frustration mounting.

"I said get off." It had become a battle of will, of subjugation. "Seb just let me go." He felt a constriction in his chest as he breathed.

"Calm down lil' brother." Sebas ordered through gritted teeth, one word at a time. The headlock remained firm. Paco grunted, exasperation building. "Calm the fuck down or I'm not letting you go." Paco hit a weak blow to Sebas' back, the only place his trapped arm could manoeuvre. "Cool it. I'm warning you." But Paco continued to struggle finding a little more space to jockey his body. Sebas realised he was breaking free and loosened his grip but as he did so he grabbed his brother by the nape of the neck and swung his other arm round to land a heavy slap. The force of it threw Paco back onto the floor but he bounced up again in a flash.

"You dick," Paco raged. But his brother was also on his feet. They faced each other, the younger's cheek smarting from the strike. Sebas stood before him like an immovable wall a hand or so taller, two hands or so wider. The adrenaline focussing his steadfastness, his drunkenness superseded for the moment. He lifted both his hands and slowly, deliberately held them towards Paco's chest, imitating a push in slow motion, daring a response. Then he rested his hands on Paco and with minimal force pushed against him. Even in his anger Paco knew there was no contest and this time didn't rise to the bait. The fight was over, he swivelled and stormed into the house. Sebas stared after him, his breathing heavy then turned towards the street but the air was too warm and heavy to offer relief. His chest rose and nostrils flared as he stood trying to calm himself. He didn't question how, what started as banter had spiralled out of control, how they had come to blows. Paco had been put in his place, he had been asking for it for weeks now.

Some 20 metres away Jimmy stepped onto the street dragging his dog behind him. He raised a hand and Sebas automatically reciprocated, but thankful the Englishman wasn't any closer. He wasn't in the mood to be civil. As he watched the stubborn black dog raise a leg against a car wheel, Paco pushed past him down the stairs pulling on a t-shirt. Sebas watched him go in silence, satisfied with the outcome. Once Paco reached the street he paused then decided to head towards the beach. As he crossed the road he realised who Sebas had been waving at. It was he who had run over his dog. It was that bastard that started all of this.

Chapter Twenty

Ibiza 2016

Five days had passed since Maria Dolores told Father Gabriel about her stolen baby. After that painful revelation she had fled. This was her custom when overwhelmed, unable or unwilling to be consoled. There was much that he wanted to ask and he hoped that she would come back sooner rather than later. He was sure she didn't know about the Church's efforts to reunite these children with their birth mothers. How would she? There was undoubtedly something to be done to help her. Perhaps, The Church owed it to her. When that prompt return hadn't materialised Father Gabriel decided to take matters into his own hands. *He* would track her down.

The obvious place to start was the food bank where they had had their first encounters. However like Father Gabriel no one had seen her recently, but several people knew that she lived up the hill by the old windmill. Strangely, he thought, although they all knew who he was referring to no one knew her by name. No one knew Maria Dolores.

Following those directions he climbed the hillside street that ran parallel to the sea, thankful the blazing sun was at his back. Their previous meetings had taken place in His House and Father Gabriel felt somewhat apprehensive as he neared her home. He recognised the ramshackle house immediately, it was just as it had been described, the only unkempt one in the vicinity. From the street its entrance was totally obscured. There was no invitation here. He had not dressed in his priestly uniform and attracted a few stares as he banged on the rickety gate. He smiled at passers-by as he shouted her name. Nothing, nothing except some geckos rustling in the undergrowth. Undeterred he reached up and removed the loop of chain that kept the gate closed and stepped inside.

"What do you want?" The unmistakable rasping voice came from the little porch above him.

"Maria Dolores, good morning." No reply. Father Gabriel climbed the remaining stairs to find her perched on a weathered plastic chair. The kind normally found on the terraces of the cheaper bars along the seafront. "Good morning," he repeated. "You're not so difficult to find are you?" His jovial smile was met by a scowl and he feared again he had offended her. Unmistakable also was the stale musty odour that always accompanied Maria Dolores, in that cramped gust-less space it was almost overpowering. She nodded to another plastic chair. He removed a pile of old magazines which Maria Dolores seemed indifferent about and sat opposite her.

"I really just wanted to check in on you. You left in a bit of a state the last time we met." Maria Dolores looked past the priest as if concentrating on the neighbouring building. "How have you been?"

"Hmm," she grunted.

"I was worried that I had upset you."

"Huh, worried?"

"Well, yes I was, we talked about some very personal

things didn't we?" She glared at him again for reminding her of their last encounter. "Erm your baby." Father Gabriel could see that he had, within a minute of arriving, pushed her too far too quickly but he held her gaze and her stoney face did eventually soften.

"I have water."

"Ah, yes that would be perfect, thank you. It is very humid *again,* and that hill." The priest left the words hanging and half rose to help her as she struggled to her feet but she waved him away and shuffled into her home. He watched as she entered the house and closed the door behind her. His eyes wandered around the cluttered porch. Everything on the terrace was covered in dust and it seemed nothing had been moved for years; bottles and jars, a child's stuffed toy or a dog's. The place had a sense of melancholy about it, a forgottenness that reached out to the priest. The straggly dog was half-concealed behind a cardboard box, motionless and wilted, it never took its eyes off him. The vast bougainvillea that obscured the entrance from the street gave some vital shade, but its branches hung limp in the dead air. Maria Dolores returned and handed Father Gabriel a plastic tumbler half full of tepid water. The priest thanked her and placed it at his feet. They sat a few minutes in a stewing silence, listening to a quarrel escalating in the neighbouring house. Maria Dolores closed her eyes and summoned the words she had been ruminating upon.

"Who knows where he is now?"

"Perhaps."

"Retired. If he's still alive."

"Yes, retired probably, considering his age, but that doesn't mean," Maria Dolores cut him off.

"A whole life, done, finished and I know nothing about it. Not even a name."

"Hmm," Father Gabriel reached for his water. "Not

necessarily finished."

"Maybe he has children, my grandchildren."

"This was what I wanted to talk to you about the last time but you, um, well, anyway it's really why I've come round today. Did you know the Church offers a service to put people back in touch with their birth mothers? And of course mothers in touch with those children. Some of them, adults now of course, have actually been reunited." The words flew from his mouth before they could be halted. This time she had heard everything. Her head slowly rose. A crooked finger parted her white fringe, her eyes drilling his, her attention piqued.

"They do that? Your Church does this?"

"Yes, well we, eh, here in Ibiza haven't yet traced anyone but it is happening on the mainland. Yes." Maria Dolores stared in disbelief. They took him away and now they can give him back.

"You, you do this now?"

"Well, *I* haven't done it but it is being done, umm, generally. The Church has admitted to some of the mistakes of the past." His words softened as if he weren't fully convinced of their veracity.

"Can you do it?"

"Would you like us to try?"

"Yes, yes of course." Then in the pause that followed, the reality of what she was asking struck her. "No, no don't."

"But why?"

"I don't," but the visceral emotion rising inside her couldn't be verbalised.

"Why do you say that Dolores?"

"What if he doesn't know? If no one told him, he won't know I even exist, his own mother."

"I agree, but think about this carefully. This is what you've been wanting a long time." The priest's words were lost on her. Maria Dolores felt her heart pound, heard the force of it inside her. Something was telling her this wasn't a good idea. "Dolores?"

"No, how can that be done now? After all these years. Who knows where he is?"

"The Church and the State have records, written papers, Dolores. Judge Garzón says there could be as many as 30,000 babies taken and now those records are to be made available to the public, they already have, most of them." Maria Dolores felt faint. She hadn't been expecting the priest to arrive at her door, she hadn't expected this conversation and she certainly never expected to have the one thing she had lost decades ago thrust upon her again. Hope.

Father Gabriel continued, "I have a feeling that it would be easier for children to contact mothers rather than the other way round but we could look into it." He stared at the bewildered old woman waiting a response but again she hadn't heard him. The possibilities were too overwhelming.

"What if he's dead already? No, no I'd know, I'm his mother." She sat shaking her head.

"Dolores I know how you feel. It's an awful lot to take in."

"How would *you* know how I feel?"

"I didn't tell you this but the same thing happened to an aunt of mine. She was pregnant when her husband died and because she already had 5 children they took the baby away from her. I have an older cousin out there somewhere." Maria Dolores struggled to see the connection. "I understand. This is also something close to my own heart."

"What do you know about it? Thinking of him everyday. What do you know?" Her voice trembled and rose an octave, gathering pace.

"Maria Dolores I'm not trying to," but again she cut him off.

"You're a man. You've never had a child." Anger grew

with every breath, her skin began to prickle and burn with it.

"I was only trying to explain that something similar happened in my own family. That I empathise."

"Have you *ever* even been with a woman?"

"Please, don't get so upset, I came here to offer help." Humanity and charity had brought him to her door offering solutions but it had blinded him to her vulnerability and the depth of her loss. Pain that refused to abate with time, now intensified within the old lady. Baby rose to her feet at the sound of her mistress's distress.

"You're not even a real man." Father Gabriel shuffled uncomfortably, the heat of the afternoon suddenly more intense. He hadn't expected this reaction. He sank back in the chair, deflated.

"Men just let you down and you'd do the same."

"I only came to let you know there may be a way to put you in touch with your son."

"Men always do." She turned away, her defensive attack delivered. She wanted to be alone again and the priest felt it. He rose scraping the cheap plastic chair across the broken floor-tiles. "Perhaps we can talk about this again. You can come back to see me at any time Dolores." He wasn't sure if she would. He had said what he came to say and that could not be taken back. The seed had been sown. Now it was over to her.

Chapter Twenty-One

The Mountains, Spring1947

The bus driver from Cardeña took one look at Maria Dolores and allowed her onto the bus without paying. She held out the few coins Rocio had given her but he refused them. He had watched her climb the stairs like some old arthritic crone in some considerable discomfort and had taken pity. Her youthfulness was obvious but exhaustion had taken its toll. Her eyes however still sparkled with life, that would never be stolen. He was clean shaven and had his hair slicked back with a neat side parting, as was the style for a young working man. She didn't notice his handsome appearance or warm smile and asked to be let off just before the village of Los Caballeros de La Sierra. He tapped a cigarette packet on his leg as he watched her advance down the bus in the rear-view mirror. He could never know that her cumbersome movement was caused by vaginal swelling, red inflamed skin that cried out in protest against being compressed by her clammy underwear. It burned as she walked. She had given birth less than 48 hours earlier.

It had been only a few months since her departure from the village but so much had changed. She sat with her forehead pressed against the cold window. For a moment she saw her own reflection, the tiredness shocked her. A smile tried to break through but it was feeble and unseemly on her heavy face. Again she wondered how she would confront her treacherous mother not to mention her father. There was no way they would allow her to go to Marbella. But that was her plan, she had to find her son. The mountains became more familiar and although still inside the bus, she felt the air clearer. Her spirits lifted at the thought of seeing Juan Diego again but she also worried that she had had no contact with him all the time she was in the hospital. How could that be? Had he not wanted to see her? After the revelation of her mother's deceit, her part in the adoption, she and Rocio had concluded that she must have also lied to Juan Diego. Maria Dolores would seek him out first and tell him everything that had happened. He would help her get their son back.

As promised the driver dropped her off before they reached the village. It was early afternoon and she calculated that most people would be at home. She prayed Juan Diego was not with her own family. As she made her way through a pine copse the branches pushed against her, tugging at her already dishevelled hair. Animal paths that ran beside lichened dry-stone walls and criss-crossed the valley were tracks she knew like the back of her hand. She hoisted her heavy skirt to her knees to quicken the pace but progress was slow over the wet ground. Nature working against her. Her own country telling her not to advance. The first bluebells poked their heads through rough thickets of mountain pastures. Maria Dolores looked at them as she paused for breath. Her whole life had been spent in this high valley. She knew the flowers were early, they wouldn't last if there was a late frost.

As she approached Juan Diego's house her pace quickened

but then she stopped. The adrenaline that had carried her there suddenly abated. Anxiety almost overwhelmed her, her breathing became rapid and loud. Her actions seemed ill thought-out but there she was in front of the cottage, their cottage. She had come this far and could not go back but there was something amiss, something warning her. The cottage was not only empty, but even in the bright spring sunshine, it seemed lifeless.

Less than a kilometre away Maria Dolores' family sat in silence around the table. Conchi ate as she had been ordered to but Pascual hadn't heeded his own words. He pushed his food around on the plate, as he had done at every meal since Juan Diego's unceremonious burial. It tortured him to think that he had been responsible for the young man's death. He agonised over it. It filled his every waking hour and haunted the little sleep he was afforded. Remorse was an unforgiving companion. He had even thought about going himself to Seville to tell Maria Dolores but Dora had persuaded him not to go. For the sake of the baby, she had told him, echoing Father Alberto's advice.

They had attended Franco's address to the nation as normal the previous Wednesday. There had been a stunned silence afterwards as it was announced that José Blanco would lead out the Virgin this year. What had been more surprising was that Pascual hadn't raised any objection. He had sat staring at the floor, assessing his losses. Father Alberto's words battered him, that smug grin mocked him. Pascual didn't know why José Blanco had visited Juan Diego that night but of course he had told the priest that he had found the young man's lifeless body. They buried him together with the help of Miguel Guerrero in a shallow grave a few kilometres from the village and only 20 metres or so from where the body of his friend,

Manolo Jimenez, lay. But now he was beholden to José and the priest, forever in their debt. The priest had told the village Juan Diego had been exposed as a wanted Republican and worse, a Catalan, but he had fled before he could be held accountable for his actions and beliefs. His escape, however, proved his guilt.

Pascual did not know what was happening in Seville and of course had no idea of his own wife's complicity in it. Likewise he had not taken his wife into his confidence, he could not, she was a religious woman. The burden of Juan Diego's demise was his and his alone, at least within his own house. He missed his daughter, her absence was more than he could bear. He rued the day he met Juan Diego and wished he had never invited him into his house but that was no reason to kill a man. He yearned for the warmth of the home they had had together, for his family. He reconciled himself with the fact that Maria Dolores would soon return. And she would bring with her his grandchild. He had accepted that, the child now had no father. There was at least that, a chance of a new beginning.

Maria Dolores' last few steps to the house were the hardest to take but she forced herself onwards. She became more aware of her physical self. How would she look to Juan Diego, her dress was wet and dirty, her hair hadn't been washed in days, it clung to her head. She pressed on. The door opened easily but as always scraped across the stone step just inside the house. She shrunk back a little, fearing that the noise would carry across the valley and bring unwanted attention. The stone walls were cold, they sucked the warmth out of her as she passed her hands over them. Somehow she expected to feel Juan Diego in those walls but she knew this house had not recently been lived in. The air held the staleness of inactivity and was heavy with mildew. The cinders in the fireplace were white with decay. Where was Juan Diego? Dread started to build up inside her. It weighed her down, slowed her progress. She pushed on further into the house, looking but not daring to see. The crib in the bedroom, half built, was as she had last seen it. There was no food around. She peered into the dark recesses of the house looking for clues, anything, but found nothing. His work shirt and some other clothing lay crumpled on the table. She touched them as she passed. The shirt felt soft but it was cold and damp, lifeless. The only sounds were her light footsteps, cautious and careful.

As she rounded his chair her foot nudged a hefty square bottle on the floor. She recognised it immediately. It was her father's Gran Duke d'Alba brandy bottle. Why would that be here? Juan Diego didn't drink brandy. As she bent down to pick it up, the change of light reflected something near the door that she hadn't noticed before. There was a darkness on the floor, a black lucent stain. A pool of dried blood that still half-glistened in the daylight. Maria Dolores started backwards, a quick half step away from the evidence before her. She looked at the bottle still in her hand. And even though she tried to reject the thoughts that were taking form, they would not be dismissed. Her father had taken revenge. She thrust the bottle away, trying to refute its existence. It clunked against Juan Diego's dried blood then skipped across the floor. The anxiety that had been lurking inside her began to make itself known. It screamed at her as it rose in her chest, she felt it fight for her breath. Then the palpitations boomed and reverberated until they consumed her. Her whole body telling her to flee, run from the house and escape the truth.

* * *

And so she did, she ran from the cottage and vomited a thick bilious fluid. She had to rest at the corner of the house, gasping for air, dizziness too beginning to overcome her. She stood there supported by the wall, taking deep desperate sobs. Then the tears started, they mixed with the green vomit that still clung to her lips. They fell between sobs and anguished cries of grief. They flowed through her fingers when she raised her hands to cover her eyes to deny them vision, to deny her what was so obvious. Her own father had killed Juan Diego. The minutes passed, she cried in fits and starts and mumbled his name. She took a few hesitant steps towards the door again but couldn't go in. She sank to her knees and wrung her skirt tightly, letting the misery and heartache flow through her hands.

What would she do now? She had no choice, she was alone in the world. She started the short walk from the cottage to her own home.

Pascual pushed his plate back, the fork fell from his hand with a dull clunk on the wooden table. More than half the food remained but Dora knew better than to challenge him. Since Juan Diego had left his mood had been volatile. She had spoken several times to her confidant, Father Alberto, about it. He bade her be patient and not tell Pascual about the adoption. When Maria Dolores returned from Seville he would talk to them. He would counsel them, offer guidance. They could take the Sacrament of Penance together as a family and would be absolved of their sins. Dora took hope from this, some optimism in this darkness. She knew Pascual didn't like Father Alberto but he was a holy man and spoke with experience and the authority of God.

Pascual stood and made his way towards the door. Pirri also

stood, hesitated, then trotted behind. Outside the air was crisp and the clear skies allowed the sun to stream down onto the yard in front of the house. He grabbed the large axe that laid propped next to the door and marched over towards the roughshod outhouse. Pirri who had become accustomed to his master's recent behaviour, lay on the ground at a safe distance and observed. Pascual rolled a large trunk over to an area of hard ground and began to chop. He swung the huge axe through the air bringing it down on the defenceless wood, which jumped in response as splinters sparked off in all directions. He swung again with the same result and again the axe pounded the massive trunk. Pascual grunted as the metal blade this time wedged into the wood. He pulled it free and repeated the movement with more force, crying louder each time. As on previous days the grunts took a life of their own and formed words as the catharsis continued.

"God forgive me," he spat as he pulled the axe out of the wood and swung again. Then with all his might as if trying to split the Earth itself he smashed it down again. "I'm sorry," he wept. The words drowned in a sob. "Bring me back my daughter," he hissed through clenched teeth. Anger blinded him. Self loathing hounded him. Then another powerful blow and with it a wild cry "Arrgghhh." Frustration and despair forcing their way out of him, their shackles broken and also given life. As remorse broke free, again he asked God for forgiveness, but he knew he was not a religious man, who would exonerate him? The dead can't forgive. Between blows and bellows of his own outrage he muttered the names of his absent daughter, his dead farm hand, and that bastard priest.

Maria Dolores heard her father before she saw him, she stopped and spied him from behind a rock half buried in the mossy hillside. His angry voice not what she had expected, she shivered as its pain reached her. She saw his anguish and even from a distance felt his fury. She paused there watching the man she knew to be her father but he looked different. He was thinner; an unshaven, gaunt version of that other man. He looked afflicted by some malady, something that had ravaged his body. She cowered behind the rock and listened as her father pulverised the trunk both simultaneously outraged and pleading forgiveness. He was perhaps only 100 metres away, with her house a little further. She could stand up but she didn't know if she had the strength. She was trapped. The thwacks of the axe on wood continued, each one followed by a grunt or a yell. Mostly wild indistinguishable bellows that formed no words, that made no sense but then she heard her name in amongst all that anger. Juan Diego's name was also called out. Yes their names *were* yelled out as the axe pounded the defenceless trunk.

If she stood up what would happen? How would he respond? Juan Diego was not there to protect her. Her name was cried out again. His own daughter fuelled his rage. She shuddered as she sat and again burst into tears, her fingers dug into the cold soil below her and she pressed herself hard against the stone fearing she might be seen. The sharp edge of the rock dug into her back. She was alone now. Her mother had colluded in taking her baby away and her own father had killed her lover. No. No. There was no way she could go back home.

Her shoulders shook and trembled in their own erratic rhythm as she cried into her forearm, terrified to make even the slightest noise. She started to rock, her mind unable to focus. How could this be happening to her? At only 17 she had lost everything: her son, her lover, and now her family and home. Then Maria Dolores felt something touch her hand. She withdrew it but opened her eyes again. Pirri jumped over her, ecstatic to see his mistress again. "Pirri, Pirri," she sobbed. The dog exploded with excitement. "Ohhh, Pirri, cariño cariño." But seeing him made her more anguished and she cried again unable to control her emotions. "Pirri, shh, shh." She reached out and hugged the exhilarated animal. After the initial thrill of seeing her friend again she breathed and remembered her situation. "He can't see me here Pirri. You have to go." The dog looked up at her and barked. "Shhhhh, Pirri cariño you have to go." She pushed him away. "Pirri, GO." And with that she crawled away from the rock and stumbled to her feet and without knowing her final destination headed back towards the village. Tears made her vision hazy. The sun began to dip below the mountains, the fading dusk light would give her cover. It was unlikely that anyone would see her but she wasn't thinking about that. Nor had she considered her inadequate clothing for the cold mountain air. She turned to make sure Pirri wasn't following her, but she was alone. She stumbled towards the only place she had a friend. Dark sinister shadows grew longer in the receding afternoon light, creeping towards her. Foreboding, forewarning. At that time the bar should be closed but Ana would surely be there. She was, and luckily she was alone. She slapped a hand over her mouth, her eyes bulged as much as beady bird eyes can, as Maria Dolores pushed the door open and staggered in.

"Uhhh, Maria Dolores. I," she gasped but could say no more. The sight of her old school companion in such a state shocked her into silence. She rushed around the bar and grabbed her arm, ushering her into the warmth of the kitchen. And it was in that kitchen that Maria Dolores broke down, drained of all strength. Ana sat beside her, hand on her lap, and listened open mouthed, her stare darting around Maria Dolores' face and body for verification of the story. Between sobs Ana grasped that Maria Dolores' mother had planned the adoption from the beginning, about the Sisters of Clemency and Grace, finding Rocio and returning home to find out that her father had killed Juan Diego.

"But Lola, Juan Diego isn't dead." She cocked her head backwards, the extra flesh of her neck swallowing her chin. She stared at Maria Dolores who didn't appear to have heard her. "Lola, Juan Diego escaped. Father Alberto told us." Maria Dolores looked up, tears still streaming down her face but she had quietened.

"What?"

"It's true. Father Alberto told us a few weeks ago. He told us Juan Diego escaped before he could be arrested. He's alive."

"No, he. I, I saw his blood, in the cottage I saw his blood. I heard Papi say it." The words broke free from her between gulped breaths. She turned to look at Ana, wiping the tears away from her blotchy eyes. "Ana?" she pleaded.

"It's true Maria Dolores," came the solemn voice from behind them. Both girls spun round, Ana gulped dramatically and almost fell from her chair, as her father, Miguel, entered the kitchen.

"Papi."

"Juan Diego did leave the village more than a month ago." His calm authoritative voice, hid the rising alarm that had started to grip his stomach. He stepped further into the room, his every movement followed by the girls. "I don't know where he went, I don't think anyone does." He paused "But Maria Dolores, what are you doing here?"

Maria Dolores ignored his question. Her tone was becoming desperate again. "But I heard Papi say he was dead."

"I don't think he would have said that but we can ask him.

He'll be happy to see you," Miguel interrupted. And not for the first time that day Maria Dolores felt totally overwhelmed. She felt herself sway on the chair. "Bring her some water Ana," Miguel instructed. Over the next quarter of an hour Ana fed Maria Dolores some left-over food from the bar and Miguel left them alone without giving an explanation.

"I don't think I want to see Papi," said Maria Dolores looking down at the pastry she pulled apart in her hands.

"But what else can you do?" They sat for a while without talking, void of ideas. Already life had begun to take its toll on them. Ana's daily routine in the kitchen and bar had added inches to her waist and bust but she retained her youthful face. Maria Dolores on the other hand, at least physically, looked defeated, her face gaunt with exhaustion and dehydration, her jet black hair limp and lifeless. Not so long ago they had sat together as schoolgirls but since then circumstance had led them down very different paths. Ana fated to remain safely in their childhood village, Maria Dolores' destiny lay somewhere else.

"Uhh Lola," Ana exclaimed, suddenly energised by the brilliance of an idea. "Maybe Juan Diego has gone to Seville to look for you. Did he know where you were? Did he know about the hospital?" Maria Dolores looked at her, stunned.

"I don't know. Yes, he knew I was going to hospital. Mami said she told him." And although there was a doubt about the truth of her mother's words, she dismissed it. This was at least hope, it offered an alternative, a way forward.

"He would definitely go and look for you Lola. He would. I know it." They both stared at each other forgetting that Ana hadn't even known about the relationship, let alone the pregnancy until the day Maria Dolores left the village. Their innocence and desire to find a solution eclipsed their thinking.

"I have to go back to Seville. He'll be there, Ana. You're right." Maria Dolores straightened up wiped her eyes and for the first time in days a semblance of a smile crept across her face. Their enthusiasm fuelled each other. "But how do I get back? How do I find him?" They sat in silence for a moment holding each others hands.

"I can give you money from the till." She paused then gripped Maria Dolores hands, thrilled by her own idea. "I'll ask my father, like before when he took you to Cardeña." Maria Dolores squinted at her. It had crossed her mind that Miguel had gone to fetch her father, he had already been away for some time.

"Ana, give me some pesetas, I'll take the bus back. There's a bus every night" she blurted out, her decision made. "I'll pay you back someday, honestly I will."

"I will Lola. I'll get it now." She ran from the room leaving Maria Dolores alone. The size of the kitchen belied the industry undertaken there everyday. Bowls and small porcelain plates, cooking utensils, dirty glasses and coffee cups cluttered the worktops. She thought she had lost Juan Diego. She felt foolish that she had allowed herself to react as she did at the cottage but the sensation of loss was so overwhelming. But then why was Papi so angry? She squeezed her eyes closed hoping that it would help her concentrate, praying for clarification. So much had happened so quickly.

After a few minutes she heard Ana and Miguel's voices in the bar. They had arrived together and began to discuss something that Maria Dolores couldn't make out. They entered the kitchen, Ana behind her father trying to suppress a smile behind her jowls.

"He said he would take you," Ana blurted. Delighted that

her idea had worked. She ran round her father knocking him a little off balance in the process. She grabbed Maria Dolores and hugged her. "Lola, you can go. You can go find him Lola." Maria Dolores looked over her shoulder at Miguel.

"You *should* see your father." Miguel added addressing Maria Dolores but looking at her feet. "But if this is what you want." His voice trailed off. Ana hugged her again. "We can leave in 10 minutes. Ana, give her some food to take with her, and a coat." And with that Miguel left the kitchen again. Maria Dolores accepted Ana's embrace but could not fully reciprocate. She was a bit perturbed by Miguel's willingness to help her. It wasn't what she had expected. Why should he help her? Was he not her father's friend? So much just didn't make sense.

When Miguel returned, wearing a jacket and cap, he motioned to Maria Dolores. As she stood, she caught his eye and for a moment they held each other's stare. A private moment, that pushed Ana's wittering into the background. But Miguel conceded nothing. Maria Dolores was still young and naive. She hadn't yet learned to read a man's face, to recognise treachery in his eyes, to know the lengths he is willing to go to.

"Yes," she replied. "I'm ready."

Maria Dolores was hesitant when Miguel suggested that she travel in the rear of the van, at least until away from the village. It did however make sense, even though to get beyond the town's boundaries would only take a few minutes. It smelled as awful as it had done a few months earlier, of staleness and rancid earth. She kicked away a rag which looked like it had been a piece of clothing at one point and sat down on a folded blanket that Ana had given her. Miguel watched her settle and closed the door, without saying anything else, leaving her in the pitch black. She bounced as the truck moved off.

Ana had been discrete when slipping her some money as they hugged goodbye, she was thankful for that. In her mind's eye she saw the village as they set off; the bar, the cobbled street to the old well and finally the church with it's imposing tower and great black cross. She wondered when she would return. When would she see Conchi and Mami again? When she thought of her father she could only see his anger and it filled her with panic. She tried to focus on Juan Diego. First she had to get back to Seville and return to Rocio. Ana watched as the small van trundled into the night, the weak headlights half illuminating the road ahead, knowing that she could keep a secret.

Ten minutes or so later, the van slowed down and lurched as it slid off the road. She heard Miguel's voice but it was impossible to make out what he was saying. She stood and took a few steps towards the back of the van holding her hand out in front of her, edging her way through the dank air. The door opened onto the darkness of the night. The only thing she could see was the amber glow of a cigarette as it was being inhaled. As she held her hand out for assistance that orange light was flicked away and someone jumped into the back of the van. She sprang back, an innate sense of preservation prevailing, in her escalating confusion.

"Hello Maria Dolores." The voice was very familiar but before she could register who it was she felt a blinding pain in the side of her face as something connected with her jaw. The force of it knocked her sideways and she fell to the floor. She screamed in agony and surprise, but there was no one around to hear. Then he was on top of her. He grabbed her hair and slammed her head against the floor of the van. Once, twice, three times. Then he thrust her head down again, got up and pulled the door closed. The van's engine started and once more it continued its journey. Maria Dolores, stunned, raised herself up on one arm and gasped for breath. The speed of the attack had left her dumbfounded, nothing registered except shock and pain. Now they shared the same enclosed space.

"You didn't say hello." Perhaps because of the darkness or perhaps because of the movement of the vehicle the kick José Blanco aimed at her stomach missed its intended target and connected with her thigh. Maria Dolores howled a deafening cry and fell flat again. Then he was a second time on top of her and started to lift up her skirt. She struggled and kicked back at him but to no avail. She pushed with her hands to lift herself from the floor but he slammed her down again. Dirt entered her mouth and nose as she tried to gulp air. Rank air that nourished him, driving him on, the same putrid air that refused to fill her lungs, refused to give her strength.

"Nooo." She screamed not only in protest but also at the sudden realisation of his intent. Then his left hand punched her in the kidney. Another blow to her chest took her breath from her. Why didn't Miguel do something? Her father's friend.

"Shut up. Shut the fuck up," he hissed at her, malice riding his voice. He fumbled underneath her skirt until he had hold of her underwear. He yanked it violently up, the rough seam cut into her, ripping across her already inflamed skin. His knee dug into her thigh where he had kicked her. "No one's coming, so shut up." But she couldn't. She couldn't keep quiet so he struck her again and held her head to the floor. The rough earth embedded in her face, it lacerated her eyelid. She tried to grab at his arm but she was hampered by her coat and couldn't reach him. She tried to lift herself to her knees again but his weight was too much. She tried to scream again but she had no air in her. She tried.

As he penetrated her, her body jerked its objection. She had no breath but still squealed in pain, an animal cry that reverberated around her enclosure. Her fingers tried to grab the metal floor, its cold hardness unyielding. A fingernail broke in half and was ripped off leaving a bleeding tip exposed. His weight was on top of her but the heaviness of her own body restricted her, as she struggled to move. For a moment she saw herself in the dark, detached, a third person looking on. She saw the violation taking place, blow by blow. "Stay still whore." He pulled at her coat to bring her closer to him, to trap her under him. The buttons held and the collar dug into her throat strangling her, making it even harder to breathe. He pushed himself further into her. The darkness hid his face but she sensed he was smiling. He wasn't, his twisted grimace contorted more with each thrust, spittle spraying though clenched teeth as he panted.

"No, NO," she spluttered. Blood and dirt fell from her mouth. And he went deeper into her, again and again. He pulled her head back by the hair. Then he ejaculated and was quiet. For José Blanco it was over in a matter of a minute, for Maria Dolores it would last a lifetime. He leant over and tried to kiss her cheek. When she squirmed away from him shaking, he grabbed her hair again and pulled her closer to him, his putrid breath doused her. She tried to swallow but the saliva wasn't liquid enough, the congealed blood a mass trapped in her throat, trapped as she was. She wanted to vomit.

"Ughh," he grunted. "Where's Juan Diego now?" He paused as he recovered his breathing. "I'll tell you where. In a hole in the ground," he hissed into her ear and as he lifted himself off of her he spat on her hair. "And your own father killed him." His vitriolic words whispered yet reached Maria Dolores like the crash of a falling pine. A few more deep inhalations. He knelt behind her, her petrified, used body motionless. He pulled at his softening penis, and in the dark wiped the semen and blood on the back of her coat, an ultimate insult. He stood up and buttoned his trousers. As she lay there paralysed, Maria Dolores heard him laugh, a self satisfied snigger as he banged on the cabin wall.

The van pulled over and José Blanco left her there on the floor and climbed into the cabin. She heard talking then him laughing as they drove off again. For a while she dared not move, she lay pulling her coat around her, a protection that came too late. She had no perception of time, locked there in the dark. Then after what could have been minutes or hours, Maria Dolores inched across the dirty floor away from the cabin and the voices until she could go no further. She spat dirt from her mouth. She gagged at the metallic taste of her own blood. What would in a few days become black and purple bruises were already evolving, pink tender blotches on her flesh, a visual testimony of the night's violence. Her body stung and throbbed. It screamed pain as she curled up to make herself as small as she could. She lay there foetus-like, trembling, agonised, then she blacked out.

Chapter Twenty-Two

Ibiza 2016

Bernarda had already left with the twins on the daily trudge to school. They moped behind her, awaiting the day to grow upon them. She stopped and turned to them, her annoyance didn't need to be verbalised. They didn't quicken their pace. Not yet teenagers, she wondered if in their adolescence their temperament would change. Which of their elder brothers would they take after? She knew which one she would prefer, but as a mother she didn't let herself dwell on that.

Back at the house Paco was ready for school. It wasn't even a quarter to eight, yet Sebastian was also ready to leave. He couldn't remember the last time he had seen his father this early in the morning. Something didn't feel right.

"I'll come down with you." It wasn't a question and Sebastian was at the door waiting before Paco had found his mobile phone. It flashed through his mind that 'I'll come down' meant that he was going to accompany him to school, which made him feel even more perturbed. They left together in silence. Once on the street, Paco looped over the rusted bike lock that hung from the gate post to close it. It was a practice he hadn't lost even though there was no longer a dog to confine.

They continued their way down the hillside towards the town centre. Sebastian almost skipping as he shared with his indifferent son his plans for the day. Meet with someone or other, go to an office and discuss work for the summer, Paco pricked up his ears. Perhaps this uncharacteristic excitement was just down to nerves or even the actual possibility of employment. Either way his father's exuberance was beginning to rub off on him and he permitted himself a smile. When they reached the town the air was more dense, more noticeable in the cool morning. A few people, office workers and school children, navigated the early streets. When they reached the main thoroughfare, Avinguda de Espanya, Sebastian halted.

"I'll just nip in here and have a coffee," he signalled to Paco a bar where three dishevelled men had already gathered. Before each of them a small espresso cup and an empty snifter glass. The men sat together in a silent fellowship, not feeling the need to communicate. Paco looked at his father, suddenly angry then walked on without uttering another word. The news from the television in the bar became audible as Sebastian opened the door unaware of the change in Paco's mood. The sense of deception and disappointment was almost overwhelming, he should have known better. His father wasn't looking for work, it was a decoy. An excuse to have an early morning drink. And he had allowed himself to be taken in by it. He walked the further 10 minutes to school with an unshakable resentment building.

It wasn't going to be a taxing morning for Paco. Catalan, mathematics and English, a break then Modern Studies, Social Politics then home. One more week of exams then summer holidays, it would be a breeze. At the end of his

English class, Sñr Alves, asked him to stay behind and gave him a book to read over the summer. 'Of Mice and Men' It was a second hand book, maybe his own. Sñr Alves told him kids of his age in America would be reading the same. It was a compliment on his linguistic ability. He felt a surge of something inside, an elation that made him want to smile, to let his emotions show but he didn't. He took the book with a solitary 'OK', thankful to be given the book in private, then made his way to the recreation area outside.

After arriving late and unable to see his friends, he settled under a huge triangular canvas. He pulled out his mobile phone eager to make the most of the school's free WIFI. With class finished and nothing to occupy his mind his thoughts soon turned again to his father. He imagined him at home half drunk or perhaps still in that bar talking 'business', a personal amalgam of bullshit and invention. The aggravation that had been simmering in him all morning crept again to the fore.

At first he didn't notice the commotion over towards the school building, but as more children gathered the noise intensified and Paco's curiosity got the better of him. He rose and ambled towards the rabble. Two senior boys were pushing another kid, passing him between them like some medieval game. Each shove was accompanied by a stifled '*olé*', the onlookers wary of attracting too much attention. The performance was tracked at various angles by adept hands recording on phones. The perpetrators' jibes focussed more on the fat boy's slavic roots, calling him 'Dracula' and 'Romanian piece of shit'. The fact that the boy was actually Serbian was of little relevance. Paco eased through the throng to get a better view. Their target wasn't saying anything, no retaliation, physical or verbal, apart from an occasional grunt of exasperation.

"What happened?" Paco asked a girl beside him.

"Nothin, just these two being dicks as usual."

"Bullying for nothing?"

"Yeah, I think so. He don't talk a lot, that kid. Don't think he understands that much."

Paco squeezed to the front and stood arms crossed observing the scene. He stood solidly as those around him jostled for position. Then a more forceful shove, another '*olé*' and the boy tripped and fell. Both giggles and groans rippled through the onlookers. Paco stepped forward.

"That's enough." The two bullies turned to the voice.

"Says who?" Questioned one of them.

Paco didn't answer, he stared at each in turn daring further reaction, the day's vexation bursting for a release. He laid his back-pack gently by his side. His normally soft eyes, sharpened and confident. He was shorter than them both but considerably wider, a bull in comparison. Paco was a daunting opponent and they knew it. The gathering looked at the three of them waiting to see where this would lead. From the ground the Serbian boy looked bewildered. The bully who had spoken took a step towards Paco but his companion grabbed his arm. Then the fleeting moment of tension was over. An anticlimax, mobile phone cameras fell in disappointment. They knew better than to mix it with a gitano, there were more of them in the school and they would come running. Anyway for now they had had their fun and left sharing a smile and a slap of the hands. A girl came forward to help the Serbian boy to his feet and the small crowd dispersed. Paco also walked away. Two words, an unswerving stare and his sturdy frame more than enough to diffuse the fracas.

The afternoon continued without further incident. The Social Politics class had, for most of the year, been tedious. Recently, however, they had entered a time when his parents were alive, they would remember the death of Franco and The Transition. His teacher, Señora Brotons managed to capture his imagination by going off curriculum, teaching how Franco's death also lead to cultural change and *La Movida*. She talked of another kind of freedom, of music, fashion, literature and of Pedro Almodóvar. She spoke of that time as if she had experienced it herself. Paco noted her dreamy eyes but thought she couldn't be old enough to have lived through that time. He had heard of *La Movida* but hadn't realised the significance of it. The thought of being given such sudden freedom to believe resonated with him.

The last class of the day was given over to the students as exam preparation time. They sat in rows at their desks, a few books open but no one actually studying. Some chatted with neighbours, most were glued to their phones. Paco thumbed through Of Mice and Men. He felt something for this book without even knowing what it was about as he fingered its fragile spine. Its rough, yellowing pages smelled a little stale, almost of dampness. It reminded him of the stuffy reference room in the Puig d'es Molins archeological museum. He didn't want to start reading it until he was somewhere quiet, private. He sat and subconsciously toyed with a cheap biro. Spinning it on the desk, stopping it and spinning it again. Over and over. Contemplating his father, over and over. The soft repetitive scraping noise of the pen attracted the teacher's attention. Approaching Paco she was drawn towards his unkempt hands, the stubby fingers, the chewed nails and torn cuticles: bitten enough to expose reddened nail beds. She hadn't thought Paco a nervous kid. A pang of melancholy hit her, having this sudden insight into one of her brightest students. There was perhaps in her a mother's instinct as she hovered over him. She saw a fragility that made her want to protect him. Paco felt observed and looked up at her just as the bell rang. The kids stood simultaneously, classes were finished. School was over. The summertime was theirs.

Hundreds of teenagers diverged and took their own routes home, many to the same neighbourhoods. Paco said goodbye to a few around him then started home knowing he would see them during the holidays. One block away from the school he paused for a second, then decided to return via the Figueretas promenade. It was only a few minutes longer but he would avoid the bar where he had left his father that morning. He surely wouldn't be there but Paco didn't want confirmation either way. As he waited to cross the road he felt a presence beside him.

"Hola." It was the bullied Serbian boy. "I need say thanks. For today." The broken words in his eastern accent were soft and almost inaudible amongst the traffic. He fretted with the strap of his satchel as he smiled at Paco. It wasn't convincing, he still looked scared. His dumpy face and pale skin looked ruddy in the midday heat. His sweat stained t-shirt was tight across his torso but the collar had been stretched and remained out of shape.

"It's OK." Paco returned an equally unconvincing smile, then turned to look back at the traffic.

"Those boys do this more times," he began but Paco cut him off.

"Look, I don't know you. I stopped them because what they were doing was wrong. No one should bully kids. It's not right."

"I. I," the boy stammered, nervous again, shrinking back and looking feeble.

"I told you. It's OK." The boy didn't take his eyes off his saviour. "Look, we're not mates. They were wrong. End of."

Paco stared again at the boy, this time with a slight frown. "We are not friends," he repeated. His eyes sharp again, brow furrowed. The traffic stopped and Paco felt the people around him move so he followed, crossing the road. The Serbian boy watched as his hero disappeared with the crowd.

The commotion coming from the Moreno household greeted Paco long before he reached the house. Without realising it his pace slowed. As he neared, he saw Maria Dolores hobble out lugging a grocery bag. Paco held the gate open. "Hope you're ready for good news." Paco couldn't tell if she was being sarcastic or not.

"Why, what's happened?"

"You finish school yet?" she added, ignoring his question.

"Yes, just today."

"Huh. Well, maybe we'll see more of you then." And again Paco was left puzzled by her meaning. They were both distracted as the noise levels from inside peaked once more. Maria Dolores chortled to herself and ambled off to her own house. Paco braced himself as he climbed the stairs, it was lunch time and he was hungry but it seemed there was a party just beginning.

Sebas shook and opened a can of beer then laughed as the foam spurted into the middle of the room. He accompanied that with a vulgar cheer, which the twins repeated. Their father Sebastian sat in his chair looking pleased with himself. Paco couldn't tell if it was alcohol induced or not. What difference did it make? There he was in his habitual position, slumped back on his armchair. King of nothing.

"Hey, here's the smart-ass of the family. Where you been lil' brother?" Paco ignored Sebas and proceeded across the room, dumping his open school bag onto the dining table. His summer reading poked out.

"Don't be touching any beer, lil' brother." The last words drawn out, an unnecessary dig at the clearly irritated Paco. He walked into the kitchen and scanned the worktops, looking for something to eat. Nothing.

"Paco, come back through here. Your Papi got a job today." Paco was a bit taken aback by the tone of Bernarda's delighted voice. He peered more closely at his mother. The wide grin across her face showed off her white teeth. She looked radiant. Genuine happiness shone out of her as she pulled one of the twins closer. In that moment he realised he hardly saw her like this, so animated, so natural, so beautiful. He turned his attention to his father who had slid forward to perch on the armchair.

"Rest of the season Paco. Hotel handyman." He too smiled broadly and rolled his sleeve up and flexed his tattooed biceps in a show of strength. That morning's apprehensions began to flood back to him; the derisive thoughts, scornful feelings, the general lack of sympathy he had for his father. His heart pulled a little inside his chest, the embryos of self-reproach.

"All summer Papi?" The words stuck in his drying throat but Bernarda saw a smile take form, she laid a hand on his forearm. Paco took a step forward, back into the heart of the family.

"Leave him be, grumpy little bastard." Sebas snapped, with a glaring dart in Paco's direction.

"Sebas!" But he ignored their mother.

"Why can't you be happy for him? Why you always acting like a brat?" Sebas reached over for another beer and gave it to his father. Bernarda felt Paco tense and tried to tighten her grip on his arm but he flinched, breaking free. He stood in a rage not knowing how to control himself. Yet again Sebas had managed to antagonise him with just a few words. He glanced over at his father, who as their eyes met lowered his head and toyed with the beer can held between his hands. Before the lump that was forming in Paco's throat exploded he made a retreat into his bedroom, the one that Sebas had appropriated, slamming the door behind him. He sat on the end of his bed close to tears but denying them life. The smell of Sebas' freshly laundered clothes filtered through the stink of stale smoke. Mumbled voices came from a few metres away but he didn't try to listen. His name was shouted, something hit the bedroom door and then the front door slammed. The silence that followed didn't comfort Paco. When, soon after he heard the twins leave, he inched the door open. Bernarda was bent over in front of him, as she stood she handed him a book, parts of a book. She placed the broken copy of 'Of Mice and Men' into his opened hands. Three parts of the same but yet not the whole, having been broken down the spine.

"I'm sorry." His mother offered the apology but it was clearly not she that should be apologising.

Chapter Twenty-Three

Marbella, Spring 1947

"Isn't it strange Father that I still remember so many things that happened to me when I was young? I remember how the air smells just before it snows and how the lavender floods the meadows in spring, it gave the ground as much colour as the sky." On another day memories of the valley that she still held as clear as photographs could make the hardened Maria Dolores wistful. This day, however, she was reliving yet again the terror of José Blanco's attack on her, the last memory she had of the mountains. "But I don't remember how I got back to Seville." Father Gabriel sat with his hands folded, a natural position but covering his groin, a subconscious reaction to what had just been divulged. He wondered if the old lady sat opposite actually could remember the journey. He had heard of such traumatic experiences being obliterated from the victim's memory in a desperate attempt at self preservation, pain so profound that it just cannot be tolerated. But she had just described to him the attack which surely must be the most horrific aspect of it. Not for the first time Father Gabriel felt perplexed by Maria Dolores and her tale.

"I don't know how I got back to Rocio, but that was where I

woke up. Just like the day they took my baby away. She was there wiping my brow, soothing me. I was covered in bruises, it hurt to breathe. The cut in my lip stretched and bled every time I opened my mouth. She wouldn't show me the mirror but I didn't need to see it. I saw all I needed in her eyes. I must have been there weeks recovering, maybe a month, I don't know. I couldn't bear to tell her what had happened. I didn't know how to say the things he did to me. After a while she stopped asking. I never left her room those days, even when she went to work at the hospital. At first she slept on the floor but as I got better we shared the bed just like I did with Conchi. I missed her so much. Rocio tried to persuade me to go back to the village. But back to what? No. I wanted my baby. I wanted Juan Diego. I told myself he was looking for us and he would find us. I was sure of it. I was such a stupid girl." Maria Dolores sat motionless, staring through the floor. "I was there a month and he hadn't come for me. Maybe I should have known, but I couldn't give up hope."

"It took me so long to get better, to feel like normal again. Well not feel normal, just look it on the outside. When I was ready to go Rocio said she would come with me." Maria Dolores looked at Father Gabriel and smiled, her eyes sparkled as she remembered her friend, as she remembered the compassion of someone else. Suddenly she didn't look so old. Something in her changed, something ignited in her soul, he could see it. She had disclosed the most damaging, horrendous event of her life and shown that she had survived. That she was still surviving. "Rocio hated that hospital and what those nuns made her do. She wanted to run away as much as I did. We took the money she had and got a bus to Malaga then to Marbella. Just like that. Two girls, we were just two girls." Her voice trailed off but her nostalgic smile remained.

* * *

"Marbella was another world for us. We drove along the coast. I couldn't believe it, we had never seen the sea before. It was amazing how the sun shone on it like a mirror so you couldn't look at it too long. Rocio just sat with her mouth open and head pressed against the window. At first I stared as well, pushing against her to get closer to the window. Then I giggled and jumped up and down on my seat and before long I was laughing out loud. I don't know why, there wasn't anything funny. I laughed until I cried, people were looking at me and that made me worse. Rocio grabbed my hand and she started as well. We laughed and we hugged and we stared at that never ending sea."

"There wasn't really a bus station like in Seville, the bus just stopped on the seafront. We ran to the beach throwing our bags in the sand. It was like a dream, it was so warm and soft, it swallowed my feet as I ran on it. I took my shoes off but Rocio ran straight into the water up to her knees. And I went in after her but holding my skirt up, and we kept on laughing and screaming. Then we were splashing each other and everything got soaked." Maria Dolores paused to take breath. As she recalled that first encounter in Marbella her words spilled from her as fast as those two young girls were running across the beach to taste the Mediterranean for the first time. "It was all so warm; even the sea wasn't cold like I thought it was, and the sun so bright, much brighter than the sun in the mountains. I never knew the sea had a smell or tasted funny until that day. When the waves came they pushed us around like the floating seaweed, our skirts swayed first one way then the other. And we watched like it was all magic, our hands skimming on the surface. Rocio thought it was the ocean and asked if America was out there. And we laughed again until we fell into the water. We were like little children, hah, but now I know we were just children, even after all that had happened to me." Then that shadow encroached upon her again, as the recollection of that freedom and adolescent innocence was usurped by the memories of what had taken her there.

"We sat on the sand, drying in the sun and talked about what we were going to do. We only had a few hundred pesetas, in a town where we knew no one, we knew nothing. I was more worried than Rocio but she had lived in a city. We paid for one night in a pensión and didn't leave the room after dark. Our wet clothes hung around us but we slept with the window open, the air was so warm and filled the room with jasmine. I shouldn't have worried so much. The next morning the man who ran the pensión told us of a hotel that was hiring chamber-maids. They gave us a job with a room for us to share, that very same day. Just like that, a job with money and food and a room and we hadn't even been in the town for 24 hours. Summer was coming, there was work for everyone."

"All of a sudden everything changed for me. We cleaned the rooms in the morning and worked in the restaurant in the evening. Rocio told them we had been waitresses in Guerrero's Bar in our village. That made me laugh. We worked every single day, even on Sundays but we didn't care. Every afternoon after lunch we went down to the beach. Men came back with their boats full of fish and octopus, prawns and lobster and Rocio squealed because we had never seen creatures like those in real life. Tourists from Madrid with parasols sat on deck chairs as we ran between them. We laughed at the different languages; German and English and we giggled like schoolgirls as we mimicked the Spanish with their funny Galician and Asturian accents. The work was easy and everything was just so different. I was discovering what it was like to have a life. I had never thought of such a thing before. I had never even thought of earning money. After the first week when we were given our wages by Señor Vasquez I didn't know what to do with it. Rocio said we should hide it somewhere. I hid mine under the mattress and Rocio took it before the day had ended. 'You have to be smarter,' she laughed at me. I always had to learn the hard way."

"We felt so far away from our village although we were still in Andalusia. It was just another world. Everybody was happy, I even started to believe." Father Gabriel saw and heard the change in the old lady that sat in front of him; her tone, her posture and more that he couldn't put a finger on. She had become animated from within. Neither did she elaborate on exactly what she had started to believe in, but he was encouraged that something had changed in her younger-self's life.

"But I never forgot why we were there; my son," she continued. "Every time I saw a baby I would go over to the parents and ask to see it. I'd ask how old it was. I didn't know what he looked like, my boy. I counted the months and guessed how big he would be. How much hair he would have, how many teeth. I never once saw a baby who I thought was mine. I knew that when I saw him I would know him, because he was part of me."

"We started to go out with some of the other workers from the hotel. We would go to a bar and there was music. I drank Coca-Cola. Rocio even drank beer. For the very first time I bought clothes, and even a swim suit. Men would talk to us and we would giggle. Sometimes we danced but we were still girls I wasn't even 20. In those days the fascists were everywhere. On Sundays the *Frente de Juventudes* marched around town, boys and girls our age, and younger, dressed like a little army. Franco's little army singing 'We are the future.' They would stare at us like we were animals, like we were dirt. But I didn't care, they were jealous because we had our freedom. One night we even went to the cinema. I sat in amazement the whole time. Less than a year before I listened to Franco's address on a crackly radio and there he was, talking to me on the newsreel on that huge screen.

"Old Vasquez and his wife were good to us. He treated us well, always paid us and he never asked anything of us girls. And when summer season finished he let us stay in our room. It was the oldest and most well known hotel in town and even in winter people came. One afternoon 'El Dominguin' came to the hotel. The others were so excited, and squealed like my little Conchi. The matadors were our royalty and he was so elegant, even more handsome than his posters. We had even seen him on the newsreel at the cinema. We lined up to see him and the girls hid behind their hands and giggled. I stood still and smiled at him. The others were so jealous when he spoke to me." Maria Dolores broke free from the past and looked directly at Father Gabriel and laughed. "He only said 'Buenos diás señoritas,' and smiled at me but it was enough to send them all into giggles. I smiled back and corrected him 'Buenas *tardes* señor Gonzalez' because it was after lunchtime and that made him laugh too."

"It was in the hotel that I first saw Alfredo. I should have learned not to trust another man, but stupid me, I did. It was our second summer and I had seen him quite a bit, drinking with his clients in the bar. He was the deputy mayor for the town and everyone knew him. He had seen me too, I could tell. Always taking time to smile at me, say good evening. I was getting a lot of attention from the boys we knew and the men we saw in the bars but I didn't want another boyfriend. I was still waiting for Juan Diego to turn up."

"But Alfredo, oh, he was different. So charming when he spoke to us. Always a real gentleman. One day he invited us to a party at his house. We were so excited, we bought new dresses and even new shoes. A car took us to this mansion, that had gates, a driveway. Oh, I thought it was a mistake and we were to work there, at the party. But he had servants, who asked us for our coats and bags. I laughed because I didn't even own a real handbag. We were given champagne in those funny looking glasses and taken to a terrace which looked down towards the sea. Rocio squeezed my arm, too afraid to speak. All the women were elegant in summer dresses and high heels. I felt very young, we didn't belong there. But when Alfredo saw us he told us we were beautiful and took our arms and walked with us around that enormous villa. In one room he had a television with two big dials on it, like a radio. His swimming pool was bigger than the dining room at the hotel and we ate food I had never even heard of."

"He introduced us to people who smiled but no one talked with us. No one was interested except Julia, who laughed and told us we should be careful with Alfredo. She wore trousers, trousers that pinched in at her waist, they looked really uncomfortable on her. But she stood out, she looked more out of place than I did. She was incredible. She leant over and blew a perfect smoke ring across my face. Her drink spilled when she slapped Alfredo on the arm but just she shrieked with laughter. I thought maybe she was drunk but he didn't mind. He just grinned and let her talk. Then he joked about her being jealous because she was 30 already. I could tell by the way they looked at each other, there was something there. We didn't stay too long that first night. We both started to feel a bit drunk from the champagne and I said we should go. Rocio wanted to stay, she said she felt like a film star. Alfredo walked us to a car which took us back to our room. As he helped me get into the car he said to me, 'Dolores, anything you need I can help you. Anything at all, just you come and ask me,' and he smiled at me, that beautiful smile and twinkling eyes that had won him so many women. 'Anything at all.'"

"That was it, he had said the magic words. I knew who he was and what people said; the money and the power. A man that got what he wanted. *And* he worked in government. I thought of nothing else, I was obsessed. He was the solution to my problem. Rocio asked me what I was going to do when I found my son. I couldn't answer because I had no plan. No ideas at all. But I knew finding him came first. After that when Alfredo came to the restaurant I made sure I saw him and he saw me. If I heard he was in the bar I would take him a drink. And every time I saw him he would touch my arm and give me that smile of his. He had a way of making you feel special, important. Then at the end of the summer he invited us to another party."

"This time we knew what kind of dress to buy, and shoes and even an evening bag. I didn't care that they were expensive, I had to make an impression. And we did, we certainly did. This time people talked to us. And Julia was there, she took me by the arm and showed me how to eat mussels. Alfredo must have been watching because when we spoke later, he joked about what I could learn from Julia as she was the woman of the house. His housekeeper he said. I didn't know what he meant but oh, how I found out. She was the woman of the house. That whole evening I had only one glass of champagne. I think I already knew, or maybe it was just the girl in me wishing that Alfredo would kiss me. And at the end of the night he did. He invited me to stay the night and I said yes, but we didn't have sex. He could see I was nervous, I hadn't hardly even kissed anyone since, well since Juan Diego, so he said we should wait. We slept together in his huge bed, me lying in his arms. How could I not fall for that man Father?" Maria Dolores looked up at Father Gabriel. She paused then continued without waiting for an answer. Father Gabriel shuffled in his seat, embarrassed at missing his cue.

"A few days later he turned up at the hotel, just to see me and asked me to dinner. I knew the time had come and I had to do it with him, I even wanted to. He was a man who could have any woman he wanted. He was a man, and he wouldn't wait for ever. In the end the sex wasn't as bad as I had expected, I even liked it. Looking back now I see things so differently. But I wanted my son, I wanted that life and I wanted him." Father Gabriel had been immersed in the story, still seeing in his mind's eye the innocent violated girl. The same girl as before but now in the sunshine, by the beach or at a party. Her candidness about sex, about using sex, had made him look at her differently. That girl was replaced by someone strong and resolute who knew what she wanted. It was difficult to reconcile the hunched old woman in front of him with either younger version that he had conjured up. He got the feeling however that her narrative was changing, that Maria Dolores the woman had entered the story.

"Not long after that I moved into an apartment that Alfredo had on the edge of town, it had views of the sea. It had a telephone, although I never had anyone to call. A radiogram that looked like a cabinet until you opened it. It played vinyl records. We had mostly Spanish records but also a few American ones a Major from the army base gave him as a present, well, a bribe really. It was music I didn't know and wasn't really interested in but I had fun playing them. These things helped me forget my old life, they took me a million miles from the mountains. I wanted to show Conchi everything, she would have been even more amazed than me. Rocio came round sometimes but she also had to work. I saw less and less of her. I missed her but she had a boyfriend, a handsome man called Marc from Barcelona. She had her own life to lead."

"Alfredo paid for everything and brought me gifts, gave me money. At first we spent every night together, he would be so charming and fun. We ate in restaurants. Everyone knew him and treated us like royalty. Then there were the parties, like the ones at the villa but just for a few selected people in the apartment, normally after he had done one of his business deals. It didn't take me long to figure out what he was doing, he didn't even try to hide it from me. Business men gave him millions of pesetas for land, land that wasn't his. He made sure the building permits were approved by the council and a new hotel was built. They gave him money for roads, for contracts, for the new marina. They gave him money for everything. He was everyone's best friend. I saw bags full of pesetas, suitcases full of money. I saw so much money that after a while I hardly noticed it. And I waited and I waited. He promised me if my son was in Marbella he would find him."

"Looking back now I know he was a man that I never really loved but I liked him and I felt comfortable with him. I trusted him to be himself. I thought he was good to me because he didn't hit me and he never forced himself on me. That was how we judged men not because of the good things they did for us but because of the bad things that they didn't do. It wasn't long until I realised he was good to everyone until he had no more use for them."

Chapter Twenty-Four

Ibiza 2016

Paco's displacement from his bedroom had become tedious. The sofa was no substitute for his bed. His young body woke most mornings with complaints, aches and pains befitting a much older person. He was tired and irritable. Bernarda noticed this but had little control over the situation. Sebas had mentioned that he had rented an apartment but it wasn't quite ready to move into. A concocted story that she didn't fully believe. It was Ibiza in the summertime, affordable apartments were impossible to come by. Owners easily rented to tourists for double the going rate. It was an annual occurrence, part of the seasonal culture. No, it was clear Sebas was quite comfortable at home and truth be told she was happy to have him there. But that didn't stop her worrying about Paco and his increasing frustrations.

One afternoon Paco found the car Sebas had acquired half parked on the pavement again, abandoned on the narrow street with little consideration for others. A man he didn't recognise was sitting on the hood of the car wearing fake aviator sunglasses. He was clearly also gitano; his closely cropped and contoured stubble, cinnamon skin and hand inked tattoos that disappeared up his arms were worn like gang markings. Indiscreet insignia warning danger lies here. A pristine Tupac t-shirt didn't reflect as much his musical taste as the misplaced kudos he thought it gave him. He flicked his cigarette stub at Paco as he passed. Paco sucked his teeth in return. There was recognition that they were of the same tribe. This wouldn't escalate, not yet at any rate, just emerging beta males maintaining their ground.

"Heyyyy, there's my lil' brother. Where you been?" Paco wasn't fooled by Sebas' cordiality. He threw his backpack on the floor without replying and trudged on to the kitchen, where his mother was preparing a sandwich.

"You should just answer your brother," Bernarda whispered, not lifting her head from the task at hand.

"School's finished so I went to the library." Paco shouted back at him. "It's where you go to learn stuff."

"Paco!" His mother scolded, her voice controlled but stern. He sighed, grimacing with his back to them as he opened the fridge door. The flickering light inside revealed the only drink available was half a carton of full fat UHT milk. He slammed the door closed again but before he could say anything Bernarda, sensing his frustration interjected.

"I'll go to the supermarket later, after lunch. I said I'd get a few things for Dolores." She ruffled his hair causing him to recoil. He hated it when she patronised him and was further angered when he saw her hand the sandwich to his brother who took it from her without thanks or acknowledging her efforts.

"Don't know why you bother with that old whore." Sebas interjected as he dropped into his father's armchair and picked up his can of cola. It left a glistening wet circle on the tiled floor.

"No need to talk like that Sebas."

"The old crow is just sponging off you. You don't owe her nothin'." Paco snorted both at the irony and knowing that Sebas wouldn't get it. It was true, he would never consider that he was taking more than giving. What he did know was that Paco's riposte had been directed at him.

He scoffed the sandwich without taking much time to breathe between bites. A drop of mayonnaise landed on his trousers. He pressed his thumb on it, rubbing forcefully until it disappeared, all the time glaring at Paco. Bernarda sat on the sofa, in her usual place, sensing the hostility in the room. The only noise in the stifling air was Sebas' graceless chewing.

"Don't worry about dinner tonight." Sebas mumbled through his food, then swallowed. "I'll be working late," he added, slurping from the can of cola. Bernarda forced a smile, she wouldn't ask about his work, there was no need to invite lies into the house. It was not her way, she would take any money when offered, no questions asked.

"What's up with you?" Sebas turned his attention back towards Paco. "You still crying about that dog of yours. I told you I'll get you another one." Sebas stood up leaving the remnants of the sandwich on the chair's arm.

"I don't want another dog."

"Well stop sulking about it you little faggot." His voice carried an edginess, a weapon in its own right, but Paco didn't react.

"Sebastian, please." Bernarda's words bounced off him. Taking a step towards Paco he addressed his mother.

"I'm sick of seeing his face like this." He reached into his pocket and pulled out two scrunched up twenty euro notes and handed them to her.

"What would you know about it?" Paco retaliated. The heat of the day had infiltrated the room. The back of Sebas' shirt clung to him, sweat beading on his temples.

"Paco, don't fucking push it." Sebas' stare matched his words, daring another response. Bernarda interjected herself and brushed a few crumbs from Sebas' shirt. The gesture diverted his attention, he looked down, flicking her hands away.

"Go. Your friend is waiting." But Bernarda's soothing words did little to ease the tension. Sebas glared at Paco then turned again to his mother.

"Gracias Mama." Then without another word walked out the door without closing it behind him. Paco stared after him, a fiery confrontational glare that would wilt many a grown man's resolve. The breeze from the open door brushed his face as he heard Sebas outside greet his waiting companion.

Bernarda did as she had promised and went to the mini-market. She lay the few shopping bags on the floor beside the table where Paco was playing with his phone.

"Where are the twins?" She asked. "It's too quiet in here."

"Papi took them fishing again." Paco mumbled to the table. Bernarda raised an eyebrow. It was unlikely there would be fish for dinner but there would be at least some contented boys in the house, husband included.

"Paco, when you finish can you take a few things to Dolores next door please?" Paco nodded.

"I'm done already," he added. Bernarda smiled, pleased with her son's decency.

Paco hadn't been inside Maria Dolores' house, no one had. He called her name as he climbed the concealed stairs. She was sitting on a plastic chair watching him as he reached the little porch without feeling the need to acknowledge him verbally.

"Mami sent me over with a few things," he offered the bag, stating the obvious. The little dog growled as he approached.

"Shhh Baby," she hushed. "He's the good one." Paco laid down the shopping bag and turned to leave.

"I hear everything you know. I'm old but my ears work perfectly." She raised a fragile arm towards the Moreno house. Paco followed her hand and saw, that only a few metres separated the dwellings. She had explained this before but seeing it from her perspective clarified it. Furthermore, the old lady never made any noise so her presence went unnoticed.

"I suppose."

"Yes, I do. I hear a lot." Maria Dolores smiled at Paco, it was a warm smile that she didn't often share. "Your bother thinks he's the man of the house. He's the same man now as he was when he left. A few years older but none the wiser." Without being invited Paco sat down on the top step. At that level he noticed the old neighbour's shoes were in tatters, one heel had almost separated from the sole and in the other the toe was so frayed that a fleshy bunion was beginning to poke through. Baby crept a few cautious steps towards him but then decided against it, turning and taking refuge behind her mistress's chair.

"Even when he was little he was a handful. Aways fighting. Showing no respect to your mother, I don't know how she put up with it. Pffft, and then your father, well, he didn't help much." She took a breath and relaxed back into her chair leaving her thoughts on Sebastian unspoken.

"You lived here that long then?" Paco's eyes were opening to the fact she was more than just the crazy who lived next door.

"Oooooh, Paco," she giggled. "Except for that windmill, which even worked when I came here, I'm older than the rest of the houses on the street. I watched them being built around me." She leant forward and stared at Paco a moment. "When I came here there wasn't anything on that side there. I had views down to the sea. Right down to the sea." She repeated with a wave of her hand. Paco turned and tried to imagine the place she described, this same street in another incarnation. "It was so beautiful then. Before they ruined it." Paco studied the old lady's face. Hidden amongst the deep-set creases he saw those blue-green eyes full of life.

"You're a good boy Paco. Don't let that brother of yours bully you. That one will end up in jail, or worse. I've known men like him before." Her smile disappeared and her eyes darkened again. "You won't remember the night the police came to arrest him. He jumped the fence, right there, and he hid in my house. Didn't ask me. Told me to shut up or else. He thought he was so brave but you could see the fear in him. Anyway what was I going to do? I've been an old woman for a while now." Paco sat upright at the news.

"Is that true?"

"Oh yes. Ask your mother. Well, when it was safe for him to leave he told me at least I was useful for something. No thanks for hiding him. He looked at me like I was dirt. Still does." Maria Dolores sneered as she recounted the incident. Paco felt at first embarrassed then again angry with his brother.

"Was that when he left?"

"No Paco. No, that was another time, a few years before." They sat in silence a long minute. "He was right about one thing though. I was a prostitute. I can't call him a liar for saying that." Paco felt his cheeks blush. He didn't know how to respond. Sensing his unease she added. "That was a long time ago now though. I'm almost a hundred you know."

"Are you?"

"Ha, ha. No, not quite. Cheeky bugger." And she allowed herself a subdued little giggle. Paco smiled back at her. There was an unexpected ease between them and they both sensed it.

"But you were alive when Franco was dictator?"

"Yes, of course. That was an evil man. Did no good for anyone except himself and his kind."

"What was it like?"

"It was better towards the end but to begin with it was terrible. Everyone lived in fear, folk just disappeared. No one trusted anyone. People were shot in the street. And when I lived in Marbella there were fascists everywhere. They were proud to show they were monsters." She looked directly at Paco. "It was good for your lot when he died."

"What do you mean?"

"Your people, the gitanos, Franco never cared about them either. They had it hard, some were sent to the camps or lived in slums. Now they are just like anyone else, well, that's what they say." Paco didn't quite understand what she meant by this. After a pause Maria Dolores changed the subject.

"I know how much you loved your dog. She went everywhere with you. She was a big dog, she scared my Baby, but you had good control of her. I think Sebas was jealous that she took to you and not him. Dogs have extra senses you know." Maria Dolores awkwardly reached down and hoisted a squirming Baby onto her lap.

"When she came he said we could only keep her a while, until she was an adult. That she wasn't really ours." As he talked, Paco watched Baby turn and settle into Maria Dolores' lap.

"Hmm, I remember," she murmured.

"But then Sebas left and Tyson stayed." Paco paused. "I wish it was still like that, with him not here." He began to feel free to talk about Tyson. Free from Sebas' oppression. Free to unburden himself.

"A boy's dog is his best friend," Maria Dolores interrupted, reading his mind. "You'll never forget her Paco but you'll see there are more important things in life. You won't go down the same path as Sebas. Don't worry, you won't end up like him. I'm sure your mother would say the same thing if she could. She's no fool."

They sat again in silence for a minute, Maria Dolores peering into the shopping bag, Paco reflecting on what she had said. What he had said. He had never had such a conversation with her before, nor with anyone, and started to see why his mother wanted to help her.

"You want me to take it inside for you?" He offered, noticing her interest in the bag.

"No," she smiled. "You've done enough." They both turned to face the road as they heard a scooter approach and slide to a stop. Paco shuffled himself to see through a gap in the foliage. Maria Dolores grunted her disgust beside him. Her face now stony, lips curled. It was the neighbour, Jimmy.

"He's another bad one," she spat, speaking as much to herself as to Paco. "I was here watching when he ran over your dog." Her voice became harsh. They watched together both hating the man they saw. Jimmy dismounted the scooter and pulled out his phone and started tapping the screen, oblivious he was being watched. Oblivious to the antagonism aimed at him from across the street.

Chapter Twenty-Five

Marbella 1951

Three flags cracked and snapped in the relentless buffeting winds above the Town Hall in the heart of Old Marbella. The yellow and red Spanish flag complete with black eagle, the Spanish Falange banner with its characteristic black vertical band and the green striped standard of Andalusia. There was no doubt that this was Francoist heartland and there was no doubt that even in this modernising landscape the decrees of one political party were The Law. A very visible military presence ensured that was never forgotten.

Maria Dolores, strode with a confidence that bordered on arrogance along the Parque de la Represa. When she reached the old castle walls, she turned towards the local government buildings. She had never really got used to living in the city and passed through these green spaces whenever she could. The foliage, although different from her mountain roots, soothed her. It took her back to that other place more than she realised. The park at this hour of the morning wasn't exactly tranquil. Colourful parakeets and bee-eaters chattered and bickered as they jousted for shade in the palms that bordered the walkways.

* * *

The leather satchel that she clutched to her side was uncomfortable and clammy against her skin. The shiny metal clasp that only just held it closed dug into her but she didn't dare loosen her grip. Her cotton beige pencil skirt shortened her stride. It was an inappropriate choice for such a hot day but Alfredo insisted she dress suitably. Every now and then perspiration trickled down her back cementing her discomfort. She climbed the few steps under the noisy flags, the clacking of Italian high heels announced her arrival. The bespectacled and inept Mariano, the armed guard whose responsibility it was to ensure that nothing unpropitious occurred on government property, looked up from his newspaper. She nodded curtly, he smiled back scratching his greying beard, knowing he too would receive an envelope. A small recompense for his silence and the canny ability to know when to look the other way.

Despite feeling uncomfortable in the heat and humidity she cut an elegant figure as she passed from office to office distributing envelopes. Each payment marked with a numerical code, no name or initial. She quickly got used to handling such large amounts of money. The novelty of it had well and truly worn off. Before she left her village she had seldom seen a large banknote. Now she helped Alfredo fill envelopes from carpetbags of cash that he kept in the apartment. Afternoons counting out pesetas whilst he marked amounts and codes in a ledger. Money that her family had never had, lost it's meaning. If she wanted something she bought it. Alfredo didn't care if she used money but she had never thought of keeping any for her self. Why would she? It was always there, always available.

That afternoon she took a taxi to Alfredo's villa. Julia was standing by the sitting room window, looking down over the town. She didn't at first acknowledge Maria Dolores, seemingly entranced by view below. The sunlight bounced off her beige trouser suit giving her a warm aura. As usual Maria Dolores felt inferior in her presence, despite her own expensive attire she knew she was no match for Julia's natural elegance.

"Ah Dolores, how was your morning?" Julia was the only one to call her Dolores.

"The same as usual. I handed out the envelopes, they took them." Julia twisted the smouldering cigarette butt out of its long black holder and dropped it into an ashtray. Maria Dolores watched the last of the smoke escape into the midday heat.

"So what's your plan for the rest of the day? Going to the cinema again."

"I guess, there's not much else to do." Maria Dolores secretly cherished her solitary time when Alfredo left town. She had become fascinated by the cinema and the heroines she saw there; Sara Montiel, Sofia Loren and Lana Turner. Icons of the big screen beguiled her, beautiful determined women living the dream. There was nothing they couldn't achieve.

"Would you like a sherry?"

"Julia it's only 11."

"Is that a no then?" Julia strode over to a cabinet and poured herself a glass. "Actually it's 12.15, when else would you have an aperitif?" She held the bottle out to Maria Dolores who shook her head. "Just something to stimulate the appetite." Julia smirked to herself.

"No thanks." Maria Dolores watched as Julia paced the room.

"You enjoy it when he's out of town, don't you Dolores?"

"You know what he's like when he's working on some

deal. He stresses a lot."

"Yes, he can become just a little unbearable." Julia rolled her eyes and picked up the little clutch bag she had been looking for.

"He works hard for himself but when it comes to helping others he…" Julia prevented her from finishing her sentence.

"Oh, not on about your boy again."

"Well he hasn't done very much to find him. The big man with all his contacts. I'm beginning to think his heart isn't in it."

"No, his heart isn't in it. His heart is in making money and that's why we, you and me, live the way we do." Maria Dolores dropped her head. Julia continued. "Look, I'm sure he tried, he told me as much. The Church's doors are firmly closed, even to Alfredo. I knew a couple that adopted one of those babies. There's not a lot that can be done to trace them. *They* don't even know where their little girl came from." Julia reached out and stroked Maria Dolores' forearm before turning away.

"Adopted? My baby wasn't adopted he was stolen, it's kidnapping."

"Oh, don't be so melodramatic. You watch too many of those movies."

"He'll be four years old Julia and I don't even know his name. Or what he looks like. One day I'll probably just forget about him." She turned away deflated and thought of those screen idols. They would have found their son by now.

"Come and sit here." Julia patted the space beside her on the chaise longue. "This is a depressingly masculine world we live in Dolores. Men like Alfredo love us but mostly when it suits them. The gifts, the apartment, the money. You've been here long enough to know that. Stop being naive. We have to make the most of it. Do what we need to, to survive. Survival, Dolores is the most important thing we can do for ourselves and if your son *is* out there waiting to be found, *you* have to survive. Put on a face and smile when you have to." Julia lifted her hand to Maria Dolores' cheek. "Above all smile when you have to," she repeated. They sat in silence a minute, the older woman searching the younger's face but Maria Dolores continued to stare at the floor. Julia sighed and turned her attention to the clutch bag which sat between them. A moment later she pulled out an ornate silver pillbox. A detailed wasp engraving covered most of the lid. "You have to look after yourself. You're still young and beautiful, but the day will come Dolores." Julia took a white pill from the ornate box and placed it at the back of her tongue, then swallowed it with another large sip of sherry. "What? It's just a little something, you know, to suppress my appetite." Again she smirked to herself.

"What is that?"

"An amphetamine, everyone is doing it. Don't look at me like that."

"It's drugs isn't it?"

"A pharmaceutical Dolores, nothing else. My doctor prescribes them." With that she dropped the box back into the clutch bag and snapped it closed. "If you think our precious Alfredo doesn't do this sort of thing, then think again."

"What do you mean?"

"Well amphetamines of course, to keep him going. All those hours he works. And cocaine, Alfredo loves a bit of cocaine. I can't see the fascination with it myself but if it keeps him happy."

"Cocaine? I don't even know what it is." Julia laughed at this reply.

"Oh Dolores really! At heart you're still that innocent little mountain girl aren't you?" She rose and walked over to the drinks cabinet feeling the younger woman's eyes track her.

"Stop saying that, I'm not that innocent girl anymore."

"Well sometimes you act like it. Waken up to what's around you." The clinking of the sherry bottle against glass punctuated the air as Maria Dolores thought on Julia's words. "He's back tomorrow you know. He wants you to meet him. They're having lunch at Casa Manolito."

"What for?"

"You know what for. They'll have had a few drinks and if this deal for the new marina isn't going well you'll need to bat those pretty eyes of yours, show a bit of leg or cleavage and help things along." Maria Dolores shrugged. She knew very well what was expected of her.

"You make me sound like a common prostitute."

"Well aren't we?"

"Julia!"

"That naivety again, Dolores. We're both in the same boat. You're just 15 years younger then me, well 20 really but don't tell Alfredo. We have to use our femininity, this is the only power we have over men like him. Are you not listening to me? It's our greatest strength." Julia slipped another cigarette into the holder. "If you need something to wear take a dress from my wardrobe. Trousers don't suit you. You have a more er, traditional body." Maria Dolores knew she was being dismissed.

"Maybe I'll go have a look." Julia lit the cigarette and watched as Maria Dolores trudged out of the room, relieved that Alfredo hadn't asked for her.

Maria Dolores heard the ruckus from outside Casa Manolito and steeled herself as she entered. There was only one occupied table in the dimly lit room. The subdued light from the art deco lamps gave the room an intimate almost romantic feel. It was not wholly suited to the party of men gathered there. Alfredo was seated with his back to her, the three other men whose clamouring voices vied for attention didn't even notice her arrival. A shroud of smoke hung around them but hid nothing. Two ashtrays were overflowing, one smouldered with a half-smoked cigar. A vast array of glasses in varying states of emptiness cramped the rest of the table. The middle-aged waitress that sat forlornly by the bar had tired of her customers and service was down to a minimum. She inhaled deeply on her cigarette sighing as she exhaled, then came to greet Maria Dolores. Her pinafore was a snug around her chest, it's crispness had been replaced by the tiredness of the day's toil, but remarkably hadn't been soiled.

"I'm sorry señora, the restaurant has been closed for the evening. The owner has taken leave of his senses and is onto his second bottle of brandy." She gestured towards the noisy table, making no attempt to conceal her disdain.

"It's OK, I'm a friend of Señor Montes." The pout fell from the waitress's face at hearing of Maria Dolores' acquaintance with the restaurant's best customer. She rolled her eyes.

"Of course you are. Well I hope you're taking him home. They've had quite enough for one day."

Maria Dolores smiled back. "I'll try my best." As she approached the table she placed a hand on Alfredo's shoulder and leant in towards him, allowing him to kiss her on the cheek, her cleavage catching the attention of the other men.

"Maria Dolores, you've arrived at last." His voice loud in the empty room. As the other men stood up to welcome her, one knocked his chair over, then grabbed at the table to regain his balance. The others cackled. The waitress scowled at the man but made no attempt to pick up the chair.

"Please, please sit down with us. Would you like some French champagne?" The man who Maria Dolores presumed to be the owner, dragged over a chair and slid it into the space between him and Alfredo.

"Thank you, that's very kind." Maria Dolores grinned, and raised an eyebrow at the beleaguered waitress. She acknowledged each of the men in turn, holding their eye, lingering there just a moment too long, making sure her sexuality wasn't lost to them. She perched half on her chair, ankles crossed underneath her, a posture that straightened her back and pronounced her breasts. A pose she had perfected after seeing Ava Gardner play Kitty Collins in The Killers. Alfredo was delighted she was playing her part.

Señor Luis Closas, made a great deal of coming round the table to kiss her hand. A nondescript man of medium height, he wore a white shirt that he had outgrown. The only outstanding feature was a lopsided mouth, which when he smiled, seemed to pull down the left side of his face. There was something else that unnerved Maria Dolores that she couldn't quite pinpoint. An unnatural gait gave him a graceless, damaged quality. Again she smiled back at him, holding back her revulsion as he closed in on her. His breath reeked of heady brandy whilst the sickly smell of body odour was strong enough to permeate the cigar smoke that clung to him. Closas, an Argentinian, had an importation business. Marbella, he proclaimed, had the potential to become the largest port in the Mediterranean. Maria Dolores could see the attraction in that for Alfredo. The youngest and drunkest of the group just nodded and beamed a witless grin and made no further attempt to engage with her.

The restaurant owner brought her a bottle of Juvé & Camps Gran Reserva, which he struggled to open. White cava froth effervesced from the bottle and splashed over the table. Maria Dolores tittered politely, inwardly cursing his ineptitude. She sipped the cava whilst listening to the owner prattle on about his plans for expansion: another, larger restaurant and a classy chiringuito on the beach front. Americans, he declared, were coming and they liked to spend their money. He grappled at Alfredo's arm for attention, practically begging his collaboration. Alfredo nodded noncommittally, this paltry negotiation would have to wait for another day.

The drinks lasted almost an hour longer. Even in his escalating drunkenness Alfredo picked up on Maria Dolores' impatience and announced that it was time to call it a day. There was a moment of relative sobriety and calm as the group said their farewells. The restaurant owner guided the younger drunken man to the door. Closas walked with her and Alfredo.

"Luis, why don't you come back for a night cap. My place is only a few blocks from here."

"Fantastic idea," retorted Closas, "Perhaps we can put an end to the business talk now that we're in more refined company." His eyes alighted on Maria Dolores. She smiled but something in his expression suggested she was the main focus of his interest. Despite the evening warmth she asked Alfredo to cover her with her shawl as they walked off.

In the apartment Alfredo offered Luis a drink. "You'll have a Scotch won't you? On the rocks as it should be or American with soda?"

"Straight up for me Alfredo." Closas threw his jacket onto the dining table and took the drink from Alfredo with a grunt of acknowledgement. His eyes glued to Maria Dolores who was fixing her own drink.

"Now my friend, just how are we going to make Marbella the biggest port in the Med, eh?" Alfredo dropped into an leather armchair by a glass coffee table, its gaudy chrome legs clashed with the rest of the room's soft wooded interior.

"Really Alfredo, are we still talking business? I'm sure the señorita is sick of this tedious chat." Maria Dolores glanced over to the men. Luis took a big gulp of the Chivas Regal and dropped the tumbler onto the table, the amber liquid jumped in the glass but didn't spill. From his pocket he pulled out a little purple leather pouch and without a word threw it onto the glass table next to Alfredo.

"Ahh, OK Luis. Perhaps we can leave negotiations until later." The men were suddenly on the same wavelength. Maria Dolores took her Martini and sat at the end of a long leather sofa next to Alfredo's armchair. She crossed her legs and pulled down her dress so it touched her knees.

"After you Alfredo." Luis lumbered across the sofa to sit closer to Maria Dolores, his weight pulled her towards him. Instinctively she grabbed the arm of the sofa, but remained focussed on Alfredo and the purple bag. She watched as he pulled out a tiny metal spoon. He then loaded it with the white powder and inserted it into a nostril. He inhaled deeply and the cocaine disappeared. He threw himself back into the armchair with a self-satisfied, if somewhat exaggerated, 'ahhhh'. It was the first time Maria Dolores had actually seen cocaine, for the brief moment it was visible. She was brought back to the present when Luis reached across her and lifted the pouch and spoon and offered it to her. She laughed at him dismissively, another instinctive response but his eyes were serious, bordering on intimidating.

"No," she replied to the unasked question. She looked towards Alfredo for support but he had his eyes closed, a stupid grin on his face.

"It's only a bit of cocaine Dolores, you should try it." Luis pushed the pouch into her hand but she withdrew away from him.

"No thank you, Señor Closas." Her voice trembled, as she reverted back to his surname hoping the formality would provide distance. He sensed her distrust and laughed at her, and again his face melted to the left.

"Dolores, please, Luis, call me Luis," he crooned in his Argentinian accent, tapping her forearm. Then he turned his attention to the pouch, dipped the spoon in and helped himself in the same manner as Alfredo had, inserting the little instrument into his nostril.

Maria Dolores stood and retreated towards the kitchen area pretending to busy herself. She felt dizzy from the alcohol and suddenly quite threatened. She noticed that Alfredo had sat forward in the chair and was staring intently at Luis who's lilted voice was extolling the beauty of Spanish women. A moment then passed between the two men, the silence alerted Maria Dolores. They were staring at each other, smiling inanely, enjoying some connection. A corroboration perhaps that they were more than just businessmen and shared other pleasures. Luis turned to face Maria Dolores. She had seen that look before, she felt it before she had time to process it. Luis' intentions struck her like a blow to the abdomen. A dread filled her that she hadn't felt in a long time, provoking memories of distant places, forgotten men. But Alfredo was there, he would protect her. She folded the small towel she had been toying with and returned to the salon. This time she perched on the arm of Alfredo's armchair and placed her hand lightly on the back of his head.

"Dolores, are you sure you don't want to join us? It's only a little pick-me-up." Luis' penetrating eyes had followed her to where she sat.

"I don't think so Señor Closas. To be honest I feel a little drunk. I should have a lie down." She leant a little closer into Alfredo who didn't react.

"Oh, don't leave the party just yet." Luis grabbed his glass and drained the remnants and as before with an cloddish hand banged the glass back onto the table. His ungainly movements gave him added an ugliness.

"Let her go rest if she wants to Luis, we can talk," Alfredo interjected. He patted her thigh but his eyes remained closed. Maria Dolores took the opportunity to exit.

"It's better I go. I'm sure you two have a lot to discuss." She rose pulling her dress down again. Luis bowed his head in farewell, at last conceding defeat and reached again for the little purple pouch.

She was glad to reach the security of her bedroom. The sharpness of the cold door seeped through her dress as she backed into it. She stood there a few moments trying to relax, trying to liberate herself from the anxiety Luis had triggered. The men's voices lifted and fell with snorts of laughter or a giggle as they entertained each other. Moments later as the tension began to ebb away she sneaked across the hallway to the bathroom. From there the conversation became clearer and she was the subject of it. She smiled as she heard Alfredo talk about how they first met and how happy he had been to meet her but alarmed as he told Luis the sex had been fantastic. She stepped into the bathroom leaving the door ajar.

"You can have her if you like." Alfredo's voice was matter of fact, void of expression.

"Alfredo!" Luis exclaimed. "YOU are drunk and too bloody high already. You don't know what you're saying."

"I'm serious. Have sex with her if you want to." This was no flippant remark, there was no jest in his tone. Maria Dolores froze. The door handle rattled it's displeasure as the panic flowed through her hand, the intensity of the grip whitening her knuckles. Both men glanced towards the bedroom but quickly faced each other again, satisfied there had been no movement.

"No more cocaine for you." Luis laughed. "Ha, or maybe I *should* give you more." His voice trailed off and Maria

Dolores lost what was being said in the whispers. Rooted to the spot, she dared not move, unsure that her legs would carry her. What was happening? Was Alfredo serious? Had he lost his mind? Anger and fear rose in her in equal measures, she wasn't sure which to embrace or which would embrace her. Luis laughed again, she imagined them huddling, heads together, plotting just as José Blanco and Miguel Guerrero had. It had been a while since she had thought of those monsters. The putrid staleness of that van overwhelmed her once more. Then silence. In the dim light of the bathroom she glanced frantically around not knowing exactly what she sought. The window was small, there was no way she could fit through it. There was no escape there and she remained pressed against the door. The thought of arming herself with something burst into her head but nothing presented itself as a weapon. Her heavy breathing echoed round the airless room. No sounds from outside. A light prickling flushed across her skin as the hairs stood on end, alert. 'Lola. Lola. Calm down,' she whispered to herself. As she started to concentrate on her breathing she began to feel foolish then angry with herself that she had reacted in such a manner. But she certainly hadn't imagined it, Alfredo had offered her like a piece of meat. She took another deep breath and closed her eyes. The loud bang jolted the door in it's frame and made Maria Dolores start. She inhaled sharply, adrenaline suddenly exploding through her, focussing her fear.

"Dolores is everything all right?" It was Luis' voice, softer though, almost compassionate.

"Yes, thank you. Umm, I'll be out in a minute." The hesitation ir. her voice almost palpable. She saw the handle turn, silently moving and became overwhelmed by the urge to flee. She wanted to lose herself in the little bathroom, not wanting to be cornered like an animal again. The only escape was forward. She grabbed the door and violently pulled it towards her, revealing Luis' astonished face.

"Dolores," he started but she was already pushing past him. He made for her arm.

"I just need some air," she interrupted again. Once passed him she stopped and faced him, she felt petrified but the fear gave her fortitude. Her eyes boring into his.

"Is everything alright?"

"I'm going out." She replied. He began to lift his hand again but she batted it away. "I'm going outside," she repeated defiantly.

"Would you, would you like me to accompany you?" Luis, a little stunned, leant back a little.

"No," she blurted before he could ask her anything else, her eyes still fixed on his. Maria Dolores sensed a modicum of control come back to her and she felt herself swell, filling the space between them. The danger seemed to be averted, his softening expression spurred her on. "I just need a little air." She repeated and turned towards the door. She grabbed an overcoat and left the apartment. Later she would wonder if it was all in her imagination. Luis had tried to touch her arm, no more than that. Perhaps a genuine gesture of comfort and nothing else, but perhaps not, after all he was a man. Alfredo's actions on the other hand had distressed her more than she could have imagined. She had foolishly allowed herself to believe that Alfredo had in some way, in his own way, loved her but it was obvious that he valued her more as a possession, a pawn to be used to obtain what he really coveted. His intentions were now confirmed. She wouldn't be able to stay there much longer.

Chapter Twenty-Six

Ibiza 2016.

Jimmy was suffering from the night before. The fluorescent corridor lights a lot brighter than normal as he drifted towards the nurses' office. Those same passageways were also more congested, the spaces smaller, as patients and colleagues alike seemed to gravitate towards him. The voices and the general hubbub of the A&E bombarded him with little sensitivity for his physical and mental state. He sidestepped an approaching hospital trolley, the porter pushing it smiled at him. Jimmy didn't reciprocate but decided he needed a moment alone so he slipped into to a nearby storage cupboard. Work could wait. He sat down on a box of intravenous solutions and took a deep breath, hoping that would somehow revive him. A few seconds later the motion sensor light turned itself off.

He had been trying to avoid Santi ever since their visit to la Fragata. He didn't want to relive that night, and knew Santi would insist upon it. He didn't need to be reminded that they had had sex with a prostitute. Together. Santi would think it hilarious. What the hell had he been doing? At first he blamed it on the drugs. It was true they had over-indulged.

Alone in his apartment the night before he mulled it over sipping whisky. Sipping whisky to take the edge off the memories. It hadn't worked, he had slipped into drunkenness with only self reproach for company. He couldn't really remember if he enjoyed the sex. He hadn't even given that woman a thought in all the time they were with her, doing things to her. He remembered the drugs and the alcohol and the hangover. He remembered her, the look on her face. "Fuck's sake," he muttered, disgusted with himself. Over a fortnight had passed and he was still admonishing himself. He took another deep breath and sighed. Santi's laughing voice screeched around in his head.

But then they had bragged about it, laughed about it with Sebas and he felt powerless not to join in. He wanted to be accepted. He was as bad as they were, no, worse because he knew better. Perhaps the guilt was being amplified because he knew he couldn't avoid his partner-in-crime any longer. "Bloody Santi." He sat on the uncomfortable cardboard box, head in hand and tried to ignore the racket going on outside. He felt the tension mount as a tightness developed between his shoulder blades, soon that pain would spread up to his neck.

A few moments later the door opened and the light flickered back on. Another nurse, Cati, entered the store but if she was surprised to see him sitting in the dark, she didn't show it.

"OK Jimmy?" Her rhetorical question was nevertheless answered with an unintelligible mumble. She didn't ask him to clarify. "The police have brought a woman in from the airport. Can you deal with it? She's English." She picked up a box of bandages and left him sitting there without waiting for a response.

"Don't I always?" He answered the closing door. It was

mid-summer, tourist season in full-flow, what did he expect? It was his unofficial role, an undesirable obligation to fellow countrymen. His colleagues thought that being from the same country automatically engendered some sort of brotherhood, friendship even. It couldn't be further from the truth. He despised it.

A few minutes later Jimmy pushed open the door to the 'soft' room. A furniture-less, window-less space with a rubber floor and walls, where unmanageable patients would be brought to await psychiatric assessment. The only feature was a bed bolted to the floor with a variety of straps and restraints to contain even the most physically aggressive person. Patients paradoxically tended to become less collaborative, more volatile once they had been incarcerated in this cell. Where the walls met the floor had been rounded off, even the dust here had nowhere to hide.

"Hello," Jimmy said to the handcuffed woman perched on the edge of the bed. He simultaneously greeted the uniformed policeman standing in the doorway with a nod and a smile. "Are you all right?" The woman didn't answer, she kept her head bowed but looked up through her fringe at the policeman standing beside Jimmy. "I'm one of the nurses here." A pause. "Do you understand what I'm saying?" Another pause then the woman nodded. Her dark lank hair which covered most of her face, swung a little, a half-beat behind the movement of her head. Jimmy turned to the policeman, who he recognised, and signalled that he step out into the corridor with him.

"Hi," he smiled at the policeman. "Why is she in cuffs?"

"She's cuffed because she was being a dick and causing a disturbance on a plane. We were waiting to arrest her when they landed. She resisted, totally fucking lost it and bit my partner. He's being stitched up in here somewhere."

"What?" Jimmy thought he'd seen it all but even he found this a little incredulous.

"Yeah, like I said. She bit a hole in Rodrigo's arm. She's a fucking animal." The policeman directed his speech to the closed door. There was no mistaking his vitriol, nor the defence of his partner. Jimmy wondered exactly what it was she had been resisting.

"Why is she here then?"

"She's bleeding from her mouth. She lost a tooth when she bit him. We can't take her in if she's bleeding like that." Jimmy rolled his eyes, not sure what to believe and entered the room again.

"What is your name?" The young woman stared at the closed door. No answer. "He's outside now. He can't hear you. I don't even think he can speak English." The woman looked at Jimmy sceptically, then glanced over his shoulder again to confirm they were alone. She pulled her cuffed hand along the bed rail and slid it under her slender thigh, an action that made her look even more fragile, childlike. Her size and vulnerability reminded him of the woman they had met at La Fragata.

"He said he was going to rape me." This time she looked Jimmy straight in the eye, a glare that bored into him. Her voice was coarse, as if she had been shouting. Her eyes were heavy, the mascara had followed the tears down her face. Her jeans had a few blood spots on them, as did her sky blue blouse which was missing buttons and was ripped at the collar and sleeve.

"I don't think so. You must have misunderstood what he said." Another pause. "Come on, tell me your name." Jimmy crouched to her side bringing his head closer to her level, mindfully keeping out of her leg's reach.

"Monique." Clearly she wasn't English, her accent sounded German, or maybe Scandinavian. He sighed heavily, frustrated at being duped by his colleague. Monique thought it was directed at her.

"He did. He told me when we get to the police station he's going to rape me," she hissed at him. She stood but was restrained before she could stand upright, the metal cuffs pulling back on her wrists. As she spoke Jimmy saw that she was indeed missing a front tooth. The tooth's neighbours still bore witness to its violent recent removal; dark dried blood stuck to the white enamel. He recoiled at her sudden movement.

"Calm down Monique. No one's going to hurt you here. You're in the hospital. Do you know that?" Jimmy fought the urge to place a hand on her knee. A simple human, humane gesture to let her know kindness had not deserted her.

Monique sobbed. "I am not lying. He said it to me in English. I know what he said." She sat down again just as quickly perhaps aware that the policeman was just the other side of the door. "You can't let me leave here with them. Please. Pleeeease," she pushed her face forward towards Jimmy again as she emphasised the last words, her eyes bulging wildly. Jimmy took a moment to study her. She seemed coherent but easily distracted. Her facial expression desperate, borderline manic. She was volatile and prone to outbursts. An element of fantasy, the potential rape. She was missing a tooth and there had been a disturbance on the plane, otherwise the police wouldn't have been called. Maybe she was on the cusp of some psychotic episode or maybe she was just a scared drunk woman who believed she was actually going to be abused. Jimmy wasn't sure what to believe.

"Have you ever been in hospital before?" A vigorous shake of the head. "Monique what have you had to drink today?

Any alcohol?" To some that question could have been provocative but Monique answered carefully her voice still edgy, her breathing rapid.

"A bottle of champagne. Two bottles. We're on a hen weekend, there's 8 of us. Nothing else." All words were spoken individually, deliberately. "I am not an alcoholic."

"I didn't say you were. Any drugs?"

"Of course not. I'm 32!" The offence evident in her voice. She glared at Jimmy again.

"Well listen, we're going to need a urine specimen all the same. I'll get one of the female staff to come in and help you."

"No, no, no. No, don't leave me. Don't leave me with them," her voice became frantic again. Jimmy tried to calm her but soon realised she wasn't listening, reasoning was useless. She pulled more vigorously on her manacles as he backed out the room. Outside the policeman was waiting, he looked over Jimmy's shoulder as the door juddered closed.

Jimmy continued the questioning. "How's your partner?"

"Haven't seen him yet. What did *she* say?" The policeman added without taking his eyes off the closed door.

"Nothing much. She's quite upset. I'm going to get the on-call psychiatrist to assess her. She's not just some drunk who got out of hand. Her behaviour isn't quite right."

"She's under arrest you know." He turned to face Jimmy adopting a well practiced pose his stance intimidating.

"That's fine but she has to see the psychiatrist before she goes anywhere." Jimmy shrugged, unperturbed by the policeman's tone. "I'll call them now."

"What else did she say to you? Did she say I was going to beat her or rape her or some shit like that? Told you, she's a fucking psycho." The policeman knew as the words came out of his mouth that he had divulged too much information, his self-betrayal complete but he didn't care.

"Well, did you say that?"

"Of course not." But his grin and his smiling eyes said otherwise and with no attempt to hide the lie he was inviting a confrontation. Jimmy just walked away determined to find a female colleague to sit with Monique until the psychiatrist arrived although he knew that would be impossible. For now she would have to fend for herself.

Jimmy had managed to spend most of the shift without bumping into Santi. He had heard his hearty voice a few times but by luck or design they hadn't actually seen each other but he knew it couldn't last. Then whilst standing by the medicine dispenser he felt a great whack on his shoulder.

"Jimmy, Jimmy," Santi chirped. "Where you been hiding?" Jimmy gritted his teeth as the medicine cupboard door opened and a little drawer dispensing two paracetamol tablets pinged open. "Hate that fucking machine. You can't steal anything these days," Santi continued.

"I've been here all morning. It's busy," Jimmy replied typing in another medicine to be dispensed.

"Well I know that. I meant generally, I haven't seen you about. What, you not talking to me? You still shy about the other night?" And there it was, exactly what Jimmy had wanted to avoid. It had taken Santi about 12 seconds to bring it up.

"Well yeah Santi. To be honest, I don't think we were at our best. I don't know," his voice trailed off as he turned to face Santi for the first time. He immediately noticed that he had dyed his beard. Gone was the mainly white goatee, the new colour didn't match for his hair. More noticeable now were the grey hairs that remained on his temples. It made the beard look fake, and ironically made Santi look more mature. Jimmy didn't comment but it was obvious he had noticed it.

"Jimmy, she was just a bit of fun."

"Fun? I'm not sure I...." Jimmy started but was interrupted by another nurse.

"Jimmy, the shrink is looking for you. She's in the medics' office. About the woman from the airport. Is that the one who bit the policeman?"

"That's her," Jimmy replied. "Thinking maybe she is a bit psychotic. She's in a right panic. Just coming." Santi scoffed before Jimmy could explain any more. "What?" Jimmy probed.

"Nothing. Just, them being them," Santi chuckled again.

"What d'you mean?"

"Nothing, they were just winding her up a bit."

"I knew it. Fucking arseholes," Jimmy protested.

"What? Wait a minute Jimmy." Santi sounded offended. "She fucking bit someone. She deserves a bit of a slap."

"Deserves a slap?" Jimmy repeated incredulously. "How can you say that?"

"Fuck her. She's just some piss-head. They think they can get away with anything because they're in Ibiza. Getting totally drunk, probably pilled up as well. Then acts all innocent after biting a policeman." Santi didn't realise the contradiction; this was exactly the behaviour he expected from the women he pursued.

"Or maybe she does actually have a psychiatric problem."

"Doesn't mean she can bite someone." Santi's retort sounded childish.

"Of course not, but Santi, you can't threaten to beat or rape someone either. That's well out of order."

"Shut up Jimmy, they weren't actually going to do anything. Can't believe you're sticking up for her." The two of them now stood face to face in the doorway of the medicine room. Both genuinely disbelieving of the other's attitude. The tension Jimmy had felt over the last week had found a vent but he was feeling increasingly stressed. The situation was curtailed when Cati poked her head into the small room.

"Jimmy, the psychiatrist is looking for you."

"Coming," he replied. "I'm done here." And with that he pushed by the open-mouthed Santi.

None of the paths running up and down the Los Molinos were straight. They contorted and twisted between the irregular rows of apartments; buildings that appeared to have been placed on the hillside at random. They carried pedestrians from the town to the beach and back again. A one-way narrow road curved up the hillside and down the other side giving the traffic an exit again. The quicker, if slightly more arduous route across the hill, was to take one of these many footpaths. It was difficult to get lost but the winding nature of the paths, combined with the wild honeysuckle and trumpet vines that grew unchecked meant that sometimes immediate and practical visibility was at most only a few metres. Jimmy took the steps two at a time then waited at each turn as Wayne bobbed slowly behind him, his short legs compelling him to take an additional stride on each stair.

The rest of the shift had flown by. A trip to the pub hadn't been planned but he felt he needed to be out of his house, and a few cold beers in this heat wouldn't go amiss. Santi could be a dick sometimes. He knew of Santi's reputation and hadn't judged him for it, but experiencing him first hand had brought it home how much of a predator he was. Worse than that Santi thought it was all hilarious. 'Just a bit of fun.' Jimmy felt the shame rise in his face again as he thought of the prostitute. Valeria. That was her name wasn't it? Why did he remember that now? He stood and watched as Wayne plodded his way down the last steps then stopped for a sniff. He was brought back to the present by the voices of some kids running up the stairs behind him. He instinctively brought Wayne towards him with his foot. The dog made his annoyance known with a sultry huff.

The first of the kids to reach Jimmy almost ran right into him still shouting something about how his jump from the rocks had been the most impressive. The boy of about 15 slowed and looked at him suspiciously. Jimmy's weak smile wasn't reciprocated. A second or two later three other boys of about the same age caught up. They were all wearing only shorts which still dripped water. Their hair tousled and damp, their tanned skin smooth and peppered with glistening drops of sea-water or perhaps sweat. Suddenly, after the din of their voices the evening seemed very quiet. He recognised the last of the kids to reach him as his neighbour. Jimmy bent over and hooked Wayne to his leash and urged him to come. Wayne continued sniffing.

"This is the guy who ran over Tyson." Paco announced to his friends by way of introduction. As a pack they took a half step closer to Jimmy, who's instinct pressed him against the little wall.

"You know that was an accident. The dog ran out in front of the car." Jimmy looked around at the young faces. All but one of the boys were the same height as him, and Paco was considerably wider. Now, close up Jimmy could see that he was solid, despite appearing to be a bit flabby with a T-shirt on.

"You know they sent my dog away you fucking queer." Paco continued facing up to Jimmy who now started to sense the peril he was in.

"I told you it wasn't my fault." Jimmy felt a nudge from

behind from one of the other boys. "We'll see what Sebas says." Jimmy noticed the hesitation on Paco's face at the mention of his brother's name.

"You'll fucking pay for this. You'll see. Its not fair." Paco squinted his eyes and brought his face closer to Jimmy's. "Come on," he said to the others and together they turned and ran up the path and out of sight. It had been a quick exchange but Jimmy felt the relief as the sound of their laughing echoed around the hillside and disappeared.

Chapter Twenty-Seven

Marbella 1951

Although she had never been rotund, the last vestiges of adolescence had completely left her, and now in full womanhood she was remarkable looking. Sculpted, shapely, every inch a woman. She wore an aquamarine dress although a little longer and more orthodox than she would normally wear. Julia said it brought out her sparkling turquoise eyes. Her shoulder length black hair had been mostly tied back leaving a centre parting. Classic, simple, elegant. Her smooth neck was subtly exposed, just the way Alfredo liked it. Small creamy pearl stud earrings matched the necklace just visible above the dress's round collar. Subtle mascara and thin eyeliner emphasised those eyes even further. As she looked in the full length mirror Maria Dolores knew she looked stunning. She should have felt fantastic. With an open palm she flattened a slight wrinkle above her hip, then went to join the other guests at the reception downstairs.

The first person to approach her was Julia who greeted her with her usual smile and commented on how graceful and appropriate she looked. Their friendship had become sisterly, their closeness punctuated by the occasional flare-up usually fuelled by Maria Dolores' jealousy. However it was Julia who lived in the villa and was always the hostess. The more recognised although still informal partner for the wealthy bachelor. That they were still lovers was a reality Maria Dolores tolerated. What choice did she have? She had quickly learned that she was the second woman, even if it pained her to accept it. Alfredo had made that explicit: his love, like his generosity, could never be limited to just one woman. Educated and savvy, Julia was more important to his operation, furthermore she had accepted that he would be periodically 'distracted' by other women. Maria Dolores studied Julia and wondered if Alfredo had offered *her* to any business associates, something to sweeten the deal. Did he love Julia? If he was capable of truly loving anyone it would be her.

Since Alfredo's crude revelation Maria Dolores had felt betrayed, sometimes petrified and often furious. She wanted to confront him but couldn't find the words, it sounded ridiculous. Had he really been serious or had alcohol and drugs corrupted his mind? She was consumed by her precarious predicament. She felt more relaxed back in the villa, amongst people, engaged in the preparation for the party. Alfredo, too preoccupied by the event, hadn't come to her for sex and she was thankful for that. This wasn't uncommon, despite outward appearances, the more important negotiations stressed him. He wouldn't return to her until it had been concluded. It agonised her to feel so alone, but who could she talk to? She wasn't as close to Rocio now they moved in different circles and she could only confide in Julia up to a certain point. No, this was something she would work out for herself.

Julia had also dressed more conservatively. Despite their

differences Maria Dolores felt safe and reassured in her company. Alfredo, when he saw them together complimented them and smiled his approval, but his attention was fleeting. He mingled with Marbella's dignitaries, shaking and kissing hands, with the occasional, less formal peck on the cheek. He was well practised in the art of seduction. Maria Dolores sipped her champagne and watched as he enchanted wives with an aristocratic air. Husbands laughed loudly also beguiled, inwardly envying the natural manner with which he mastered everyone around him. It was all so effortless.

There were around 50 guests for the reception. They huddled in cliques, occasionally accepting someone else into their group or parting as a waiter offered canapés or champagne. The doors to the spacious terrace were open allowing a light breeze to pass between them. It lifted the stuffiness of the room even though the heat of the day lingered on. In preparation, the room had been cleared of furniture, except for the occasional small table that held only ashtrays. The lavishness of previous parties replaced by a more meagre, formal ambience. A portrait of Pope Pius XII had been placed next to that of El Generalísimo, specifically to impress the ecclesiastical visitors. The less customary sight of military regalia gave the evening a more ceremonial and solemn atmosphere. The attendees talked in hushed voices perhaps subconsciously aware of the irony that corruption was being celebrated under the gaze of both the head of State and the head of the Church.

An hour or so later Maria Dolores found herself talking with one of Alfredo's trusted colleagues, Manuel Lomas. A respectable man who had previously propositioned her and was surely working his way towards doing so again. There were rumours that he was homosexual; such an attractive and wealthy man who never seemed to have relationships with women. She was on her fourth glasses of champagne and was wondering if he would be a good sexual partner. He was a tall handsome man not unlike Alfredo, furthermore he was single. He had a wide generous smile. She had never seen him without glasses but this made him all the more attractive. His previous advance had come the year before, when Maria Dolores was still intoxicated by Alfredo and the lavishness of her new lifestyle. She had thought his attentions scandalous and wholly inappropriate. Julia on the other hand had laughed when Maria Dolores confided in her, adding that he was indeed an attractive man and a good catch for the right woman.

"You know there are rumours that Alfredo will run for office next year. Have this whole operation to himself." Manuel's open implication that this was an opportunity to further unlicensed dealings surprised Maria Dolores.

"That's what they say." She confirmed although she had never actually heard anyone say that.

"Leaves a space for Deputy Mayor. I'm thinking about it. You know joining Alfredo at the Town Hall."

"Really? Oh Manuel, I think you should. You work so well together. What does Alfredo think?" This time Maria Dolores wasn't improvising. Manuel smiled to himself, hoping the allure of a powerful man might win her favour.

"I'll talk to him about it after the Monseñor's visit." Manuel suddenly stopped talking and looked around. They both became aware of a general commotion spreading throughout the room. The arrival of Monseñor Bocanegra and his entourage. The whispered voices gathered pace then were silent as the official party entered the room. The small groups amalgamated then separated, dispersing like detergent on oil leaving a gaping hole in the middle of the room which the half dozen holy men stepped into. Maria Dolores, like many in the room, struggled to get a good view of what was happening. She saw Alfredo's back as he walked forward to welcome a slender balding man, who was surely the guest of honour. His heavily starched black robes kept their rigid shape as he walked. They were pulled together in the middle by a fuchsia cincture which sat uncomfortably across a little paunch. Mother of pearl buttons nestled neatly in matching fuchsia buttonholes the whole length of his cassock. Silver buckles on his shoes flashed with every step forward. A heavy looking pectoral cross was ornamented at each apex with deep blue sapphires which matched that of his bishop's ring. He was a man who wanted to make an entrance, to be seen with the riches of the Church in full view. If the meek were to inherit the earth they would not belong to the echelons of the Catholic Church.

Alfredo greeted the Monseñor formally underneath the central chandelier, the yellow light reflecting off the sheen of the cassock. Behind him his entourage waited reverentially. All robed in black they watched attentively as their master exchanged words with their host. Maria Dolores took hold of Manuel's arm to maintain her balance as she peered around the woman in front of her. She gaped at the Monseñor and his lustre for a moment then casually let her attention wander to the others not expecting to see anything interesting. Then she saw those piercing eyes looking directly at her. Their gazes held. Recognition flashed across his face. Those black raven eyes narrowed almost imperceptibly. His head cocked and turned slightly. He peered closer.

"Dolores! My arm." Maria Dolores gasped and loosened her embedded fingernails from Manuel's arm.

"Sorry, I," she spluttered as she stepped back, shielding her body behind the woman in front of her, lowering her head, hiding her face as much as she could from that devious penetrating stare.

"Are you feeling OK? You look very pale. Dolores?" The words flitted past her, she perceived little but an increasing sense of doom. The shock of seeing her old parish priest Father Alberto had taken the breath from her. Her heart thumped in her chest. She was immediately transported back to the village and everything that had happened to her there. She tasted the blood and dirt in her mouth, from the violence of that last journey away from Los Caballeros de La Sierra. It had been around five years since she had last seen him but there was no mistaking it and he had seen her. He had recognised her. They had both felt it. Her heart and stomach, suddenly heavy, sank and pulled her body down with them. As she lurched forward Manuel took a step with her.

"Come sit down. You look terrible." Bewilderment strained his voice as Maria Dolores shot him a quick look he didn't know how to interpret but he reached around her and pulled her away from the onlookers. She turned into him hiding her face but she knew it was too late. A sudden surge of adrenaline galvanised her as she allowed Manuel to steer her away. Father Alberto stared after her knowing it prudent not to break away from the Monseñor, not just yet, but the corners of his mouth curled up slightly at this unexpected but more than welcome surprise.

Maria Dolores let Manuel guide her towards the large open doors and onto the veranda. She had no option her legs refused to carry her further. She took great breaths but the humid air did nothing to revive her. She collapsed onto an antique chaise longue, not releasing her grip on Manuel's hand. Her head swam with memories, flooded with fears and fright. She felt both dizzy and alarmed. Manuel offered to bring her water but she shook her head, unable to let go of him. The darkness beyond the terrace walls looked inviting, an escape to nowhere in particular but anywhere would be better than being in that room. Her dress started to become restrictive, the thick seam of her brassier dug into her ribs the deeper she inhaled. Minutes, which seemed like hours, trudged by as she fought to regain her composure.

"Señora." Maria Dolores felt his presence loom over her before she saw him, his voice was soft however, not quite as she remembered it. Still, it teased her. Father Alberto nodded, in mocking etiquette but when he raised his head again his eyes sparkled with glee, a hunter who had his prey cornered.

"Father," she replied in a low rasped voice without looking up.

"Oh, I'm not a priest any more, well not exactly. The Church has bestowed upon me a greater honour; to serve the Monseñor." His smile broadened as he puffed out his chest. "I'm his personal prelate. I have no congregation, not in the conventional sense. I assist the Monseñor with his duties." He leant a little closer, the tips of his fingers danced together on top of his bulging stomach. "We administer Church Law. But sometimes we even help lost sheep back to the fold." He inched forward as he delivered these last words. Maria Dolores withdrew herself back on the chaise longue."How have you been child? Although I see that you're not quite the child I remember," he taunted. Maria Dolores looked up, her face remained pallid but before she could muster a reply Father Alberto continued. "I knew it was you the moment I saw you. There are some people you never forget. Now what could you possibly be doing here in the company of these fine people?" He lifted his arm, a half gesture towards the crowd around the Monseñor behind them. His eyes widened, emphasising the question, but remaining fixed on his old parishioner. Manuel watched this strange exchange develop a little bewildered. The curate clearly knew Maria Dolores but she had only uttered one word and could hardly look at the plump man.

"Buenas noches señor." Manuel stretched out his hand towards the holy man who slowly turned towards him with a disdainful look. Father Alberto didn't reciprocate the greeting and looked back at Maria Dolores.

"This cannot be your husband, you're not wearing a ring." A pause. "Huhhhh. A lover? Maria Dolores." he smirked in feigned astonishment.

"Excuse me!" Manuel interrupted taking a step towards Maria Dolores, partially obscuring her from this brutish adversary. He stared at the priest, face to face, awaiting confrontation, but his demeanour betrayed him. As gallant as his intentions were, he was an implausible hero.

"Maria Dolores, you haven't told him. Cat got your tongue? As I remember you weren't always so shy, quite the opposite actually." In the absence of a reply he continued. "Let me see if I can jog your memory. Seville wasn't it? The Sisters of Clemency and Grace Hospital." He paused for dramatic effect, his penchant for performance unwavering. "For unwed mothers. Teenagers and whores mostly." Maria Dolores stood unable to tolerate him any longer, pushed past Manuel and headed for the door.

"How dare you speak to her in that manner." Manuel watched as she disappeared into the throng of people.

"It seems," continued the priest, "that I am more acquainted with the err, young lady than you are." He brushed the sleeve of his cassock, ridding it of some mote of dust, some unsavoury particle and placed his hands behind his back then rocked gently, smugness oozed from him like a heady fog. Manuel edged closer, incensed, his fists curled into a ball, the priest's foul breath crashed into him.

"If I ever see you again, I will not hesitate to give you what you deserve, whether you hide behind that cross or not." Manuel pointed at a silver crucifix sitting askew on the apex of the priest's belly with an unconvincing aggression that did not befit him. Father Alberto guffawed then with an exaggerated sweep of his hand covered his mouth, ridiculing his would be aggressor. He then swung on his heels and strode back to the Monseñor delighted. There would more fun to be had with her later.

Maria Dolores slammed the door to Julia's room. Blind panic consumed her breathing. The whole situation was out of control. How could that priest be here? Had he even been looking for her? If her destiny had not been fully decided a few nights before, then his sudden appearance had convinced her. She could not stay in Marbella. She pulled at the restricting dress, it ripped easily releasing her chest, allowing great heaves of noisy air to be sucked in. In a rage she kicked her shoes off then tore off the rest of the dress and threw it against the wall. Julia would have something to wear. The previously impeccable hair had loosened, broken free and clung to her face. Spittle burst from her mouth as she sobbed, half cries of fear and frustration. Her hands worked frantically through Julia's closet, discarding any unsuitable clothing to the floor, shoes followed until she found something she could use. Like the clothes strewn around her, her mind became a frenzied jumble of thoughts; Juan Diego, her child, Conchi and her parents, things she had tried so hard to repress, the pain she tried to run away from. And for the second time that week, she was tormented by the face of José Blanco.

A few minutes later she was running along a basement corridor and out the servants' entrance. She just managed to remain calm enough to ask Joaquin to drive her to her apartment. He didn't hesitate, most of the young men that worked for Alfredo would do anything for Maria Dolores. As she distanced herself from the villa and all that it contained she waited for the tension to ease but it only intensified. At her apartment she thanked Joaquin and kissed him tenderly on the lips and said goodbye. He returned to the villa with the biggest grin on his face and a story for his friends.

Her apartment near the marina seemed suddenly smaller and full of Alfredo. The smell of his cigars followed her into every room. His shirts that hung in her closet were thrown to the floor. She knew that he would be busy at the villa for hours but also managed to convince herself that he was going to come through the door at any moment. When Maria Dolores arrived in Marbella she brought with her no past, no heirlooms, no family photos. She had nothing to weigh her down. The tears that her anger and fear had fought to control now broke free. She wiped her eyes furiously as she collected clothing and stuffed a small travel bag with blouses, trousers and underwear. She took another pair of shoes and grabbed a jacket. A hair brush and a few random pieces of make-up that lay on her dresser, were squeezed into the side pocket and then she pulled the zip closed. She changed into her own clothes then as she sat on the toilet she noticed that everything outside of her own body was so peaceful. The sprinkle of her urine echoed in the silence.

It was after 10pm, there was no public transport, she didn't know how to drive even if she did have access to a car. The panic rose again. How could Father Alberto have shown up at the villa? Seeing him had propelled her so violently back to the ghosts of her past that it had left her trembling, the fright still lingered. Her alarm amplified the humidity of the night, making her sweat as she wandered back to her bedroom wondering where her escape lay. From across the harbour, a low bassy rumble sent vibrations through the air and she knew that was her opportunity. Leaving her bag by the door she went to Alfredo's desk. The deep bottom drawer was locked but that was no obstacle, she knew where the key was. It slid open and Maria Dolores took one of the small carpet bags out, it didn't weigh much, but then she knew that. She didn't have to look inside, it contained exactly what she needed.

The short walk to the marina took an eternity. She looked conspicuous, wearing an overcoat on such a balmy night. There were few people around but still she expected someone to grab her arm, take her back. The only vessel with any signs of activity happened also to be the largest boat docked. Maria Dolores slowed her stride as she made her way down the wooden quay, past the clinking of the ropes against masts and the gentle gossiping of splashes on the boat's hulls. She steeled herself as a scruffy middle aged man stepped up to her as she approached the small ship.

"We're going to Palma, Mallorca señora. Is that what you're looking for?" The expected confrontation didn't materialise, the pleasantness of his tone took her by surprise.

"Yes, yes it is," she snapped back at him, a little flustered. "I'm sorry, it's just that I didn't have time to buy a ticket."

"No problem we can sort that out on-board. Come on then let me help you up." She handed him the clothes bag squeezing the smaller one into her as they climbed the rickety gangplank. "It's not a long journey. We stop in Ibiza first, should be there midday tomorrow, then Palma early evening."

"Perfect." she breathed to his back. And for the second time in her short life, Maria Dolores was running, leaving everything she knew, everything she had behind her. But this time she had a carpetbag full of pesetas.

Chapter Twenty-Eight

Ibiza 2016

"You shouldn't do that." Jimmy continued regardless, not particularly convinced that the only other person in the room was talking to him. "Heating that kind of plastic in the microwave releases dioxins and phenols into food and can give you cancer," the toneless voice persisted. Jimmy closed the microwave door, turned the dial and looked round.

"Eh?"

Nurse Ana sat opposite him, she continued to rustle through her handbag, oblivious to the fact she was now being observed. The staffroom's window shutter was still closed from the night before. The pale yellowish hue from the overhead light gave her skin a waxen, sickly look.

"So how do you suggest I heat the water then?" The steady hum of the microwave behind him failed to break the awkward silence that followed.

She shrugged her shoulders. "Just read that you can get cancer. It could kill off your sperm, make you sterile." She glanced up at him, a pause and a smirk to mock his masculinity.

"You're a nurse right? And you believe that shit?" Jimmy talked to the top of her head whilst her search continued. He loathed her: her pompous arrogance, the misplaced self-confidence. She was not a good nurse, on the contrary she was clumsy, unprofessional and led with her mouth. Her brown hair was, as always, pulled back into a paltry ponytail. Jimmy thought balloon faced people shouldn't do that with their hair. She lay a cigarette paper on the low coffee table then began to finger some tobacco onto it. The microwave pinged bringing Jimmy's mind back to the previous task. He groaned when he saw that the plastic cup had buckled slightly in the heat. Her little victory riled him.

"So rolling a fag's good for your health is it?" He retaliated, shielding the plastic cup from her view. She stared at him expressionless, raising her eyebrows slightly. "You talk about phenolines in plastic."

"Phenols," she corrected him with another wince of a smile.

"And smoking doesn't do you any harm? How many chemicals in tobacco? Eh?"

"I was just saying."

"Well keep your nose out of it," Jimmy snapped. He turned his back to her again and started to pour the hot water into another cup, adding a tea bag. He wondered if he had been a bit too aggressive but then decided no, fuck it, she deserved it.

A minute later as Jimmy was squeezing the teabag, the staff room door opened and an auxiliary nurse flounced her way into the room and perched herself on a chair between them.

"I can't stand those black men." The first words out of her mouth. Spat out. Jimmy turned towards the voice. Carolina.

"What men?" Ana didn't sound surprised by her colleague's racist outburst.

"The BLACK men," her heavily mascaraed eyes bulged as she repeated her contempt. "The looky looky guys that sell the crap sunglasses and shit." With both hands she lifted her long peroxide-blonde hair back behind her head, ruffled it and let it fall back into place. It landed exactly how it had been before. Dave Lee Roth on a bad day. Numerous bangles clacked off each other as her arms settled on the back of the chair.

"Ahh, the vendors." Ana agreed, nodding. "Yeah, they're a pain in the arse." Jimmy's skin prickled. The confrontation with Ana and now this. He dipped the thumb holding the cup into the hot tea and held it there. The liquid stung, burned him, his skin complained but he didn't remove it. It distracted him, saved him from opening his mouth. He breathed deeply, deliberately.

"What happened?" Ana prodded, dropping her bag between her hefty thighs, confirmation that Carolina had her full attention.

"We just brought one of them into the Resus room, he was vomiting blood everywhere. It was disgusting, I've had to change my uniform." Carolina flicked her hand towards her trousers. Without much of a pause she held her other hand up signalling there was more. "Jenni, the one that's shagging Miguel, couldn't get a cannula in his arm. Three times she tried. I don't blame her, you can't see their veins." Her eyes bulged again as she concluded her hostile gossip with a nod of her head.

"Maybe it's because he's hypovolaemic, you know, the bleeding and vomiting," Jimmy interjected. "Eh, did you think of that?" Carolina turned to Jimmy and looked at him a little bewildered, as if she had just noticed that he was in the room, then turned back to Ana.

"What's up with him?"

"Grumpy as usual."

"You know, these *black men*, are smuggled here, live 20 to an apartment, take turns sleeping on mattresses on the floor.

They sell crap on the beach because they have nothing else. Then the mafia that brought them here take whatever they earn for rent. No money. No state aid. Do you think these *black men* have access to health care? When they've a problem they make do until it's so bad they end up here. They're refugees. They're not on fucking holiday." Jimmy pulled his thumb out of the tea, the skin red and angry, inflamed but no longer painful, the neurones spent. He waited for a response from the pair who sat before him gawping. "He lived I guess, no thanks to you."

"What you talking about? Course he did. We didn't treat him any different."

"No you just talk about him *different*." Jimmy stared at them.

"Oh God, you coming for a cigarette?" Ana shuffled forward on the low chair and struggled to her feet.

"Yeah, come on. I really need one after that." Carolina flicked her hair again without specifying if she was referring to Jimmy or working with the black man.

The minor injuries room was unusually quiet. The majority of patients seemed to have more urgent problems and were directed to another area. However, it gave Jimmy time to ruminate over what Carolina had said. Her racist attitude towards someone probably trafficked to the country under false pretences. Like the prostitute they had visited. The same. That thought gathered pace and ferocity. A slave. A body to be used. The more he thought the more it tormented him. The room began to suffocate him. He stood abruptly, sucking in a sharp breath, his chair crashing against the wall behind him. As he left the treatment room he saw the ward manager approaching him. "Bloody hell," he muttered to himself.

"Jimmy. How are you today?" Jimmy guessed from the

formality in her voice that this was an official visit. He stepped back into the small room, she followed closing the door behind her.

"Mercedes. I'm very well thank you and how are you?"

"Good thanks Jimmy. Ana mentioned that you were a bit out of order with her earlier," Mercedes said staring into his eyes, smiling. She edged closer encroaching on his personal space.

Jimmy shrugged. "She's a total cow. We don't like each other so why can't she just stay out my way. I didn't ask her to talk to me."

"Relax Jimmy. I know her, she's an idiot and she came to me just to get you in shit. But if she complains about you swearing and being aggressive, I have to follow it up." Mercedes half sat on the table, pulling out her pager.

"I'm just sick of these useless bastards doing the absolute minimum and thinking they're God's gift. She's a fucking embarrassment."

"Don't hold back Jimmy," Mercedes sniggered. "Tell me what you really think." Jimmy half reciprocated the laugh and felt the tension in his shoulders ease a little. As he leant on the table beside her it slid a fraction under his added weight. Mercedes lurched clutching at his thigh, a deliberate and wholly unnecessary act. Jimmy pulled back, he wasn't in the mood for flirting.

The atmosphere darkened again when she mentioned Santi. Jimmy sighed loudly and turned away, focussing on some imaginary point on the floor.

"I'm sick of people asking me about him. We're not joined at the hip."

"Oh, sorry I spoke. I just thought you two were friends. He's been a bit of a pain recently and I thought," Mercedes began before being cut off.

"Maybe we are friends, were friends, but I'm not his keeper. He does what he does and that's that."

"OK." Mercedes stood holding up a hand. The intimacy of sitting so close seemed all of a sudden inappropriate. Jimmy looked at her expecting some kind of comeback. "Well, umm OK, we'll just leave it then." Her reply stumbled awkwardly out of her mouth. "I'll catch up with you later," she patted his thigh again and was gone.

Jimmy felt he should go after her and explain but decided no. Santi could sort out his own problems. He sat a minute mulling over what had happened. He wasn't sure how he felt about Santi. Mercedes was right, he was being a pain in the arse. Others had made similar comments. They hadn't spoken for weeks. That in itself was strange but Santi's attitude had changed. Perhaps his own attitude had as well. It had been a month or so since their night out at La Fragata. What at first had felt like harmless fun seemed now to border on the criminal. He didn't know what disturbed him the most: the things they had done to that woman or the fact that they had done it together. Enjoyed it. Shared it. It was freaking him out. Was he was more like Santi than he wanted to admit? Valeria, her name was Valeria. Jimmy couldn't get it out of his mind. Why did he remember her name? Why did he care? He rose again and left the room. He needed some air.

Outside in the baking heat a few people had gathered by the ambulance bay. A dozen or so cigarette butts littered the ground under the 'No Smoking On Hospital Premises' sign. The collective noise emanating from the group was louder than their small number might warrant. Jimmy recognised them as gitanos and felt himself tense. He cursed his conspicuous uniform, an illusion of importance, and prayed that he hadn't been noticed as he veered off towards the public entrance. Too late. Bernarda, his neighbour, had already broken from the group and was making her way towards him. An older woman scuttled after her but was firmly instructed to stay behind, which pleased Jimmy, he certainly didn't feel like being bullied. A nephew had been brought in by ambulance and they hadn't been told anything. A nephew of the Clan, she didn't feel the need to specify who. Her voice was calm, demure, the antithesis of the gaggle she had just detached herself from. She was glad to see him, a sentiment Jimmy often heard when people needed something. She would send her son to talk to him. Jimmy protested, he was finishing his shift soon but Bernarda took his hand briefly and thanked him, then returned to her family. That was all he needed, Jimmy felt his day was about to get worse.

Twenty minutes later Sebas was shown into the minor injuries room.

"Jimmy." He called ebulliently, giving him a ferocious handshake and slap on the shoulder. "You enjoy what I gave you last week? Quality no?" A quick reminder that Jimmy was somehow indebted to Sebas.

"Yeah good. Thanks. What's up?"

With the preliminaries over Sebas explained the situation. A cousin had been involved in a car accident but he'll be OK. As the story unfolded Jimmy knew that some kind of intervention was about to be solicited. He felt the room become warmer. His heart rate quickened as Sebas pushed by him and sat on the chair by the desk. Jimmy's chair. Sebas' large hands carefully turned the PC monitor around to face Jimmy.

"He'll be on here somewhere. Nando Moreno Moreno." An invite for Jimmy to locate the cousin's records.

"He will be," Jimmy confirmed. "But what's actually wrong with him?" His mouth began to dry, the words struggled in his throat but he didn't move.

"He's waiting for x-rays or something, maybe a broken neck. He's in the corridor just out there." This information didn't add up. Serious head traumas or vertebral fractures would be in the Critical Observation room being immobilised and monitored awaiting a definitive CT scan. They wouldn't be on a trolley in the corridor. "He's got one of those things round his neck," Sebas continued.

"A cervical hard collar," Jimmy muttered. He looked up. Sebas was staring at him. He nodded slowly back at Jimmy his eyes cold and fixed, not a confirmation that he understood, just that he was listening, that the dialogue was heading in the right direction.

"Do you want me to find out if they're doing the scan? See if there's a bed for him somewhere?"

"No, not that."

"What then?"

"I spoke to Santi already." And there it was, the missing piece that allowed Jimmy complete the puzzle. Santi.

"No." Jimmy said without waiting to hear the imminent request. "I'm sorry but I can't."

"You don't even know what we need." The deliberate change of pronoun increased the stakes, it wasn't just Sebas that Jimmy was denying but the Clan. "It's easy. The piss has to be changed. The alcohol and drugs can't be found in his system, he'll go back to jail."

"Someone else was involved," Jimmy exclaimed. "Were they hurt? Santi told you to make sure the drug screen was changed, swap the urine sample." Not questions but rhetorical statements that Jimmy already had the answer to.

"Jimmy, Jimmy. It's easy. I've spoken to my cousin and he hasn't even done the piss yet." Sebas spoke with authority, but he had obviously been well prepped.

"Fucking Santi," he mumbled to himself. "No, that's it."

Jimmy's enraged words were directed at the absent Santi, at their relationship, at their terminating friendship but were taken by Sebas as a flat out rejection.

"Jimmy. There's no one else to help us. No one will find out. The other woman from the crash is a tourist. She's gone to the private hospital. When you get the sample swap it with another one, register it into the system using someone else's computer. It won't be linked to you." Jimmy couldn't believe what he was hearing. The words came from Sebas' mouth but they weren't his.

"Where is he?"

"He's out there on a trolley."

"Not your cousin, that fucker Santi?"

"He's in Barcelona. He said I could count on you." Sebas stood and took a step towards Jimmy. A practiced tactic, his physical presence an oppressive and menacing weapon in itself. "I need you to help me. Come on we're mates. I would owe you one." Jimmy felt suddenly very intimidated, utterly trapped. He couldn't see a way out without offending a dangerous man. The plan was more than plausible but he didn't know if he could bring himself to do it, to act so illegally.

"You know my brother is still very upset about his dog," Sebas added. More emotional blackmail. "You know we had to send her away." This strategy hit a different chord.

"What do you mean?"

"Tyson was always supposed to be a fighting dog. She had great potential, came from good stock. A gold mine. That's why we called her Tyson, like the boxer, a killer in the ring." Sebas bobbed his head a little to each side, imitating a boxer. "We were just waiting for her to mature a little, have some pups then fight her. Once they're mothers they become more aggressive. Did you know that Jimmy? They attack as if the lives of their young depended on it." Sebas paused, it appeared he was searching for a more succinct explanation but he knew exactly how this was playing out. "But of course after her injury she was never going to be a champion like we hoped." Sebas sat down again and began to twirl a pen that had been sitting on the desk.

"Sebas, I can't."

"But *all* dogs fight Jimmy." Jimmy didn't understand what he was getting at but felt even more threatened now that Sebas had backed away a bit. His voice had become less urgent, the pleading had disappeared from his tone. "It's just a matter of circumstance," Sebas paused allowing Jimmy to assimilate what had been said. His penetrating stare unerring. The only sound in the room the rhythmic scratching of the pen as it spun propeller-like under Sebas' heavily tattooed hand.

"Sebas," Jimmy pleaded.

"Please, I'm asking. You would be doing me a big favour." Asking, one step before telling.

Jimmy felt he was on the brink of urinating. Palpitations like jungle drums filled his whole body, whilst Sebas just sat there and smiled at him. The placid countenance of a confident man used to getting his way, knowing again that he was about to attain exactly what he wanted. Jimmy also knew he was going to do it but couldn't bring himself to verbalise it. There he was at work, in the environment in which he was charged with the welfare of the patients under his care but was being coerced into a criminal act. An act which would have serious consequences if discovered. But there was no doubt that refusal would also have consequences. His thoughts weren't on how to change the urine specimen, that, as Sebas had been briefed would be fairly easy. No, it was his anger towards Santi that was mounting, churning him up inside. This situation was his fault. This was all that bastard's doing.

* * *

An hour after Jimmy's shift had ended he was sitting on the toilet in his own apartment. Wayne had traipsed in after him but after a minute had lost interest and had wandered off again. He stared at the mirror opposite wondering who it was that looked back. Weary hands rubbed tired eyes. He was exhausted. Before coming home he had passed by Jock's Bar and downed a pint, then another with a double whisky and left without even greeting any of the regulars. As the lager and whisky left him, he felt some pressure diminish, a physical relief he could not duplicate emotionally. He was both mortified and angry that he had done what he had done. Furthermore he had the indignity of providing his own urine for the specimen. Sebas had said no one would find out but he didn't understand. Jimmy would know, he would always know. He would know he had let himself down not only professionally but worse, morally. The face that stared back at him was that of a tired soul, deflated and defeated. Crow's feet wrinkles had deepened, eyelids drooped heavily matching the bags underneath. The sclera red, bruised, those of an habitual drunk. With both hands he pulled his hair back lifting it up above his slightly receding hairline. Free of hair the face that he saw reflected back at him was that of his grandmother. A traditional cockney woman, a matriarchal head whose authority was never challenged. It was there in the eyes, the exact same grey-green eyes, the same spent tiredness. What would she think of how he had behaved? He leant over and turned the tap on. The hot August day had persevered into the night, it invaded his apartment but he felt if he immersed himself in the bath he might feel better, the water might rid him of his shame. Then there was the dog, Tyson. Not a family pet but a business opportunity, something disposable, a piece of meat. If not a challenger in the ring, then as fodder. Live flesh to be practised upon, so another dog knows the taste of blood, what it's like to kill. The brother, the younger one that always scowled at Jimmy surely didn't know that.

He glanced at his mobile phone, Santi hadn't yet seen the text. He submerged his body below the tepid water allowing it to swell around him. He had initially called Santi, but unsurprisingly there had been no answer. It was perhaps just as well, after a double whisky chaser Jimmy didn't feel like holding back. The water washed over him, bubbles slowly formed and escaped from his nose. He urinated again in the bath, another gratifying release.

He dried himself next to his bed and pulled on a pair of shorts, uncharacteristically discarding the towel on the floor. A long sleep was exactly what he wanted, what he needed. But first he would take Wayne out again. It would mean a longer lie in the morning. A few minutes later he stood on the pavement watching the French bulldog sniff around the car wheels, fastidiously choosing the exact point to leave his mark. The dying rays of the evening sun reflected on one long solitary stratus cloud that hung just above the horizon. The rose coloured glow bounced off the sea and onto the white houses that terraced the hillside dousing them in a pinkish hue. The scraping of a garage door or metal gate off to the right attracted his attention, he looked along the street then towards the Moreno household. Nothing. Jimmy was thankful that Sebas wasn't visible. There was no movement around the house nor in the garden. Just as he called Wayne back through the gate, he noticed a face looking out through the bougainvillaea in the old lady's garden. Even twenty meters away Jimmy felt the stare penetrate him, a hateful glare that reached into him. Paco realising he'd been seen, stood up confidently, defiantly, unconcerned that he had been discovered. 'Here I am. What are you going to do about it?' Jimmy felt distinctly uncomfortable and exposed under the boy's gaze.

They looked at each other for a moment, neither reacting. "Wayne, time for bed." Jimmy's subdued words hardly broke the air between them. How could a child make him feel so vulnerable? The pressure on his own bladder again prompted him to move. He reached around Wayne with his right foot and nudged him towards the gate. "Time for bed big man."

Chapter Twenty-Nine

"There wasn't a cloud in the sky the morning we sailed into Ibiza. I didn't sleep, I sat on the deck most of the time holding that little bag close to my chest. In the end I was glad I had taken the coat, the sea is its own master and cold at night even in the summer. We passed between Formentera and Ibiza to reach the port. I watched as we passed the small towers along the coast. In the old days they set bonfires on top to warn the island's people when danger was approaching. But the danger that day was only me. My escape. I thought about Alfredo and Julia, if they'd even noticed that I had gone. I doubted Alfredo would have cared, but I think now maybe I misjudged him. I thought of Juan Diego, about being further away from him and gave up on him ever finding me. He probably *was* dead despite what Ana told me. Every time I thought of him like that, a bit of me stayed with him. Dead." Maria Dolores leant over, lifted her skirt and scratched her knee. It somewhat distracted Father Gabriel. He had noticed various lesions on her legs, embryos of venous ulcers, but hadn't ventured to enquire after her health. Varicose veins with bumpy nodules ran alongside them, the unavoidable topography of old age.

* * *

"It was so different then, the port was really that small corner, just there." She lifted her arm indicating to the priest what he already knew. "This church was here of course," she continued. "It was the biggest building down here." A forlorn look passed across her face. Father Gabriel studied her, perhaps she was remembering something else, digging deeper into an old woman's memory reclaiming something that happened half a century before. "And of course the castle, d'Alt Vila with the Cathedral on top of it all, looking down on us. That hasn't changed. That'll never change. Hah, The Church will always be there," she added with no sense of derision.

"Our boat came in beside some fishing boats with sails. The noise they made in the wind sounded like they were clapping me in. That was it, a few barrels, people getting boats and nets ready to go out. No tourists, no stupid market stalls, not even the hippies. All the women wore big black dresses, it was like a funeral every day, but it was just their way. They dressed like that after they married, like a funeral," she chortled to herself. "I was glamorous next to them, not that they knew anything about that." And again she laughed a self-depreciatory giggle. "The town was no more than the harbour, the castle and the square. A few buildings but nothing else. Nothing at all. I wandered around and thought about what to do. My boat left for Mallorca, I watched it go and thought nothing of it. What choice did I have?"

"Everything was so different to Marbella. Ibiza was lost in time. There were the two hotels and one pension. I got a room in the first hotel because the owner, old Josep Ribas, was the only person I met that spoke good Spanish, they all spoke Catalan or something like that. I never understood it, still don't." She looked up to Father Gabriel for confirmation that the indigenous language was irrelevant. He, however, was born on the island, Ibicencan was his first language. He smiled weakly at her, ignoring her dismissive tone. When she didn't get the sought after reassurance she rolled her eyes with no attempt to disguise it and continued. "At first Josep was very suspicious of me, a young woman travelling alone, a woman who paid for herself. But I got to know him well, he was a good man. His son, Pepe, who helped him in the hotel, was nothing like his father." And again she paused. How quickly her face changed as she recounted the two men, the differences between father and son. "Why are men like that?" she asked, but there was no answer to that question.

"I stayed in the hotel a week or so and looked for work. But there was nothing. Everyone was poor, they worked the land or fished. Everyone had big families and they all worked together. No one could afford workers, especially a woman and an outsider at that. It reminded me of my village a bit, people just doing what they need to, to get by. The only other work on the whole island was in the salt flats, Las Salinas, and like I said, no woman would ever get a job there. There were no proper restaurants like now, no waitress jobs. Josep found me a room overlooking the port. It was above his cousin's house, like I said it was all in the family in those days. It wasn't much and had no toilet but it was mine and had a lock on the door. I paid him for three months just like that. The first night I sat there alone thinking about how I ended up there. I doubted I had done the right thing, running away like that. Maybe Alfredo would have let me stay, then I remembered how he offered me to that pig Closas like I was a piece of meat. I started to cry. I was so alone and helpless, but then decided, just like that, that I wasn't going to feel sorry for myself anymore, and I would get on with life. I bought a few things for the room, and a dress like the local women wore. The clothes I brought with me were Marbella clothes, tight skirts, high heels and Hollywood dresses. I thought they were useless for Ibiza, but they soon came in handy." At this she permitted herself a wry smile, a private acknowledgement of what was to come.

"I thought the money I had would last a while, a year or maybe more but then one day I came back to the room and it was gone. The bag was open on the bed and it had only a couple of notes left in it, like the thief had felt bad taking everything from me. I was so angry I screamed and threw the bag out the window, then had to run down to get it, for those last few pesetas. It must have been some sight." Something in that image made her smile. "I knew who it was. Old Josep wouldn't have done that and he had the only other key. No, it was that hijo de puta Pepe, the son, I'm sure of it." She lowered her eyes, realising the profanity had escaped her in the vestibule where they had been sitting like old friends passing the time. They sat then a while without speaking. Two heat-wilted tourists climbed the stairs stepping around the ragged old dog that lay waiting for her mistress. They peered through the mighty church doors into the duskiness of the vestibule but decided not to enter, perhaps put off by the ragged old woman sitting beside a pristine priest. The sullied and the unsullied.

"Then it hit me, the money I had would only last a few weeks and I had no job. I even went to the seminary to ask if I could clean or cook. A priest there told me they had nuns. Nothing else. 'We have the nuns.' Then he slammed the door in my face." She half rolled her eyes in resignation. Father Gabriel cleared his throat and was about to explain that the church had changed in the intervening years but she carried on, not giving him the chance to defend his predecessors.

"A few nights later when I was eating in Josep's hotel I saw some men come in. They were buying salt, from the Salinas, to take to Germany. They didn't have much salt in Germany. I remember thinking how strange that was, not having salt. They sat and drank beers and celebrated, they reminded me a little of Alfredo, loud and they liked the sound of their own voices. When I left one of them followed me into the street. He asked my name, he was drunk but polite. His name was Kasper, something else I remember from that night. He followed me a bit, trying to talk to me, trying to get me to talk back. He teased my shyness and I stopped and turned ready to shout at him, scare him away but he was right there almost on top of me. At first I thought he was going to do something, attack me maybe, but he didn't, he just held out 100 pesetas. I looked at it and took a step away shaking my head, knowing what he wanted. Then he smiled and nodded at me, pretending to turn. I said nothing, I froze so he walked away. But then I called out to him. 'Come back.' I only thought of the money, 100 pesetas was my rent for a week with more than enough money left over to eat. 'Come back.' I said it and he did." Maria Dolores paused, replaying the events of that night in her head. Reliving it because saying the words wasn't enough. "I let him have sex with me. In an alley close to here, over there by the castle wall. He put my hand over his crotch and he was already hard. I felt sick the whole time, but I forced myself do it. Then he just turned me around and did it. Against the wall, the humidity of it was freezing against my face. The cold bricks against my arms, spread out across the wall because I was afraid I would fall. But he wasn't rough. He just did it. Afterwards he didn't say anything and neither did I. He held the money near my hand and I grabbed it. I couldn't face him. He just walked away and left me there. There were no lights but it wasn't all dark and I was afraid someone would see me. Nothing else, just that I might be seen. I pulled my skirt down and that hid everything bad that had happened. I wanted to look normal, huh, on the outside at least. I hated myself. I held back tears until I got to my room, but even then I didn't let myself cry. I kept the tears in. I washed myself, inside and out, with the cold water squatting over the basin. 'Come back,' *I* told him. 'Come back.' It was me, father. I started it."

Father Gabriel had heard enough confessions in his young career to recognise those who sought true absolution and were indeed sorry for past actions, and others who like acquiescent children, endured the ritual of confession to appease a higher order. Maria Dolores was neither of these. The old woman spoke with a self confidence that her younger self was only discovering. The self-recrimination of those first days, that guilt had long been expelled if not wholly forgotten. He was not one to exonerate, then again he was not even sure that that young woman would have asked for it.

"Dolores, do you regret what you did?" He knew the answer to this question but felt obliged to ask it. She looked at him scornfully, it was a question she didn't want to be asked. Of course there were regrets, but acknowledging them gave them life.

"Of course I regretted it, I saw him again a few mornings later outside the hotel. I was petrified that people would know what happened just because we were walking in the same street. But of course no one said a thing. We didn't talk, he just smiled and walked on. I didn't like what I had done but who was I hurting? I was angry, furious that I had allowed myself to be upset again by a man. So I promised myself that I wouldn't care what people thought of me. And plenty of people have had opinions over the years." A curl of the lip revealed the contempt she held for those detractors, but those memories galvanised her to finish her story. "That night I went looking for him and I found him and I took him back to my room. No man was going to control me. And I saw him four or five times more before he left again for Germany." She looked towards Father Gabriel defying him to disapprove or reproach her.

"It sounds to me like you are asking for forgiveness, even though you might not see it that way." He said, wary again at causing offence. She grunted in response. A non-committal act that left Father Gabriel none the wiser.

"The money I made from him and then his colleagues was enough for the rest of the year. I just thought every time I did it, I had 100 pesetas more and I can live a week longer and that's how I got through it, that first winter. Not long after that tourists started to arrive, from then on making money was easy. Of course I sometimes worked in bars and restaurants, but no one really wanted me. Maybe they knew what I did, Ibiza was a small place. They didn't want me dirtying their respectable places, working with their women. So I did the only thing I could. What else was there to do? Of course I hated myself, but if you don't think about it so much, it's not so bad. I thought of Kasper often, of how easy it was for him to offer me money, how easily I took it. Maybe in Germany things were different. Maybe prostitutes were common. Then I realised that was what I was. I had become a prostitute, maybe the first in Ibiza." They sat again in silence with only the bustle of the street to distract them. Father Gabriel watched as Maria Dolores looked into the distance or perhaps the past, her face expressionless. He wondered where she took herself on these occasions and expected that at any moment she would stand and walk away without explanation nor farewell. This time however she continued to sit beside him. Perhaps the slow unburdening over the summer months had at last reached a climax. Perhaps her story was over. Finally, it was the priest who spoke first.

"Do you require absolution Dolores?" She looked at him quizzically as if he had understood nothing. "No," he said answering his own question with a nod of the head. "I asked you that question a few months ago, when we began to talk," he continued. "I asked you once why you had decided to talk to me." His words hung in the air, not a fully formed question but none-the-less begging an answer.

"Who else would listen to a crazy old woman?" She looked past him towards the street again. "Is that not what you priests do?" she added mocking him. It had crossed her mind that perhaps she should offer him a reason, owed him something for his summer's patience, but the truth was, as she said, there was no one else to hear her story. "I have just one more thing to tell you. You'll soon be rid of me."

Chapter Thirty

Ibiza 2016

The simple way of life in Ibiza comforted Maria Dolores in a way she had never anticipated. It took her back to the honest and frugal existence that she enjoyed in the mountains. There was no pretentiousness amongst the Ibicencan people and in the days before the town became a city there was an unspoken if somewhat limited acceptance of her. It was more scandalous that she not attend church. This new life was a stark contrast to the socialite lifestyle and illicit dealings in which she had been embroiled in Marbella. She did not miss it.

To begin with she passed each day contemplating an existence she had neither planned nor wanted. She reasoned, however, that life and circumstance had given her an opportunity to make a living and so she did. There was no going back. Juan Diego was not going to rescue her and her son was lost. Although neither were forgotten, there would be no happy ending. She spent the best part of sixty years catching glimpses of Juan Diego in the mannerisms of other men. The way they walked or the way they ran their fingers through their hair. A part of her withered at the acceptance of this loss and the planned future they never had. The memories of their short time together became more embedded and embellished as she shrouded herself in them. Another protective skin.

These early days on the island heralded the start of a change in her, a hardening, building on the foundations of her stubborn determination. A strength of purpose that carried her through life. But the protective barriers that she fiercely constructed around her worked both ways and she was determined they would not be breached. An emotional internment that became impossible to release herself from. No man would love her and she would love no man. She hid in her skin to avoid the realities of living. Her painted face, a mask presented to her customers. She was unaware as the best years of her womanhood came and went, it dragged with them her lust for life. The days passed slowly for that young woman, the nights more so but somehow they turned into months which turned into years. The island evolved around her as men like Alfredo took advantage of lax laws and corrupt officials. Hotels and resorts multiplied as the peaceful summers were given over to plagues of tourists. But no one complained, there was work for everyone, Maria Dolores included.

She was reminded of these changes every time she walked out onto her street. The seemingly constant need for development, redevelopment. The new replacing the old. She wondered how long she could last before she was evicted and all traces of her, her home and her life were erased in the name of progress. Her hillside was after all a prime location. That morning she left Baby behind as she again made her way to the Church of San Salvador de La Marina for what she believed would be her last meeting with Father Gabriel. She had never been convinced she would be able to free herself. But something had grown between them, a friendship of sorts. If he judged her, he didn't show it and so she had been able to talk openly. Over that hot summer she had grown to believe that burden could be lifted and today would be the day, of that she was determined.

"'FRANCO HA MUERTO'. I can still see it, all over the front page of the Diario de Ibiza. At four forty in the morning it said. They must have been waiting for him to die if they noticed the time like that." Maria Dolores tried to conjure up an image of the dead dictator but the name was enough to fill her with animosity. "Didn't die soon enough. 1976."

"I think it was 1975." Father Gabriel interrupted. An automatic if unnecessary correction. Maria Dolores looked at him through narrowed eyes. The air in the chancery was sweet, the remnants of some burnt frankincense still lingered. She didn't like it.

"Yes, well, he didn't die soon enough. He was an evil man. So many people died because of him, so many lives ruined. A few days later there was a photo of him in his casket." She stopped again, this time able to recall his sunken dead face and shuddered. "There were street parties, not officially but there were. He never cared for Ibiza and I don't think Ibiza cared for him. Around here most people were happy even though we were told to mourn. A few of *them* wore black but I paid them no attention. Huh, you probably weren't even born." She peered at the priest again, with an accusatory glint.

"No. 1978 I was born." The jeans he wore that day didn't really befit him and in that moment she saw him younger, he could have been her grandson, alien to the times she was describing. He stood to pour some coffee. Despite the midday warmth she nodded, accepting the drink but also feeling a slight victory. He hadn't lived through those times like she had. They had grown used to each other. He no longer felt he needed to be so attentive to her every word. Somehow she didn't seem as frail as she had earlier that summer. Telling her story had given her life, some vibrancy.

"Those days after he died were sunny but cold. The bars around the Plaza del Parque and up the old town were busy." She motioned with her head in the vague direction of the plaza, her eyes not leaving him. "There was a change in the air, everyone felt it." He placed her cup and saucer on the little table then offered her a biscuit. She took one without thanking him. They sat a minute in silence whilst she broke off little chunks and nibbled at them. "And of course when men drink they come looking for women like me." They may have become used to each other but her candidness regarding her profession could still surprise him. Or perhaps, as a priest, as a man, he wasn't quite as accepting and tolerant as he thought he was.

"I never talked much with my clients. Why would I? Then one night I talked too much. That afternoon I met a man, he was so drunk I thought it would be easy money, something quick. We went to his apartment, up there by the school. Then from nowhere this man, he hit me in the face. I can't even remember what I said but I know it was about Him, Franco. I thought he'd be easy but then I turned round and he punched me so hard I fell to the floor. He stood over me, shouting at me. Telling me not to move, not to get up. I waited for him to do those horrible things to me. I was terrified. It had been a long time since I was scared like that." Then Maria Dolores stopped talking. That far off look crossed her face again. The place she took herself to when the details became too painful to voice.

"Dolores, if this is too difficult," Father Gabriel started, offering her a way back, an alternative to again describing her torment. His sympathetic tone spoke as much as his words. She looked down to her hand and the biscuit she was crushing between her arthritic fingers.

"I stayed there on the floor, like I was told. When I tried to move he came to me and kicked me. I hardly felt it the second and third time. He pushed his cigar up to my face and told me he'd burn me if I said anything. Then he poured himself a brandy and sat on his sofa. He just sat there watching me on the floor like a dog. At first I was glad he was so drunk because men like that can't do what sober men can. Huh," she shrugged her shoulders in resignation. "Until he hit me. The drunk ones are always most violent. But I knew by looking at him all I had to do was wait. He slurred when he called me a whore. His head bobbed when he said those awful things. His eyes closed and he tried to drink but it spilled down his fat belly. The ash from his cigar dropped onto him but he didn't even notice. And I stayed on the floor just looking up at him. Watching and waiting." She took another sip of her coffee and rubbed her fingers over her thighs, ridding them of the crumbs.

"Err, Dolores," The priest repeated a little hesitantly.

"Wait Father, this is the end. This is why I had to come." Father Gabriel after all this time hadn't expected that there would be a finale to her story. He had asked her on numerous occasions why she needed to open up to him and every time she had dismissed him. But he had been caught off guard. Spurned on by his apprehension she continued.

"I could see it happening. The glass slipped from is hand and fell over his trousers. He never even moved. I reached over for my shoes. Then when his cigar fell onto the sofa I grabbed my coat. He mumbled something, who knows what he said. I crept along the floor, terrified to make any noise. When I stopped and stood at the door I saw the smoke already coming from the sofa. He hadn't moved. Then a flame, just a little yellow flame." Maria Dolores' words slowly ground to a halt. Father Gabriel was surprised by her lack of expression. She leant over and picked up her coffee but her trembling hands forced her to place it down again.

"What happened?"

"What do you think? A fire happened."

"Do you feel you were responsible?" Said Father Gabriel regaining a bit of composure.

"I shut the door on him and left him there. I could have saved him but I didn't. I could have woken him, told him to get out or maybe even put the fire out. But I didn't." Father Gabriel couldn't argue with her reasoning. Still her expression didn't change.

"Yes but,"

"Responsible?" She repeated. "Of course I was. I left him there. I locked the door and took the keys. It was me. I did it, then I sat on that little wall and watched the place go up in flames." She stared at the priest, defiant eyes daring him again.

"Dolores,"

"It wasn't the fire that killed him they said. They got him out before the building burned. He breathed in all the smoke and suffocated. That evil man died in the hospital, I read it in the paper."

"You can ask for forgiveness if you are remorseful. God *will* forgive you." Still, his natural instinct was to offer a solution through prayer.

"I stopped believing in salvation a long time ago Father. I won't ask for forgiveness from a God that was so cruel to me."

"Repentance can be yours if that is what you truly want." An anxiety began to creep into Father Gabriel's voice.

"A God that took my son away."

"But Dolores,"

"No, I won't do it." She shuffled in the seat, preparing to stand up. He reached across and placed a hand on her arm.

"It's never too late."

"You priests are all the same. No. I won't do it." Her face reddened as she struggled to her feet. "I'm telling you this because I never told anyone and someone needs to know."

"Please Dolores, you don't need to go. Sit and,"

"Achh," she raised her arm in protest suddenly frustrated with the priest. "I told you. Someone needs to know, only that." She pushed the chair away. "Nothing else. Just that someone knows," she repeated as she hobbled towards the door.

Chapter Thirty-One

Ibiza 2016

Every other morning during tourist season, without fail, Baby was awoken by the same thunderous crashing, as glass bottles were emptied from a height into a recycling truck waiting below. The little crane then crunched gears as it unceremoniously dumped the vast recycling container back onto the street with a thud. This happened about fifty metres from Maria Dolores' house, too close for the little dog's comfort. Baby bared her teeth in response and growled at the outside without getting to her feet.

"Shhhh cariño," Maria Dolores soothed, "It's done. They've gone." On hearing her mistress's voice she lowered her head resting her chin on her crossed legs but the low guttural grumble continued. Maria Dolores ambled over to the pane-less window and watched as the lorry rumbled its way round the hillside road and out of sight. She let the curtain fall again, it was another bright morning and although it was not yet seven, it was time to make a move. Upon waking every morning her first thoughts were the same. It was a new day but it was the same day. Although she had become numb to her excruciating poverty, it was, like her aches and pains a constant in her life. If she wanted a free breakfast it was always good to get there early before the paying customers arrived.

There was no reason for her to take note of the olive green Opel Zafira parked close to the recycling bins. In this street, cars and vans were packed in, nose to tail, bumper to bumper. Finding a parking space in this neighbourhood was indeed fortuitous. What was unusual was the sturdy well groomed man sitting in the back of the car. Maria Dolores passed by concentrating more on each step, than the vehicles beside her. The occupant watched her as he had done the previous three days, glancing occasionally down to his notes. Her house was partially hidden but he had chosen his strategic vantage point well, he had full view of her as she approached then as she passed. When she and that mutt could no longer be seen he climbed out of the airless car and stretched. He ran his hands through his heavily lacquered hair, pressing it firmly against the sides of his head. In his mid-sixties he was too old to be sitting in cars for hours on end. He was a respected successful man, really, this was beneath him. There was no need to follow the old lady again. His experience had held him in good stead; he had already learned that she was a creature of habit, and would return home before midday to spend the most punishing summer hours indoors. He abandoned the car and took a path perpendicular to hers, one which meandered between the houses and gardens with their overgrown foliage to his sea front hotel where he slept sporadically until midday.

After showering again, he dressed slowly, meticulously, studying himself in the mirror at every stage as he did so. Even though his shirt hadn't been worn, he had asked the hotel to iron it and his trousers again. Finally cufflinks and black brogue shoes. He smoked a cigarette on the balcony overlooking the sea, only 250 meters from the bench where he had watched the old lady the previous evening. The same view, but one which he could and would escape the following day. Despite the heat he slipped on a navy blue blazer, gelled his thinning hair and made his way to the hotel restaurant. He ordered lobster salad which, when it arrived, he couldn't eat. He pushed the succulent white meat around his plate unable to concentrate. After so long, after all these years mentally preparing himself for this moment, he still hadn't decided what to say. He assumed that the words would form by themselves. Perhaps in the emotion of the moment words, to begin with at least, would be superfluous. He had contemplated this moment so many times, each time burying his feelings deeper. High Noon was approaching and he had better be ready. He poured himself another glass of wine, and stared as he swirled the straw coloured liquid around in the glass. In his opinion Ribera del Duero wasn't Spain's worst viticultural area, it was just a pity the hotel stocked this specific wine, but it was the best the meagre wine list had to offer. Never mind, he wouldn't be in Ibiza much longer.

At 17.30 exactly he closed the door to the Zafira, laid his neatly folded blazer on the passenger seat, lowered both his and the passenger window and waited. A little after an hour later Maria Dolores came out of her house, taking one step at a time always leading with her right leg. The little dog, her Baby, plodded slowly behind her, also one step at a time. He waited until she was on the street to ensure she was headed his way.

"Señora Benitez Herrero?" Maria Dolores stopped in her tracks. It had been years since she had heard her name spoken like that, decades probably. But it was her name, she hadn't imagined it. She turned round, slowly shuffling her feet, to confront the voice that had spoken to her. She instinctively pulled Baby a little closer. The man who faced her had slightly covered his face with his hand, shielding his eyes from the afternoon sun.

"Señora Maria Dolores Benitez Herrero?" The voice continued. She stared at the man before her, a little bemused. A policeman? It was clear he wasn't a young man, but his sturdy frame and his well tailored clothes took years off him.

"Yes," she replied. The man removed his sunglasses and lowered his hand. The thinnest of smiles twitched on his lips but then faded quickly.

"My name is." He cleared his throat and repeated, adopting a more formal tone. "My name is Francisco Garzón Ortega." Although the sun was behind her, Maria Dolores squinted her eyes, there was something in this man's face she recognised but she was convinced she had never met him. An old client? She took a small step to the side, intimidated by his posture and solemnity.

"What do you want?" She lowered her eyes slightly, some deep intrinsic reaction to avoid confrontation. But she continued to study him, eyes darting to take it all in. He was obviously well to do, he looked immaculate, his large hands lacked the roughness of a labourer, his fingernails pristine. A silver signet ring adorned his third finger, a thin cross etched into its surface, the symbol of Opus Dei. A priest?

"You are definitely Maria Dolores Benitez Herrero?" He paused. "Of course you are, you confirmed it and I already knew it," he sighed. The absurdity of his question annoying him. "I had to come, I promised myself many years ago that I would find you. And I have." He inhaled deeply, knowing what had to be said but fearing the reaction it would trigger; both in himself and this woman. Could he still walk away? Maria Dolores looked up at him again and for the first time their eyes properly met. Suddenly she felt as if she had received a blow to the chest. She was instantly thrown back; back half a century, back to her village, to a another existence.

"Juan Diego?" She staggered a little, feeling her legs weaken, suddenly short of breath. Her eyes bulged, widened to assimilate what was before her. "Juan Diego!" A slow grimace stretched her face, her trachea tightened, her heart pounded, increasing the tension in her chest. Francisco Garzón reached forward to steady her and for the first time in his life he touched his birth mother.

"No Señora, not Juan Diego. My name is Francisco." And although he held onto her arm, there was nothing there. He had expected some feeling, some sensation, stimulated by their meeting, their physical contact. Something. But he felt nothing. Maria Dolores started to heave as she panted to regain her breathing. She hadn't heard him, her whole being overwhelmed by the past. How could it be Juan Diego? Was this the mind of an old woman playing tricks on her? But it was. It was his eyes, his face, older but it was him. He held onto her arm until she lowered herself against the small wall. Then he let her go.

"Señora Benitez," he breathed and started again. "I was adopted at birth, the 9th of April, 1947, from The Sisters of Clemency and Grace Hospital in Seville. You are my mother." He waited for some sort of response. She looked up at him again, stared into his eyes awaiting some truth that had already been revealed. "Would you like to sit down?" He thought about taking her back to her home but he had already been inside, examined it. He could not go back there. It reeked of neglect, a disregard that now he was close to this woman, he saw that it had been transplanted also on to her. Slowly Maria Dolores began to absorb what was happening. She grabbed the wall, fearing she might collapse, feeling the earth fall beneath her.

"Your name?" Her voice was released in slow rasps, hardly

more than whispers.

"Francisco Garzón Ortega, General Garzón Ortega." He felt uneasy, standing there over the old woman. An old woman whom he had investigated, tracked down and now seen. It was a disappointment he had anticipated the more he uncovered who she really was. A disappointment that bordered on displeasure, even disgust.

"How can it be my son?" Her voice broke into his thoughts disturbing his guilt. She had not thought of her child in many years, that part of her life had waned and died. "Francisco? How?" she repeated now addressing him directly.

"Señora, I can assure you that it is true. I'm sorry if this has come as a shock to you." He paused, the regret he had feared and knew was unavoidable began to take hold of him.

"Señora?" she mimicked scowling. Maria Dolores also knew it was true. She could see Juan Diego in him. She could feel it, this was her son.

"I am sorry, I wish I had never bothered you," he continued, apologising as much to himself as to her.

"How did you find me?" Her voice began to find form, belying the tumult she felt inside.

"I am a Lieutenant General in the Tenth Brigade, Córdoba, just like my father." He paused and corrected himself. "I was, I'm retired now." When he saw that his professional standing meant nothing to her he explained. "Many years ago, after my father died my mother told me of the adoption from the Sisters of Clemency and Grace. I was a General in the army." His haughtiness came naturally to him, but this emphasis was lost to Maria Dolores. "I have contacts, it was easy to obtain the paperwork."

"Your father was Juan Diego Martos." He stopped, she was looking past him up the street, towards the safety of her home. "You look just like him. He was a proud Catalan." He began to take a step forward, to perch himself beside her on the crumbling whitewashed wall that supported her, but he couldn't, something stopped him. Perhaps he feared the physical proximity would bring with it an emotional closeness.

"Juan Diego Martos. A Catalan!" he echoed. The disappointment evident. "There was no mention of the father in the documents, only your name, a priest and the parish he served in. I went there, to the village, to Los Caballeros de La Sierra and asked for you. It's a small place and I found a Señora Conchita Benitez Herrero, the only one there with the same surname. She was your sister."

"Ayyy ayy, Conchi." Maria Dolores inhaled sharply, then almost shrieked, another part of her past reaching out to her, reaching into her. "Conchi, my little sister," she moaned.

"She gave me a letter for you. But, that was about 5 months ago. I'm sorry but she was very ill," he added reaching into the left inside pocket of his blazer and pulled out a small plastic wallet and removed a folded envelope. "You can, erm, you can read can't you?" A genuine question delivered coldly, oblivious to how it ridiculed her. Maria Dolores stared at the envelope, ignoring his callousness, then took it reluctantly as if it were something contagious. She did not touch his hand.

"My Conchi, my Conchi." Tears welled, her eyes pained her as the pressure increased. She rocked almost imperceptibly, small rhythmic movements, a subconscious solace. The past was attempting to maul her. But she did not cry. She was yet again transported back to her house, her sister, her parents, Pirri and the smells of spring in the mountains. And this man before her.

"Are you all right? You look pale. Señora?" She heard the voice but didn't react, there was no concern in it, no compassion to embrace. Francisco felt increasingly more uncomfortable and not for the first time doubted that he had acted prudently. The woman appeared to be a little in shock but he had no idea how to comfort her. He remained detached. In the awkward silence he continued despite her agitated emotional state.

"Once I had your name, your full name and date of birth it was relatively easy. Although you have never paid social security, you do thankfully, have a police record; 4 arrests for prostitution and various claims of assault." Maria Dolores was incapable of absorbing anything else. She stared at the letter, holding it as tightly as her arthritic hand allowed. One written word 'Lola' was still clearly visible in the centre of the envelope. "And you haven't moved from this address in over 27 years at least." In the quiet of the afternoon, Maria Dolores became slowly aware that life carried on around her. Above her a seagull cried, somewhere a dog barked and another responded, some private discourse or difference of opinion. The bustle of the main street below them continued as it did every day oblivious to this most unsentimental of reunions.

"Why are you here?" Her voice found a strength her body was still to recover.

"I promised myself I would see where I came from and I have done it. I have been to the village and now I have seen you." His lack of empathy fuelled her rising indignation. "If that were judicious or not I am now not sure," he added to himself. He was, in short, embarrassed by her.

"WHY?" Maria Dolores shouted angrily. How could this man show up here and do this to her? Her child would not treat her so coldly. She didn't deserve this. Did she?

"I'm sorry that I have upset you, I just," his clipped voice was again interrupted.

"What do you want?" She snapped at him. She pushed herself up ungainly and tugged Baby towards her again. She glared at him with a sense of purpose he didn't understand, her lips trembling, his stomach fluttering. This old woman was his mother. No this old woman gave birth to him.

Nothing else.

"I shouldn't have come. I can see that now." His mouth was dry and he swallowed painfully as he tried to compose himself. "Can I, can I give you some money?" Maria Dolores cried out in anger, exasperation at this man who was treating her so mercilessly. She took a step to correct her balance, he reciprocated by moving one away in an awkward dance.

"No. No. No," she spat through gritted teeth shaking her head. "No." She wanted to return home, to the paltry sanctuary of that run down shack. But at least it was hers and she could close the door on him. She had no more words. Rational thoughts were flooded by a grief she never imagined possible. He stepped aside as she scuttled past him.

"Señora," he begged, but any attempt to induce her back would be empty, he too wished that the whole scenario was over and he could leave this woman alone. She stopped and looked back at him, her whole body shaking with rage.

"Señora? Señora? You call me señora?" Suddenly unable to control the fury that consumed her, she screamed again, a wailing cry that echoed along the empty street. He took one step towards her, one single step after his mother, but then stopped and watched her as she marched as much as her body would allow back to her house, with Baby being pulled behind.

Maria Dolores continued mumbling as she climbed the last few stairs to her house. When she opened the door she looked back but the space where he had stood was empty. Uncontrollable tears ran down her face. For so many years she had refused to cry, refusing to allow any man to hurt her again, but she had succumbed. She took deep noisy breaths but didn't feel the air enter her lungs. The breeze softly clicked the door closed behind her, gently so as not to upset her more. She staggered forward and tried to grasp the back of a chair but didn't have the strength to hold onto it, she slipped and fell to the floor. Baby danced around her body. Maria Dolores continued to cry, great weeping sobs as she pushed herself across the floor until she reached the wall below the window, where she curled up to make herself as small as she could. She lay there foetus-like, trembling, rocking in despair until exhausted, she fell asleep.

Chapter Thirty-Two

Ibiza 2016

The late September sky had been crowded out by low-lying monochromatic cloud. It muted the sea's usual aquamarine shimmer and drained the green foliage. Even the late blossoming *kniphofia*, the Red Hot Poker lilies, that punctuated the hillside like flaming torches looked washed out. That afternoon Maria Dolores watched the planes take off, they climbed before being sucked into that blanket of dense greyness. The remnants of that summer's tourist plague heading home with suitcases stuffed with souvenirs and cheap cigarettes. Duty-free bags filled with local liqueurs sat at their feet. Obscure drinks that would soon be abandoned at the back of a cupboard. Friends nudged their neighbours on budget airline seats and giggled, embellishing for the dozenth time some unremarkable anecdote, preparing it for the home audience. Sunburn, tightly braided hair and new tattoos, the visible trophies. Damaged livers unseen but nevertheless bragged about. Not quite so widely appreciated were the shared bacterial infections they also carried, that special present for the partner back home.

Maria Dolores had earlier walked Baby. The little dog had

trudged along more slowly than usual, despite her mistress's coaxing. It had been a long hot summer, they were both old and they were both exhausted. She had left her companion at home as she sought the last of the day's heat. Another aeroplane passed overhead, the wind amplifying the engine's roar as she contemplated, yet again, her physical confinement and her failing health. She thought of the letter awaiting her at home. Why couldn't she open it? She didn't want any more bad news. Life had already been too unkind. The pain of having the past thrust back upon her would be unbearable. She didn't want confirmed what she had long suspected. She was truly alone. The sun broke through the distant cloud just before it dipped beyond the horizon and momentarily blinded her. It's low rays piercing her cataract stricken eyes. But she liked the feel of it on her face. Thoughts of that man, Francisco, thundered into her head uninvited, but she was quick to shut them out. She would not allow herself to think of him. She couldn't. No man was going to hurt her again, of that she had been determined. But he had. The cruelty of the reunion raked at her heart and tormented her soul. As much as she rejected him he would not go away.

Jimmy's melancholy continued. He was stuck and he didn't know how to get out of it. With the end of the summer, work had quietened down so he had taken some days off that were owed to him. He had spent them mostly in Jock's bar but was unable to find answers at the bottom of the glass. A return to England seemed imminent. His son now lived in Madrid and that was easy enough to get to from London. The only thing tying him to the island was Wayne. Santi had sent him a text, a cowardly way to try and resolve their quarrel. The friendship was over and Jimmy was glad of it. "One for the road, and a chaser," he called to the barman. "Then I'll go home."

* * *

The setting of the sun was normally Paco's signal to return home. That evening was different though. He and his friends had congregated at the rocks but hadn't swam. The lack of sun had given the breeze an uncomfortable edge. The afternoon was spent larking around. Horseplay that sometimes pushed hierarchical boundaries within the group. Tensions sometimes resurfaced but were quick to dissipate. The three of them sat on a rocky crag adjacent to the beach. Roco toyed with his phone eventually settling for a video of Shakira. The tinny sound from the mobile's speaker complemented the rhythmic splash of the breaking waves below them.

"That's crap?" Paco actually liked the song but relished another opportunity to tease, as adolescent boys do. He grabbed his own mobile from his back-pack. The bag that also contained the other 'supplies' Sebas thought no boy should be without.

"Shut uuuup," Roco sang. "She's brilliant."

"Yeah brilliant tits," added Wilson. They laughed and chanted the chorus together, allowing the music to wash over them. Paco delved again into the bag.

"You want these?" Paco held up the cigarettes he'd had stored for months. He hated smoking but knew Roco would take them.

"Where you get these?"

"Brother."

"Cool brother." Paco threw a look at Roco but he was too busy tearing the cellophane off the packet to notice. Paco then showed his companions the other items.

"These, I'll be keeping," he beamed, brandishing the condoms. His friends joined him in a nervous laugh. The three of them were virgins, although this was never discussed. That others in his class weren't didn't bother Paco.

He never felt the urgency to have sex. Finally he pulled out a knife, the heavy rubber-handled Bowie knife.

"Woahhh," breathed Wilson a little flabbergasted. The stubby handle exaggerated the size of the steel blade. The reflected amber sunset made it look as though it had been recently pulled from a forge. Paco showed it off with some pride. Held up against his other hand the blade reached beyond his fingertips. It's double edged tip looked to have been sharpened with samurai precision.

"FUCK, look at that," gasped Roco. "Let me see."

"No way," Paco quickly flipped the knife up, catching it again by the handle, a practiced move. Then he made a short thrusting movement towards Roco's face.

"Watch it, dickhead," Roco snarled. The other two laughed.

"Where'd you get that?" Paco didn't answer. He twirled the blade slowly, pointing towards one, then the other of his friends.

"Did your brother give you that?" Paco nodded. "Give it me," Wilson continued reaching out.

"No way."

"I'd love a brother like Sebas," added Wilson nodding his head.

"Yeah, he's the coolest."

"He's not all that." Their admiration of his brother irritated Paco, if only they knew.

"You wouldn't use it though," Roco added snidely. "You're all mouth."

"All mouth?" repeated Paco as he flashed the blade towards Roco again. "You'll see." Paco sucked his teeth and pulled his hand back. As he glared again at Roco he felt resentment rising in him. How quickly the atmosphere could change. A gruelling summer of Sebas' intrusions had taken its toll on Paco. The acrimony was always there, just beneath the surface, waiting an escape. There was no question that he would hurt his friends, but he felt things were coming to a head. Reluctantly and with a scornful stare he passed the blade around.

Maria Dolores pushed herself up from the bench and staggered a few steps until her old bones woke up. It was time to go home. There was a sandwich that she had saved from breakfast for dinner, jamon serrano y queso. It wasn't much but it was enough for her and would stave off the hunger until the morning at least. It was tightly wrapped in a plastic bag so the bread would soften and be easier to eat. She ambled along the front leaving the tourist restaurants behind her and headed for the stairs that lead to her house. Shortly after she passed the neighbour. He was sitting on a bench asleep, phone in hand. From a safe distance she examined the slumped body. He had the laboured breathing of a drunk. Still resentful, she sneered and spat in his direction and continued on.

Jimmy grunted which woke him from his stupor. He was quite a bit drunker than he had thought, falling asleep on a bench like some stray tourist separated from the pack. He blinked a few times, wiped an eye with a finger and stood. It really was time to go home. His mouth tasted rank. He was already feeling dehydrated and desperate to urinate. This end of the promenade, where the beach gave way to the rocky shoreline was quiet. The only other person he could see was the old lady who lived across the road. He was sure it was her, she had that distinctive gait. He walked as straight and as fast as he could, overtaking her with a wide berth. He wasn't really in any mood to exchange pleasantries.

Paco and friends abandoned the rocks and jumped onto the promenade just as the night lights automatically switched on.

The three of them froze as if they had triggered the sudden illumination, caught in some illicit act. Roco nudged Paco in the arm and signalled to the approaching man but Paco had already seen him. It was that queer who had maimed Tyson. They stood still, unnoticed and watched, as the neighbour turned and started up the hillside.

Jimmy's progress was slow but he comfortably managed the first set of stairs. He passed the streetlight with the bin that always seemed to be overflowing with pizza boxes and onto the narrow path which led to the second ascent. His mobile phone pinged in his hand. He looked at it. A text message. The battery was at 7%, he'd read it at home once he'd plugged the phone in.

Maria Dolores reached the bottom of the stairs just in time to see three kids disappear round the corner. One of them was Paco, but in the dim light her eyesight often tricked her, so perhaps not. She stretched out and grabbed the barrier and pulled herself up, one slow step at a time.

Jimmy stopped, he took a deep breath and wondered if he should urinate over the small wall or wait the three minutes it would take to arrive home. He didn't hear anything out of the ordinary, a motor bike revved some 30 meters or so beyond the bushes. Nothing else. He concentrated on his bladder, contracting his pelvic floor muscles a little. It was a little uncomfortable, a niggle, he could wait. Suddenly he found himself lurching forward. Did he stumble? Was he pushed? He instinctively threw his arms out but the only thing within reach was a rhododendron branch which snapped as he grasped at it and he fell to his knees on the hard ground.

* * *

Hissed whispers bombarded him. *'Maricon de mierda'*, *hijo de puta'*, *'capullo'*. Then he felt a blow as he was knocked off his knees. He lay there on his side stunned but simultaneously being pulled from his drunken state to see a blurred face, no two faces bear down on him. He raised his hand to shield himself but shrank back again as he received a kick to his flank. He jerked and coughed in response. Something else, someone else struck his head. His crotch felt suddenly warm as urine escaped him and flooded his trousers.

Then nothing as he withdrew into himself. Buzzing reverberated through his head and the dull intensifying aches that seemed to be both inside and around him began to overwhelm him. He rolled out of the foetal position and collapsed onto his hands, retching, saliva pouring from his agonised mouth. He pulled himself up scraping his forearm on the coarse wall as he rose.

And as he staggered onto his feet he felt someone pull him up by his shirt. Assistance? A rescuer? No, the same face as before but no voices just a stifled snort. Paco? The person, the people holding him shook him, pushed him forwards, hauled him backwards again. More words and muted laughs. Someone held up something close to his face but he couldn't focus on it. Then he saw a glint from it, a blade? His captors once again thrust him forward and the blade pressed into his throat. He felt a sharp nick of the skin as they yanked him back again. His legs began to tremble, the merging of drunkenness and fear.

"No." A pathetic appeal as he came face to face with his aggressor. Then that lunge forward again. More forceful, less controlled. He lost his balance and his legs gave way. The knife wasn't thrust into him, it didn't need to be as he collapsed onto it. The steel didn't feel cold as it plunged into him. His life didn't flash before his eyes. Not yet. As he fell his left leg found some purchase and he stumbled forward onto the blade, widening the wound. Then the all-embracing pain so blinding that it drew all the air from him.

An arm retracted and the blade was clumsily removed from his neck, sucking air and further lacerated his trachea. Jimmy didn't see the terror in their eyes, nor hear the horror in the young voices as they ran away. Their own nightmare just beginning. His scream turned in on him as he fought to inhale. The only outward sound was a gurgle as his own spurting blood impeded his every effort to breathe. Then less than two minutes after it started he was alone. Alone with his panic and his torment and the life draining out of him.

Maria Dolores rounded the corner to be confronted by a writhing shape on the floor. She hesitated, unsure whether she should proceed or not. But as she inched forward she saw it was a man then a few steps closer noticed it was that neighbour. She had seen many things in her long life but nothing like this, nothing that had stunned her into inaction. His screaming eyes fixed on her and called out. 'Do something,' they pleaded. Another step closer. She awkwardly crouched a few feet from him, her body imposing its own restrictions on how low she could get. One of his hands clasped at his throat, an action that made him look like he was strangling himself. Blood spewed between his fingers. The majority however, was forced by his own hands, inwards, into his lungs. The other hand flailed wildly, clutching at the blood stained mobile phone which jumped as he slapped it, sending it scuttling towards the old lady. Maria Dolores didn't say anything. She spoke no words. She reached down and picked up the phone which flashed as another message appeared. Someone trying to contact him. Then she stood up and looked down on him. They stared at each other, but there was no emotion in her eyes. She took a half step back as a leg jerked towards her and slipped the bloodied phone into her pocket. Another half step back, not taking her eyes from him. They still pleaded with her. 'DO SOMETHING' but even in his panic he could see she was not his salvation. She wondered if it had been Paco. Another step back and to the side. Then still with no words spoken she turned and walked away, climbed the next set of stairs and was soon back on her street.

Absconding from the scene had put a spring in her step, she felt both exhilarated and panicked. Once her house was in view her breathing slowed and she was thankful for it. An old lady shouldn't have surprises like that. As she crossed the road she saw the knife in the gutter. In the streetlight it was clear what it was. A large knife covered in blood. Paco must have dropped it as he fled, or was it one of the other boys? Either way she couldn't leave it there in plain sight. She picked it up and was surprised by its weight. Without looking around Maria Dolores rushed on. As she passed the glass recycling container she dropped the mobile phone into it. It bounced against the bottles inside; clink-clink, clink, clink, then stopped and came to a rest. She thought about throwing that knife in there as well but it seemed too important, too vital to be discarded like that. A minute later she was back in her house. She wrapped the knife in a towel and laid it in the sink. Tomorrow's problem. Baby came to greet her as was her custom, so she stooped and lifted her up onto the sofa. They sat, the two old ladies, and stared into the darkness of the living-room. The sounds of the ambulance sirens arrived after what seemed like an eternity and then, when they had waned and she could no longer hear them, as the adrenaline subsided, she allowed herself to sleep.

Chapter Thirty-Three

Ibiza 2016

There was hardly a visible surface in the cramped, neglected hovel that Maria Dolores called home. Layers of dust covered everything. Each one was overflowing with papers that had been dropped there over the years; crinkled letters from electric companies offering change of supplier incentives, flyer publicity for optometric tests or teeth whitening, and pizza delivery menus. None of which Maria Dolores could ever take advantage of. Behind, beneath and between these redundant documents were various ornaments, hairbrushes and remnants of what once could have been called make-up; a dried out lipstick, an empty foundation palette and a mother of pearl compact, the mirror of which was cracked and split through the middle. The odd items and artefacts of a life, present but discarded and forgotten.

It had been three days since Maria Dolores' abrupt and acrimonious exchange with Francisco. She had hardly ventured outdoors since, preferring not to stray from the safety of the house. Perhaps he was still out there. A dread that she had never felt before, nor understood, consumed her. His offensive words still rang in her ears and no matter how much she tried to dismiss them she knew there was truth in them. But how could a son say these things to his mother? Why he had sought her out only to treat her like that? She had indeed been a prostitute and had been arrested for it, but how could he judge her for that? She had to eat. To live. To survive. She wished he hadn't come and although she could not bring herself to think of that man as her son, she knew that he was. Her eyes were failing her but there was no mistaking the resemblance to Juan Diego. Then there was the police who were still investigating the death of the neighbour. No, it was best to stay indoors.

The letter Francisco had given her sat by itself in a space cleared of debris, debris which now lay strewn on the floor. The envelope was crumpled but she could still see her own name staring at her, it called to her in her sister's voice. She had picked it up a few times, held it in her hands, held it to her chest but still hadn't had the courage to open it knowing it contained only bad news. 'She was your sister' he had said. Was? 'You can read can't you?' The words still derided her. The truth was that it had been years since she had read anything. But of course she could. Her lip curled in contempt for him, what did he know? She had been the brightest student in her class and had managed thus far. But he had said worse, 'she was very ill'.

With the envelope she made her way to the stairs, her gateway to the outside world. Here in the bright September sun she could see more clearly. The faded pale blue envelope almost stung her hands. She turned it over a few times, it was thin, there weren't many pages inside, perhaps only the one. With difficulty her deformed arthritic fingers picked it open, careful not to damage the paper inside. Baby waddled over and flopped down by her side and groaned with satisfaction, happy to be in contact with her mistress. Maria Dolores glanced down at her, at least someone needed her, then she turned her attention back to the letter. She spread it out on her thigh and began to read each word out loud in a low cautious voice.

Lola,

So many years have passed. I don't know how to tell you things, so much has happened.

A man arrived today and told me he was your son. I am still in shock. This man says he's going to find you. Lola I am trembling. I don't know what to think but I'm writing this in the hope that he does find you. And that you are alive.

I am an old woman now, nearly 80, I think I was only 11 when you disappeared, maybe younger. Everyone thought that you had gone off with Juan Diego because he disappeared at the same time. I always hoped so and you were happy with him. But I wished you would come back and see me or even write. If you are alive, why did you never write? Mami wouldn't let me visit you in hospital because I was so young. Then one day she came back and told us the baby died and you had gone, run away. Lola, I cried, I cried so much, we all did. A hole in my heart appeared that day and has stayed with me ever since. We were all devastated and Papi was never the same after that. He blamed himself for not accepting the baby. Every year we sang Happy Birthday to you and Papi would say the same thing every year, that he would go to Catalonia to look for you but he never went. He died in 1955 and Mami in 1971, they are buried here in the village.

So much has changed here but I still live in our house although it's not quite the same. The house might be different but the mountains never change, it still feels like our village. After Papi died, I married José Blanco. Do you remember him? He was a bit older than us and was not such a bad man although I cannot say I ever really loved him. He left many years ago now after our daughter Catalina died, she was only 16. My heart was broken. But I still have a son, Luis, who lives in Jerez. He's a teacher and a good man and phones me every day. I have two grandchildren, they are so beautiful. Their mother, Zaira, is from Morocco. The children are all grown up now. Angel lives in Berlin and my granddaughter in Madrid, she's a doctor. They called her Dolores. They never met you but they knew how much I loved my sister.

Lola, a few years ago I had treatment for a cancer in my breast and all was good, but it has come back. They gave me medication which I take every day but the cancer is in my bones now so we shall see what happens.

I'm sorry my letter is like this, telling you people are dead or dying. I even feel like I'm writing to a ghost. It's so difficult to think of things to say when this man Francisco is here in my house waiting. Lola if he finds you, my phone number is here. Please call me. He says he is a military man, a General and he will find you. You must be very proud of him.

My sister I have never stopped thinking about you and I never stopped loving you.

Conchi

Maria Dolores only realised she was crying when a tear hit the page, dissipating the ink beside her thumb. The second time that week she had cried, only the second time in decades. She drew her fingers across the paper, those written words, reaching out to touch her sister, little Conchi. Why had she kept on running? Conchi's words pounded Maria Dolores creating an abyss in her chest, thrusting profound grief onto her. She sat on her step and rocked as she sobbed, oblivious to the world outside. This was too much information to absorb. She thought of their home, their village, of Juan Diego's cottage. He had disappeared? Perhaps he did go to look for her. What did it matter now? Maria Dolores became aware of an intense throbbing behind her eyes. She had a nephew, there was a family for her. She tried to imagine Conchi as an old woman, like herself, but she could only see that young girl so full of life, running around the kitchen of their old home. Did her little Conchi really marry José Blanco? Could she have done such a thing? She thought again of the terrible events he had subjected her to and felt anger grip her as she thought of the same happening to her sister. She reached down to Baby, who had stayed by her side and crushed the letter with the other hand rubbing it vigorously up and down her thigh. 'My Conchi,' she moaned. She wanted to know, she had to know what had happened. She looked at the now torn letter again. She would take it to Father Gabriel, let him make the phone call.

The following morning Maria Dolores banged on the door of The San Salvador de La Marina church where she had for the last few months revealed her story to Father Gabriel. Although her knocking could not be described as forceful, it hurt her hands. She decided instead to take off her shoe and bang the wooden doors with the heel. She didn't have to wait long before a young cleaner unlocked the door. But before it could be fully opened Maria Dolores had pushed past her and was scuttling down the nave of the old church. When she couldn't see Father Gabriel, she turned back towards the cleaner who stood open mouthed watching this excitable old lady.

"Where is he? The priest, where is he?" Then she heard his familiar voice, he appeared as if she had summoned him herself.

"Maria Dolores, Good morning." Father Gabriel smiled at her in his usual manner, still fixing the collar on his shirt. "A nice surprise to see you so early," he added.

"You have to call her. I have the number here , but *you* have to call her." Maria Dolores took the last few steps towards the priest and thrust the broken letter into his hand. He took the damaged paper from her and opened it delicately, treating it as if it were the first discovery of an ancient manuscript. Parts of the letter were torn and unreadable but the last few lines were legible. "My sister I have never stopped thinking about you," he mumbled to himself, then read out the number below. "Is this from your sister?"

"Yes, yes," she confirmed irritably. "She has a telephone. You call her. Now." She bowed her head and pushed at him like she was opening a heavy door.

"Ahh, yes," he acquiesced. "Of course, come with me." He had never seen her with such verve, so energised. He opened the door to his office and Maria Dolores barged past him coming to a halt beside the telephone. He followed her in and lay the paper on the desk and flattened it out.

"Let's see." His words floated into the room as he picked up the old dial telephone, Maria Dolores watching his every move. She grabbed the back of the armchair, that same chair she had sat on as she told him tales of the younger Conchi and willed him on as he dialled the number.

"It's ringing." He looked up at Maria Dolores who's stare remained fixed on the telephone. "Dolores, it's ringing," he repeated and held the receiver out so she could hear, to corroborate his words. Father Gabriel replaced the earpiece against his ear. The adrenaline surged through Maria Dolores as the realisation of what was happening. Her heart rattled and skipped beats, every hair on her arms and neck stood on end, a wave of nausea rocked her. Father Gabriel looked on concerned. He was just about to say something to her, when someone answered the phone. Maria Dolores heard a thin, tinny voice.

"Yes."

"Good morning, I'm sorry to disturb you so early. My name is Father Gabriel Ferrer, I'm calling from Ibiza. I am, erm, looking for a Señora Conchita," Then Father Gabriel paused and looked again towards Maria Dolores, suddenly realising he didn't know her full name.

"What's your surname? He whispered a little too loudly.

"Benitez Herrero." Both women answered simultaneously.

"Yes, that's me," confirmed the voice over the phone.

"Good, good. Err, I have someone here that would like to talk to you." And with that he held out the receiver to Maria Dolores.

Chapter Thirty-Four

Ibiza 2016

Fuchsia bougainvillea flowers tumbled down the streets of the Los Molinos neighbourhood. The first autumnal winds carried respite to everyone, bringing in changes, heralding the cooler months ahead. Maria Dolores felt she could breathe again. The sun still shone but the intensity had been taken out of it. She had survived another summer. The reunited sisters talked every day since that first phone call. A visit had been arranged, a family reunion with people she had never met, hadn't even known of their existence. A deep contentedness filled her, emotions she couldn't remember having experienced, but in quieter moments anxiety also crept in. Conchi had cancer and cancer killed people. Father Gabriel had told her to take it one step at a time and that was what she intended to do.

A week had passed since Jimmy's death. It had been scandalous, a death, a murder in the neighbourhood. The rumour mill had quietened down but people still whispered and pointed out his apartment. A common theory was that it had been a drug deal gone wrong. These things sometimes happened. More fuss seemed to surround the future of the dog, who had been taken in by one of the dead man's colleagues. The police had interviewed everyone but no one had seen anything. Maria Dolores had admitted to occasionally saying hello to the man but had never asked his name. Bernarda and Sebastian had been at home and swore Paco had been in his bedroom at the time. Sebas had been working in a bar, dozens of witnesses would testify to that. Jimmy's mobile phone hadn't yet been recovered. The battery finally petered out an hour or so after Jimmy had died and lay deep in a mountain of glass at the recycling plant. There was no word either about the murder weapon. Black stains remained where Jimmy had fallen, where he was found already dead, where the emergency services could do nothing to revive him.

Paco had barely come out of his bedroom since that night. The walls closed in as the room became his cell. Cracks in the ceiling's paintwork mocked him, imaginary smiles twisted into laughter when his insomnia made him delirious. The strain of it forced him into fits of crying, fear and frustration overcoming him. He buried his head deep into his pillow to suppress the sobs until he could breathe no more. Afterwards, exhausted, he stared at the ceiling again, dreading the next attack. Anxiety stripped him of any appetite to eat and once, even provoked vomiting. He resolutely resisted all attempts by Bernarda to take him to the doctor. She worried of course, but knew her son to be stubborn and introverted and hadn't pressured him too much. The family put it down to Paco being a moody teenager as he had been all summer.

Thankfully there had been no contact with Roco or Wilson. He assumed they were also living the same hell but he didn't want to see them. See the guilt on their faces, their swollen crying eyes, their features torn and gaunt from sleep deprivation. See his own misery reflected. There had been no incriminating texts or calls, he was thankful also for that. No incriminating texts, but what about the knife. The knife. The knife that Sebas had given him. He assumed one of them had it since the police hadn't kicked down his door. Assumptions were all he had, what else was there? The knife had all three of their fingerprints on it. He was reminded of it in the few moments of sleep afforded to him, tormented visions of his marks on a blood-soaked blade. It was as damning as being caught in the act. School started soon, he would be forced to see them again. Until then the plan was to stay in the room and wait.

Outside on the terrace, Bernarda and Maria Dolores were in high spirits.

"I've never been on an aeroplane. I don't know what it's like."

"Well, you'll find out soon enough." Bernarda giggled and rubbed Maria Dolores' shoulder. She'd never seen the old lady so animated.

"And you'll keep Baby here with you?"

"Yes, I told you a hundred times already."

"I know, I know."

"I'll get Sebas to take you to the airport if you like."

"No." The change in Maria Dolores' tone went unnoticed. "No, it's ok, the priest's coming and Luis, he's my nephew, he'll will pick me up in Seville."

"I know who he is, you already told me. A hundred times."

"And Conchi will be there too. I hope my heart can handle it."

"I still can't believe it though. After all these years you have family out there and you'll see them tonight." Bernarda shook her head again and entered the house, reappearing with a small travel bag. "Here it is, it's a bit old and battered."

"Bit like me then," and the two women giggled again.

Bernarda broke away. "Paco. Paco." It took a minute until he answered.

"What?"

"Take the case over for Dolores please." The women studied the gaunt looking boy. "He's not been feeling great," Bernarda explained. "A bug going round I think." Paco sighed loudly, unconcerned that they could hear him. "Go on, it'll just take a minute."

"Thank you Bernarda," she said clasping the other's hands.

"No problem Dolores, I'll come and see you off. And pick up Baby of course."

Paco grabbed the case and trudged over to the hole in the fence that connected the two houses. Maria Dolores wasn't nimble enough to climb through so she walked down to the street and entered by her own door. Paco waited, clearly displeased.

"You want it inside?"

"Er, yes Paco, please." She opened the door and they both stepped in.

"OK, there you go."

"Paco, just a minute." Maria Dolores closed the door behind her.

"Listen I need to go, like mami said I'm not feeling great." His voice was despondent.

"I know."

"So, what is it?"

"I know Paco, I know what happened. To that man, the neighbour. I saw it." She continued to stare at him. Paco knew immediately what she was referring to. He wanted not to believe her but the look on her face told him it was true. He shook his head, slowly at first then more vigorously. A wave of nausea and dizziness enveloped him and he thought he was going to vomit.

"No. No. You better not say a fucking word." The words that flew out his mouth were replaced by heavy breathing, spittle spraying through gritted teeth.

"Paco, Paco relax. Of course I'm not going to say anything." She raised an arm to touch him but he flinched away then a step closer, over her, an inch from her. In that moment she felt Sebas in the room, the naked aggression. A man's breath on her. The toxic masculinity she had faced her whole life rearing its head again. "Paco, it's ok." She raised her hand again, her scrawny fingers reached out and clasped his muscular forearm. This time he let her touch him. The tears started to roll down his face. No sounds, just a lost boy crying. Then she hugged him. Her fragile arms around his broad body. A motherly instinct. He rested his head against hers, and kept on crying. They stood in that position few minutes, an old woman hugging her young neighbour. Tears and mucous mingled in her hair.

Paco was the first to pull away. "I don't know what to do. It's so fucked up."

"You've worried yourself sick son. It'll pass."

"How's it gonna pass? We killed a man. He's fucking dead. They won't stop till they find us." The sobs again threatened to overpower his breathing.

"They won't find you Paco."

"Don't be stupid, the police can do anything. It's just a matter of time."

"Paco, I have the knife. I've got it. I found it outside. It's buried there, in the garden." Paco took a step back, staring in disbelief. "No one is going to find it. I was going to take it to the cliffs and throw it in the sea but I couldn't throw it very far so I buried it."

"What? You buried it here? Right next door to me?"

"When I get back I'll show you and you can take it and go to the cliffs and you can throw it in. But it's safe for now."

"Why would you do that?" Paco took another step back, struggling to comprehend the news. "You've had it all this time and I've been dying." He could feel his pulse harden, his heart pounding again in his chest. "Why would you do that?" he repeated.

"I found it in the street, what was I going to do?"

"Jesus Christ." He barely controlled his voice, shouting in a whisper.

"Paco, I've never done anything good in my life. My own son hates me. You're a good boy, I know you are. I can see it in you. You don't deserve that life. You're not your brother."

"And you're crazy."

"Don't you want to do things, go to the university? Have a different life? Well don't let this stop you."

"Dolores we killed a man. Don't you get it?"

"There's nothing linking him to you or your friends. Only the knife and we can get rid of it." She shuffled closer to him.

"For God's sake." He turned and began to pace the small living room muttering to himself.

"I've been thinking about it Paco, but we, we have no other choice."

"We? WE? I need to go, need to get out of here." He turned to face her again and she saw the anguish in that young face. A wearied face convinced there was no future.

"OK, but listen, this is the way out. Don't be your brother Paco, you're better than him." The words fell against Paco's back as he pushed through the door and she was left alone. A minute later the silence was broken by an angry Sebas. 'Where the hell have *you* been?' Maria Dolores couldn't make out the reply but as the Moreno's front door slammed she knew Paco's afternoon was going to get worse. She winced again at the thought of the young man's aguish. "Don't be your brother," she repeated into the emptiness.

Sebas' mood continued into the afternoon. Another moment of panic hit Paco as he overheard Sebas complaining on the phone that Jimmy owed him money. Sebas' ire alternated with laughs, he didn't seem to care that someone had died. He was only interested in the drug money he had lost. Paco listened until the conversation ended. When he heard Sebas call his name he got up and closed the door and returned to the chair in the corner of the small bedroom. He picked up the broken 'Of Mice and Men' and again thought of how it could be repaired. He didn't really know how but he knew that it could be done. Broken and battered perhaps but it could be done.

An hour later Paco stood on the terrace watching his mother hug Maria Dolores, then help her into the priest's car.

"I can't wait till you get back and tell me all about it." Bernarda seemed more excited than Maria Dolores. When there was no answer she leant in and stroked the old woman's arm.

"What's wrong Dolores?"

"Nothing, just that,"

"We better get going." The small car bounced a little as Father Gabriel threw himself onto the seat.

"Normal that you feel nervous."

"It's not that. Everything just feels so strange.

"Don't worry about it, you'll have a great time." Maria Dolores fumbled with the seatbelt, when she looked up again Paco had joined his mother. "Won't she have a good time Paco?" Paco nodded holding the gaze of his elderly neighbour. "Everything will be alright, I promise." Bernarda added.

"Yes, everything will be alright." Paco echoed and the merest of smiles crept across his face. Maria Dolores beamed back as the engine started.

"You ready?" Asked Father Gabriel.

"Yes." Maria Dolores took a last glance at her neighbours and then looked forward. "Let's go." The priest slipped the car into gear and they set off down the street.

Acknowledgements

Thank you to everyone who gave me feed back throughout this long process. Your patience and kind words have been invaluable. To Mike who read the very first efforts and gave me belief, Mary for proof reading, Eithne G for keeping me going and thank you Linda for the classes and encouragement.
Also Gordon, AndyP & Amanda and the others who dipped in along the way.

Finally to Manuel without whom I would never have known Ibiza nor the real Maria Dolores.

Printed in Poland
by Amazon Fulfillment
Poland Sp. z o.o., Wrocław